GIVE ME THE WIND

Also by Jan Jordan

DIM THE FLARING LAMPS
A Biographical Novel of John Wilkes Booth

GIVE ME
THE WIND

by

JAN JORDAN

PRENTICE-HALL, Inc., Englewood Cliffs, N.J.

Give Me the Wind by Jan Jordan
Copyright © 1973 by Jan Jordan

Printed in the United States of America

Prentice-Hall International, Inc., London
Prentice-Hall of Australia, Pty. Ltd., North Sydney
Prentice-Hall of Canada, Ltd., Toronto
Prentice-Hall of India Private Ltd., New Delhi
Prentice-Hall of Japan, Inc., Tokyo
10 9 8 7 6 5 4 3 2 1

Library of Congress Cataloging in Publication Data
Jordan, Jan.
Give me the wind.
1. Ross, John, Cherokee chief, 1790–1866—Fiction.
2. United States—History—1783–1865—Fiction.
I. Title.
PZ4.J8197Gi [PS3560.0725]   813'.5'4   72–12587
ISBN 0-13-356824-5

TO
ARTHUR IRVING JORDAN
For Many Reasons
But Especially for Building
SHANAWAN
Where All "Those Kids" Enjoyed a
Beautiful Childhood

"*There is only one man there upon whom I now rely for strength and loyalty and I know he will get information to me if he is alive. He is John Ross, Chief of the Cherokee Nation. He shall not fail the Union.*"

ABRAHAM LINCOLN, *1861*

I

THE NUDE, SCALPED BODY OF A YOUNG MOTHER LAY spread-eagled on the blood-soaked mattress of the bed, and the dried flow of the red fluid which had once filled her veins stained the floor of the cabin. A naked baby, placed bizarrely upon the mutilated breast of its mother, reached with tiny hands, even in death, for the nipple which was not there. Huge horseflies, flashing an ominous blue in the early afternoon light, droned a terrible song as they swarmed over the bodies.

Outside, the bodies of the men of the family—the father, two young boys, and an old man—hung by their heels from a low branch of a nearby tree. Their stomachs were slashed open and their heads scalped. The same breed of flies, boring into the vitals of the deceased, were feasting unmolested.

Andrew Jackson, not yet twenty-five years of age, had lately come to the land of Tennessee to establish his life in the new town called Nashville. Now he staggered from the bedroom where the stench and the horror were overwhelming. He wiped his trembling hands on the long deerskin jacket he wore, and he had to run his tongue over his dry lips before he could speak.

"By God, I swear!" he told the frontiersmen with him; "If it takes me the rest of my life, I'll avenge these people. If I ever have the power, I'll remove every bastard Indian from this land of ours."

A bearded young man was wiping blood from his hands with grass he pulled from the ground. He was a frontier scout guiding Jackson through the frontier settlement area of Tennessee, and this was not the first time he had seen scalpings, tortured bodies, and burned homes. He shook his head. "Truth is, Andy, the Hopewell Treaty says this here land belongs to the Cherokee. Oh, I ain't sayin' what they done here ain't the work of savages, but the fact is this cabin was put up on Cherokee land, agin the warnin's of our own Congress."

The wind was blowing out of the north. The branch which

was already bending earthward under the weight of its awful burden swayed and dipped, and the lifeless fingers of the dead brushed the ground.

Andy Jackson, the wind tangling his long red hair, felt a rage rising in him such as he had never experienced. "Get those bodies down from that tree."

II

THE SECRETARY OF WAR, GENERAL HENRY KNOX, HAD COME to the President's house at 190 High Street in Philadelphia. The Secretary hurried through the cold March wind into the warmth of the mansion, while a black slave tended to his baggage and directed the coachman to drive the vehicle around to the Coach House for protection against the on-coming blizzard.

A young Negro servant helped the Secretary shed the wooden-soled, leather-topped start-ups which he wore to protect his silver-buckled shoes. Relieved of his blue wool cape, hat, and mitts, the Secretary paused a moment in front of the Chippendale looking glass in the reception hall to adjust the Steenkirk scarf around his neck. He smoothed the hair of his wig and turned to check the black ribbons which tied the hair back. The servant assured him he looked well by bowing to him.

President Washington was seated by the fire in a brocade-covered wing chair, his feet comfortably placed on a beautiful grospoint rug. He wore a brown velvet suit and his powered wig was like shining silver. He rested a leather-covered packet of papers on his knee. The President smiled and nodded but he did not rise from his chair.

Marvel, a black servant, had set a burning taper to the candles in the room, replaced the shining glass chimneys over them, and lighted the whale-oil lamp on a table by the window. She carried it to the President's round, hinged-top side table so that he could read by it.

The Secretary eyed the brandy and glasses which a male servant was now bringing into the room. Marvel offered a curtsey, and the two servants left and closed the door to give the President and his guest their privacy.

"May I pour you a brandy, sir?" the Secretary asked.

"No, thank you, Henry. Not just now. But you better have one."

The Secretary poured brandy into a glass and took the hoop-backed Windsor chair across the hearth, lifting his coattails and seating himself. "Why is it, Mr. President, that a winter in town these days seems so much colder than the ones we endured in the wilderness?"

"It's not the weather chilling us, it's old age."

"You, sir? You'll never age. You could still scatter the enemy, if we had one."

The President was solemn. "We have one, Henry. It's called Shina."

"Shina? Oh, yes, The Cherokee word for Evil, the Evil Spirit, the enemy of the Cherokee. Correct, sir?"

The President touched the papers on his knee. "Your reports carry shocking facts, Henry. Land speculators buying Cherokee land for a penny an acre!"

"Sir, there are worse things. There are instances of acreage going for a bottle of whiskey. Many of the Indians are simply robbed, thrown off their own land and their cabins burned, their stock run off, slaughtered."

"It appears the Cherokee Nation is in a state of seige."

Secretary Knox cupped the brandy glass between his hands. "Mister President, there's fault on both sides. I had word today by way of an Army scout that there has been an incident of cannibalism in the Cherokee Nation. Three white men were set upon, killed, dismembered, and their flesh roasted and eaten. I'll have a report prepared for you."

President Washington arose and moved to the table to seize a feathered pen. "The violence, the hatred has to stop. The honor of our Nation is at stake here as well as the future of the Indians. We're going to set forth a new treaty."

"A treaty? Sir, there isn't an Indian out there in the Cherokee towns who can possibly have any faith in a treaty. They consider the Treaty of Hopewell nothing but an imbecile promise. They know our people are laughing at it."

"Agreed. Certainly the Treaty of Hopewell is lost." The President gave the Secretary a long look and his heavy-lidded blue eyes sparked. "Henry, we'll create a treaty which will do the task it ought to do."

"Do you think the Senate—"

"Yes, we'll get it approved."

The President concentrated on writing, not bothering to go to his table, despite the awkwardness of his standing position. "I'm going to issue a call to the chiefs and the people of the Cherokee tribe to attend a meeting to negotiate a new treaty. It will be the law, and all our citizens will be obliged to honor it. It will give the Indians perpetual right to their lands."

"Sir, the Treaty of Hopewell was supposed to do that," the Secretary commented quietly.

The President straightened his posture. "I'll appoint a reliable group. It will include the best interpreters I can find. I believe the Indians will understand us all right. It is our white citizens who may have some difficulty in translation. I will therefore be very specific and firm. And I must rely on your ability to convey not only the meaning of the words of the treaty, but also the spirit behind it to both the participants in the conference."

"I am dedicated to the task, sir," the Secretary commented.

The President stooped to write again. "Do you agree that a convenient meeting place would be at White's Fort on the Holston River?"

"Yes, it's well located in the Cherokee Nation and known to all white travelers, too."

The President nodded. "Would the second of July be a proper date?"

"The weather will be good and travel easy. And it's far enough ahead to allow planning."

President Washington finished writing and he sprinkled the document with sand to dry it.

"I noticed you mentioned a man who seems particularly active within the Cherokee borders along the Tennessee: Andrew Jackson."

"Yes, Jackson. Of course, he's only one of many who are operating against the Indians in their own land, but he's very outspoken in his hatred of the Cherokees. He and his friend are amassing an empire in acreage. I've heard it said he has sworn to rid Tennessee of every Cherokee. He considers them without any rights whatsoever. I have to admit he's but reflecting a general feeling on the frontiers."

"This man Jackson—is he young?"

"Yes. I'd say not yet thirty by some few years. He has a partner in his land dealings. John Overton. They jointly own at least fifty thousand acres of land which the Treaty would term within the confines of the Cherokee Nation. And each of them owns acreage in his own name."

"Do they plan to sell it?" the President probed.

"I believe so. At least I know that Jackson acts as a kind of land agent for others, working on a commission basis." The Secretary leaned forward. "Mister President, Andy Jackson and his friends won't take kindly to a new treaty to protect the Cherokees."

"I don't expect the new treaty to be popular with our citizens. But I am hopeful I won't have to use military force to impress them with the fact that it shall stand as the law. We'll make the new treaty stick if we have to send the Army into the Cherokee Nation."

"You'd do that, sir?"

"I've said so. I have no patience with land grabbers and speculators. I'll not have our national word dishonored. When the Indians are secure, they will cease their raids on white settlers. I suspect," concluded the President, "that Andrew Jackson of Tennessee does not share my hopes for the Cherokees' future."

"He calls them savages. But, our missionaries give us reports contrary to such opinions as Jackson holds. The Cherokee children are reported as being very bright and eager students in the missionary schools. And Christianity has already taken a powerful hold in the Indian Nation."

"Yes," President Washington nodded. "I've read the reports with immense interest. And I tell you this, Henry. One of the greatest influences in changing the Cherokees from a tribe of hunters to a nation of civilized persons will be the consistent mixing of their blood with whites. I have personally been able to observe that a mixed-blood child in the Cherokee Nation is often white in appearance and personality, but deeply Indian in spirit and inclination. To all purposes, the white blood in them is dominated by the red. They are brilliant and handsome people and devout in their Cherokee ties."

"Do you believe the civilizing process will take effect before the Indians are totally scattered to the four winds?"

"It will depend upon the character of the Cherokee people themselves. If there are men enough like Sequoyah in the tribe, the Indians will come through any crisis as a united people and a civilized one. Sequoyah is only one of many mixed bloods who will build a great civilized Indian Nation in time, if we allow it. They need our help."

The Secretary cleared his throat. "You're speaking of George Gist, aren't you? He is called Sequoyah?"

The President spoke again slowly: "Yes. I consider George Gist the finest example of a mixed blood."

The Secretary, knowing of the President's friendship with Nathaniel Gist, picked his way carefully through the subject. "He is the son of Nathaniel Gist, I understand. His mother is Wurteh, full-blood sister of Chief Doublehead?"

The President's gaze was stiff with dignity. "There was a Cherokee marriage ceremony between Nate and Wurteh. Did you know that?"

"I've heard some say so, sir."

The President moved to the brandy and poured a little into a glass, and sat down. "The Cherokee marriage ceremony was very simple then. Nate and Wurteh, both clad in white doeskin, surrounded by family and friends, exchanged the traditional ceremonial gifts. Nate gave his bride a cut of venison to pledge he would always provide for her, and Wurteh presented him with an ear of corn to promise she would be a good wife. Then there was dancing and singing as the tribe rejoiced."

The Secretary asked: "Nathaniel Gist performed a mission for you, didn't he?"

"Yes. He brought Cherokee warriors to our assistance when we were desperately in need of them. No one else had been able to persuade the Cherokees to join us against the French and Shawnees. Nate is beloved by the Cherokees. It was then that he first met Wurteh."

"That was over thirty years ago," the Secretary figured. "Yet today Nathaniel Gist's son is still living in the Cherokee Nation, unrecognized by his Virginia relatives."

"True, although he often sees his father who visits him in the nation. Of course, Nate married Judith Cary Bell some years ago and they have a fine marriage. Wurteh has raised her son by herself and done a magnificent job of it. Nate has helped as much as he could."

"It's your observation, sir, that George Gist is exceptional in intelligence and personality because of the white blood in his veins?"

"Not exactly, Henry. I believe rather it's a combination of the red and white racial characteristics in him. But the benefit to his people is that this immensely brilliant man considers himself wholly Cherokee. Whatever he does in life will be to their good. They regard him highly already and call him Sequoyah."

"His white father has had no influence on his life, then?"

"To the contrary, Henry. Sequoyah is fully civilized and has an attitude toward the future development of the Cherokee people and Nation which his father holds. He wants the children educated by white people and raised in the Christian faith. Yet above all his hopes for them lies his Cherokee heritage and pride. He wants his people to advance in life, but to advance as Indians. His white blood inspires the Indian blood. Do you understand?"

"Yes, I believe I do." Knox knew enough about the Cherokee to know that the children were always raised close to the mother and her people, and that in this way their real heritage came to them without taint. The women of the Cherokee Nation were held in high esteem, sat with the men's council and were heard in meetings, and their opinions heeded.

"I don't have to tell you about the mixed bloods though." The President reached for the papers and, thumbing through them, began to read: " 'The mixed bloods of the Cherokee Nation, resulting from marriages between white men and Cherokee women, include such names as McIntosh, Vann, Dougherty, Galpin, Wafford, Adair, Pettit, Watts, and Ross'!"

"Ross," repeated the Secretary. "I saw Daniel and Mollie Ross recently when I passed through Tennessee. They have a new son, John. A red-haired boy, bright in looks and personality. They're very proud of him."

President Washington looked up from the papers and smiled. "Red-haired, eh? I suppose his father is Irish or Scottish?"

"Scottish, sir. The boy's mother is Cherokee. A really fine couple. They have a large home on the river, and a mill which is already on its way to making Daniel Ross rich. They have an eye to building a larger home on the Georgia side of the river. Very fine people."

The President lifted his brandy and said: "Henry, a toast: To the Cherokee Nation, may the good Lord bless their lives."

III

FORTY CHEROKEE CHIEFS RESPONDED TO THE CALL TO negotiate a new treaty with the United States of America. They came to the meeting grounds on the Holston River banks in Tennessee in the company of twelve hundred of their people. As the red and white men gathered under the trees, the hot July sun beat down upon a diverse-looking group of people.

There was one woman among them: the Beloved Woman, Nancy Ward. Years earlier, she had earned the title *Ghigau* when she had gone to war in place of her warrior husband who had died in a battle. In the years since, Nancy had become the leader of the women's council, and she and a group of the women always sat in on the men's council meetings and stood to give advice which was always considered and often taken.

The Beloved Woman, in her declining years, was becoming a pacifist. Secure in her own hold on the ancient tribal ways and religious beliefs, she nevertheless saw that the white missionaries who had come to her land were having an amazing success.

Nancy, envisioning a day when a Cherokee Chief would rule over a Christian nation, cast her vote for a new treaty with the United States which would bring the white and red nations closer together. Nancy smoked the pipe of peace with the commissioners of the United States and told them that the Cherokee people "are now under the protection of Congress."

The chiefs were eager for the benefits the new treaty would give them. They would be implements for farming, a miracle of sorts. The President of the United States would help them to become herdsmen and cultivators, removing them from the necessity of hunting. One thousand dollars would be paid to the Indian nation each year. In return, the Cherokee Nation granted the United States the exclusive right to trade with the Cherokee, who disavowed any trade with any other nation, state, or individual.

Good listeners, the Cherokees heard silently the words of the white commissioners who spoke to them on behalf of President Washington. They heard that the President promised them perpetual peace; that he would forbid inhabitants of the United States to enter onto Cherokee lands without authorization; that no white man would ever hunt on Cherokee soil. Their boundaries were defined to their satisfaction, and guaranteed.

Crimes committed by Cherokees against white citizens of the American Union would be punished by the laws of the United States. In turn, white persons committing crimes against the Indians were to be tried and punished according to the laws of the Cherokee Nation.

The Treaty of Holston was accepted by all the clans of the Cherokee tribe: the Wolf, Deer, Bird, Blue, Red, Twister, and Wild Potato. But although the treaty was signed, it was not fully satisfying to all. Some chiefs, trusting no white man, were resentful that the treaty carried no provisions for arms and ammunition. They determined to negotiate for weapons on their own with the Spaniards in Florida and the English in Canada.

Dragging Canoe appeared at the meeting in warlike dress, vivid paint striping his body and face, feathers bright in his headgear, making no effort to hide his hatred of the white men. A tomahawk was belted to his waistline and his fierce appearance was disturbing to many. "Why have you not come to this peace meeting with a hoop of scalps?" Nancy chided him. "Or do you save that for the hour when the moon shines upon us and you perform the Scalp Dance?"

"There are scalps here which deserve to be hung on hoops," Dragging Canoe replied: "The clans make a mistake here today. It will end in blood." He gave a grunt that signified he had spoken and would speak no more.

President Washington, upon ratification of the treaty, termed it: "A promising beginning for the future of the Cherokee people." But the Holston Treaty did not make men of peace of all Cherokees. Chief Doublehead, accompanied by his brother

Pumpkin Boy and their nephew Bench, waylaid and murdered two white men, Captain William Overall and a companion. Having slain and scalped the men, the Indians sat beside the bodies and drank heavily. Under the influence of the liquor and spurred by their hatred of all white men, the Cherokees carved the bodies of their victims with hunting knives, made a fire, and held the awful meal over the flames to roast. Later they explained that they had devoured the enemy because they wished to partake of the courage they had shown in fighting for their lives.

Doublehead and his two cohorts rode through the Cherokee towns to display the bloody scalps of their victims, strutting their victory to arouse the people to war against the whites who were still coming into the nation despite the Holston Treaty. Young men began to join them in their wild war dances around fires, their eyes on the scalps attached to poles.

IV

HAVING ALREADY SENT LEWIS AND ANDREW OFF TO SCHOOL, Mollie Ross was still busy trying to get John, her youngest, ready for his first day at the missionary school. During the hot summer months she had spent long hours in weaving, cutting, and sewing the clothing and had just finished his the last evening. Her eyes were tired and she felt a stabbing headache, but looking at six-year-old John, neat and trim in his outfit, she was proud of her work.

She smoothed his bright red hair back from his forehead, lifting the shoulder-length ends of it so it did not catch in the high collar of his jacket.

John shrugged her hands away. "Couldn't I wear my other clothes?" He was as close to whining as she had ever heard him.

"Now, John, it's time for you to go. Go directly to the schoolhouse, take a seat, and pay heed to whatever the teacher says, you understand? You'll sit quiet and you'll mind everything you do."

John squirmed in his new suit, tugging at the collar, pulling the material out from his knees. His underlip was beginning to protrude in resentment. "These things itch," he said.

She rubbed her aching forehead. "They do not. And you look very handsome. Now you stop your fussing and come along."

He stood with his legs set apart and he put his hands behind his back. "Mother, Stand and Pine and me, we're building a fort." He cast an anxious glance toward the bedroom window. Out there where he wanted to be, the Tennessee River was shining in the morning sun. "The Long Person expects we'll be there," he explained patiently.

Mollie Ross, the dark eyes of her Cherokee ancestry alight with love for her son, knelt beside him. Would he ever be able to understand his own mixed blood? But to be honest with herself, was she so certain that she wanted her son raised as a white child? Yet, what was the choice? In a historic move, the Cherokee Council itself had decided to renounce its ancient tribal posture and let down the bars against whites being allowed within its borders. It had voted to permit white missionaries into the Nation to set up schools for Cherokee children. More astounding, the children were to be taught the ways and things of white men. The Christian teachers would instruct the Indian children in reading and writing English, and the studies were the same as to be found in any white school.

"John, the teacher will not understand you if you speak of things like 'the Long Person' when you mean the river. Or if you say something like 'Ancient Red' when you mean fire. John, you are to learn to speak like a white boy now. You must try to remember the white words."

"Why?"

"Well, because our people have decided it is best. And because your father is a white man and wants you to speak as he does. That's why."

John, always respectful toward his father, accepted her explanation. When she reached again for his hand, he let her take it. They went to the front door of their comfortable home which stood grandly on a hill above the river. The Ross mill, a thriving business in the Cherokee Nation, was operating at full scale. Mollie could hear her husband's voice as he worked near the water with his employees. There were Negro slaves, too, lately acquired.

Mollie kissed her son on the cheek and gave him a little shove toward the open door. He stood in the doorway and gazed up at her with a pleading in his eyes but he said no more. He left the house and did not turn around to wave her a farewell although she waited for it.

Seating herself on the stone steps of the entrance to the house, she watched John head down the path which would take him through some woods along the river and to school, at last. She mused about the boy. He had been so beautiful and so strange at birth. Instead of being dark-eyed, bronze-skinned, black-haired, his red hair had been only a copper-colored fuzz and his eyes had seemed so blue and so round, so contrary to her expectation that her sons would inherit the look of her people. The Scottish background of his father was physically obvious in John, but his mother's Indian nature was surfacing in his personality.

As an infant John had not been attracted as much by white children's toys as he was by all the things of nature: the flight of birds, the wind, the rain, the scents of grass and flowers. He was fascinated by anything which sparkled or moved: the glitter of the river in the sunlight, the nesting birds in the trees gave him hours of delight as he lay in his cradle set out under the trees or walked through the forest by his mother or was taken by his father for a drifting canoe ride.

Born across the river near the base of Lookout Mountain in Tennessee, John was often a visitor at his Tennessee home, crossing the river from Ross, Georgia, with his family for stays at their first home.

When John was old enough to roam the area, he made friends of everyone. The Cherokee people called him Tsan, "Little John." He had Indian children as playmates, though some of them, even as he, were "mixed bloods." Because the Ross home was set beside the river and forests surrounded it, the boy was allowed to play in freedom. He wore buckskin jackets and leggings in the winter and almost nothing in the summers. Really, she decided, he had been very good about going to the white school this day—especially since his two Cherokee friends, Stand Watie and Pine Moseley, both full bloods, were not yet old enough for school and would no doubt devote the day to working on their fort under the watch of "the Long Person."

Mollie went to her bedroom, filled the washbasin with cool water from the pitcher, dipped a cloth in it, squeezed it dry, and held it to her throbbing forehead. She lay down on the rose-decorated quilt covering her bed and closed her eyes. A short time later she awoke at the sound of her husband's footsteps.

Daniel Ross was a large man with a square jawline and steady blue eyes. His sandy-colored hair was thinning and a slight pouch was beginnning to spoil his fine physique, but he still had the look and vigor of youth. Seeing her lying down, he frowned. "You sick?" He always felt a strange kind of resentment when she was ill.

She lifted a hand to him and smiled. "Oh, no. I had a little headache. It's almost gone." He was beside her, holding her hand. "I got John off to school. He hates his new suit."

Daniel smiled, too. "He'll get over it."

"I'm not too sure," she eyed her husband. "He's so much like you—so independent."

"If you mean he's got a mind of his own, you're right. I've noticed that in him. Well, I know what that is. I set my mind on having you—"

She squeezed his fingers. "It just never mattered, did it? My Indian family—your white one."

"It mattered. It gives our sons a proud heritage, one to make men of them. Lewis and Andy, though, don't seem quite as affected by their mixed blood as John does. But it's going to give him an interesting life."

She glanced out the window which had a view of the rock walk from the river to the door. She sucked in her breath. "Dan, look!"

Leaning over her shoulder, he looked, too, and expelled a roar of laughter. Mollie was on her feet, running to the front door.

She opened it to look down in astonishment at her youngest son. John was standing there totally naked, his suit of clothing neatly folded over one tanned arm, his shoes and stockings dangling from his other hand. He gazed soberly up at his mother and silently handed her his clothing.

She drew him into the house, shutting the door behind him. Daniel's expression was very stern. "What is this, John? Have you been to school?"

"Yes, Father." He turned to his mother. "I want my buckskins."

Daniel held up a hand to his wife. "Did you go to school without your clothing on?"

John shrugged his bare shoulders. "When I got to the woods, I just was itching, Father."

"And so you took your clothes off in the woods?"

"Yes."

"And went to school naked?"

"Yes, Father."

"John, you have done a very bad thing, you know that?"

John's wide blue eyes looked in puzzlement from his father to the clothing in his mother's hands. He said nothing.

Daniel squatted in front of his son. "Listen, John. I'll try to explain. You're my son. You are a Ross. Through me, you're white." He looked up at Mollie who was standing hugging the clothes, her own eyes shadowed. "Through your mother and her people, you are Cherokee. We're proud that you have both bloods. But I want you to learn now to love the things that I love. You've learned a lot of Cherokee things and now it's time for you to understand about white men and their lives. I want you to honor the things I honor. Do you understand, John?" He gripped the boy gently by the arms. "You are to wear the clothing of white boys at school."

John's mouth had firmed as he listened, and his shoulders squared more. "Are Stand and Pine white, too?"

Daniel shook his head, "No, John. They are Indian—Cherokee. They have no white blood line."

John bit his lip. "Do they have to wear white clothes?"

Daniel stood up. "No, I suppose not, unless their families decide upon it."

John's eyes were misted. "Father, will it be all right if I wear my buckskins when I go to build our fort at the side of the Long Person?"

"The Long Person, huh?" Daniel grinned. It was going to take a while to educate John Ross to speak in English terms. "Yes, John, it will be all right." He put the boy on his feet. "Go on, get your buckskins and find your friends. Greet the Long Person for me. But tomorrow, off you go to school in the clothes your mother made for you." He paused. "And you'll say 'the river' during school hours."

His father gave him a playful punch in the ribs, and John giggled. Then he ran off to his room in search of the buckskins.

V

BY DECEMBER OF 1796, JOHN HAD TURNED FROM HIS obstinancy to an eager fervor for learning. He was so excellent in his studies that his father hired a private tutor to accelerate the boy's progress. Yet the father did not neglect John's instinctive and rightful need to know of his Cherokee heritage. All his sons learned of it.

When the Cherokee Council called a very important meeting in mid-December, the Cherokee people came from all points of their nation to the temporary capital at Ustanali, Georgia, a town of sixty log-constructed homes on the Coosawatee River. The public meeting hall, known as the Town House, was set in a cleared public square, its heavy timbers secured against the weather by a covering of clay.

Daniel Ross took his son with him. The boy was accustomed to attending council meetings, as were the Cherokee children, but tradition held that the children always sat with their mother and her people. "This day I want my son with me," Daniel had told Mollie. "The Council is to hear the Farewell Address of President Washington. He is my President, and he is John's. We will sit together to hear his words."

The one door of the building was narrow and the way dark until the turn was made into the immense hall. The tiered seats arose in a semicircle from the center of the rotunda where there burned in perpetuity the sacred Eternal Fire of the Cherokee people, the symbol of their own eternal life.

John's eyes smarted from the smoke of the fire and the lighting of many pipes in the windowless room. He walked close to his father as they moved toward their sofa but he kept his gaze on the fire and watched the smoke spiral upward, drifting lazily past the rafters overhead before it vanished through the small opening in the roof. His father had told him that the flames came from seven different kinds of wood.

"There are seven clans in the Cherokee Nation," Daniel told

his son, "and they are the clans of Wolf, Deer, Bird, Blue, Red, Twister, and Wild Potato. These are like separate families, yet they are related. And each clan has its own wood to burn in the eternal fire to assure its own eternity. As long as the fire burns in the council houses of the Nation, so shall the people live forever. The home fires are kindled by brands lighted by the eternal fire."

John wondered if the blue haze in the room was coming from the wood burning for the Blue Clan.

As he and his father took their places on the sofa set halfway back from the front tier, John looked to the sacred area where sat the Town Chiefs. The White Chiefs of each town were seated closest to the fire because they were Peace Chiefs, and peace was in the land at the moment. The Nation was quiet and in all the towns and valleys there was heard only the sounds of peace: children at play, the jingle of the bells on the sheep and cattle in the fields.

John had never seen the War Chiefs take the place closest to the fire. His father had told him about it though, and John hopefully looked for them anyway. But they were not in war dress today, and he would not see them with their faces painted black and slashed with scarlet stripes. Today they had not struck the war pole outside the Town House, nor had they sent the war hatchet to all the towns of the Nation and to their allies. Today there was peace.

John, a little disappointed, saw that the Beloved Women had taken their seats in the area set apart for them near the White Chiefs. The women, their hair fixed into shining braids which they had wound around their heads into a crownlike appearance neatly held by bands of silver, wore semilong petticoats over leggings, their briefly cut jackets decorated with beads.

He was fascinated by the sight of Nancy Ward. She wore a ceremonial dress woven of white swan feathers, and a headdress of the same downy beauty. Colorful beads were brilliant around her neck and she wore silver armbands. As she moved gracefully toward her place on the sofa among the Beloved Women, the musicians, from their place near the White Chiefs, tendered her a musical offering. A red-stained water drum, its drumhead of skin resounding to the beating hands of the drummer, tattooed loudly and was accompanied by the chattering of gourd rattles and the piping of flutes.

John looked across the hall to where he usually sat with his mother. She was there, smiling at him across the space between them. Her hair was swept back in the popular style of the day, pulled into a glossy mass tied in place at the back of her neck with a dried eelskin—a fad which had swept the tribe when word went out that the skin of the eel could make hair grow long and lovely. Mollie was wearing the customary short skirt, leggings, and brief jacket of deerskin with a yellow calico shirtwaist underneath.

The meeting was beginning. Major Ridge, called always "the Ridge," arose from his seat and went to stand by the fire to be heard. He was a full blood, a young man of fierce expression, dark skin, and a generous head of hair. A few years back he had fought a battle with his own view that the Cherokees must practice strict racial purity. He had fallen in love with a mixed-blood girl, Susie Wickett, and he had married her. Their son, John, sat with his mother near Mollie Ross. John was the same age as Mollie's son, and Mollie smiled at him, too, and pointed out her son to him. The boys waved to each other.

The Ridge introduced an interpreter who would put President Washington's message into the Cherokee language.

John heard the name *Washington* spoken with such reverence he knew it was the name of a white man who was a friend of the Indians. Before he sat down and gave the floor to the interpreter, the Ridge said, "We as a people have lost a friend. Our brother, the great Washington has put away his right to be Chief of his people. He goes to quiet years now. He leaves us. We are alone."

The Farewell Address of President George Washington was read and heard. The silence was so deep in the rotunda that the hiss of the fire could be heard throughout the place.

When the message was finished, the Cherokee chiefs of the Upper, Lower, and Middle towns of the Nation arose to acclaim Washington. John did not understand everything that was said, but their emotion-filled voices, their dramatic ceremonial white doeskin clothing, all affected him very much. They used terms that John understood: Warrior, Chief, Friend, Brother, Brave. He swung his gaze to look around the hall and he saw the same spellbound expression on everyone's face.

The enthralled boy thought: They're talking about a white man! John looked at his father. White, like Washington.

Then the praises were finished. The people stood a moment

at their seats and chorused, "Toeuhah." Daniel spoke the word aloud in English, offering the President his own praise: "It is true."

Now a War Chief came forward from his ranks and stood by the fire to speak.

Chief Tellico was aging and the mark of it showed in the darkening of his skin and the shadows in his eyes. Yet he took care with his appearance. He affected the old warrior's style of headdress, his head shaved except for the bristling top part which he had decorated with glistening beads and brightly dyed feathers of purple. His buckskins were new and his moccasins tied with snakeskin. His old hands bore tattoos of flowers he had pricked into the skin long ago, using gunpowder to create the stain. His war deeds entitled him to be taken seriously. He wore no warpaint on his lean face, but in a harsh voice he cautioned that there was a white man who, unlike Washington, was not their friend.

"There are many white men who rejoice this hour that our brother, the Great Chief Washington, is no longer to sit in power. Already we have endured the greed of the white men who hate us and who come among us to steal our land and to send us away."

The people said again: "Toeuhah!"

Chief Tellico held an arm high, turning slowly to look at everyone seated in the semitheater.

He lowered his voice to a husky tone. "There is a white man who is our enemy and the enemy of our protector, Washington. The man is called Andrew Jackson."

A rumble of voices told him the name was known.

The old Chief held his arm aloft again in a gesture for silence. "I am ancient. I will not stay long among you. I speak wisely to you now and I want you to remember my words. Andrew Jackson is the enemy of the Cherokees. He has already robbed some of us of our lands. He covets all our Nation. He has said that he will remove us all away from this land which was given us by the Great Spirit."

Again the people in the rotunda talked to one another, and once more their voices spoke out: "Toeuhah!"

Chief Tellico raised both arms, turning from left to right to gain quiet, and spoke with renewed vigor. "He is called the Honorable Andrew Jackson, a new member of the United States

Congress from Tennessee. This man of honor has said to the Congress: Impeach Washington!" The old Chief paced the dirt floor. "He would impeach Washington for several reasons, but largely because he accuses him of being too friendly with all Indians in general and with the Cherokee in particular. Because Washington would honor the Holston Treaty and bring troops to our protection against the invasion of white men who want to steal our land, Andrew Jackson, the honorable man from Tennessee, suggests his impeachment.

"If I am a wise man, I have spoken a wise warning to you. My last word now is: Cherokees, beware of the Honorable Andrew Jackson. This white man Jackson will drag us away from the land of our fathers. We will no longer see the graves of our people. Our ancestral home will be under the feet of white men." He gave a mighty grunt, his speech finished.

The chiefs and the people left the Council with hearts heavy. Where would they be heard, now that Washington was gone from power? John asked his father if Andrew Jackson were colored blue. Daniel, leading the boy out of the Town House, was puzzled. "What do you mean, John?"

"Blue is the color of trouble, you know. Blue is defeat."

The white father realized his young son was associating color with deeds. "Well, I guess that's right. If Chief Tellico speaks the truth, and none deny it, then Andrew Jackson is colored blue for the Cherokee people."

VI

DURING THE NEXT DECADE, JOHN ROSS RECEIVED HIS education and attended an academy at Kingsport, Tennessee. He excelled in his studies and concentrated on governmental systems, but always he returned with tremendous satisfaction to the home of his parents. The land grabbers were still operating, and now the legislatures of Tennessee, Georgia, South Carolina, North Carolina, and Virginia were beginning to experiment with laws to declare the rights of Indians null and void.

On June 22, 1807, during John's final year of school, the British frigate *Leopard* overtook the American frigate *Chesapeake*, which had enlisted some British sailors as part of its crew. The sailors, deserters from other British ships, were demanded as prisoners by the commander of the *Leopard*. When the American frigate refused to deliver them, the *Leopard* fired across the *Chesapeake*'s bow and then fired directly into her, hitting her three times. The shots killed three American sailors. The British seized the deserters.

The United States was teetering on the brink of war, but President Thomas Jefferson held it off through economic measures against the British.

The British, for their part, were certain that war would ensue, probably through an invasion of Canada by American troops. They sent emissaries to the Indians all along the far-flung border, seeking active allies against the Americans. Their argument was persuasive; supplies of food and guns and ammunition reached the Indians. Chief Tecumseh and his brother, the Prophet, already driving for a confederation of all Indian tribes to war upon white Americans with the aim of their annihilation, traveled among the tribes of the American nation to urge war.

John, approaching his eighteenth year, went home. His mother was not well and his father seemed to be lost in an increasing vagueness of mind and action. John, somewhat set apart from his childhood friends by the years he had spent at a white man's school, went in search of his people, riding daily among them, traveling the nation, renewing old friendships and making new ones.

At a town in the center of the Nation called Cita, John rode in on his sleek black horse in time to celebrate the fifth festival of the Cherokee year, the Ah, Tawh, Hung, Nah event which signified the beginning of a renewed life for every Cherokee. The chant-like phrase called for a "turn around to a new life." He came to town as every Cherokee family brought their old clothing and furniture, all old and worn possessions, to the flames of a mammoth fire in the center of the public square. This was the time when the sacred fires burning in the town houses of each community were extinguished and renewed from the flames of the central fire. When the flames had died away to embers, the people came forward and scooped the red-hot leavings into vessels and carried them home to start their own home fires once more.

Cita was a Town of Refuge, a place to which those who had sinned, even murderers, could come to live in immunity, and because of Ah, Tawh, Hung, Nah, forgiveness and a new life was theirs.

The ceremonies included a dipping in the river and a drink of a black liquid which was said to purify. John, still damp from the river, was sipping the drink slowly when his gaze went to the girl known as Quatie.

She was standing not far from him, beside handsome Jim Henley, a full blood whom John had known slightly from childhood. Quatie's white teeth were in bright contrast to the deep bronze of her skin. Her hair was thick and very black, and she wore it shoulder-length, free of combs and ties. Under the loose folds of a white doeskin dress, her small-boned body was enough to entice the eye of any man.

As they talked, Jim reached for her hand, and they laughed together in some private understanding. Their open affection in public meant only one thing: they were pledged to marry. The ceremony tonight was a good time to celebrate a coming marriage which, too, was a kind of renewed life.

John was pierced by a pang of jealousy. Until now he had viewed the meaning of the archaic ceremony in its more staid connotation: friendship, beginning. But now, tantalized by the dark-eyed beauty of Quatie Brown, he knew its real significance: intimacy between a man and a woman was the real meaning of Ah, Tawh, Hung, Nah.

Quatie had turned from Jim to John at his approach, but the smile fled and awe came into her expression. The dark-haired Cherokee girl and the red-haired man stared at one another as though they were alone.

The sound of Jim's voice, introducing them, brought them back to their surroundings. Quatie managed a smile and held firmly to Jim's hand: "John Ross," she repeated, "I'm glad to greet you."

John, with never a glance for Jim, asked, "When are you to be his wife?"

Jim's fingers gripped hers more firmly. "Tomorrow," Jim answered John's question.

Quatie said not a thing. John, hardly realizing what he did, offered the Great Spirit of the Cherokee people the silent prayer of a man who seeks his perfect mate. Through his mind flashed the words all Cherokees offered for love—I promise this: Give me this woman as my mate and she will never be lonely. Her soul has come into the very center of mine, never to turn away. She is mine. I take her.

But John turned away from Quatie and offered his hand to Jim Henley in congratulations. The Bear Dance was just commencing, and the dancer, hidden by the burden of the bearskin in which he was wrapped, was starting his wild dance to the thumping of the drums. But without daring another look, John strode to his horse and rode away. The reverberations followed him and the drumbeats seemed to be repeating: Quatie, Quatie, Quatie.

His Cherokee blood told him: Take her. His white blood said: You cannot have her. He wondered, tormented, if the ancient ways of the Indians were not the best ways. Not long ago, it would not matter if Quatie did marry Jim Henley. She would be able to take as many husbands as she wanted. No! He would not want it that way, nor would she. I have found her and I have lost her, all in a moment, John thought. He knew his only remedy was to interest himself in other women and in the affairs of his Nation.

Yet even as he became popular as a young leader, he found no woman who could really make him forget Quatie Henley. Often he saw her from a distance, riding through town. He liked Jim Henley, and whenever they met they exchanged ideas on the topics of the day and parted in friendliness. He avoided seeing Quatie alone, and whenever she appeared in any group in which he was included, he always made a quick departure.

He berated himself for his hopeless love. When he saw that Quatie's young body was swelling with the growth of a baby, he rode blindly out of town. What it must have been like, to plant that seed of love in her! John rode to the river, tore his clothing off, and plunged into the cool waters. Rising from the dive, water spilling from him, he made his way back to shore. He looked up at the blue sky and he begged: "God help me. Take her from my mind and soul."

VII

AT NEW ECHOTA, THE ROUNDED TOWN HOUSE WITH ITS dome-shaped roof was set amid the communal gardens in the public square, but the harvesting of the gardens had taken place over a month ago and now the grounds lay frozen and black on the November evening which was to witness John Ross in speech for the first time before the Cherokee Council. The Eternal Fire burned in the center of its floor.

The chiefs of all the towns were there, as were the Beloved Women. Many citizens had come to hear John Ross, who had requested permission to speak on a matter he deemed important.

The place seemed excessively hot when John entered it through the narrow doorway. He was among the last to arrive, and was pleased to see the Beloved Women sitting on the sofas—the places they occupied when they were to give advice. They were dressed in new wool outfits and they sat on blankets which they would wrap around themselves if the rotunda became cold. Their dark eyes were friendly, watching him.

He strode to his place beside the Eternal Fire where Elias Boudinot [Buck Watie], the elder brother of Stand Watie, awaited him. A brilliant man known only in his youthful days as Buck Watie, he had gained his new name of Elias Boudinot when the aged white President of the American Bible Society, impressed with the young Cherokee, asked him to adopt his full name in life. Stand Watie, only a few years older than John, was unlike his brother, unquestionably Indian in looks and personality. He put an affectionate hand on John's shoulder as they faced the assembly together.

Gazing down upon them from their places on the sofas were John's parents and his brothers, Andrew and Lewis. Mollie Ross held her husband's hand. Even though the place was very warm, the father shivered. Mollie gave him a glance and pulled his coat collar up a little higher around his neck. She forgot her own headache, but lately they came so often she had almost forgotten

what it was like not to have one. Seated near them were the Ridge, the uncle of Stand and Elias; Sequoyah, Going Snake, and Ira Parkins, the government interpreter whose services were permanently offered to the Nation through the Holston Treaty. Custom decreed that all Council meetings be held in the Cherokee language, so Parkins was not always heard from.

Elias, dropping his hand from John's shoulder, began. "Beloved Women! Brothers! We come to hear John Ross. He has earned the right to speak to us not only because his age permits, but because he has earned the respect of his elders. He is strong in heart and honorable in tongue. He cherishes the ways of our people. He is ours. We shall hear him if it be the will of this Council. Shall we hear John Ross?"

The routine question Boudinot asked was always put to the Council when a young man came to speak for the first time. The little silence that always followed the asking seemed a long time to John. There had been cases where a young man had not been heard.

He took a deep breath as Elias Boudinot, accepting the silence as the approval it was, left him and went to his seat next to the Ridge.

Instinctively, John knew that this was the last minute of his life in which he would be claimed as a friend by every man and woman there. When he finished speaking this evening, things would be changed.

He requested Ira Parkins, the wiry man clad in a hunter's jacket and trousers of red wool, to come forward. "Mister Parkins? Will you oblige me? I'll speak in English, but I'd like an interpretation of my words into the Cherokee language."

"Certainly, Mister Ross." If Parkins was surprised, he did not show it, but the same could not be said of the Council members and the guests.

Parkins came down the dirt steps to John's side at the fire. There was a hasty, whispered conference between the Ridge and Boudinot at the level of the fifth step above the fire and then the Ridge stood. Clad in a dark suit and calico shirt; he had a robust physique and now his fleshy but handsome face was darker than normal and there was no serenity in his eyes. His heavy gray hair was cut short and brushed back from his broad forehead, standing out from his head in a kind of feathery effect.

The members of the Council silenced themselves to hear him.

The crackling of the fire and the little sounds of a restless audience filled the room. "Does John Ross appear at this Council as a white man?" the Ridge inquired.

John faced him. "I am a Cherokee yet, also, I am white. I am both, now and always. As a Cherokee I want my people to prosper and to be blessed with the good things of earth. As a white man, I know what the red men must do to gain these things. I want the red men to be equal to the white men in all things. A start must be made if this is to be. I begin with a request that I be allowed to speak to this Council in the English language and that my words be interpreted in the Cherokee for any here who do not understand English."

The Ridge was furious. "No, no, no! There shall be no English spoken in Cherokee Council business. You shall not stride in here in all your swagger of twenty-one years and dictate to this venerable body the language it shall use. You shall not break our customs. You shall not be heard!"

John stood with his fists clenched at his sides, his blue-eyed gaze sweeping the hall quickly. Would they support the Ridge, whose influence was undeniable? Or had he dared right?

Going Snake hefted himself to his moccasined feet and he let his blanket fall off his shoulders. His aged voice was not powerful, but it was clearly heard. "This Council has voted to allow John Ross to speak. Brother Ridge, you violate a rule of this body. Let not your anger, however just it may be, topple you from that which is right. The floor of this Council has been yielded by our vote to our son, John Ross. We shall hear him."

The Ridge's wary eyes saw that with a few exceptions, Going Snake had expressed the attitude in the hall. "My brother, Going Snake speaks wise words. Yet I cannot take my seat until I have said this: I have always regarded John Ross as one of us. Now, hearing him, I am shockingly aware of his white blood and his white education." And the Ridge grunted and sat down.

The expressions on many faces had altered, and the rotunda was humming with subdued remarks as Going Snake and the Ridge took their seats. Motioning to Parkins that he was ready, John began to speak. He spaced his words carefully, giving Parkins time enough to interpret his words.

"My sisters! My brothers! These are days of bad trouble for the United States of America. The time is perilous for all Americans, be they red or white. And because this is so, we must unite.

The British, the French, the Spaniards have sent warriors to our land and seek to use any Indian, or tribe of Indians, against the white Americans. No frontier is safe from their plottings. Indians are uniting with the enemy of the United States and dealing death and destruction to white men. It is true many Indians have suffered death and losses due to some whites, and for this reason the British, the French, and the Spaniards are using these red men against the white in America."

Elias Boudinot and the Ridge had their heads together again, whispering. John lost his pacing for a moment, and decided to take the offensive. "Do my brothers wish to make a comment?"

"Yes," Boudinot said, unabashed. "We wonder why our young brother gives us a history lesson. It is well known that there are murders and burnings on the frontiers and that many red men wish to annihilate the white race. We know many are joining the foreign powers against the Americans. Does our brother have something else to say?"

John's voice was cool. "Three years ago the first serious legal conflict between white natives and red occurred when several Cherokees led by Chief Doublehead in Georgia, our homeland, accepted bribes and sold some sacred land of our Nation to white land speculators. I need not say that no Cherokee can legally own the land which the Great Spirit has given us all, but may only lease it so long as he tends it. Therefore, the sales were illegal. More, it is a matter of treason, punishable by death at the hands of he who apprehends the perpetrator of the deed."

"Go on," said Boudinot with a deliberate note of resignation in his voice.

"Doublehead was murdered for treason—"

The Ridge was standing and his breath came in a heaving gasp: "Murdered! I executed Chief Doublehead, as our law demands."

John bowed his head to the Ridge: "The execution of Chief Doublehead was accomplished by the Ridge with a blow by an axe to the head of the victim whom he had found hiding in the attic of a schoolhouse. The criminal had been put to death viciously and without the due process of law recognized in the world of white men. The United States Constitution—"

"What are you saying?" The Ridge spoke through gritted teeth.

John took his time. "It is time the Cherokee people organize into a republican type of government patterned on the Constitution of the United States of America, with a view to becoming a state in that American Union. In this way alone will we ever claim perfect equality with the white men. We can lay no claim to that equality until we are ready for it."

Going Snake was on his feet. "Suppose you're right. Where do we begin?"

"We have begun," John said. "We're speaking in English for the first time in the history of this Council. But before we can go further, we must unite. We must hold our lands, and to do this we must write an unbreakable and just law regarding the ceding of any Cherokee land to any white man."

"We have our ancient law, and it is unbreakable and just," the Ridge interrupted. "It gives to any who violate the law against ceding our land the just treatment he has earned: death! It is the Law of Blood. It serves us well."

"No, it is an old custom and it is bad. We must become a proper government, not just a loosely flung organization of many Town Chiefs with a Council which can meet only infrequently. We must create a government like that of the United States if we are to gain international respect."

Going Snake commented: "You ask for unity—"

"Unity!" the Ridge broke in. He flung an arm wide: "Out there is Tecumseh, the great Chief, seeking to unite all Indians against all whites. Yet his plans are lost in the wilderness today, the guns of the enemy have destroyed him. Tecumseh is hunted. Yet you stand here in all your magnificient wisdom of twenty-one years and advise your elders to seek unity against the white man?"

John whispered to Parkins: "I want to be quoted as accurately as possible so there will be no misunderstanding of my words." He turned back to the Ridge: "I say we must unite in order to gain strength as one people, and when we have that strength we will be able to organize into a republican form of government. Then, as such, we will be a free and independent nation, gaining recognition in the nations of the world. Then we could be admitted into the American Union and know true equality with our white brothers."

The Ridge replied as though the wind had been knocked out of him: "You advocate unity in order that we may obtain statehood—in the white Union—"

"My brothers," said John, addressing the entire assemblage, "I pledge my life to this ideal for our Nation. As a civilized state in the Union, we would follow a destiny we can know in no other way. No battle shall swerve me. No friend, no enemy, shall move me from my path. The future of the Cherokee people can only be reached through the high road of constitutional government, the same trail already blazed by white Americans."

The members of the Council were stilled, forgetting their pipesmoking, forgetting their whisperings. The Eternal Fire flamed unnoticed. Outside there was a sudden squall of snow and hail, and the hailstones rattled on the roof like gunfire.

The Ridge shook his head and announced bitterly: "We have heard this night the Oracle of Delphi!"

Going Snake asked: "Have you spoken all your words?"

John batted a hand at the drifting smoke. "I have a request. I ask that the Council send me to Arkansas on an official visit to our brothers there. Let me go speak to them. Let me see how they live under their self-inflicted exile. Let me see how they do after three years alone in a new land."

"What purpose would that serve?" Going Snake asked.

"I want to know what happens to our brothers who sell their lands—our lands—and move away from us. I want to know if the crime of selling their land, the move west, the money they received, has been worth it to our departed people. We cannot realize our strengths, until we are aware of our weaknesses. That is why I must go."

The request sent a stir among the members. The Beloved Women hastily drew together at their benches and conferred. The men discussed the matter, word going from man to man around the semicircle of seats. Glances were directed at John as he stood motionless beside the fire, awaiting the verdict.

The Ridge stood and looked toward the Beloved Women. "We seek the advice of our most wise."

A tall, thin-bodied woman of forty years arose from a sofa, shedding her bench blanket like a coccoon to stand regally clad in a full-length white wool dress. Black braids, tightly wound around her head, glittered with the glass beads strung through them. Her voice was unhurried. "'We are impressed with John Ross. We believe he is wise to suggest the mission. We think that he has expressed here tonight the ideas of our young men and that he must travel to Arkansas. We want him to go and talk to our wandering brothers. But, as mothers, we fear for him. The path of Arkansas is a long and lonely one. It is not good for any man to travel through such dangers without a companion. We ask only that he be accompanied by another young man. If this is done, let him go." The woman took her seat again on the bench, rewrapping herself securely in the warmth of the blanket.

The Ridge and Elias Boudinot leaned their heads together again in consultation. Then Boudinot sat down and the Ridge began to address the Council. "Before a vote is taken on the mission to Arkansas, I offer a suggestion in support of the advice of the Beloved Women. Let Stand Watie, who numbers his years at eighteen and who is a friend of John Ross, accompany him." He waited, but the suggestion was not challenged, and thus accepting the silence as agreement, he went on: "One more point, brothers, sisters: Let John Ross and Stand Watie be instructed that under no conditions shall they attend to policy matters of our people. They shall not enter into any political or policy discussion with our brothers in the west. Let it be clear that their mission is to obtain information only and that they hold no authority to speak for the Council. If this is agreed, let the mission proceed."

The vote was taken, and it was unanimously agreed that John Ross, with young Stand Watie as his aide, would travel west to Arkansas to ascertain the living conditions of the Cherokee who had voluntarily removed themselves west on profits from sales of their homelands in Georgia.

Stand Watie looked as Indian as John Ross looked white. His face was squarely constructed with level, dark eyebrows, broad nose, and a firm mouth with its slight downcast pull at the corners. His skin, naturally dark, was tanned further by the weather. His abundant hair hung to his shoulders, but he kept it well washed and brushed. His pride in being a full blood among a people who were becoming mixed bloods gave him a haughty, even a belligerent manner. He believed himself superior to John Ross. During their very young years they had disagreed more than they agreed, yet so evenly were they matched in their capabilities that they sought each other's companionship. They had a respect for one another, but no warmth; yet their lifelong friendship had endured and they were often hunting companions, friendly competitors at sports and rivals at dances.

Now, although John might have preferred a more friendly

companion in the wilderness, he recognized the choice of Stand ›
Watie as a good one.

Stand was as eager to travel westward as John. "If I had not
been chosen, I would have trailed along, anyway," he admitted.

"I know," John grinned. "But let's have no misunderstanding
on the trail. This is my mission and I am in command. I won't
be responsible for you as a companion unless you agree that my
word is law throughout the mission."

Watie's gaze was steady enough, but there was a flare in the
depths of his dark eyes. "I understand. But when I am twenty-
one, I shall have my own mission."

"All right. But now, I hold the vote. My first decision is that
we'll travel by water to Arkansas. It's faster and easier."

"Water!" Stand objected. "That's the long route. And practically frozen."

"We'll ride horses to Chattanooga and embark by canoe at the
point there, taking the Tennessee River north to where it joins
the Ohio, and south on the Ohio to the Mississippi, going down
to Arkansas on it."

"That takes us into Missouri Territory."

"Why not? The settlement we go to visit is on the border,
claiming Arkansas by a hair's breadth."

Stand's face was washed by a frown. "You think a canoe is
adequate on the Mississippi? It's got a mighty pull, you know."

"We'll trade ours in at Paducah for the toughest new one we
can find. Are you worried?"

Stand denied it. "But I would think we'd use the Federal road
and go by way of Nashville."

"I've decided upon the river trip," said John.

Stand accepted the decision outwardly, but he thought: John
Ross thinks like a white man, and worse, he acts like one.

As they readied for their mission, word came from the north
that the warriors of Tecumseh had gathered together once more
for a planned raid on the Indiana Territory. General William
Henry Harrison had attacked them, losing nearly two hundred
of his men, but nevertheless breaking the back of what he termed
a major renewal of Indian warfare centered at the Tippecanoe
River.

Once more the warriors Tecumseh led were scattered by white
soldiers, and the elusive chief was banished. Reports circulated
that he had been killed at Tippecanoe, but rumors of his death

were never rare. One thing was certain: Harrison and his troops had destroyed the village of the Prophet, and Tecumseh's cause of a united Indian war against the whites of America had received a bloody setback.

John and Stand's trip up the Tennessee and on the Ohio was marked by very cold weather and the fall of snow and sleet. Ice blocked their progress more than once, and John wondered if he had chosen the most difficult route. It was a mean and wet canoe ride from Chattanooga to the Mississippi to Arkansas. But the flow of the Mississippi carried them swiftly, and one snowy day they were greeted at the Cherokee settlement of Tahlonteskee.

John was appalled at their situation. The displaced Cherokees in Arkansas were living a rugged life. Their borderline neighbors, the Osage, demanded the removal of the Cherokee, calling them interlopers on their lands. Frequent raids brought death and terror to both sides.

Although the Cherokee had been there three years, their farms still looked like they were newly hacked out of the woods. Poorly stocked, they offered almost nothing in the way of a living. Their homes held no comforts except for the few items which had traveled west, such as the trunks of hide gaily painted with flowers, in use as needed chests and cupboards. There was absolutely no formal government in the settlement, nor any schools, and the children were being taught very little.

John saw all that he needed to know: the sale of the productive Cherokee acreage in Georgia had brought these people near to disaster. He knew what he would say in his report to the Council upon his return.

But Stand Watie looked at the same settlement and he saw an independent people, free of white men, carving their own future out of the wilderness, dedicated to their own way of life. He was inspired by the hardworking, meagerly rewarded red men. "You're looking at these people through the eyes of a white man," he told John. "You want them to live in a civilized white town. Why? Leave them alone. They are Indians and they want to stay Indian."

John had promised the Council he would not speak of his policies, and he aimed to keep that promise. He would not discuss it with Stand, either, lest Stand rightfully protest to the Council that John Ross had put forth his own political opinions among the people at Tahlonteskee.

Their mission done, John and Stand began the arduous trip back upriver. It was bitter winter weather in mid-December as they traveled up the Mississippi toward the white settlement of St. Louis.

VIII

ON THE FIFTEENTH EVENING OF DECEMBER, THEY MADE CAMP on a wide bank of the Mississippi under a high-towering, tree-covered bluff. The freezing night was exceptionally clear, and the stars were like distant campfires, flaring with color.

They built a fire and allowed themselves the luxury of coffee made in a small clay pot which Stand had packed along with a few knives and their few items of prepared food. They ate in silence, and giving up trying to warm themselves by the small fire, they wrapped themselves in their blankets to lie down beside the flames, Within an hour, however, the cold ground became a misery under them so they moved into the canoe, which gave them some added protection. Huddled in the bottom of the craft, they soon slept. John was not even annoyed, as he usually was, by the weight of his money belt around his waist. The campfire, untended, went out and nothing disturbed their sleep, not even their half-sitting positions in the canoe.

At a few minutes after two o'clock that morning, there was a rushing noise, a thunderclap, and a flash like lightning. They awoke, startled, but there was no storm. The stars were still shining.

They sat up, turning startled faces to each other. The canoe gave a pitch, the ground heaved, and massive waves arose out of the dark waters of the Mississippi, reaching for the small boat.

The bluff above began to crumble, and rocks and trees began a tumbling ride to the river. The tree to which their canoe had been tied toppled, ripping the mooring rope. The ground beneath gave way, and water from the river lifted the boat and tugged it into midstream. John and Stand, slumped together in the canoe, held on to each other, dazed, knowing only that the earth was quaking, and that the river was rising, falling, shifting, gone amuck.

The canoe was carried erratically downriver, all but submerged, threatening to overturn at each wash of the monstrous waves. They were drenched, helpless, clutching to the sides of the craft.

The swells of the river spilled water onto the land and the backwash drew trees and mud back into the river, to add to the debris. The heaving waters grew murky and discolored, and with the discoloration came a sickening, sulphurous odor to burn their nostrils and plague their seasick stomachs. The turbulent waters played with their canoe as though it were a cork.

Lifting his head, John exclaimed, "My God!" above the roar. Stand pushed himself up in time to see an island disappearing just ahead of them. The peculiar light of the atmosphere, hovering somewhere between dawn and daylight, provided sufficient illumination of the terrible happenings to give the men all too good a view of the catastrophe. As they looked, the tree-covered piece of land submerged amid the pulling and hurling of the river's savage run. Where the island had stood but moments before, there was now a rapid billowing, an ugly cresting of the darkened waters. Then, terrifyingly, against every law of nature, the Mississippi reversed its natural flow and a great wave of water swept upstream, carrying the canoe northward with it.

The men weakly turned themselves around in the craft. Trembling, Stand wiped his wet face and choked on the odor of the sulphur.

A broken canoe, turned upside down, floated near them until it was snatched away by a new funneling of waves. The water was filled with debris of all kinds.

John felt as though his lungs were bursting from the combined water, cold, and odor. He watched the shoreline and saw the land split, trees felled, forests leveled as if by an unseen axe. Squirrels, rabbits, deer, game of every type were swimming in the unfriendly waters.

Something hit John's face and he reached for it with icy fingers. It was a fish desperately seeking peaceful shallows. He tossed it away.

As a floating tree began to tumble past their canoe, John grasped hold of its leafless branches, his numbed hands not even feeling the cuts he received. Stand, understanding what John was attempting to do, moved to help him. The canoe would not stay afloat much longer. They hauled the tree as close as possible to the side of their canoe and on the makeshift raft rode together upriver.

Stand hit his head on the edge of the canoe, and blood streamed from his nose. John's left thumb was broken, but he did not yet know it. The tree branches scraped his face and slashed him across the forehead.

A whirlpool grabbed the little canoe and tore the tree from the hands of the men, sending the craft into a spin, around and around. Beyond, much too close, huge boulders suddenly shot up from the river bottom, forming a chain of rocks from shore to shore. The craft stopped its wild turnings, and then plunged down, waterlogged, toward the chain of rocks.

"We're going to hit!" John warned. Kneeling in the boat, water swirling over them, they covered their heads with their arms as the canoe rammed into the side of a massive boulder.

In the water, barely conscious, buffeted and bleeding, they gained a handhold on the slimy boulder where waves dashed and receded wildly. They made an exhausted climb upward, hauling themselves wearily to the top of the rocky haven where they lay for some time, unable to move as the river jumped toward them only to fall back.

After a seemingly timeless age, John felt the cold wind. He was shivering and even as he shook from the icy blast, the temperature of the wind altered drastically and it felt hot to him.

Stand got to his feet carefully and turned his face into the wind. His voice was crippled with fatigue. "The wind is Black. It comes from the west and it is Black." He shivered from a sense of doom.

John touched him reassuringly. "No. It's not the wind that has done this. There is no such thing as a Black Wind. Stand, you speak of ancient Cherokee fables. There is no wind which brings death."

Anger chased the terror from Stand's eyes. "There is truth only in the Cherokee. The wind from the east is Red and brings success, and the wind from the north is Blue and brings defeat in battle, and the wind from the south is White and brings peace. So does the wind from the west bring death, and it is a Black Wind."

"Stand—"

"You are sightless if you do not see this wind which blows upon us. It is Black. It has brought death to the Long Person. The Black Wind blows upon him."

Stand's shock continued to manifest in recalling the teachings of his people. "Shina, the Evil Spirit, has stirred the Black Wind against the white people. He takes their land from them, swallows it, even as they take from us." He gazed vacantly at the waters.

John's thumb hurt and he knew it needed to be put between sticks and bound securely. "I need to bind this," he said, choosing to change the subject. If they were going to make their way to safety, they had to think clearly.

Stand looked at the injury. He said solemnly: "May the Great Spirit heal your left knee which is sore and swollen."

"Don't, Stand," John scolded. "All I need is to find a couple of sticks."

Stand's dark eyes glistened. "I have prayed the formula prayer of confusion. I have fooled the Evil Spirit. By telling Shina that your injury is in the knee, I have confounded him. Now his power knows not where to go and it will leave you."

"Come on, Stand," John said. "The good God has given us a way over these waters—a bridge of boulders."

They made their way, slipping, climbing, jumping, swimming from boulder to boulder until they reached the new shoreline of the Mississippi River. They rested only for a while, and then began walking over water-pocked earth which rumbled and shook.

John's thumb, expertly bound at last with sticks and strips of bark, was more of a nuisance than a misery. They plodded on, stepping time and again into hidden crevices cut in the ground by the quake. Once their feet were sucked at by quicksand which bubbled unexpectedly from a deep pit in soggy earth. The wind continued to blow hot and cold, and the light of the atmosphere fluctuated as though lightning came and went.

At St. Louis, John was thankful that he had chosen coins as

his money medium. He brought forth his water-stained money belt and paid for food, lodgings, new clothing, weapons, horses, and equipment. After eating and resting there for a day, and exchanging stories with the natives, they mounted and rode toward Nashville.

There they learned more about the earthquake which had afflicted more than two million square miles, from Canada to Washington, D.C. It had been worst at New Madrid, Missouri, not far from where Ross and Stand had camped. Log cabins had shook, fine buildings had trembled, and people had fled in their night-clothes into the dark and cold night, struggling to maintain their equilibrium. Fissures in the earth had opened from lengths of six hundred feet to five miles. The valley of the Mississippi had undergone a geographic change, in convulsions. Miraculously, there had been very few reported losses of lives. Most of the dead and missing were said to have been claimed by the Mississippi River.

They took a comfortably furnished room at a popular tavern. John eyed the feathered mattress on the canopied and curtained bed with some concern, placing his hand on its downiness. "It's too soft. We'd never sleep in it. Too much give." He lifted the mattress to look at the ropes strung beneath it. "Use that wrench by the foot of the bed and get some know-how into these ropes. They're sagging."

Stand twisted the bed wrench and the ropes became taut. "Now," he said, "let's go find a venison steak."

By the time they had finished a big supper in the taproom of the tavern and sat back to enjoy an extra pot of coffee, they were surrounded at their little round table by half a dozen men who had heard them speaking of the earthquake. Except for the breaking of dishes and the shaking of homes and the fall of chimneys, Nashville had escaped the worst of the disaster. The men listened in astonishment to the report of the two travelers.

Their recital was abruptly halted when a tall, redheaded, lantern-jawed man, probably in his mid-forties, arrived in a group of six others. He was dressed in the long jacket and fancy shirt of a planter, but the burning blue eyes told he was a man of high spirit with a temper. He went to the bar, joined by his companions, ordered a hot rum which the servant striped generously with butter, and turned, mug in hand, to raise it to John.

"I believe I've interrupted you. I'm sorry, friend. Perhaps

you'll let me—and my friends—share in your talk. From the way everyone was bending their ears to you, sir, you're mighty interesting. Will you let us in on the latest news. It's hard to come by, you know." The stranger smiled. "I'm Andrew Jackson."

John got to his feet, as did Stand. This was the man who a few years back had termed President Thomas Jefferson a coward in his foreign policy for not warring upon the British when American ships were fired upon and American sailors seized; he who probably owned more lands rightfully belonging to the Cherokee and Creek tribes than any other white man; who itched to lick the British and the Indians and looked hopefully for a war and a command which would let him do both.

John, knowing these things, still put forth his hand to meet Jackson's.

"I'm John Ross," he told Jackson. "And this is my friend, Stand Watie. We've just come from St. Louis on our way home to New Echota in Georgia. We were talking about the Mississippi River during the earthquake—"

A cooling came to Jackson's voice. "New Echota? Are you Cherokee?" He gave John a strange look, and turned his gaze on Stand.

"Yes, sir," John replied, "we're Cherokee."

Andrew Jackson turned to the counter to put his mug down. He looked again at John, now with no interest in his expression whatsoever. "Well, tell us about the earthquake, if you please."

John shook his head. "Your pardon, General Jackson. I finished my report before you entered. I'm sure you have official facts on it. I bid you goodnight, sir."

Surprised, General Jackson grinned. "By God, I believe I'm sorry I missed your report. Tell you what you do, John Ross. Next time you're in Nashville, ride on out to the Hermitage. Perhaps I can coax you into telling my wife about the earthquake over a proper dinner?"

John bowed his head. "Thank you, sir. It would be an honor."

The General gave them a nod of his head, and they departed.

Undressing in their room, Stand muttered, "Damn Jackson, white robber!"

John pulled his boots off. "I think I'll accept his invitation some time."

Stand threw himself naked on the bed: "He's our enemy! You'd do better to leave him alone."

"No," John said. "And until we earn the respect of men like Jackson, our people have no future."

"Respect! Why, he all but kicked you in the teeth when he found you are a Cherokee."

"True enough, at first. But when I let him know he wasn't going to get the report, I had his attention and his regard. That's why he invited me to the Hermitage."

"You think he meant it?"

"He meant it. And I'm going to hold him to it. I'll visit him."

Stand was puzzled. "Why?"

"Because he hates Indians," John smiled.

Several hours later, General Jackson and his men rode out into the night toward the Hermitage where Rachael Jackson waited up for her husband, a sleeping child on her lap and a lamp in the window.

John stood again before a meeting of the Cherokee Council at New Echota and gave his report on the condition of the Arkansas Cherokees. He summarized his findings with the dire prediction: "Unless we stand as an organized nation against the sale or transfer of our lands to others, we shall perish as a race. Together we are whole. Separated, we are broken. I have seen it. Our brothers across the Mississippi are deprived people. They battle a new enemy, men of their own blood. They are lost to us and we to them. Soon white settlers will move on down to their new lands in Arkansas, and they will lose them too. We must stand together and never again yield so much as an acre of our land to any man. This is my word."

The Council members cast glances at each other and began to confer in whispers, as before. The Beloved Women grouped together and talked to each other. Going Snake moved from his sofa to kneel in front of the Ridge and their foreheads all but touched as they conferred.

Going Snake got to his feet and faced the youthful speaker. "Your elders ask how you would unite the people. Could the wind blow your thoughts out of your head? Tell us how to unite so that no man among us shall sell or give our land to the whites."

There was a new hush in the hall, and the firelight sent shadows scuttling over the people. John began: "Three years ago our wise chiefs and warriors and the Beloved Women revised some of our tribal laws to a form much like the constitutional laws of the United States. It was a beginning. Now we must go further and organize a national Cherokee government with an executive, judicial, and legislative system. Then shall we have control over our own destiny. Then can we protect our land. There is no other way."

The Ridge was standing, his yellowish-colored face bearing a scowl which made him look older than his forty-five years. "You have exceeded your right to speak here. You gave your report on your mission west and that is all you were to do. Now you dip your tongue into a feast which is not yours. You have no right to speak of a national government, nor of policy matters at all. You are not a member of this Council. Your tongue wags as did that of Tecumseh the Shawnee, who wished to unite us only that he might rule all Indians."

John held up a hand to ask for silence. "Elders! Listen! Your ears have heard the sound of my voice, but not my words. Your eyes see but behold no vision. I tell you this: The Cherokee people must begin a new way of life. The old ways are for ancient days long gone past. Under a republican form of government we may not only be equal to the white men, we may surpass them. We have only to organize."

The Ridge sat down with a deep scowl. He knew John Ross had become a man to contend with, but this was not the time or the place, not when the young liberal had the floor. The Ridge clamped his lips tightly together. He would say no more this day, but his lively black eyes missed nothing.

Stand Watie, present to hear John's report, watched too, with a rising sense of jealousy. He did not agree with most of the things John had said, but the Beloved Women, who might have blighted John's future, stood together to chant: "You have spoken the truth."

The chant was taken up by the warriors and then by the chiefs. It was a chant which almost always brought an emotional release to the speaker. John, his hands at his sides, hearing the verdict, bowed his head in gratitude.

IX

IN THE SPRING OF 1812, THE BRITISH STATIONS IN CANADA were again supplying the Shawnee with the means of warring upon Americans, promising them lands and power when victory was achieved. There was terror on every frontier of the American Union. The white settlements were being burned out in the false name of Indian unity.

In June, news from Washington excited everyone in the Cherokee Nation. President James Madison, his long patience at an end, had asked the Congress to declare war upon the British.

"Our attention is necessarily drawn to the warfare just renewed by the savages on one of our extensive frontiers—a warfare which is known to spare neither age nor sex and to be distinguished by features particularly shocking to humanity. It is difficult to account for the activity and combinations which have for some time been developing among tribes in constant intercourse with British traders and garrisons without connecting their hostility with that influence and without recollecting the authenticated examples of such interpositions heretofore furnished by the officers and agents of that government."

The President held his complaints against the British to five general issues, including their support of the Indian raids and massacres against white settlers. "The Redcoats and the Redskins!" was the battle cry.

On the evening of June 18, 1812, the courier Billy Phillips delivered the message to Governor William Blount of Tennessee that Congress had declared war upon England. He then rode on to the Hermitage where Jackson, Major-General of the Tennessee Volunteers, was recuperating from a gunshot wound in the shoulder which he had suffered in a duel.

On the twenty-first of June, Billy Phillips rode away from the Hermitage carrying a letter from the General in which he offered the President his division of twenty-five hundred Tennessee men. He enthused that within ninety days he could have them standing at the door of Quebec for an invasion of Canada.

John Ross began to share sympathy in the American cause, but once more he found himself at odds with the elders of the tribe. Visiting at Elias Boudinot's home as a dinner guest along with Stand Watie, Sequoyah, and Going Snake, John was eager for the moment when the women would leave the men alone with coffee and pipes to pursue the real topic of the day: war.

The Boudinot home, as well furnished as many to be found in far-off New England, and boasting large rooms as well, was a hospitable place to spend an evening. John hoped no one observed his startled interest when Harriet Boudinot smilingly remarked she had spent a few hours lately at the home of Jim and Quatie Henley and was entranced by their small daughter, Jane. Finally the men, seating themselves in the front room around a cheery fire, with coffee and bowls of fruit handy, settled to an hour of talk.

Stand, sitting cross-legged on the floor, tearing a juicy plum apart, looked up at John. "Would you fight in the white man's war, John? You know, all we ought to do is stay out of it and watch them destroy one another. That way, we'll be the victor without taking up the hatchet ourselves."

John stood at the fireplace, staring into the flames. He was elegantly dressed in a long tunic-style black jacket, belted with a wide sash of emerald green, and skintight black trousers, tucked into riding boots. Snugly wrapped around his head was a Turkish-type turban of heavy silk, also emerald green. His wardrobe held a half-dozen of the jackets and turbans in different colors.

He had found the outfit useful for several reasons. The tunic and turban were derivatives of an early dress style among the Cherokee which had been long forgotten. It was comfortable to wear, but most importantly, it attracted attention, and he aimed to become personally known to every Cherokee in the nation.

When he rode into the many towns and villages and valleys of the Cherokee country, often before he could tie his horse to a hitching post the people had him engaged in serious discussions. He always took the opportunity to offer advice and to tell them of the need to unite in one government. They began to look for John Ross, astride his black horse, handsome in his strangely exciting outfit.

There were times, of course, when he wore the simple broad-rimmed black hat, white shirt, plain dark jacket, and trousers of any southern planter. His growing wardrobe also included buckskins and several imported Scottish warriors' habits of his father's family plaid.

John took his time answering Stand, moving to accept a cup of coffee from the hand of Going Snake and seating himself near Sequoyah. "I'll fight with my brother Americans when and where I'm needed. As a matter of fact, I've been thinking of volunteering." John spoke to the aging Cherokee slowly, hoping by the use of the right words to gain his understanding. "At the time of the first geese of coming winter, General Andrew Jackson sent out a call from Nashville asking young men to join the Tennessee militia. His words have stayed in my heart because through those words his spirit has touched mine. The General called: 'Come to the Tented fields . . . to promenade into a distant country . . . to see the grand evolutions of nature . . . carrying the republican standard to the heights of Abraham.'"

The Ridge had just arrived to join in the conversation and coffee. "You would stand with Jackson?" he asked sharply. "Then you are no longer a Cherokee!"

John got to his feet and the Ridge took the chair which John had vacated for him. John went to stand again by the fireplace.

"America has been attacked. We are the first Americans. Our land is coveted by the British. I say I am an American, born one, live as one, and I shall die American. My Cherokee blood gives me the right to call myself American. My white blood, too, gives me the right to fight as an American. If I go to war, against the British, I go as an American."

The Ridge arose, not giving John so much as a glance, and walked to the door. Stand got up from the floor and quickly followed, going ahead to open the door for the Ridge.

"The trouble is, John," observed Going Snake, "you don't understand him."

John shook his turbaned head and his clear blue eyes were bright. "No, the trouble is that the Ridge understands me. And he does not like what he understands."

"And you would fight at the side of General Jackson?"

John allowed the question to hang in the air a moment. Then he said: "I think even the Ridge will take up the hatchet in behalf of the United States and that he, too, will serve with General Jackson. The Cherokee people will do that which must be done."

X

TECUMSEH'S EFFORTS TO UNITE ALL INDIANS AGAINST THE whites did not go completely unrewarded. The Upper Creeks who lived on the Coosawattee and Tallapoosa rivers, in the depths of the area to be called Alabama, rallied to his call to war upon the white settlers they considered their enemy. They were liberally supplied with war chests by the Spaniards in Florida, who wished them every victory against the homes and forts of the vast area surrounding their homeland. The Lower Creeks, those settled on the border of Georgia, rejected the war and took no part in the raids on white settlers.

Two mixed bloods, Peter McQueen and William Weatherford, led the Upper Creeks into war against the white settlers. Weatherford was called Chief Red Eagle and he had already proved himself to be an able and merciless warrior.

In the years 1812 and 1813, the frontier families of the Alabama River gathered at the one point of safety: Fort Mims, forty-five miles north of Mobile. There they settled into a temporary kind of life, making the best of their predicament. Chief Red Eagle swore he would yet kill them all.

On the thirtieth day of August, 1813, four hundred settlers, including women and children, were within the walls of Fort Mims in the protective custody of a hundred armed volunteers. There had been no sign of Indians. It was noon, time for the big meal of the day. The stockade was so airless and the day so bright that it was decided the gates could be opened and the people, including some children, allowed to roam as far as the river waters to take up fresh buckets and bathe. Some black slaves assisted their people with the bucket brigade from river to fort.

The cry of a baby was heard clearly from a room in a separate building near the front gate. The young mother went running. Her friends chuckled at the way she jumped at the sound of her child's cry for attention.

William Weatherford, Chief Red Eagle, also heard the cry of

the baby. He watched the noonday activities from his hiding place in the heavy undergrowth. He saw children running back and forth, delighting in their hour of freedom. The odor of cooking meat wafted to him. He saw the busy mothers carrying serving dishes to a long table in the center of the shaded grounds where the settlers planned to eat. He was curious when he saw black men and women scurrying, with dishes too, busy about their chores. He saw the Mississippi Volunteers, standing around with muskets over their shoulders awaiting food, some coming and going from the river, casting occasional glances toward the underbrush, river, and sky. They were obviously not on patrol.

Chief Red Eagle gave the signal to his hidden warriors who surrounded the fort.

The water-bearers—man, woman, or child, white or black —were the first to fall. They died on the trail, in the water, at the gates which were wide open. The water buckets crashed to the ground as the victims were felled, their bellies slashed open, their scalps taken.

Screaming Creeks rushed through the gates and met the surprised whites with flashing knives, guns, and firebrands.

A few of the white men escaped and made their precarious way downriver to Mobile with the awful story of the massacre at Fort Mims. It took ten days for troops from Mobile to reach the burned fort. They found 247 dead lying in the heat, mutilated, unapproachable. Some of the black people had been spared, but had been taken as prisoners.

The word of the Fort Mims massacre went to the Governor of Tennessee, and to the President of the United States, and to Andrew Jackson.

There was an immediate call for volunteers by both the state and federal governments. It was specifically stated that there ought to be volunteers from the Indian nations, particularly from the Cherokee and the Lower Creeks. Fort Mims was to be avenged.

General Jackson assumed the command of twenty-five hundred troops from the western section of Tennessee. General John Cocke, in charge of men from eastern Tennessee, was to join his army with that of Jackson at Fayetteville, on the Mississippi, and at Knoxville. General Jackson swiftly sent troops under Major-General John Coffee to Huntsville with orders to send scouts into Creek country, even in advance of the mounted riflemen, to locate the fleeing Chief Red Eagle. Jackson himself lingered at the Hermitage as he awaited response to the call for volunteers.

The seventy-five Red Chiefs of the Cherokee Council stood at a meeting held to determine whether war was fact between the Cherokee and the Creek. They spoke in sorrow that war must be waged against the foe who had brought shame upon all Indians at Fort Mims. Their brothers had done a great wrong and must die for it.

The Ridge, magnificent in a gold-dyed jacket and leggings and a towering headgear of gold and flame feathers, arose in his ceremonial splendor to be heard. Flashes of light danced from a wide silver bracelet on his right wrist as he raised his arms over his head and shouted: "War! Death to the Creeks! Let the honor of the Cherokees wipe out the stain of dishonor on the Creeks, on the name of the Red Man! We shall follow the fleeing enemy into the haunts of his wilderness. He shall not escape our vengeance. Death to the Creeks!"

Elias Boudinot, the Cherokee war belt of beads carefully laid over his outstretched arm, moved toward the Ridge.

Around him were stacks of war clothing and weapons which the Beloved Women had collected from the homes of the men. The moment war was voted, the young men would come forward to claim their gear. Boudinot was joined by Going Snake, who took one end of the lengthy war belt, and they backed away from each other, stretching the embellished leather between them. Any man who came to touch it would be casting his vote for war.

The Ridge held his arm stiffly toward the war belt. "I say this. The Creek has become our enemy. He has murdered white women and children and now looks toward us. Already he has turned in his path and comes closer to our lands. He has raised the tomahawk. He allies himself with the white men from over the wide waters who would rule us. We dare not allow him to do this." The Ridge's voice became shrill: "It matters not that the United States has asked us to war upon the Creeks. It is of no importance that the State of Tennessee has requested us to come to its aid. If the Cherokee did not know his own enemy, hear with his own ears, feel with his own soul, then well might the white men remind us of our duty. Let them all know: The Cherokee knows when to dig up the war hatchet and when to touch the war belt." He paused, paced a few steps to the left,

retraced the steps, stood, arms upraised, to shout: "Brothers! Come forward and vote. Touch the war belt. Now!"

Before any man could move, John arose, and addressed the Council. "Brothers! It is good to touch the war belt. By ancient ways, it is right. Yet surely this Council of the Cherokee people, a civilized people, does not declare war in such a manner? Are we not to take a vote in the manner of civilized men in order that we may convey proper reply to the United States of America and to the State of Tennessee? Are we to say to them: Our young men have touched the belt of war and so we go to battle? Brothers, this is no way!"

The Ridge turned an angry face toward John. "You speak without permission. Your words are sharp against your people and their customs."

"And you speak of touching the war belt, even as did your father's father. But the touching of the war belt, the digging up of the war hatchet, and the sending of it to our allies is no more than a symbol. We must also give a responsible written answer on the war issue, else we remain primitives of the wilderness."

There was a quiet in the hall. After a few minutes of consultation, Going Snake, Chief Junuluska, Elias Boudinot, and the Ridge went to the sacred area where the Beloved Women were holding their own low-voiced conference. Then they broke apart and the Ridge went back to his stand by the fire.

He let the Council members wait, getting their attention. When he spoke, he held back his own feelings and reported the decision in a monotone. "We believe John Ross has spoken a truth. It is right that this Council send written reply to the United States government and to the State of Tennessee announcing our decision for or against war upon the Creeks. Yet we are reluctant to forego our traditional custom. We have come to this agreement: We shall first take our traditional vote by a touch of the war belt. The result of that vote shall be duly recorded in the writing of English and relayed to Governor Blount of Tennessee and to the President of the United States. We shall select a courier to take the word to the Governor who will convey it to the President. We suggest the courier be John Ross."

Elias Boudinot and Going Snake took their places in the center of the rotunda and once more held the war belt. The Red Chiefs came first, leading seven hundred men, each of whom filed past the belt, reaching out to touch it, voting for war.

When it came to putting the vote into writing, there was some delay. The Cherokee language had never been transferred into print. There was no Cherokee alphabet. Lately, though, Sequoyah, the silversmith, had developed a deep interest in the writings of white men. He was consulted. What was the proper method of writing the war message to the white men?

Sequoyah, removing his long-stemmed pipe from his mouth, shook his head. "In the time since I first saw a talking leaf of the white men, that which they term a book, I have studied to see how I might do the same with our language. Lately, John Ross has encouraged me in this. I am beginning a work on an alphabet of our language, but it is tedious. Now we must write in words of English."

It was voted that Sequoyah would prepare the document of war and that John Ross would carry it to General Jackson in Nashville.

XI

JOHN, DRESSED IN BUCKSKINS, THE DECLARATION OF WAR against the Creeks folded securely into a leather pouch tied to his waist, rode swiftly toward Nashville.

As he kept an eye alert for the blazed trees to keep him on the right trail, he thought about the new National Road which Congress had authorized to be constructed through Virginia, Ohio, and the Indiana and Illinois territories. The contract specified it was to be cut sixty-five feet wide, surfaced with stone and gravel, augmented by stone culverts and bridges, and graded!

He rode on, his troubled thoughts going to Elias Boudinot and the Ridge. One thing was certain: there was a growing separation between himself and his elders. Was he wrong to oppose them in Council when he really had no legal right to do so?

Thinking about it, he saw some hope. It was the Ridge, he was told, who had suggested he be selected to speed the war message to General Jackson. Then the older man must have some trust in him after all.

Riding toward the front door of the Hermitage, Jackson's home on the outskirts of Nashville, John was inspired by the sight. The fields had been lately harvested, leaving the rich, black soil bare under the sun. The trees were luminous with scarlet and gold.

Down a lane stood the stables where slaves were grooming and exercising the General's horses. General Jackson's interest in racing was well known and his stables were fast gaining recognition for holding some of the nation's finest horses.

The house was impressive, its windows reflecting the blue October sky, and its colonnades gleaming. John promised himself that someday he would possess such a place and men would ride to it with admiring eyes, even as he rode now.

As he waited for a response to his knock on the front door, he took the Cherokee war document from the leather packet and smoothed it carefully. A black servant in a long-sleeved white dress covered with an oversized white apron led him in.

General Jackson sat before a fire, his left arm in a white sling. His face was very pale, but he set aside a map he had been studying and got to his feet. He bowed his head in greeting, but offered John neither hand nor chair.

"You have a communiqué for me, Mr. Ross?"

John held the paper toward him. "The Cherokee Nation has appointed me to hand you this document. It states that a condition of war exists between the Cherokee Nation and the Creeks of Tallapoosa. My instructions are to hand you this paper with the request that you give word of it to the President of the United States and the Governor of Tennessee."

General Jackson sat down again, broke the seal on the paper, and quietly read the text.

John, hands clenched at his sides, crossed in front of Jackson and deliberately settled into the empty chair opposite the General's.

Jackson appeared not to have noticed him, but continued reading. His face, however, was not so pale as it had been. "I am advised," he said, looking up from the paper, "that the Cherokee Nation will support the United States and the State of Tennessee in any military effort against the Creeks. Do you have any details? How many men? Who will lead them? When may I expect them?"

"There will be seven hundred Cherokee warriors at your command, sir," said John. "The warriors will ride under command of Gideon Morgan, Major Ridge, John Lowrey, and Richard Brown. These men have had war experience and have served in the Lighthorse Brigade of the nation. All are capable and excellent with weapons."

"And you? Will you be riding with them?"

"Yes, sir."

"Have you any military experience, Mr. Ross?" Jackson probed.

"No, sir."

"I thought not," said the General, with heat in his face again. "You were not invited to seat yourself. As a courier, it was your duty to stand in my presence and to await my disposal of the message you handed me. It was an affront to me that you dared to reprimand my manners by taking that chair."

John got to his feet. "I took the seat as the official emissary of my people. It was an affront to them that you did not have the courtesy to offer me your hand in greeting or a seat while you read the message I have ridden miles to bring you. Therefore, I took the seat as a matter of honor for my people and a clarification of my own status."

Jackson heaved himself to his feet. "By God! Damned if your people haven't chosen the right man! You're a worthy adversary." He held out a hand in belated welcome.

John, wondering at the choice of the General's language, nevertheless accepted the handclasp.

The hospitality of the Hermitage finally came his way. Rachel Jackson presided over a candlelit table set with a lace cloth and shining silverware. Later, because of the hour and the night which threatened a storm, the General insisted his guest stay until the morning. John slept dreamlessly in a cozy room with a subdued fire.

The day at the Hermitage began before sunup. The General, as was his custom with all his guests, walked John to the stable area to show off his horses. He had several special prize racehorses trotted out for inspection.

"You know, Ross," he said, eyes squinting, "I believe that if the Indians are ever to be civilized, it will be through mixed bloods like you. You're good for your race."

John kept a silence a moment as he reached out to rub the nose of a racehorse. "The Cherokee people are civilized. They are Christians."

"If they are, they've changed a hell of a lot since I first came face to face with them."

John followed the General's lead and spoke frankly: "I understand you hate all Indians, sir."

Jackson's eyes narrowed, but he smiled slightly. "It's true, to some extent. I feel the white settlers ought to have the land the Indians are squatting on. The whites would farm that land and make it pay. The Indians have no legal right to it."

"And shall I take that word to the Cherokee warriors who are to ride with you?"

The General handed the horse's halter back into the hands of the Negro trainer. "You tell them anything you want."

By mid-morning John was ready to ride home with General Jackson's orders for the Cherokee troops to join him at Nashville at all possible speed. The General had John's horse brought from the stable to the front of the house. He offered John a hand in parting.

"Thank God there are exceptional men like you among the Indians, Ross," the General remarked.

John eased his booted feet into the stirrups. "You wrong my people—"

"Oh, what the hell, Ross!" Andy Jackson was impatient. "Don't tell me about those savages! I've fought a few in my day. I've seen what they do. And how about Fort Mims? Everyone trapped there was butchered. When I get my hands on Chief Red Eagle, I'll show him no mercy."

"Chief Red Eagle is a mixed blood, General!" John gave Jackson a half-salute and spurred his horse away.

XII

SEVEN HUNDRED CHEROKEE WARRIORS FROM ALL PARTS OF the Cherokee land gathered at New Echota. They stood beside their horses and listened to the prayers offered for them by the Reverend Gideon Blackburn.

The Presbyterian minister stood apart from them, near the women and children who had come to witness the men's leave-taking for war. Glancing from the heavy Bible in his hands to the flock beyond him, the Reverend felt the hair at the back of his neck bristle.

The warriors, young and middle-aged, whom he had known for a long time as friends and converts to Christianity, were not recognizable to him. Wide streaks of red, white, and yellow war-paint were slashed across their faces and torsos. Their hair, usually hanging loosely in long bobs, had been carefully combed and parted in the middle, braided and interwound with varying decorative items, from strands of scarlet cloths to husks of corn or beads. Silver bands encircled their arms. Some wore breech-cloths only, and others were more warmly dressed in buckskins. A few wore headgear of painted feathers. Some had attached tiny bells to the fringes of their leggings and on ankle bracelets. The ponies and horses were similarily bedecked.

The Reverend Blackburn gave up trying to determine their identities. He read a passage from the Bible and then he offered a prayer in which he implored God to protect the Indians and to keep them in the right.

He was finished with the prayer service, yet the warriors still stood waiting, as though they expected more. Puzzled, the Reverend Blackburn turned to John, who stood near him, head bowed.

John, dressed in buckskins, wore no warpaint. He was bare-headed and his hair was brushed and unbraided. "Thank you, Reverend," he said. "Now I believe my brothers wish me to lead them in a warrior's prayer long chanted by our people."

The Presbyterian minister stepped back. John held his right arm up and faced the warriors. "We will pray." They raised their arms toward the sky and seven hundred masculine voices lifted in the prayer of the Cherokee warrior: "Great father, I go now to war. My enemy are many. My enemy are sly and quick and concealed, like the fox. Great Spirit, give me, your child, the strength and the brave heart I need to be a warrior. Give me the wind, that I may detect where my enemy hides. Give me the wind, that I may ride swiftly home to my own."

The prayer done, the warriors mounted their horses. John shook hands with the Reverend Blackburn. As the seven hundred warriors moved down the path which would take them to Nashville, the women pushed a bit toward them, but did not shame them by running to them with their tears.

John, whom General Jackson had ordered to rally the Indians to the meeting place by the Mississippi, led the troops, In command of the Cherokee volunteers were Colonel Gideon Morgan, Major Ridge, John Lowrey, Captain Richard Brown, George Gist (Sequoyah), John Drew, Whitepath, Arch Campbell, Going Snake, Chief Junuluska, George Fields, and Charles Hicks. Stand Watie and his friends rode at the rear, instructed to follow orders to the letter, since this was their first ride to battle.

Jackson was not waiting at Nashville for the Indian troops to reinforce his army. He had already plunged into the wilderness, advancing from the Coosa River into the Creek lands. He directed the hasty construction of Fort Strother and there awaited the arrival of the reinforcement troops, including the Cherokee.

On November 3 he dispatched troops under Major-General John Coffee to the Creek village of Tallassahatche in a surprise raid. Coffee's victory was almost complete—at the end of the day's annihilation he had lost only five of his men and counted but forty-one wounded. He scored 186 warriors killed, reporting to General Jackson later that not one of the Creek men had escaped. The real tragedy was in the deaths of uncounted women and children who fell along with their men when the attack came at dawn.

Within a few days, word came to Jackson at Fort Strother that 160 friendly Creeks were surrounded and entrapped by hostile Creeks at Talladega, about thirty miles to the south. The General, not without foresight, had white feathers and deertails to distribute to the Indians among his troops. "In the heat of battle,

I'm going to want to know which Indian is friendly," he told his subordinates. "So mark our allies."

Two thousand troops, including the Indians with their identifying tags, marched southward with Jackson. The General had expected to be reinforced by Brigadier General James White, but White was not within striking distance having been counterordered to join the eastern command under General John Cocke.

Jackson attacked the Creeks before dawn, closing in on them in an encircling maneuver, sending the Cherokee troops thrusting into the village from the center of the circle. Upon firing, they retreated, drawing the Creeks out of their safety into the closing circle of Jackson's army.

Realizing too late that they had been outmaneuvered, one thousand Creeks broke and ran. Three hundred of them never left the field of battle, dying under the barrage of American guns. The fleeing were pursued, and only a very few escaped into the wilds. Again women and children had perished.

General Jackson rode his horse through the shambles that had been a Creek village. He reinforced his heart against the sight of it by bringing to mind the horror of Fort Mims. But still he muttered to himself, "They know damned well they're asking for battle, but they won't travel without their women and children."

John, weary from the day of death and destruction, helping to make the devastated campground livable, was approached by a Creek woman who led a small Creek boy by the hand. He was naked and he was shaking from head to toe. She thrust the child toward him and said in English well enough to be understood: "He is alone. This day he has lost everything. We cannot care for him. Take him to the General who has killed his parents. He is his now."

"Wait—" John implored the woman, who was already retreating. But the Creek woman did not turn around. She had done her duty.

John held the boy close in his arms. Cold and hungry, too frightened to cry any more, his tiny hands fiercely gripped John's battle-scarred jacket.

John took him to where tents had been erected as a temporary shelter. The women sat around a fire, huddling the children in the blankets given them by the Americans. They had just finished a spare meal of rations offered by the troops.

John held his burden and addressed himself to the women:

"This child is one of yours. Take him. Warm him and feed him."

The Creek women looked at him with faces blank with grief. They said nothing and made no attempt to take the boy. He knelt beside a young woman and would have transferred the child to her arms, but she backed away: "No! The child is alone. The white men have done this to him. We are homeless and without our men to help us care for our own children."

"But he is one of you—"

"There is no other way," she said.

John knew she meant it. He carried the boy to the tent where General Jackson stood. Several of his men were on their knees, building a fire by which the General might warm himself. He was about to light his pipe from the flames, his first smoke of a long and gruesome day.

John approached him, the child cradled against him. "General, this boy is orphaned. He's been rejected by his people. They will kill him if we insist they take him. They say you are to take him since you brought the battle here."

Andy Jackson looked at the naked child. He forgot his pipe. "Bring him into my tent. I've blankets and brandy. We'll warm him up some."

Together they knelt over the boy and massaged his cold body, the General making good use of his one able hand. The pack the General carried with him always, at the insistence of his wife, contained a few medicinal items, some of his favorite grind of coffee, sugar, tea, and brandy. He also had his own drinking cup, a small tin, in the pack. "Pour a bit of the brandy into it and add some sugar," he instructed John. "We'd better give it a taste the young fellow can tolerate."

When the boy had swallowed the drink and was snugly wrapped in blankets and asleep, the General lifted him and took him to the fire outside where he sat cross-legged, holding the child. John stood over them.

"It's the innocent who are the most hurt in war," Jackson said.

"What's to become of him?"

"Well," the General pondered, looking down at the sleeping child and rocking him gently, "we need another baby at the Hermitage. I expect my Rachel would want me to bring this child to her. I'll send him to Rachel tomorrow. He's our son now."

John turned away, a sense of awe overwhelming him. Andrew

Jackson, Indian hater, enemy of the red-skinned people, was cradling a Creek baby to his chest! He left them there, father and son.

The pursuit continued. At Horseshoe Bend on the Tallapoosa River, twelve hundred Creeks dug in for a final stand. They fortified themselves by constructing a log barricade across the neck of the waters at the upper part of the bend. Their position, on the river's bend on a land area of some one hundred acres, seemed invulnerable, and should the Americans break through the barricade, a fleet of canoes secured close to the breastworks guaranteed that they could escape across the river.

General Jackson and his troops, together with the Cherokee warriors and Creek allies, came upon Horseshoe Bend on the twenty-seventh morning of March. Jackson and his aides studied the strategical problem and determined that time was important, that the Indians would probably not expect an immediate attack. Therefore, he commenced the battle at once, ordering General Coffee and the Cherokees to a stand opposite the barricade near a point where they could best stop any Creek attempt to retreat by canoe.

To John, Stand, and Jim Henley, the problem appeared obvious. The canoes must be taken so that a retreat would be simply out of the question. Then the cannon Jackson was bringing up on the shore and aiming at the barricade would force the Creeks to escape. John conferred with General Coffee, asking him to allow the Cherokees to swim across the waters from their position on the bend and seize the canoes.

General Coffee stamped his cold feet on the frozen ground to ease the cramps and shook his head: "You couldn't do it, Ross. That's ice out there in that river. Besides, they'd spot you and slaughter you before you could reach the canoes."

"It's got to be done, sir," John insisted. "If they reach those canoes they'll make a break for the wilderness, and we'll only have to find them again and hope for conditions better than this. The water is bearable. We're volunteering, sir."

General Coffee made up his mind. "All right, Ross. Go ahead. Good luck." He and his troops would support the Cherokees with fire from the shore. Across the bend there was Jackson with cannon.

John, Stand, and Jim, together with forty-seven others, stripped and tossed their clothing into individual piles on the rocky shore. With knives and tomahawks as their only weapons, they slid into the river, grunting at the frigid shock of it. John dove under the surface quickly to get wet all over, coming up yards away to shake his head free of the icy water. Stand and Jim were nearby, and with the others of their silent company they began swimming.

Jackson's cannon were firing upon the enemy's fortifications, but the structure stood. The waters vibrated with the sound of the big guns. A pall of smoke hung in the air and streaks of fire swept over the Cherokees' heads. The Creeks behind the barricade were kept too busy to notice the dark shadows in the water moving into shore.

The Cherokees floated motionless offshore in obedience to a signal from Junuluska, who was in front of them, bobbing in the water. They trod water, all peering ahead to where over two hundred canoes stood positioned for an easy launch. There were no more than six guards and they had grouped together to watch the effect of the cannon fire from the opposite shore on the breastwork up the line from where they stood. They were totally unaware of the approach of the swimmers.

Junuluska, gesticulating, directed the men nearest him in the water to follow him. John, Stand, Jim Henley, John Drew, and Whitepath all floated close to Junuluska, ready to leave the water and seize the guards. The others were waved on to shore toward the canoes. The barricade began to splinter under the pounding of the guns; it would not long withstand.

The knives of the Cherokees made no sound. The Creek guards fell dead with hardly a moan. John pulled the knife out of the wound he had inflicted, and his hand was stained with blood. The body lay at his feet. He thought: My God, I've killed a brother! He felt a hand clamp hard on his shoulder and Junuluska said: "Get going, Ross! The Creeks are after us."

He reacted instantly, sheathing the bloody knife and running with the others to the canoes. The fifty Cherokees worked fast, damaging canoes, dragging them into the water and scuttling them, setting others adrift downstream. They saved a half-dozen for their own use in crossing back over the river to Jackson.

They were already away from shore when the retreating Creeks began to appear in search of their escape craft. The stranded enemy, aware of their desperate plight at last, began firing at the Cherokees, but the range was too wide.

Jackson's men were manuevering to take the breastworks. The Creeks, realizing escape was impossible, resolved to fight. The battle went on all day, becoming a hand-to-hand slaughter in the river, on the barricades, on the sandy shore.

By late afternoon, the Creeks scented defeat and began to scatter and to try for individual salvation. Many of them risked the freezing waters, rushing Jackson's men with bows and arrows, guns and knives. Blood churned with the water and bodies submerged amid chunks of ice.

Jim Henley, in a group which included John and Stand, Davy Crockett and Sam Houston, faced the oncoming, panic-stricken enemy in the river. Jim took an arrow in the shoulder and a bullet in the heart, falling between John and Stand. John shot the Creek who had hit Jim in the shoulder, but not before that marksman had let fly with another arrow into Houston's hip, inflicting a painful wound. Stand felled the rifleman who had killed Jim Henley.

They got the wounded to shore and carried Jim's body there, too. John thought: If only he'd had time to send Quatie a last word.

When the battle was ended, Generals Jackson and Coffee stood together by the river's edge and looked wearily upon the awful scene.

Jackson's eyes were red-rimmed from smoke and his ears rang from the pounding of the guns. He rubbed a hand hard over his stomach, which was riddled with sharp shooting pains. General Coffee ran a dry tongue over his lips and tasted gunpowder. "I've had a report that Chief Red Eagle has escaped. Likely he's retreated to his home village of Econochaca, some one hundred miles from here."

"Well," said Jackson, "We'll have to go after him, or we'll have it all to do again."

XIII

BEFORE MOVING ON IN PURSUIT OF CHIEF RED EAGLE, the generals counted their dead at Horseshoe Bend at 26 and sent 106 wounded whites back to Fort Strother. The Cherokee dead numbered 18, with 36 too gravely wounded to travel on. The Creeks who had fought with the Americans counted 5 dead and 11 wounded.

It was the enemy who had suffered the terrible losses, losing 557 warriors on land and an estimated 300 in the river. The Americans took 350 prisoners, many wounded.

The battle at the village of Chief Red Eagle again saw women and children falling victim to the guns of the Americans. The Indians were routed, most of them slain. Yet Chief Red Eagle escaped once more.

General Jackson, back again at Fort Strother, was determined to set out again in pursuit of the Creek Chief when he heard loud voices of the guards just inside the open gate. Other guards were coming from all points in response.

At the gate stood Chief Red Eagle, wearing breechcloth and a feathered headgear of brilliant orange and white, carrying a rifle in his right hand, muzzle down, and his reputation as an expert shot gave that rifle added importance. The guards, having allowed the lone Indian to approach the gate, were now encircling him, warily, their rifles aimed at him.

The tall, well-muscled man spoke very quietly. "I will kill anyone who tries to stop me from seeing General Jackson."

The General, observing the scene from his room, called out: "Let him pass."

Reluctantly the guards lowered their rifles and stood aside. They watched as the Creek moved across the yard toward Jackson, the wind blowing the feathers of his bonnet. A purpled shadow followed him, elongating the man and the rifle.

The General closed the door and they were alone. Jackson was astonished. "You dare to come here?"

"I dare."

"By God, why? You know you're a prisoner now."

Chief Red Eagle held the gun out toward the General with both hands. "Take my rifle. I surrender to you."

"You surrender?" General Jackson made no move. "You escaped the battlefields and now you walk in and surrender? Why?"

The words came bitterly: "You, the zealot, have killed my warriors. Your troops have destroyed my villages. My people are perishing. Women and babies you have killed with guns and burned with fire. Now there are only a few of my own left to me. We are without supplies. Your troops have carried away the corn in our bins and our livestock. We are hungry. The women and the children must have food and a place to be safe. I surrender for these things from you."

General Jackson's anger was ebbing. "You'd trade your freedom for the sake of your people?"

"It is my offer. If you want my life, take it. But help my people."

Jackson eyed him curiously, striving to understand. "You trust me?"

"I am here."

The General paced the floor. "I'll have all the help your people need on the way to them by sunset." He looked at the Indian's rifle. "You keep that. You'll guide my men with the supply wagons to your people."

The Chief asked: "I am not your prisoner?"

"The war between us is finished, and you are defeated. You cannot rouse dead warriors to fight again. You are free to go. Your people need you."

The supply wagons left the fort, led by Chief Red Eagle, who was provided with a mount. General Jackson went back to his room and sat down in wonder to record the visit in writing. Would he ever understand Indians?

Ross and Jackson met in a brief farewell exchange. The General stood at a small table throughout the discussion, indicating he had no time to sit and talk. John, however, was there not only to bid the General a goodbye but because a rumor was sweeping the camp that Jackson aimed to demand that the Creek people cede their lands to the United States. "What's going to happen to the Creeks now?" John asked bluntly.

"That which happens to a conquered people," the General replied: "They'll pay for the war."

"How?"

"The only way they can."

"You'll take the lands of all the Creeks?"

"I'll recommend it."

"Even those who fought here with you, the Creeks who were your allies?"

General Jackson nodded, and there was an expression in his eyes which John disliked. "The Creeks are one tribe. Yes, I'd expect the law to apply to all of them. Their land ought to be ceded to their conqueror by way of reparation for the war in which they have engaged us."

John moved to the flap of the tent, giving the officer his back. The General's voice stopped him. "Ross!" He held up a letter, saying: "Mrs. Jackson has sent me a note. She has taken Lincoyer into our home and her heart. She wants me to express her thankfulness to you for bringing the boy to us. The aide who took him to her has reported back with the note and the additional word that the child is well and happy."

"I'm pleased to know, General. My regards to Mrs. Jackson." John left the tent totally puzzled.

At his own insistence, John made a lone and swift ride home to New Echota, traveling far ahead of the Cherokee troops. By custom, the returning warriors would be greeted at the public square by their women and children amid much celebration and joy. He did not want Quatie to learn there and then of Jim Henley's death. She was entitled to hear the tragic news in privacy.

He rode directly to her little frame home. With no near neighbors, it was set in a small orchard at the base of a hill from which there was a grand view of the river and the town beyond. The fields around were already plowed for the planting of cotton with the first coming of warm weather.

John hitched his horse near the front of the house and went to the door, torn between his dread and his desire to see Quatie again. The front door was ajar. He called her name. There was no response.

The wind, sharp at his back, blew the door wide open. He went in. The fire was banked, and the place was cold and drafty. He called for Quatie again, but no sound came from the other two rooms.

He saw that her touches were everywhere. The house was spotlessly clean. The windows were carefully curtained. The kettle gleamed on its arm beside the fire. A decorated chest stood colorfully beside a table. A bearskin rug made the floor comfortable to the feet. Pewter dishes were neatly stacked in an openfaced cupboard. A spinning wheel stood in the light by the window, the work partly done.

Hoping Quatie and her child had not gone far, he set the fire to a blazing warmth.

Outside again, he found their footprints in the snow. Quatie had evidently taken the child on a walk to the top of the hill, probably hoping to see Jim ride in.

The path was well trod, but the grade of it was enough to pull at the lungs, and John took his time as he headed uphill. Pausing near the top, he looked up and she was there, holding the hand of her tiny daughter, Jane.

Quatie was startled at first to see him. She flung an arm upward in greeting, a smile lighting her face, and tugging the child along, she came downhill toward him as fast as she could, impeded some by her heavy wool jacket and deerskin leggings and boots. She came so fast he held out his arms and caught her, steadying her, reaching down to the child, too. "Where is he?" She looked beyond John, toward the house, ready to hurry on. "Where is Jim?"

Her long hair was blowing free in the wind and it slashed her face, and his, as they stood together on the hill. All he could say was: "Quatie!"

She tried to break away from his hands, still smiling. "Let me go, John. I want to see Jim—"

He held her. "Quatie, listen. Please—"

The smile was fading, frozen. "Isn't Jim with you?"

"No." He plunged into the words, his hands hurting her arms. "Quatie, I'm sorry. Jim won't be coming home."

She stepped back a few paces. "It's not true," she said huskily. "No, it's not true at all."

"It's true," he said. "I'm sorry."

"No. He promised he would come home to me. You see, John? He *promised.* "

He wondered now why he had thought he should be the one to tell her. He was doing it badly. No tears came, but she dropped to her knees, covering her face with her hands, swaying, rocking to and fro, gently, and a moaning came from her.

Jane, knowing only that her mother was sobbing, knelt beside her and with her small fingers she tried to pry the mother's hands from her face. Jane's underlip began to tremble and she, too, began to cry.

John leaned over them. He pulled Quatie to her feet and held her face close against his shoulder. His strong arms stopped her swaying and her moans ceased and she held tightly to him. Jane was on her feet, an arm around her mother's right leg, crying. John reached down and touched her head. Quatie stayed within his arms for a time, hiding her face from him, unable to move.

When at last she lifted her head, she was still dry-eyed but her lips were stiff. "Thank you for coming to me," she said.

"I wanted to come. Quatie, what can I do to help?"

"If you would see my father in New Echota—" The sound of tears now washed her voice. "Tell him I need him."

John guided her down the path toward the house. Jane stumbled and fell in the snow and John lifted her and held her easily as he strode along. The baby looked up at him with a sober expression.

When they got to the house, Quatie halted at the door. John saw her anguish at entering the home which Jim would never see again. He shifted Jane to one shoulder, opened the door, and offered his free hand to Quatie.

She saw the bright fire and felt the warmth of the room rush to her. Quickly, she scanned the scene, her gaze darting over Jim's familiar things. A little trembling sob came from her.

Holding her hand tightly, John said: "Come." He led her gently across the threshold of the home she had dreaded to enter.

XIV

FIFTY BRITISH SOLDIERS, SAILORS, AND OFFICERS STOOD IN
the President's House in Washington, blazing torches in their
hands. They were there to burn the mansion.

A dinner table had been set for the President and a half-pre-
pared meal still simmered in the pots and kettles in the kitchen.
The British laughed to think they had changed the President's
dinner plans at the last hour. They searched the house for proper
souvenirs of their visit, but the prizes they would most like to
have captured were safe. The First Lady, Dolly Madison, had
personally removed the precious original copies of the American
Constitution and the Declaration of Independence and Gilbert
Stuart's portrait of George Washington to a place of security.
The British moved outside. At a signal, the torches were tossed
through each of the windows.

The burning of the President's House was only one of the fires
set that night in Washington. Torches were put to the buildings
of the War and Treasury departments. The Capitol was afire.
The headquarters of the *National Intelligencer* went up in flames.
Ships were burning at anchor on the Potomac. The British raced
through the city destroying everything which the Americans had
not already deliberately rendered useless.

The President of the United States and his official family had
taken a stand with the military on a parcel of ground overlooking
the city. Washington was captured, but having fired the city the
British were sweeping onward. Fort McHenry at the harbor of
Baltimore was their immediate objective, and the city of Baltimore their ultimate target. Baltimore, alerted to the danger, dug
in for battle, determined that the British should not pass.

Attorney Francis Scott Key was aboard a ship anchored off
Fort McHenry. He had been on a mission to the British in an
effort to free a Washington doctor held prisoner on a British ship.
The American attorney watched the night-long battle, keeping
his gaze on the rocket-lighted fort as long as it could be seen

through the smoky night. If its flag were lowered in surrender, the American nation might be lost. By the light of the early dawn, Key noted the flag was still flying.

The British commanders of the land-sea forces also noticed it and decided that Baltimore and Fort McHenry were too difficult to seize. They began a retreat, eventually going all the way to the island of Jamaica to map a new expedition against the American nation. This time the British would try victory through the Gulf of Mexico, estimating they could seize New Orleans without facing a heavy American defense.

General Jackson was reported to be in Florida, a threat to the Spanish and the Indians as he probed the enemy's strength on America's southern defense line.

During the few months after his return from the Creek War, John stayed close to home tending to the family business which his ailing parents were finding increasingly hard to manage.

He rode often to see Quatie, who was planning on giving up her isolated home and moving to New Echota to live with her father. The day came when he rode to tell her that once more the call had come from General Jackson, appealing for Cherokee troops. Jackson was heading for New Orleans, convinced that the British were about to launch a massive campaign to take the Mississippi Valley.

"I won't be riding out here for a time, Quatie. I'm going with General Jackson's forces to New Orleans."

Quatie closed her eyes as he took her in his arms and held her, saying nothing.

"If you need anything—if you're lonely—you'll go visit my parents? I'm going to ask them to keep an eye on you." He touched her face, making her look up at him. "I'm going to say it: I'll be back. I'm coming home to you, Quatie."

"If you don't, I will not live," she told him.

He kissed her for the first time and was appalled at his fierce response to the warmth and softness of her. During the past months he had felt such compassion and tenderness toward her that his love had seemed almost holy, but the touch of her lips made him acknowledge that a near unholy need for her surged within him.

It was not until he was far down the trail that he realized he hadn't told her he loved her! If Stand Watie, who rode beside him to New Orleans, noticed his thoughtful silence, he said nothing.

After all, Stand was in love himself with a girl, Sarah. Besides, everyone knew that John Ross had been in love with Quatie Brown Henley since the first moment he had beheld her. It was to be expected he would be sobered upon leaving her, especially now that he was free to claim her.

John and Stand joined with other Cherokees and Choctaws and some loyal Creeks to travel on to New Orleans to report to Major-General Andrew Jackson, commander of all American forces in Tennessee, Mississippi, and Louisiana. It was the end of November 1814, and from Jamaica the British were sending superb troops, veterans of the Napoleonic Wars under Wellington, to attack New Orleans.

The people of the city hardly knew whether to be amused or alarmed by the appearance of Jackson's rugged-looking forces. The American volunteers had no regular uniforms and many of them sported buckskins and carried their own mountain rifles. The women of the city, seeing them pass through the streets, were disappointed in their appearance and called the weather-worn buckskin outfits "dirty shirts," a description which became the nickname for the men who wore them.

On the fourteenth day of December the British arrived off the coast of Louisiana. It seemed all too easy to deprive the American nation of the Mississippi and its outlet to the sea. Five American gunboats were taken at the very start at the mouth of Bayou Bienvenue, an all-important route to New Orleans. This allowed the British to proceed to a point nine miles below the city, in a move so swift that General Jackson was outsmarted in his plans of defense. He was amazed to learn the British were camped at plantations only a few miles to the south and seemed prepared to continue their march on the theory that American resistence could be overcome in quick order.

Jackson launched an immediate attack upon the British lines, sending General Coffee's troops to the far left in a flanking movement while he moved his own troops between the British and the city. His attack came as a paralyzing blow to the British, who were temporarily scattered, their neat lines of advance torn apart.

The black night descended with heavy fog. The American General listened and heard the troops of the enemy shouting orders and counterorders, groping to reassemble into an army. But he could not pierce the fog and dark to discern figures and faces and guns. So Jackson ordered his troops to withdraw, fearing the results of gunfire under such conditions.

He took his troops back to an abandoned grass-covered millrace called the Rodriguez Canal which ran between the two plantations of Chalmette and Macarty. The canal, approximately fifteen feet wide, provided an excellent trench for the troops, and Jackson directed the immediate construction of a shoulder-high defensive rampart from which his troops would fire upon the enemy. The mile-long trench was reinforced with all available materials, from wood posts, kegs, and rails to trees and mud.

Later, John would try to recall those days which stretched from one major battle to another on the fields five miles south of New Orleans. Only flashes stood out in his memory. Most of all, there was General Andrew Jackson, wet and chilled, sitting on a log, surrounded by his men, sipping a mug of hot coffee in the predawn, before climbing a parapet to peer through the cold fog over the dim fields toward the enemy's stronghold.

John remembered, too, the ominous, eerie quiet following or preceding the awful roar of the big guns. He recalled the sense of panic which had to be fought as fiercely as the physical enemy. He had fired into the damnable fog as they all had, not knowing for certain that the enemy was there, not sure that he was not to receive a bullet in exchange.

The night-long bombardments continued without abatement, fog or not. Some of the bombs fizzled, nevertheless terrorizing the men as they fell among them. Hundreds lay dying in the swampy land.

With the gray miserable dawn the enemy troops began to take form. The Americans, ready for the advance of the British troops, held their fire, letting them come on.

John would never forget the sight of the 93rd Regiment of Highlanders, eleven hundred strong, moving across the battlefield toward the walls of the rampart, their kilts and the bagpipes proudly identifying them. Observing their approach, the Americans had held fire through sheer admiration and awe. *This* was the enemy!

Jackson had instructed the Americans to function as rifle teams, rotating positions, one team mounting the rampart, firing, backing down, the other team immediately ascending, firing, backing down—repeatedly. The teamwork had the effect of an automatic gun which never stopped firing. The Highlanders could not withstand such an unexpected and revolutionary attack.

Word swept the British lines that the Americans had let loose with a terrible new weapon.

The enemy fell everywhere along the line of the canal. Yet the British officers kept them moving in, for north of it was New Orleans and once that was in hand, the Mississippi Valley was theirs. It was worth the battle.

They sent in black men from Jamaica equipped with rope ladders and ordered them to climb the mud rampart and kill the defenders in the trenches. They never reached the rampart, falling to the rapid fire.

There were already twenty-six hundred British troops dead on the fields, but the British orders were: Seize the American rampart! The last of their troops came onward, relentlessly. The regiments looked like a red line of blood in their bright uniforms. When men among them fell dead or wounded, they paid no attention but just kept coming.

Andrew Jackson stood on the rampart with an odd sense of unreality, watching the British attack. He saw soldiers topple, rise again, fire, and fall dead. He was stunned by their magnificent effort. At the very last, when there were not many of them left on their feet, the Americans held their fire once more, watching cautiously. Would the enemy retreat? Would they surrender?

The answer came swiftly. Taking advantage of the temporary cessation of gunfire from the rampart, the British raced across the fields, over the bodies of the Highlanders and the black Jamaicans, struggling to reach the American canal, firing as they ran.

The Americans, startled by the daring of the enemy, gave them a barrage of cheers before they opened up with their guns. The last of the British regiments fell dead.

The battle was done. Jackson and his men were standing silent in the fog, shivering for more reason than that of the damp cold which bit into their bones. Hundreds of bodies lay in the fields beyond the rampart. Death was the victor; fog was a shroud.

Jackson and his men then witnessed a sight which none of them were ever to forget. Half hidden by the fog and the smoke which drifted low over the ground, men arose from among the dead on the battlefield. Crippled, stunned, defeated, numerous survivors arose and came forward, arms raised in surrender.

"It must have been something like this—the Resurrection,"

General Jackson whispered aloud, to no one in particular. He did not know tears streamed down his face and that when he wiped them away with a trembling hand, he left a streak of gunpowder.

John and Stand, their rifles resting on the butt ends, were among the men who stood to hail General Jackson as he rode the lines of his men to give the final cease-fire order.

The men began to sing *"Hail Columbia."* John and Stand, while giving the General due attention, did not join in the singing.

General Jackson shook hands with each man. When he and John clasped hands, they looked each other squarely in the eye but neither said a word. The General passed on down the line.

XV

QUATIE'S FATHER, A MEMBER OF THE COUNCIL, MET JOHN AT the door of his home in New Echota. He was holding his granddaughter, Jane. "Quatie rode out to her home," he said. "If you must know, John, I believe she ran when she heard you were on the trail, not far from here. I have seen startled does take to the brush to avoid the huntsman in just such a way. If you want her, you had better be gentle. She is shy, this strange daughter of mine."

John, riding swiftly to the Henley home, worried about his parting with Quatie the day he had left for battle. He knew his kiss had been almost brutal. Had he repelled her? Yet, if he were to kiss her now, would it be less passionate? He knew only that he wanted her. The February day was cold and there was a drizzle in the air as dark clouds came in low over the hills.

He saw her astride a horse, racing through a field which ran from the house to the river. Her dark hair was lifted by the wind and she rode with no saddle, holding the reins easy and allowing the horse freedom. Quatie, snug in deerskin jacket and leggings, calf-length soft boots protecting her feet, was exhilirated by the ride and her face glowed.

John's horse took long strides over the frozen ground to overtake her big bay. "Quatie!" he called, as his horse came up behind hers.

She heard him, tossed a glance backward, bit her lip, and spurred the bay faster, turning in a wide, retreating line, racing back toward the house. It was a real race, but John reached the hitching post outside the front yard at the same time she did and he slid from his horse and was at her side before she could move.

She turned, dismounted on the opposite side of the horse, let the reins drop, and ran toward the house.

He caught her and held her by the arms. His eyes were bright with the chase. "I love you," he told her.

"No!" She struggled. "Let me go."

"Quatie, are you afraid of me? When I kissed you good-bye, was I too—rough?"

She looked up at him, not struggling. "Oh, John!"

"All right, then. Why did you try to run from me?"

"I've had time to think, John." She touched his face gently. "You're white. And I feel you are going to be an important man. Perhaps you ought to have a white wife. Someone who can go with you into the white world."

He looked into her eyes and cupped her face very gently between his hands. "Don't let my red hair and blue eyes fool you. In my heart and in my soul, I am Cherokee. The only important question is the one I ask you—would giving birth to children with white blood in them distress you?"

"To give you sons has been my reason for living. If I could not, I would die."

The Reverend Gideon Blackburn officiated at the marriage held in the parlor of Quatie's father's home. It was a beautiful April day and she held a bouquet of white, blue, and yellow field flowers. Jane stood quietly beside them, and when the ceremony was over the little dark-haired girl flung herself into John's arms, hugging him. She did not understand it all, but she knew that the man she had accepted as a father had indeed become just that. She loved him and pouted some when she was told she would be staying with her grandfather for a few days while her parents took a trip across the river.

They were to live for a time in the old Ross home on the

Tennessee side of the river. A party of friends and relatives saw them safely home. There was singing and dancing at the Ross house and a lavish meal. The festivities of the wedding evening were highlighted by the Cherokee wedding ceremony which John and Quatie both wanted to perform.

Mollie Ross held Quatie tightly at the door of the home as the guests departed. "I've prayed John would have happiness in life," she told her. "When he looks at you, I see my prayers answered."

Stand and John shook hands at the door. "She's beautiful, John," Stand said. "I wish you joy, both of you." Crossing the river back to New Echota, with Sarah seated in the canoe in front of him, Stand glanced back at the dark structure of the Ross home.

One candle glowed brightly in the window of an upstairs bedroom. As he looked, the candle winked and went out.

Stand thought: They are alone in the dark. The bed will creak with their weight and their movements. The only sounds will be those of love, a cry of ecstasy, a moan of desire. By dawn, John will have planted his seed in her and Quatie will no doubt be pregnant.

Stand forced his gaze away from the darkened house on the hill and turned to look at Sarah. He envied John who, this night, was in the arms of the woman he loved.

XVI

EARLY THE FOLLOWING YEAR, QUATIE GAVE BIRTH TO THEIR first son, James. John, building his family a new home at New Echota, was feeling his own power in his personal life as well as his public one.

Even as white Americans were turning their hands and minds to the rebuilding of their capital, the Cherokee Nation began its own plans for its citizens. John's voice was heard throughout the land as he continued individual meetings with the people.

"We must gain our equality with our white brothers through our ability to match them in all things," he told them. "We must, first of all, develop an educational system comparable to that of the whites. We must see that our children grow up not only speaking our language but English. We must initiate a republican form of government, exactly like the Americans. We must elect officials, write laws. We ought to develop a court system which offers all men justice, discarding our ancient tribal law of personal revenge. We must form a Cherokee Nation of free men and written law."

John rode his big horse into every village of the far-flung Cherokee Nation. His turbaned, long-jacketed figure became a welcome sight as he hitched his horse to posts in public squares to take time to visit with the residents of the town.

The people began to turn to him for advice and help in many personal problems. A minister without portfolio, he sought the people, and they came to him to hear his dream: a united Cherokee Nation, a State of the Cherokee within the Union. Equality.

John was fascinated, too, with the work begun by George Gist, he whom the people knew as Sequoyah. He was devising a Cherokee syllabary and in the few years ahead he planned to complete the alphabet, putting the Cherokee language into writing for the first time. The tremendous work would bring the Cherokee people ever closer to the equality John envisioned for them.

In Washington, new buildings were rising to take the place of the ones burned by the British. The President's House, charred and roofless, was being reconstructed within the original walls which had stood thanks to the heavy rainstorm which had pelted the city like a benediction from heaven the night Washington burned.

The city was taking a new shape, growing rapidly and astonishingly. There was a brand new bridge across the Potomac. Stagecoaches rolled through the streets, bringing important citizens to the capital. On the fifteenth of November, 1815, the Washington Canal was opened.

President Madison and his wife occupied the mansion known by some as the Octagon House, and more familiarly called the "House of a Thousand Candles." The Madisons held a virtual open-house policy. In the evenings, candles were lighted at the windows of every room and slaves with flaming torches guarded the place with dutiful walks around it.

In the spring of 1816, John came to Washington, in company with an authorized Cherokee delegation to see James Madison. The issue which General Jackson had raised regarding the cession of Creek lands was becoming a crisis. Not satisfied with the land taken from the Creeks, Jackson had lately recommended to the President that now the Cherokee, the Chickasaw, and the Creek ought to surrender all their lands in Tennessee, thus ridding the United States and the State of Tennessee of any further Indian problem in that area.

President Madison had turned a cold ear to Jackson's radical suggestion. He gave orders to his Secretary of War to maintain the Cherokee boundaries as had been agreed following the Creek War. Jackson's ire was aroused when the Cherokee and the Chickasaw had put in their own war claim upon the acreage of the disloyal Creeks. The General could see no reason at all for allowing the Indians to add to their lands.

John's delegation included the Ridge, Captain John Walker, Captain Richard Taylor, Cheucunsenee, and Colonel John Lowrey, who was assigned the duty of spokesman. John was to record the entire proceedings, since he and Captain Taylor were the only ones among the delegation who could write.

The President met them graciously, his small body full of tension. The drawing room formality seemed somehow a proper background for the colorful but dignified group. The Indians had hired a fancy coach and quietly left for the Octagon House from their hotel rooms. They were variously clad: the Ridge wore a high-collared dark suit with a ruffled shirtfront not unlike that which the President wore; Captains Lowrey and Walker appeared in fringed buckskins; Cheucunsenee wore a bright red blanket over jacket and leggings, his feet encased in moccasins and a headband with a crimson feather; and John was handsome in a dark blue heavy-silk, tunic-style jacket and trousers, shining boots, and a white sash and turban.

Colonel Lowrey stepped forth from the group at the door, bowing to the President: "Father: It is our pleasure to be in your company. We are asked by our council to take you by the hand. We say this day was appointed by the Great Spirit for us to see one another. It makes our hearts glad to enter your home even as they are glad when we enter our own."

The solemn-faced President extended his hand first to the Colonel and then proceeded down the line of the small delegation. "It always gives me great pleasure to receive my friends in my house, especially my red brethren who have fought by the side of their white brethren and spilt their blood together."

There was a presentation by Colonel Lowrey of the business the Cherokee Nation wanted to place on the desk of the President of the United States. The matters pertained not only to a reaffirmation of the borders of the Indian nation, but to such internal matters as the determination of the use of roads within the nation by the white Union. Paramount among the issues, too, was the request of the Indians that those white settlers who had come into their territory at the urging of General Andrew Jackson, following the close of hostilities in the Creek War, be removed.

The President assured his visitors that when their petitions were studied carefully, there would be other meetings. He requested that if possible they extend their stay in the city while he made his study. This agreed upon, the Cherokee delegation returned to their hotel to await further word.

President Madison gave them a treaty which met most of their demands, but it required that the Cherokees cede the acreage the nation still held in South Carolina—land whose value was less to them than the benefits they received from the Union in exchange.

The important segment of the new treaty was that which defined the Cherokee and Creek boundary lines between the Coosa and Tennessee rivers, establishing the claims of the Cherokee Nation south of the Tennessee. This was a victory of sorts and pleased the entire delegation. They also received a payment of $25,600 to be awarded the Cherokees who had asked for reimbursement for damaged property caused by the passing of the American troops through their lands during the Creek War.

The treaty benefited both the Union and the Indian Nation, offering the Americans the right to build and open roads through the nation for the free use of all in commerce between the states of Tennessee, Georgia, and the Mississippi Territory. This clause also allowed free navigation of all rivers within the nation. The Cherokee were given the permission to build taverns and other necessary buildings for the public use along the roads, thus creating a new source of income for their people.

The delegation was invited to a musical evening at the President's House in the company of Washington's highly fashionable men and women. The ladies, peeking from behind their jeweled fans, whispered about John Ross, the red-haired Indian in a formal evening suit. A matron who fluttered to Dolly Madison's side in pursuit of information about John was told in a whisper: "He's married, my dear! I asked James about him because I knew he'd be the center of attraction here this evening."

"Married?" The matron, who had a daughter ready for marriage, was unhappily surprised. "To whom, Dolly? Anyone of importance?"

The President's lady had an eye for romance and an ear for gossip: "She was a young widow. Her husband served under General Jackson and he was killed in the Creek War."

The matron gazed at John across the room to see him bowing over the hand of a young woman. "How tragic. And how romantic! Mrs. Ross, however, is not a very clever woman to let her handsome husband visit Washington without her. Just look how the ladies are buzzing around him. Will his wife visit here with him some time?"

"I would think not." Dolly Madison hid the smile in her eyes very well. "The wife of John Ross is a full-blood Cherokee. She is at home now with their firstborn child, and I would imagine she has no plans to visit Washington."

"A full blood!" The lady stared at John in amazement. "How awful!"

Dolly Madison moved away from the woman, her eyes clouding.

John danced with a few of the young ladies, the perfume and silks and satins of their gowns pleasing to him. He would go shopping on Pennsylvania Avenue, he decided, before he went home. Quatie would be more beautiful than any of the Washington women in a gown cut low over the breasts and delicately belted under them to give the female form a flattering emphasis.

As the guests began to depart the reception, the First Lady drew John aside at the front door. "I've had a glimpse of your turbans this past week. I've decided I want to wear the things, too. Would you mind if I copied yours, perhaps adding a jewel here and there?"

He bowed. "I am flattered, Mrs. Madison. I'm sure you'll set a new style among the ladies."

His prediction was right; a few months later he would hear

that Mrs. Madison was affecting turbans, creating quite a stir in the world of fashion. John had little time for gossip, though, as the events of the months ahead brought new problems from Andrew Jackson.

The General, hearing of the treaty Madison had conferred upon the Cherokees, went into a rage. "By God," he swore: "I'll undo it if it takes me a lifetime, come heaven or hell. Madison has made a terrible mistake. The treaty is a wanton, hasty, useless thing. It has got to be undone." He made particular objection to the boundary lines as set by agreement between the President and the Cherokees.

It did not take Jackson long to figure a way to effectively abrogate the treaty. Together with two friends, David Meriwether and Jesse Franklin, he secured a federal position as a commissioner to deal with the Indians in matters involving them and the Union.

"We'll get rid of that treaty, one way or another," he told his friends. "In March we will have a new President. I aim to see that he has a clearer picture of our Indian problem than Madison could ever grasp."

James Monroe was inaugurated on March 4, 1817, coming into office as a popular hero, and Jackson moved ahead on his plans. He began by calling together eight Cherokee chiefs: Pathkiller, Glass, Boat, Sour Mush, Chulioa, Dick Justice, Chickasautchee, and Richard Brown.

Jackson told them: "If you will give up the claim of the Cherokee people to the land south of the Tennessee River which you took in the Madison treaty, the United States will give you five thousand dollars cash now and sixty thousand dollars during the next ten years." He followed this offer with the presentation of individual gifts to the chiefs.

Unauthorized by the Council, and against tribal law, the chiefs accepted the deal with Jackson, ceding the land. Jackson's actions were considered a success by the War Department, which immediately followed his lead by a demand on the Cherokees that they also cede the lands they owned in North Carolina.

The Cherokee Council, already shocked by the chiefs who had used their own signatures to cede Cherokee land, sent a blunt refusal to the War Department and an appeal to President Monroe, protesting the work of Jackson and the War Department in making a secret and illegal treaty with individual chiefs.

President Monroe, sidestepping the problem, put it back into the hands of Andrew Jackson, Joseph Minn, and John Coffee.

John paced the floor of his bedroom. Quatie, lying in bed, watched her husband anxiously. He went to the window, looked out, turned, and looked at his wife. "Jackson has got to be stopped. He'll leave us nothing but the wind, if we allow it."

Quatie sat up, and the candlelight gave her naked body a rosy gleam. "You'll find a way to beat him."

He sat down beside her. "You make it sound possible."

"Because I believe in you," she whispered, kissing his mouth, leaning into his arms.

He snuffed out the candle. "I think," said he, "I'll worry about General Jackson tomorrow."

XVII

THEN CAME ANDREW JACKSON'S FIRST SUGGESTION THAT the Cherokees voluntarily remove their Nation to new lands, thus ending the racial problem in the southern states: "Exchange your ancient lands for the new of the west."

"We no longer understand our white Father in Washington," the Cherokee replied: "But a few years ago he gave us gifts of the plough and the hoe telling us we must farm our lands. He said to us it is not good for his red children to hunt for a living. We must make the earth feed us through the planting of good seeds. Now our Father tells us we will find good hunting and much food in the west if we will go there with rifles he will give us. We will not go."

But General Jackson had hit upon the method of dividing the Indian Nation through bribes. He called a meeting of the Cherokee people to be held at the Calhoun Indian Agency headquarters on the Hiwassee. The Council came to hear him, curious but suspicious.

John sat at the convention without a legal position, but only as a young man interested in the events of his people. He would say nothing but he would learn. The day was not far off, he believed, when he would stand at the head of the Council. For now, he must keep his silence.

General Jackson towered in their midst, a man of brief words and short temper. He told them that the United States wanted more of their lands in long overdue payment for the lands given the Cherokees who had migrated to Arkansas and were now squatting on land belonging to the Union. The United States government would take some of the lands in Tennessee and Georgia as an exchange. For the remaining Cherokee acreage, the United States would grandly exchange more lands west of the Mississippi to which all the Cherokees would be removed.

The reaction was bitter and swift. Sixty-seven chiefs at the meeting immediately signed a protest against the policy of land cession and the removal of any Cherokees west against their will.

General Jackson was furious. "Repudiate the written protest!" he ordered the chiefs.

The Council, in worried conference, decided the Union could take the Arkansas problem to the courts and win. But as a concession, they agreed to cede two parcels of land in Georgia and Tennessee to the Union as payment for the land occupied by their brothers in Arkansas.

Some of the Cherokee, given money by the Jackson commissioners, left their homeland and went west. The Army supervised their going and counted the number at thirty-five hundred. The United States government gave each man a blanket, a rifle, a brass kettle, and lead for his gun.

John told Quatie: "We have now lost some twenty thousand square miles to the white men since the days of our first treaty negotiations with him. Our people are right in terming the compass of the white man 'land stealers.' Our Nation now measures two hundred miles to the east of us here and to the west, and one hundred and twenty miles north to south. Most of it is within Georgia, as are the greater majority of our people. If we lose more land, we will lose our identity as a people, and our future."

"You're going to rally the people against ceding any more land, aren't you?"

"You won't mind? It will take a great deal of my time. I'll be away from home often in the next year."

"Well," she smiled, "I'm going to be busy myself. We're going to have a new son."

In the next few months, as the child grew within Quatie, and Jimmy and Jane played on the grounds of the old Ross home, John hurried the completion of the imposing mansion he was building for his family in New Echota. The two-storied house, southern in style, graced a gentle hilltop, rising above lands which would be largely devoted to cotton. John was purchasing slaves for both the fields and the house.

The plantation was a gift for Quatie, who watched its development with a mixed sense of joy and awe. When John imported furniture from New York and Philadelphia, she was stunned and tearfully happy.

John also continued his rides through the country to bring to the people the idea that not one more acre of Cherokee land should be ceded to the Union. They needed a voice in their governing Council which would represent them without fail, and urged him to become a member of the Council in order to have an official voice.

He decided to work to reorganize the Cherokee government so that one official head officer would preside over all the local chiefs. And he was determined to be that official.

He began his campaign among the people. A meeting of the Council was called for the sixth day of May, 1817, to prepare a revised governmental system to fight for their land against the whites.

General Jackson's attention was temporarily distracted when the Seminoles rose, moving from their Spanish-protected centers in Florida to attack Georgian homes, robbing, killing, and burning.

They received aid and guidance from eight hundred Georgia slaves who had fled from their captivity into the wilds and banded together in an abandoned British fort on the Apalachicola River some sixty miles below the southern border of Georgia. The British had moved away from the fort so fast in 1812 that they had left all their supplies behind. Taking over the fort, the Negroes found, among other supplies, a dozen pieces of artillery, twenty-five hundred muskets, five hundred swords, four hundred pistols, five hundred carbines, three hundred quarter-casks of rifle powder, and over seven hundred barrels of common powder.

Now, after spending nearly two years in their private fort, the blacks were in need of some new provisions, especially food to help feed the young children. From their vantage point on a bluff they could see any boat ascending or descending the water route. They became aware of the schedule of supply boats for Fort Scott, a federal stronghold upriver, which was just over the border into Georgia, and mapped a plan of attack on the federal supply ship.

Their assault came without warning, but the Americans put up a vigorous defense, losing only a portion of their supplies and escaping downriver. Four sailors were dead, and one was captured alive.

As the federal boat beat a retreat down the river, the single captive was dragged to the fort where he was tied hand and foot. Amid the victory howls of the blacks, he was drenched with tar and set afire.

Jackson ordered troops to seize the fort. Federal gunboats loaded with armed men went upriver on a hot day in July 1816. The Negroes were ready. As the Union troops came into view, guns bristled from every part of the stronghold and heavy gunfire pelted down on the gunboats.

The sailors and soldiers on the boats returned shot for shot, but the attack was over in one dreadful combustion when a shot hurled from one of the gunboats landed in the fort's ammunition room. Flames reached toward the sky, and fragments of the fort's walls were blasted into the river, sizzling in the water.

Seven hundred and ninety-seven persons were killed in the terrific explosion. The few survivors were unable to speak.

General Jackson moved into Florida with a new hate in his heart, holding the Seminoles and the Spaniards responsible for the Negroes' attack upon the American boats.

The General went about his swift campaign with no particular direction from the White House. He crossed into Spanish-held territory and helped himself to victory. St. Marks, a Spanish fort, surrendered to him.

He captured two Englishmen, Alexander Arbuthnot, a trader, and Robert C. Ambrister, a former officer of the British Royal Colonial Marines, whom he charged with operating with the

Spaniards and the Seminoles. They were given a court-martial and pronounced guilty of the specific charge of inciting the Indians to attack the frontiers of the southern states of the Union.

After seeing Arbuthnot hanged and Ambrister shot by a firing squad, General Jackson went on to capture Pensacola, where he raised the Stars and Stripes.

Word of Jackson's victories spread throughout the country. The General had sent the Seminoles scampering back into the wilderness of Florida. Throughout Florida, the Spanish were in flight, fearing Jackson would descend on them. The hero of the Battle of New Orleans was acclaimed victor in Pensacola on the twenty-eighth day of May 1817.

Henry Clay arose in the Congress of the United States to tell the world that since there were plans to purchase Florida, General Jackson's action in seizing it by military force was appalling. He warned the nation that Napoleons arise from the ranks of military chieftans.

General Jackson, hearing of Clay's attack upon him, bellowed: "Well, I'll be God-damned!"

The House of Representatives voted to recognize Jackson's victory. The Union accepted his militarily won gift, and Florida was formally claimed and annexed in July 1821.

XVIII

IN THE MONTH OF MAY 1817 JOHN ROSS AND QUATIE welcomed a new son, Alan, who was dark-eyed and dark-haired like his brother and half-sister.

The Council met as planned. Elias Boudinot arose to summarize the draft for a vote: "It is proposed that from this day forward the Cherokee government shall consist of a National Committee of elected officers, the Committee to have complete

national governmental powers over the people during the interim periods between meetings of the Council which is to remain intact. The power of the National Committee shall be invested in the new office of President of the Committee."

The vote was in favor of the revised government.

The Ridge then arose to speak. This day he was dressed in the white ceremonial buckskins and feathered headdress. "The vote will now be taken for the office of President of the National Committee. This office carries much more power than I personally feel is wise to give any one man. Our vote now must be to select a man worthy of our trust. I am told that my name is to be one of those you will consider. I first thought, upon learning this, that I would decline the honor. However, upon more selfless thinking, I stand ready to accept the vote of this Council, whatever it may be."

It was clear to the Council why the Ridge had made his little speech: the only other name entered before the Council for the presidency was John Ross.

"He's too young," went the whispers among the friends of the Ridge. "He's too radical. He's white in his views. At twenty-seven he has much to learn," they told each other.

Too late, the Ridge and his friends realized that John had been quietly campaigning for the position of President for many months, riding among the people, trading talk with them, making friends.

Elias Boudinot, only half in jest, said: "The Delphic Oracle is about to be licensed to ride among his people to bring them his revelations from heaven."

Stand Watie, a new bridegroom who had not been giving too much time to governmental policies of late, laughed. "Oracle or not," he admitted, "the people are John's friends and they hang onto every word he says."

Andrew Ross was opposed to his younger brother taking the office. He clashed with him over policies. Lewis, admiring John, wanted to see him elected.

The chiefs, having acquired immense respect for John Ross during the past months, and knowing that the revision of their government was largely due to his work and vision, did not hear the critics in their spectators' seats. The people had raised a leader and they meant to keep him. John Ross was elected President of the National Committee of the Cherokee Nation.

John, having taken the oath of office, spoke very briefly. "Our country and our people—this should always be our sacred motto and the people should always direct us in the path of duty. What I may do, I do *with* them, never against them."

In the next ten years, John led his Nation as President of the National Committee. Through the genius of Sequoyah, the Cherokee language was committed to writing and the children learned it right along with English.

The Nation founded its own newspaper, the *Cherokee Phoenix*, published in both English and Cherokee, the pages divided down the center to give each language its own space. Elias Boudinot was elected editor of the *Phoenix*, which reflected the growing feeling in the Nation, spurred by John, that once again the Cherokee government ought to be revised, this time to a constitutional one such as enjoyed by white America.

The Cherokee schools were superior and the students bright and attentive to their lessons. Fine Christian churches were constructed and well attended. New homes were rising in contrast to the old log buildings and cabins. Business was thriving as the Nation entered into commerce with the states.

John's private life now included Silas, another son with the physical appearance of a Cherokee; and George Washington, a red-haired youngster.

Quatie presided over the Ross mansion with all the quiet dignity expected of a First Lady. She was not in robust health, but with an enforced daily rest she managed to extend hospitality to all who came to see her husband on national matters. She spent hours among the blooms in the Ross gardens, and her roses, growing in profusion throughout the spring and summer, were gaining notice even outside the Nation.

The Ross home had become a cotton plantation and John was gaining a fortune. He tithed himself, contributing funds to the general national purse, earmarking a good deal of it for use in building and equipping schools and hiring teachers. Education, he was convinced, was the real salvation of the Cherokee people.

The adoption of a national Constitution in 1826 allowed the Cherokee Nation to function more effectively. The Cherokee government was now on a par with that of the individual states of the white Union. There was now a Cherokee Supreme Court and a legal system to protect all the people. But some Indian traditions held. The chiefs of the towns still held office, if only as figureheads. Under the new constitutional government, their positions were similar to governors, their power mainly on the administrative side of the law. But relations with the Union were becoming increasingly strained, especially in regard to Georgia, whose Legislature was constantly passing laws abridging the rights of the Indians. But thus far the Cherokee government had paid them little heed, instead concentrating on its own progress.

Still another honor came to John, bringing with it the power he needed to effect his Nation's unity. On a day in October 1828, the National Committee, the Council, all the chiefs and warriors, and the Cherokee people met together in the open public square at New Echota to elect and inaugurate John Ross as Principal Chief of the Cherokee Nation. The ancient tribal law provided for a head chief, but the position now embodied in written law was akin to the office of the President of the United States.

John had just celebrated his thirty-eighth birthday and he was in fine health. Garbed in the ceremonial white deerskin outfit of a Chief, he stood before the crowds gathered in the square, waiting for the attention of the people. Tiny silver bells were knotted into the fringe of the soft white jacket, playing a tuneless song when he moved. The feathers of his Chief's bonnet were red and white to symbolize both peace and war.

Stand Watie was no longer very close to John, their married lives, business, and differences in thinking had pulled them apart. "Today John Ross is Cherokee," he whispered to Going Snake. "I thought he might wear the silks and ribbons of the white men who are elected President of the Union."

Going Snake's head was white now. "Whatever he wears, his clothing covers a brave man."

John raised his right hand, resting his left on the Holy Bible held by the Reverend Blackburn. He looked to the row of seats nearby where Quatie sat with Jane and the four boys. He spoke his words firmly and loudly enough to be heard throughout the square.

"I, John Ross, do solemnly swear that I will faithfully execute the office of Principal Chief of the Cherokee Nation, and will, to the best of my ability, preserve, protect and defend the Constitution of the Cherokee Nation."

A month later, the weight of his nation's problems already heavy on his heart, John was disturbed to hear that General

Andrew Jackson of Tennessee had been elected to the presidency of the United States.

When the State of Georgia passed its restrictive laws against the Cherokees within its borders, John sent word: "The Cherokee are not foreigners, but the original inhabitants of America. They now stand on the soil of their own territory, and they cannot recognize the sovereignty of any state within the limits of their territory."

The State of Georgia chose to ignore his words and to regard the Indians as interlopers within its boundaries. They enacted more laws, touching upon the ceding of Cherokee lands to the state. "It is the fixed and unalterable determination of this Nation never again to cede one foot more of our land," John advised the Legislature of Georgia. Still the State of Georgia went ahead on its well-developing campaign to make the Indians homeless.

President Jackson had been in the White House only a few months when gold was discovered in the Cherokee Nation. The news of this hit Georgia hard. The politicians studied the problem. In the meantime, the Indians were working the mines and gold was a vital new asset for the Cherokee Nation.

Then came the staggering blow: President Jackson, in his first annual message to Congress, advocated a law to remove all Indians of all southern states to lands west of the Mississippi, beginning June 1, 1830! John, shutting himself up in his office at home, read with fury that the President also suggested that anyone who urged the Indians not to remove west was liable to immediate arrest!

John realized he would have to go to Washington, taking a well-chosen delegation to protest in person.

On May 26, 1830, the Congress passed the Indian Removal Act as recommended by the President. Chief John Ross of the Cherokee Nation, and his personal delegation, were turned away from the White House, being told that "the President is unavailable." They then went to the War Department, under which the approved exodus of all Indians was to take place. Since their visit concerned a protest over the Removal Act, Secretary of War Eaton would not meet with them.

John and his delegates returned to New Echota and John began to map a legal battle, determined to take the issue to the Supreme Court of the United States. But before he could consult in full with the white attorneys he had hired—Underwood and Harris, of Georgia, and William Wirt, who was qualified to appear before the Supreme Court—another calamity struck, by way of the Georgia Governor.

It came at noon on a hot Fourth of July, 1830, from a sweating young courier who arrived at the Ross plantation on the Tennessee.

He had ridden straight from the Governor's mansion. The slave called Alpha took the message at the front door that the Governor had a private and urgent communiqué for the Chief of the Cherokee, to be delivered only into his hands. John accompanied Alpha to the front door, ready to tend to the matter himself.

The young rider spanked dust from his clothing, his face freckled and red from the long, fast ride. "Governor Gilmer has instructed me to deliver this into your hands, sir, and to wait for your reply."

He handed him a document which had been secured in a leather packet attached to a belt encircling his waist.

John took the paper. "I'll call for you when I've got the reply ready. In the meantime, welcome to our home. If you'll go with Alpha, he'll get you a cool drink, perhaps some of the milk we have in the kitchen, cool from the springhouse."

John went to the library which he used as an office these days. Holding the paper up to catch the best light from the window, his mouth went dry.

He strode quickly to the kitchen where he found the courier seated at the table enjoying the meal and cold milk. Betina, Alpha's wife, was hovering in the background, her attention torn between the young man at the table and the dairy girl who was churning butter under her supervision. Alpha was seated on a stool, drinking a mug of cool milk himself, but when his master entered the kitchen he got to his feet, his face a little guilty. John waved him back. Betina was due to have their first child within two months, and they were being accorded special privileges these days.

"There will be no reply at this time," John told the messenger. "You tell the Governor he'll have an answer soon enough."

John met with the Council and the National Committee for the first time in the brand new Council House. It stood in the square along with other new public buildings, including the Supreme Court and a printshop for the *Cherokee Phoenix*. Nearby were the new homes of Elias Boudinot and the minister, Sam Worcester, and Elijah Hicks. The well-constructed log building boasted plank flooring, glass windows, and an attractive staircase which wound to the large meeting rooms on the second floor. Each room had huge fireplaces, raised platforms for the speakers, and plank benches for members of the committees.

"I'm going to summarize the proclamation in order that we may quickly consider each point," John told the legislators. "Governor Gilmer has just declared that all Cherokee lands in Georgia are to be confiscated. The lands taken will be distributed to white men only, through a lottery system. The authority of the Cherokee Nation—this body here now, and myself—has been declared illegal and nonexistent. We are prohibited from meeting as a governing body, as we are now doing. Indeed, we are to hold no meetings of any kind, including religious gatherings. We are to be removed west to lands beyond the Mississippi."

The rumble of voices was beginning to drown him out. "Hear me through! If we do not respond to the order of removal, we are to be punished as the white men decide. All contracts between us and whites are to be void unless they are witnessed by two white men. We are hereafter denied the right to testify in any court against any white man.

"And, lastly, but perhaps revealingly, we are not to be allowed to dig for gold in our fields from this day forward."

He waited while voices flooded the room in anger. Again John held up an arm, asking for quiet. He said: "We will answer the Governor—"

"War! Dig up the war hatchet!" It was Stand Watie shouting. His right to speak had come the last election when he became a member of the National Committee.

Andrew stood with Watie, echoing: "War!"

John waved them to silence: "No! We shall not answer with war. Brothers! Hear me!"

They quieted but they began to group around Stand, who stood with arms folded across his broad chest, anger brilliant in his eyes.

"We are civilized," John said. "Now we have an opportunity to prove it. Our law shall answer theirs. Our attorney will represent us in the Supreme Court of the United States, and in the State of Georgia. We'll bring the whites into their own courts and defeat them there."

Again the councilmen and the committeemen shouted their contempt for the federal Union and for Georgia, drowning out the words of their Chief. Stand led the shouts.

John held up both arms, pleading for silence. "As Chief of the Cherokee I take my full power of office. I tell you this—I'm going to Washington to see President Jackson. I'll carry your protest. I'll also consult with our attorney while I'm there and perhaps file our case with the Supreme Court. But I insist upon going on this mission with your support and prayers. Will you give me these things in order that we may settle our problems without war?"

He waited on the platform, not sure that he was Chief, uncertain that his Nation was not dying in front of his eyes. While he stood there, they took a secret vote on whether to support him or not.

The sure knowledge that Stand was voting against him put a feeling of emptiness in the pit of his stomach. In the other nations, young men like Stand were giving way to the removal campaign, sensing something new and romantic in giving up their old lands and removing west to a mysterious future. It hurt, too, to see Andy conferring with Stand.

He recalled all too well that just the last September the Choctaw had divided over the issue at Dancing Rabbit Creek. There had been, as a result, a hasty treaty with the commissioners sent by President Jackson, and the Choctaws had given up their lands and were going west. Their action had weakened all the other tribes.

The vote was in support of John; the talk of war was ended. But John saw that if he could not hold his Nation against the removal, it would be due to Stand Watie as much as to anyone else.

The city of Washington was continuing an amazing growth, but John had no time or inclination to roam it. He conferred with attorney William Wirt who had represented the government as special prosecutor at the treason trial of Aaron Burr. He advised John that the issue of whether the Cherokee people and their government were to be recognized as independent of Georgia was to be handled through an individual Cherokee—Corn Tassel, accused of murder and condemned to death by a Georgia court. The legal papers were being prepared, Wirt told John, and action would soon take place.

When Wirt found that John desired a meeting with the President but had been refused a prior attempt to visit him, Wirt himself made the appointment, saying only that he had impressed the President with the importance of such a meeting.

John went alone to the White House, wearing a black broadcloth suit, a white linen shirt, and a large, loosely tied black cravat and carrying a broad-rimmed black hat.

The President's desk, where he had been seated, was piled high with papers. President Jackson wore no jacket or tie. The sleeves of his white cotton shirt were rolled up to just beneath the elbows. His white hair had been haphazardly brushed back into a peruke which was tied firmly with an old rattlesnake skin. He looked more Indian than did his visitor as he stood to shake hands.

"Sit down, Chief Ross. We'll have a smoke." He pushed a box of cigars along the edge of the desk. "Or do you use a pipe?"

John declined any smoke, sitting straight and motionless in the fancy chair.

The President was striving for pleasantry. "I congratulate you upon your new title, Chief Ross."

"Thank you, Mr. President." He had a feeling that if he did not speak quickly the meeting would end with no more than the exchange of mild compliments. "I'm sure you'll forgive me if I get right to the issue between us, sir. I am here to protest the Indian Removal Act of your administration and the Congress. I also bring you the protests of my people and myself in regard to the proclamation of Governor Gilmer of Georgia who has, in effect, attempted to declare the government of the Cherokee Nation null and void and its people without any rights whatsoever. I inform you, Mr. President, that the federal and state removal acts are totally rejected by the Cherokee Nation."

"Now just a minute—"

"Mr. President, I must add that the Cherokee Nation considers the United States of America obliged to honor its treaties which have existed since the administration of George Washington, and prior. The treaties all require that the United States, rather than persecuting us as a people, are honor-bound to protect us against our enemies even as we have gone to war to protect the Union. I believe you were witness to that."

The President picked up his unlighted pipe and waved it back and forth, leaning forward in his chair. "One moment, Chief Ross! You're taking a mighty high hand here. I have no intention of discussing the Removal Act with you. You're smart enough, you know better than this. All negotiations are being conducted through the War Department and the Secretary, John Eaton. I'll not be drawn into any bitter discussions of what the Congress has done or what the State of Georgia does. I won't carry on this meeting if you intend to use it as a personal appeal to me. It's not proper for you to do so. Not at all."

"Mr. President, it's highly improper for you to advocate the exodus of a people from their native land without their consent. Since you allow me no more, I will say this: The Cherokee Nation shall not remove." He bowed his head and moved toward the door.

President Jackson shoved his chair back and arose, "We'll see, we'll see. In any case, all negotiations shall be carried on faithfully by this administration to bring a sound and equitable solution to the racial problem in this nation."

"My God! Do you know what's going on in the name of a sound and equitable solution?"

"I do. What you are not taking into consideration, Chief Ross, is my position. I must think about what is best not only for your people but for mine. And I say that the best thing is the removal west of all Indians. I aim to see it done, with or without your help, sir!"

John could do no more than leave, holding back the words which would only react against him and his people.

John went home to confer with his official family. It was decided that a visit to Secretary of War John Eaton was the only path left open to them by President Jackson. In an effort to select the men he believed most dedicated to the ideas he held regarding Cherokee unity, John sent John Ridge, John Martin, and William Shorey to Washington. He stayed at home himself this time, but kept a tight hold on the men through written instructions through the mails.

In December, the Supreme Court of the United States cited the State of Georgia to answer why a writ of error should not be issued in the case of Corn Tassel. Georgia refused to respond to the summons of the Court. After study of the case, the Court reached its decision, announced by the Chief Justice, John Marshall: "An Indian tribe or nation within the United States is not a foreign state in the sense of the Constitution, and cannot maintain an action in the Courts of the United States."

The State of Georgia carried out its sentence of death against Corn Tassel, Cherokee, for murder.

XIX

FEDERAL AND STATE AGENTS BEGAN TO RIDE THROUGHOUT the Cherokee Nation, speaking to the people about the necessity to remove, and hinting that it might be profitable to heed the law. The Cherokee government, increasingly concerned with the possibility that the government agents would bring division to their people, passed a bill stating that the selling of lands by an individual was legally considered treason, and that the ancient tribal law held such treason punishable by execution.

The act was published in the *Cherokee Phoenix* for all to note. The Blood Law, as they called it, stated that anyone selling Cherokee lands without authority from the Nation was subject to execution, upon conviction by the Cherokee Supreme Court. The act got its name, however, from the section which came directly from the ancient law:

"Be it further resolved, that any person or persons, who shall violate the provisions of this act, and shall refuse, by resistance, to appear at the place designated for trial, or abscond, are hereby declared to be outlaws; and any person or persons, citizens of this nation, may kill him or them so offending, in any manner most convenient, within the limits of this nation, and shall not be held accountable."

The Ridge faction were satisfied to see the old Cherokee law become a written document. It seemed unlikely that there would be any member of the Nation who would risk defiance of the Blood Law now.

The Supreme Court's decision only served to strenghten the will of John Ross to fight the exodus orders, but it had a different effect on some Cherokees. How could a small Nation successfully battle the powers of the state and federal governments? Wouldn't it be better to make the best deal possible with the Union and move on west to a land where the white men would leave them alone? The *Cherokee Phoenix* only dug in more firmly for a continuing legal battle to maintain the Nation on its native lands, and copies of its blazing editorials were circulated in the white nation. Outside the South, sentiment turned to the Indians and against President Jackson and the State of Georgia.

The legal break John expected came when the State of Georgia arrested eleven white missionaries in the Cherokee Nation, charging them with failure to take an oath of allegiance to the state. The new Governor of Georgia, Wilson Lumpkin, had overplayed his hand. Nine of the missionaries, displaying no sacrificial attitude toward the Indian Nation, succumbed to the pressure of the state and were given their freedom upon taking of the oath. But Samuel Austin Worcester and Elizur Butler faced the penalty and rejected the demand that they also pledge their allegiance to the State of Georgia. They were immediately given a sentence of four years' imprisonment in the Georgia State Prison.

The tale of their plight went around the world from the pages of the *Cherokee Phoenix,* inciting the wrath of peoples everywhere against the South and Jackson.

Attorney William Wirt, after a day-long conference with John in Washington, took the case, carrying the issue of the Cherokee Nation versus the State of Georgia back to the Supreme Court.

The Chief Justice of the United States, John Marshall, stunned the world with an announcement in favor of Sam Worcester and Elizur Butler: the State of Georgia was in error. It could not apply its laws to Indian matters but must give way to the laws of the Union. Where the Cherokees were concerned, the Union laws were bound in treaty agreements which excluded the rights of any state—and therefore the State of Georgia had no legal right to interfere in the Cherokee Nation.

Stand Watie, a stagecoach letter from his brother Elias Boudinot in hand, burst into John's home ahead of any other news from Washington. "John, it's over!" He grabbed his friend by the arms. "The Chief Justice has declared for us. The laws of the State of Georgia are declared null and void within our Nation. So says the highest judicial tribunal in America."

But it was a hollow triumph. The State of Georgia ignored the decision and kept Worcester and Butler in prison and would hold them for nearly a year.

When appealed to for help in carrying out the Court's decision, Andrew Jackson shrugged his big shoulders: "John Marshall has rendered his decision; now let *him* enforce it."

It had come to nothing. The missionaries were still imprisoned. Worse, pressure from the federal and state governments was increasing, and every day left more Indians homeless and destitute, forcing them to the hills where they could find primitive shelter and food.

The public lottery (Lottery Law 1802) was taking a tragic toll. The new Georgia laws provided that Indians were merely unwanted tenants on state land; that the lands of the Cherokees were open to confiscation—and the lands included their homes, large and small. State agents simply walked into private residences, guns in hand. There were some struggles and deaths, but the occupants were dispossessed. Each parcel of land, each home, was entered into an immense lottery, handled by Georgia, which entitled every male citizen, white veteran, or widow of a white veteran to draw from it.

A message came to John: "The President of the United States requests a conference with the Chief of the Cherokee Nation to discuss and consider the removal of the Cherokee Nation west of the Mississippi. The President desires to offer the Chief a treaty for the consideration of the Cherokee people."

John had no intention of accepting any treaty which would remove his nation, but diplomacy and courtesy required that he go to Washington. More, he felt it imperative that he protest to the President against the public lottery.

Before it was time to go to Washington, several incidents so disturbed John that for a time he pondered the question of war. The United States sent a commissioner to Red Clay, some miles from New Echota, to talk to a meeting of the Council called at the commissioner's request. There the Union officer offered the Cherokees an alluring version of the Removal Act.

Commissioner Elisha Chester was quiet-voiced, dark-eyed, and sincere. He talked in practical and glowing terms of the removal, pointing out all its advantages. "Removal will not destroy your Nation, it will save it," he told them. "Look at your sad position today as you follow the policy of your Chief. You suffer terrible indignities, politically, financially, and even spiritually. You're becoming weak through long legal battles which are taking you nowhere. Don't let your Chief lead you astray. You're being offered money and new lands and the assistance of the United States in settling those new lands. There is no point in battling what is to be." He clinched it with: "In the west, across the Mississippi, it will be your land alone. No white man will be allowed to step foot on your property unless you invite him."

Two young Indians, John Walker, Jr., and James Starr, had already held private conversations with the commissioner. After the meeting, they performed expert service for the Union, circulating among their brethren to bring them to the Union cause.

Among the Cherokees who listened to him were Elias Boudinot, Stand Watie, the Ridge, Andy Ross, John Ridge, William Hicks, William Rogers, and William Shorey. The removal began to seem the only answer.

Within a few weeks, a minority of the people were convinced that the only hope for the Cherokee Nation was in a treaty of acceptance in which demands could still be made for a good price for their lands. It was now being said that John Ross was stubbornly refusing to consider the future.

John sat at his desk staring at Elias Boudinot's letter of resignation as editor of the *Cherokee Phoenix*. Editor Boudinot wrote: "In my opinion the *Phoenix* has done all that it can ever do to defend the rights of our people. We have presented our grievances to the nations. We have waged a hopeless battle. Now I believe we ought to tell our people of the terrible dangers which imperil them if they do not remove west. I feel I can no longer issue the *Phoenix* to our people without telling them the truth of their situation. And from what I have seen and heard, were I to assume that privilege, my usefulness would be paralyzed, by being considered, as I have unfortunately already been, an enemy to the interest of my beloved country and people. I should think it my duty to tell them the whole truth, or what I believe to be the truth. I cannot tell them that we will be reinstated in our rights when I have no such hope."

John had no alternative but to accept the resignation. He would not change his policies. The Council appointed Elijah Hicks as editor.

The week before he went to Washington, John rode through his Nation to take a personal survey of the situation facing his people. They met him at their doors, in the roads, by the river, giving him their shocking stories: the Georgia militia had been sent by Governor Lumpkin to patrol the gold fields with orders to arrest any Cherokee found in them. They were also taking homes by force.

One woman sobbingly told the Chief: "They gave my husband liquor, and when he was drunk enough they made him sign our home over to them. Now we are going to the hills, hoping to find a cave."

A father came to him and swore: "I'll kill 'em all! They took my little girl into the barn and—" he broke into sobs, "By God, I'm goin' to kill 'em all."

John rode to a farm where the house had been burned to the ground. The family was living in what had been their spring-house. "They burned us out when we wouldn't sign the place over to them. Said the land is now in the public lottery an' we best get out. We can't. Got no place to go."

He rode up to a barricaded house where the children were kept inside at their own insistence. "They're scared," said the mother. "The Georgia soldiers pointed guns at them and told them to run. When they did, the soldiers shot around them. I can't get them to go out again."

Every town reported that women were not safe on the streets. They spoke of revenge, but in an uncertain way. What could virtually unarmed citizens do?

John warned: "Keep calm. Stay close to your homes. Keep the peace I am striving for. The alternative right now is removal west. We must continue to fight through the courts."

XX

JOHN WENT TO WASHINGTON WITH A DELEGATION OF THE Council's choosing: John Vann, John Baldridge, Richard Taylor, and Shanawan Calvin, a young full-blooded second cousin of Quatie's who had recently returned to the Cherokee Nation after an education at eastern universities. Shanawan had married a Cherokee girl who, on the past Fourth of July, had presented him with a son, Bryce, and was now a practicing attorney and considered a very capable constitutional lawyer. John warned Shanawan of the impending conference with President Jackson: "Keep a sharp ear and eye. The man is our enemy. What he plans to offer us will not come from his heart."

"The conference itself," Shanawan replied, "is called upon an unacceptable premise—that we will remove. The Chief of the Cherokee attends only as an act of courtesy to the President."

As the delegation left the Nation, Georgia lottery personnel moved in. Surveyors were everywhere, under the protection of the militia. The city of Washington had its own affliction. Upon arriving, the Ross delegation was horrified to find the city in the midst of epidemics of Asiatic cholera and smallpox. Long lines of the city's poor waited for free vaccinations offered through the Medical Society. The Board of Health was fighting the spread of the diseases through emergency action, which included banning imported fresh fruits, canceling liquor licenses, closing down public entertainment centers, and abolishing hogs from the streets of the city. The delegation awoke in the mornings to the dreadful chanting of wagon masters calling: "Bring out your dead!"

In the last days of his campaign for reelection, President Andrew Jackson was tired. Too often, Henry Clay, the brilliant pro-Indian Senator from Kentucky, took to championing the Cherokees in the halls of Congress. Jackson had known some moments of alarm when Henry Clay became a candidate for the White House. The tough President was somewhat irritated, too, when he heard of Chief John Ross's announcement to his people: "If Henry Clay is elected President of the Union, our burdens will be lightened."

The remark rankled. Jackson really did not want another meeting with John Ross, but in view of Clay's campaign and the final efforts being made to bring Ross and his majority to an acceptable treaty plan, the President had organized the conference. The record would show that he had tried.

At the meeting, no one was at ease. The four members of the Cherokee delegation sat on stiff-seated, hardbacked chairs, awkward and uncomfortable. When it came time to speak, John stood beside the President's desk.

"We are instructed to hear you, Mr. President," John stated. "Our Nation has responded to your request for this meeting. However, sir, as Chief of my people, I ask the immediate removal from my Nation of the agents of Georgia who are there to seize our lands with the intent of selling them by public lottery to white men. The treaty existing between our nations does not allow white men in our land, except by authorization of our people."

President Jackson shook his head. "The agents and the militia of Georgia are there carrying out both state and federal laws. The resistance of your people, a fruitless and tragic thing, is regrettable." His impatience was obvious. "Now, sir, be seated. I shall speak."

John reluctantly took his chair.

"The United States government is prepared to offer the Cherokee Nation five million dollars for its lands in Georgia, Alabama, and Tennessee."

John let the remark hang as he took a silent poll of the delegation. "The offer is rejected. We shall not remove from our lands."

President Jackson looked very surprised. He sat back in his chair, tapping a long finger against his chin. "The offer is rejected, sir? By you and these men here? I would expect your government would appreciate a chance to study it and, perhaps, accept it."

"We speak for our Nation at this meeting, Mr. President. The offer of five million dollars, or any amount of dollars, is refused. We will not sell or cede one more foot of our lands."

President Jackson arose. "I consider your action detrimental to your people, Chief Ross. And I am aware that not all of your people have faith in your leadership. There are men among them who would urge the acceptance of the offer. I suggest you go home and explain your rejection of it to them. As for me, I must ask your pardon now. I have another appointment."

Dismissed, the delegation headed home. John left his friends at the New Echota public square and rode on home. The sight of his home's roofs and chimneys rising from the surrounding green lands reminded him of the first look he had enjoyed of the Hermitage.

The first uneasy warning that something was wrong came when he saw that the black people were not at work in the fields. The cotton was untended. There was not a sign of human activity.

He gave his horse a spur and rode swiftly through the cultivated fields. The fires in the outbuildings and infirmary were carefully banked. The livestock was gone. The implements of the blacksmith were deserted, iron cooling. The cooper's shop was filled with half-finished work, barrels standing ready for completion, kitchenware ready for the finishing touches. The cook shop's fires were burning low, no more than embers under the huge pots of rice and corn grits and boiled meat.

John's alarm mounted as he sped his horse from the empty slaves' quarters. At the main house he jumped from his horse, dropping the reins, and rushed to the front door.

Two members of the Georgia militia blocked his entrance. "This property belongs to the State of Georgia. It is to be sold at public lottery," the lean-faced soldier recited.

John had no intention of letting the men see his fear or desperation. He thought his voice sounded normal, but it was strained with emotion: "This is my home. I'm John Ross, Chief of the Cherokee Nation. I aim to enter my house. My family is there."

The two guards gave each other surprised looks to see a white man with red hair and blue eyes claiming to be the Chief. " 'Tain't likely you're him," said the elder of the two.

"My family—they are in there?"

"Oh, yes, the Ross family's there, all right. But how do we know you're the Chief?"

"My family will identify me."

They brought Jim to the door and John hugged the teenage boy tightly. "Where's your mother, Jim?"

The dark-eyed youngster looked at the guards with resent-

ment. "Upstairs, Father. We've been allowed two rooms to wait for you. We're to leave now."

The guards let them in and John walked through the spacious rooms. The servants were gone, the curtains and draperies pulled against the daylight. He saw guards standing silently in each quiet downstairs room.

Taking the stairs with Jim, he looked down to see that his furnishings were being prepared for the public auction. Through the open door of his office he saw a uniformed man packing his library books.

John went alone to his bedroom. He found Quatie seated at a window. Dry sobs heaved his shoulders as she held him, cradling his head on her lap as she might have done for one of their children. "Should I have given in to them?" he asked: "I've hurt everyone. Perhaps I'm not even worthy of being your husband, let alone the Chief of the Nation."

"If you were not Chief of the Cherokee, your Nation would perish. And if you weren't my husband, I'd have perished a long time ago."

"Quatie, I'm not certain I know what to do. But first we'll have to move across the river to the old family lands. We'll carry on the battle from there, out of Georgia. Do you think you can be happy living in a log cabin again?"

She walked to the door and held her hand out to him, as he had done to her many years before at another threshhold: "Come," she invited.

The new white owner of the Ross plantation looked at the departing family curiously. The four handsome sons of the Chief rode horses, trotting alongside the open carriage of their parents and sister. The white man reached into his pocket for the inventory of the estate, listing everything he had won in the lottery. It was probable that his winning ticket had also included the horses and carriage. The group was moving fast down the drive, however, and the inventory was long and would take some study. The man decided he would let them go for now. If the inventory showed the animals and the conveyance belonged to him, he could always send the law after them.

The slaves had been released from a temporary stockade and brought back to the fields and the mansion to the new owner. They stood silently along the driveway in a kind of desperate farewell to the Chief and his family, many of them weeping.

Quatie lifted a hand in good-bye as they rode. They began to call to her, running after the carriage, stumbling along the edge of the field. "Take us on with you, Missus! Don't leave us!" They fell to their knees, with shrieks and moans left behind by the fast-pacing horses.

Quatie gave a last glance at the rose bushes she had planted and raised, at her pet peacocks strutting near the house, never again to be fed from her hand. She broke into tears at last. Jane held her mother's head on her shoulder, cuddling her close as John speeded the carriage to leave it all behind as fast as possible.

XXI

TO AVOID THE IMPRESSION THAT HE WAS PERSONALLY permitting terrorist action against the Cherokees in Georgia, President Jackson decided to send an investigator into the southern states with instructions to report to him upon the exact situation. The ensuing report would serve to counteract the propaganda circulating in the eastern states regarding the Jackson administration's treatment of the Indians. He selected a renowned attorney of undisputed patriotism: Francis Scott Key.

As the poet-attorney traveled the South, he became more and more horrified at the crimes committed in the name of the federal Removal Act and in the name of the states of Georgia, Alabama, and Tennessee. The report he made to the President was so critical of the removal that President Jackson took no pains to publicize it. Key was appalled at the lawlessness of the whites and the lack of all civil rights afforded Indians. His report centered largely on a murder trial in Alabama. Since Indians could not testify in courts, the defendent was without hope.

Secretary of War Eaton held his own meeting with men representing themselves as willing and able to negotiate a treaty with the Union for the sale of lands in the Cherokee Nation: Andrew Ross and John Walker, Jr., a mixed blood. Perfectly aware of the frustrating business of attempting to effect a treaty, Secretary Eaton was not averse to trying to create one through the brother of Chief John Ross. He acquired the signature of Andrew Ross on a treaty so unfair to the Indians that it was rejected by the United States Senate.

John and Quatie had taken up residence in a small log cabin, located not far from Red Clay, a convenient meeting place for all the displaced Cherokees. It was not nearly large enough for the family, but it was all that was available.

When a Council meeting was held at Red Clay and the treaty was held before the meeting, tempers flared. "Let the treaty makers die! Let them know the Blood Law!"

The Ridges' faction, held to blame for the rejected treaty, arose to be heard. John Ridge told the agitated group: "My father, the Ridge, tells us the truth: We as a Nation are on the verge of ruin." He, the Ridge, therefore was right in urging a treaty which would save the people. Yet he had not put his signature to the treaty which was so much resented. Rather, it had been Andrew Ross, brother of the Chief, and John Walker.

The Ridge, an old man, stood. "My sun is going down. It is on your account I feel oppressed with sorrow. Where are your laws! The seats of your judges are overturned. . . . I mourn over your calamity. . . . I say if you are to seek a new home in a strange land, go as true friends and brothers."

John Walker circulated on his own, urging members of the Nation to act on their own, to sell their lands to the Union. Ross's supporters, developing into a national party, heard of his activities with rising indignation. They began to speak in low whispers of the Blood Law.

But the National Party members were not to be placated. A heavily signed petition was presented which asked for the impeachment of the Ridge and John Ridge and David Vann, all accused of "maintaining opinions and a policy to terminate the existence of the Cherokee community on the lands of our fathers." The Council voted that the petition was right and the men should be removed from their official standing in the Council. However, the National Committee voted to table the petition until the defendants had been properly notified of the action against them. They were to appear at the next meeting of the Council in October.

The meeting broke up amid ugly feelings, and the Ridges, wary of the anger around them, mounted their horses and rode home by a new path.

John had not been home long from the Council gathering when a knock came on the cabin door.

Stand Watie stood there, his big chest heaving with physical exertion and emotional stress. "John Walker has been assassinated! Shot dead. On the road to his home."

"Who did it?"

Stand's fury was mixed with icy contempt: "The assassins fired down on him from the tops of trees, as he rode beneath them. The Blood Law. So death is the price of opposition to Chief John Ross!"

Stand turned his back on him and strode rapidly to his horse to ride away. Stunned, John watched him go. Could anyone believe that he had ordered the assassination of John Walker?

President Andrew Jackson was at the Hermitage when he heard the news of John Walker's death. He wrote to two agents in the Cherokee Nation at once, giving them his orders: "I have just been advised that Walker has been shot, and Ridge and other chiefs in favor of emigration, and you, as agent of the United States government threatened with death.

"The government of the United States has promised them protection. It will perform its obligations to the letter. On the receipt of this, notify John Ross and his council that we will hold them answerable for every murder committed on the emigrating party."

XXII

FOLLOWING ITS OFFICIAL ORGANIZATION ON NOVEMBER 27, 1834, in the parlor of the Ridge home, the new Treaty party led by John Ridge, Elias Boudinot, and Stand Watie, organized a delegation to Washington to request funds to carry out the removal plans of the federal government.

The Treaty delegation, together with President Jackson and his officials, made plans for a meeting in the nation at which a treaty of removal would be agreed upon and signed. The meeting would be held at the home of Elias Boudinot where, on the instructions of President Jackson, the Reverend John F. Schermerhorn, a United States Commissioner, would preside over the signing of the treaty. The proceedings would not be generally made known to the people of the Cherokee Nation or to their Chief, John Ross.

When federal agents came to the Nation to enroll all Cherokees in a government list of emigrants to the west, there was no longer doubt that a treaty had been secretly conspired. John made a hurried trip to Washington and consulted with members of the Senate. He was assured: "The Senate will never ratify a treaty which does not have the approval of the majority of the Cherokee people and of their Chief."

Upon his return, he heard that John Ridge was presenting him to the federal agents as a "half-breed nullifier" and his loyal people as "banded outlaws."

John faced him and asked the meaning of his remarks. "You know we, the majority, rule."

Ridge's fine-featured face was taut with anger. "The majority! That's a high-sounding phrase for a group who are meeting in caves, under arms, threatening their political opposition with death."

"The people in the caves are the dispossessed members of our Nation who have been driven there by the state and federal agents. If they have kept arms, I'm glad. The guns are needed for hunting food. They threaten no one. Don't you know what's happening in this Nation?"

"Yes, I know," John Ridge whipped out, "you are deliberately conducting a campaign of delay and procrastination, hoping to stall the removal until the Jackson administration is out of office. And, in doing that, you're bringing our people to their knees, for no reason. The removal will prevail."

John realized that the rumor might well be correct that Ridge had come to a secret agreement with Jackson. He turned away from the man, unable to tolerate his presence any longer.

At John Ridge's word that the men were armed bandits, the Governor of Georgia had members of the militia jail Whitepath, Elijah Hicks, James Martin, Thomas Taylor, James Trott, and Walter Adair. Alarm spread through the Nation. Ridge's campaign against the power of John Ross continued among the people and in the halls of influence in the Nation. He was effective in having the Governor "influence" Judge Hooper and William Underwood, Ross's attorneys, to desert the National Party.

While Elijah Hicks was imprisoned, Stand Watie and a group of Treaty Party members broke into his home and took away the printing press and types and many official papers of the Cherokee Nation, claiming that Elias Boudinot had paid for the presses himself. The *Phoenix* was out of business, the printed "voice" of Chief Ross stilled.

The time had come for the Treaty Party to boldly announce that a treaty had been created and signed by members of the minority party, but that the agreement for removal must be approved by the people.

John Ross agreed to the meeting, although it would be held with or without him. He knew that the majority would vote against the confirmation of the treaty, thus showing President Jackson and the Congress that the Chief was indeed representing his people when he rejected removal.

John Howard Payne, the author of *Home, Sweet Home*, came to the Nation with papers of introduction stating that the world was anxious to learn more about the Cherokee people and their way of life. There to witness the gathering of the people for the treaty meeting at Red Clay, Payne wanted to begin writing what he said would be a report of the event.

Payne noted: "The woods echoed with the trampling of many feet: a long and orderly procession emerged from among the trees, the gorgeous autumnal tints of whose departing foilage seemed in sad harmony with the noble spirit now beaming in this departing race. Most of the train was on foot. There were a few aged men, and some few women, on horseback. The train halted at the humble gate of the principal chief: he stood ready to receive them.

"Everything was noiseless. The party, entering, loosened the blankets which were loosely rolled and flung over their backs and hung them, with their tin cups and other paraphernalia attached, upon the fence.

"The Chief approached them ... and each, in silence, drew near to give him his hand. Their dress was neat and picturesque: all wore turbans, except four or five hats. Many of them, tunics, with sashes; many long robes, and nearly all some drapery so that they had the oriental air of the scripture pictures of patriarchal processions.

"The salutations over, the old men remained near the chief, and the rest withdrew to various parts of the enclosure; some sitting Turk fashion against the trees, others upon logs, and others, upon the fences, but with the eyes of all fixed upon their Chief."

The intense loyalty and devotion Payne noted was expressed in the vote John Ross's people gave at Red Clay. The treaty, carefully read to the gathering by the Reverend Schermerhorn, was rejected.

Inwardly seething at the defeat, and privately enraged because he had heard the Ross supporters refer to him as "Devil's Horn," Schermerhorn nevertheless still attempted to get the treaty ratified.

"The offer is raised," said the desperate agent, "Five million dollars, to remove; one hundred and fifty thousand for your losses in the Creek War; and eight hundred thousand more acres in the West."

The people talked among themselves, and the Council conferred.

The people shivered under the roof of the open-sided meeting place at Red Clay, bitterly remembering that across the river at New Echota was their modern council building where none of them were welcome since the advent of white landowners. They turned in trust to await the action of their Chief.

Schermerhorn spoke quietly for the ears of John Ridge, Stand

Watie, and Elias Boudinot. Elias shook his head, glancing in the direction of the beloved Chief who yet held the people's loyalty. "I'd say we'd best save our strength. If we vote for this treaty now, in view of the rising feeling here against it, we stand close to disaster. If we vote now to sell the lands, these people would consider us traitors. We would probably die by the Blood Law."

Watie and Ridge agreed. The Reverend Schermerhorn said: "You'll have to vote with the rest, then, against this treaty today."

"Yes, but we'll have it brought forth again within a few weeks, and the next time it will be signed."

"The President insists that the treaty is to be ratified before he meets again with any delegation. So I shall not leave this land until I go with a signed treaty."

"And what about Chief Ross? How can we overcome his influence and his determination?"

"There is a way to get around him," said the Reverend Schermerhorn. A little silence fell on the group, and the Commissioner looked pained. "We're all overly excited. I'll forgive your thoughts. The Chief will come to no harm."

"Well," said Ridge, "let's finish the business here so we can lay our plans. Perhaps we can confound John by appearing to compromise."

The new offer of more money and more land in the West was defeated by vote. John suggested a new delegation go to Washington to protest the invasion of the Nation by forces of the federal and state governments.

John Ridge and Stand Watie were included on the twenty-member committee, accepting the appointments as an excellent subterfuge. While they accompanied the Chief of the Nation to Washington, the cause of the treaty would go ahead in the Nation without his knowledge, ratified behind his back through the work of his brother Andrew, Elias Boudinot, the Ridge, and the Reverend Schermerhorn.

Proceeding, too, was the battle of the census takers against the people. And there was no way to stop the building of the stockades into which all emigrants were to be placed to await transportation west. Army personnel arrived in the Nation and the prisonlike walls of spiked wood went up near rivers throughout the land.

XXIII

JOHN WAS WORKING WITH HIS GUEST, JOHN HOWARD PAYNE, at a table in his cabin on the evening of the fifth of December, 1835, when the door was shoved open and twenty-five members of the Georgia Guard, soaking wet from the rainstorm which was flooding the area, burst into the cabin, guns in hand.

"John Ross?" inquired one of the guardsmen. "Are you John Ross, Chief of the Cherokee?"

John scanned the faces and uniforms. "By what right do you break into my home—"

The guardsman did not bother with courtesy. "You're under arrest, you're to come with us." The man turned his pale eyes on the writer who was standing now beside the Chief, in blank disbelief. "Are you John Howard Payne?"

"I am."

"You're under arrest."

"On what charge? Under whose order?" the writer's bearded face was flushed.

"Your writings—something you had published in a newspaper. You've violated the federal law which does not allow anyone to encourage the Indians to reject removal."

"You men have no jurisdiction here," John Ross said. "This cabin stands in Tennessee."

"That's not our concern," said the armed guard. "If you have a coat, get it. We're riding."

"I want to speak to my wife," said Ross. "She's in the next room."

"No," said the guard. "Just get your coat, if you like, and let's go."

He and Payne took jackets from the closet. Ross, near the door of the room leading into the other, called: "Quatie!"

The guard prodded him with the bayonet. "I told you no."

The door opened and Quatie was there in her nightgown and robe, her hair braided, eyes opening in fright.

"Quatie," John told her, "don't be overly alarmed. These guards are taking us to prison. I don't know the charge. But I'm positive they can't hold us for long. Now you ask the boys to ride. Contact John Ridge and Stand. Find out what's happening. Tell them I expect my release at once. Do you understand? And tell Jim to emphasize that John Howard Payne had best be released fast."

Quatie, smothering a bothersome cough, clung to her husband. "I'm going with you."

"No," he put her aside. "And don't step outside, either, darling. It's raining hard and you're not to get wet, you hear? Now you do as I ask and everything will be all right. Tell Jim and Alan to ride. They'll know what to do." He gave her a kiss on the cheek before he was led away with Payne.

It was a wet and cold twenty-four miles across the line into Georgia to the jailhouse at Spring Place. The old log jail was not rainproof. Puddles of water stood in the corners. There was no light in the place and they were pushed into it in the dark, stumbling over the legs of a prisoner who was seated on the damp ground, chained to the walls. The door was shut and bolted on them.

John, kneeling beside the man on the floor, asked: "Who are you?"

The sound of a cough came, then the prisoner gripped John's hands and he spoke in a voice thick with a head cold: "I'm Peter Smith. My father is Crawling Snake, the speaker of the Council."

"Peter! I'm Chief Ross. And John Howard Payne is here. What's the charge against you?"

"I don't know. They brought me here from the Red Clay Council meeting. I'm not sure that my father has any idea of my whereabouts." He shivered. "No one comes here except a guard with a plate of garbage each day."

Payne, standing over them, complained: "What's that terrible odor?"

Peter coughed, choked, and told them haltingly: "It's that poor devil." He pointed a trembling arm up to the rafters, and they could see a dark figure hanging there. "He stinks," said Peter. "His body has been hanging there ever since I've been here."

Payne was in the furthest corner, vomiting.

John sat beside the youthful prisoner, bracing his back against the rain-soaked wall. "We'd better make the best of this," he said. "It may be a long wait for freedom."

The President's seventh annual message to the Congress, presented on the seventh day of December 1835, gave a glowing interpretation of the removal policy, placing the United States government in the role of a concerned father with an erring son. Jackson spoke of sending the "aboriginal people" west under the loving guidance of their white superiors. "It seems now to be an established fact that they cannot live in contact with a civilized community and prosper." He told the Congress: "Ages of fruitless endeavors have at length brought us to knowledge of this principle of intercommunication with them. The plan for their removal and reestablishment is founded upon the knowledge we have gained of their character and habits, and has been dictated by a spirit of enlarged liberality."

Speaking of how the Indians were to exist in the new lands, he pointed out: "They can subsist themselves by agricultural labor, if they choose to resort to that mode of life; if they do not, they are upon the skirts of the great prairies, where countless herds of buffalo roam, and a short time suffices to adapt their own habits to the changes which change of animals destined for their food may require. . . .

"The necessary measures for their political advancement and for their separation from our citizens have not been neglected. The pledge of the United States has been given by Congress that the country destined for the residence of this people shall be forever 'secured and guaranteed to them.' A country west of Missouri and Arkansas has been assigned to them, into which the white settlements are not to be pushed."

XXIV

JOHN RIDGE WAS WELL AWARE THAT THE POPULAR IMPACT of John Ross's arrest was renewing the Cherokees' determination. He came to John's rescue as fast as he could prevail upon the authorities to take action. His maneuvering took time, however, and John spent thirteen days in the log jail. Finally he was told he was being held because he was suspected of being an abolitionist plotting to use Negroes in an army of revolution against the Union and Georgia.

In spite of the seriousness of his predicament, he grinned. "Until now I believe I've underestimated the success of the pro-treaty cause. That the opposition, including you, John, should be so desperate as to trump up a charge as ridiculous as this."

Ridge was not amused. "It's not a legal charge. No charge has been made against you at all. You'll be released."

"And Payne?"

John Ridge frowned. "The charge against him is more serious. There's some suspicion he's working for a foreign nation, opposing the policy of the American authority. His writings are very prejudiced in your favor—"

"If he is not freed, I'll take pains to see that his imprisonment becomes a national cause."

"Oh, he'll be freed, but it may take a few more days. They're still looking at his writings."

"They've confiscated them?"

"Yes." Ridge was apologetic. "And yours, too, John. But the papers will be returned upon your release."

"And the boy, Peter. What is to happen to him?"

"There's no charge. He'll go free."

John gave Ridge a long look. "Do you ever have any qualms about what you are doing?"

John Ridge paled but his eyes flashed anger. "No more than you do."

Three days after John was allowed to walk out of the filthy

jailhouse, John Howard Payne was released. He immediately penned a series of articles which were published throughout America, denouncing the segregation policy of the federal and state governments. He hailed the battle of John Ross against the enforced removal of one race from the midst of another as righteous and brave. But if Payne's articles aroused an emotional reaction in the Union, the federal agents were determined to combat it by getting the removal swiftly under way.

XXV

WITH A SENSE OF PERSONAL GUILT OVER JOHN'S ARREST and imprisonment and an honest desire to see their Nation brought from its dire condition, Ridge and Watie agreed to accompany the Ross delegation to Washington to speak once more to President Jackson. The delegation would appeal for more humane treatment of all the Indians, regardless of political viewpoint.

Since returning home from jail, John had received numerous reports of the cruelties being inflicted daily by state and federal agents. His followers were kept from buying food and other supplies on the grounds that they had not signed the enrollment list for emigration and therefore were in defiance of the law.

The afternoon before he was to leave for Washington with his delegation, his sons Alan and Jim rode into his yard.

"It's Lucy Hall." Alan snatched his hat from his head and threw it on the ground.

Jim took up the story: "The militia. No one knows who. There were three of them. They dragged her out of her cabin, stripped her naked, beat her and—and—"

"Father, she's dead!"

The horror stayed in John's mind all the way to Washington.

Andrew Jackson should have heard my sons, he thought; he ought to have been there to see their faces.

More than he knew, his own fate was in the hands of his enemy. As soon as he had left the Nation in the company of John Ridge and Stand Watie, United States Commissioner John Schermerhorn called a new meeting of all Cherokees at New Echota to sign a removal treaty.

The Council with many members absent, appeared at the Council Hall, led by Andrew Ross, Elias Boudinot, James Starr, John Gunter, and the Ridge, who had not at all approved of his son accompanying John Ross to Washington.

It was not difficult; only about five hundred people came to consider the treaty. When it was read and the appeals from a few men, including the Ridge, heard, a committee was appointed to determine whether the treaty ought to be signed. Within a few days, it reported to the members of the Council that the treaty should be ratified.

On the night of the twenty-ninth of December, 1835, the Treaty of New Echota lay on a table in the home of Elias Boudinot, awaiting signatures.

The Treaty gave the United States of America all the lands of all the Cherokee people east of the Mississippi. In return, the United States government would give the Cherokee people the five million dollars necessary for the removal. The Union guaranteed that the western lands would never be annexed by another state or territory without the consent of the Indians.

It was John Gunter who came forward first, and who nervously lifted the pen. "I am not afraid. I will sell the whole country." He signed his name with a flourish.

Andrew Ross took the pen next and showed no hesitation as he put his name to the document. Elias Boudinot signed it. Though he made no remark and his hand was steady, there was remarkable paleness to his face.

The Ridge took his time coming to the table, but when he did it was with a long stride for a man so old. He would head the delegation to Washington to hand the Treaty of New Echota to President Jackson. He bent over the paper, affixed his mark, and said: "I expect to die for it."

The Ross delegation had ridden into the city of Washington on the new steam-operated Baltimore and Ohio railroad. Mrs.

Arguelles's Boarding House offered them excellent meals and comfortable beds. Due to all the formalities and appointments necessary to see the President, they expected their visit to take at least a month.

They were greeted one day by Secretary of War Lewis Cass. He was not very reassuring, closing the meeting by telling them frankly he felt they had wasted their time in coming to the city. They were notified, however, that the President would see them the next morning at the White House.

Jackson was very polite: "This government will always be eager to consider any proposal you have to make. Just put the proposal in writing to Secretary Cass and give us time to study it and give you a formal reply."

"Mr. President," John began. "The treaty negotiations take time. The conditions in our nation are such that we need immediate relief from the crimes—"

President Jackson held up a hand, maintaining a friendly smile. "Now, sir! Haven't I just made myself clear? I thought so, at least. Put your proposals—and your complaints—in writing. Then we can deal with them in an orderly way."

"All right," John was not defeated. "I'll see that you have complete records on the crimes taking place in our Nation today. I've brought the records along."

"See that Secretary Cass gets them. Now, gentlemen, I believe we've finished our business for the day."

The Ross delegation still waited for further word from the Secretary of War and the President, when Boudinot, the Reverend Schermerhorn, and Major Ridge arrived with the New Echota Treaty safely in hand. Within minutes of being told of the arrival of the Schermerhorn delegation, Stand Watie and John Ridge, eager to affix their signatures to the document before it went to the White House, left the Ross delegation's boarding-house and moved into the hotel with the Treaty group.

Having signed it, John Ridge said: "The Chief must be told. Perhaps, when he knows it has been done, he'll accept it. He might want to sign it."

"You know better than that!" Stand scoffed.

"I suppose so," Ridge nodded. "Yet I believe we ought to offer him the chance to put his signature to this treaty. It's bound to be accepted by the United States Senate, and if he does not sign it, he will be outside the law."

They sent for the Chief of the Cherokee Nation. He entered the grandly furnished hotel room accompanied by Shanawan Calvin, upon whose legal arm he was leaning heavily since the desertion of his former attorneys.

The document lay in full view on a table in the center of the room, the signatures boldly written. The atmosphere bristled. John moved slowly toward the written treaty, hat in hand. He stood before it, not touching it, reading it quietly. Then he lifted his stricken gaze to the men who stood on the opposite side of the table. "You would do—*this?*"

Elias spoke: "John, we've remained with you as far as we can. You've lost all reason in this thing. You're pursuing a hopeless cause. You're evasive and noncommittal in your policy, dedicated only to obstructing the removal at any cost. It can't go on. It had to be done this way."

John looked piercingly from one face to the other. "I want a copy of this—document—now."

It was handed to him by the Reverend Schermerhorn. John gave it into Shanawan's hands.

There was no further word. His gaze lingering just a moment longer on the triumphant face of Stand, John left the room with Shanawan.

In the next few days, as the signed Treaty lay on the desk of President Andrew Jackson like a hard-won trophy, John was closeted with various members of the United States Senate. They all told him the same thing: the Treaty of New Echota was illegal, fraudulently obtained, and would not be accepted by the United States Senate. Not about to let the treaty vanish, President Andrew Jackson had his own conferences with members of the Senate.

On the twenty-third day of May, 1836, the Treaty of New Echota was brought before the United States Senate.

The voices of Senators Bell, Clay, Calhoun, and Webster were among those which rang out a "nay" to the passing of the treaty. Senator White, who had indicated all along that he would vote against the treaty, gave a "yea" response instead. The treaty was ratified by one vote.

John, head bowed, stood with Shanawan in the Senate foyer, hearing some of the details of the Senate's ratification. The removal deadline had been set for the twenty-third day of May, 1838. Every Cherokee in the southern states was to go west. The

Treaty of New Echota was officially proclaimed as valid by the President.

It was not long before a messenger from the War Department came to John at the boardinghouse. Secretary of War Cass had written him a note of stern warning, coming indirectly from the White House: "The President has ceased to recognize any existing government among the Cherokee east of the Mississippi. Any further effort on your part to prevent the consummation of the New Echota Treaty will be suppressed."

But the White House and the War Department could not suppress the sense of outrage which swept the country at the news that the Cherokee Nation was to be sent west by force under a treaty which was not approved by the Chief of the Nation or the majority of the people. "An infamous treaty," John Quincy Adams, a member of the House of Representatives criticized. "It brings with it eternal disgrace upon the country." His words set the tone. Throughout the land, committees were formed in order that citizens might band together and protest the treaty.

As far as the federal government was concerned, however, the exodus was under way and all the protests had not the slightest effect.

President Jackson ordered that the treaty be carried out exactly as written: "Let there be no more talk about it. John Ross is not to be allowed any further communication by mouth or pen about the treaty."

XXVI

JACKSON DISPATCHED, UNDER THE WAR DEPARTMENT, General John Ellis Wool, to command the federal troops in the Cherokee Nation with the one purpose of enforcing the treaty. General Wool's first order was to be certain that every Cherokee was disarmed.

Traveling through the stricken land where people were hungry, homeless, without recognition or rights, already helpless under the bayonets of the militia, General Wool was appalled. At his headquarters—a fine home which had been confiscated months before from a full-blood Cherokee—he sat down at a table and wrote to Secretary Cass: "I do now that which I have never even considered before in my long career. I ask that I be relieved of my assignment here as soon as circumstances permit. The whole scene in this country is a heart-rending one, and such a one as I would be glad to get rid of as soon as possible. Because I am firm and decided, do not believe I would be unjust. If I could, I would remove every Indian tomorrow beyond the reach of white men, who, like vultures, are watching, ready to pounce upon their prey and strip them of everything they have or expect from the government of the United States. Yes, sir, nineteen-twentieths, if not ninety-nine out of every hundred, will go penniless to the west."

John forwarded to General Wool a petition from the people vehemently protesting their disarmament. The General relayed to Secretary Cass their plea for a return of their arms, adding: "It is vain to talk to people almost universally opposed to the treaty. They maintain they never made such a treaty. So determined are they in their opposition that not one, however poor or destitute, will receive either rations or clothing from the United States lest they compromise themselves in regard to the treaty. Many have said they will die before they will leave the country."

However, the General carried out his duties and supervised the construction and completion of the stockades which would hold the Cherokee people. He also worked with General Dunlap, who operated in Tennessee, overseeing the work of stockade building at Calhoun and other places of convenience. Watching the log pens rise, the General felt his will for his job weaken. How could he stand by and watch the Cherokee women—young ladies, many educated in Boston and other eastern cities—herded into these foul prisons? He told his superiors by letter: "I am considering resigning. I can't dishonor Tennessee by carrying through in this. I do not want to aid in the carrying into execution at the point of bayonet a treaty made by a lean minority against the will and authority of the Cherokee people."

The Treaty Party members adjusted to the plans for their removal with goodwill and in many instances took advantage of the opportunity to remove themselves west. They were the Cherokees with money, having obtained near-just payment for lands which had been withheld from the public lottery until it was time for them to leave the Nation.

Due to a declining state of health, and the number of persons in his party, however, the Ridge accepted the aid of the government in transporting west. He went ahead of his son and Elias Boudinot and Stand Watie, traveling mainly by river route and for a time in great comfort in ships' cabin. At Decatur, Alabama, the river was low and they were taken from their boats and transported on open cars of the Tuscumbia, Courtland, and Decatur Railroad to Tuscumbia, where they continued their water journey to Honey Creek, Arkansas.

Andrew Ross, Stand Watie, Elias Boudinot, and John Ridge all went west together, making no attempt to see John before their departure. The Nation was torn by the treaty, and the majority, following their Chief, were indignant over its signing. Dire comments were being made everywhere that the Blood Law should be enforced, but John sent word among them that civilized men and nations did not kill in revenge.

The pro-Treaty Party members went as soon as their personal business was completed in the nation. They were eager to go now. En route they determined to take the time to detour to make a call on the now–former President of the United States, Andrew Jackson, at the Hermitage. The retired Chief Executive was suffering from the maladies of old age, but his sharp mind was as active as ever. He welcomed them with great interest.

There were some rumors reaching the Hermitage that there was a near-warlike atmosphere in the Nation, where now only the antitreaty Cherokees remained. The deadline for their departure was not many months away, the former President declared. Jackson inquired about the intentions of John Ross. Was he still carrying on a resistance?

Elias Boudinot replied that there was intense feeling against the treaty and the members who had signed it. "We who affected the treaty, sir, live under constant threat of revenge. We hope that in time, in a new land, all the old things will be forgotten and the Cherokee people will unite as one again." He sighed. "But the power of John Ross over the people is apparently unbreakable."

The former President briefly closed his eyes, remembering many things. "Yes," he said, "I believe you're right."

On the seventh week of their travels, late in the month of November 1837, the Treaty Party leaders reached their destination in the new Cherokee lands. They were greeted warmly by the Cherokee settlers who had been there for many years and who thought of themselves as the Old Settlers, virtually a political party of their own. They, at least, had dominated their own territory and had done well enough for themselves through an agricultural life with almost no government.

John Ridge wrote an enthusiastic note home to the Council members who were still resisting the idea of removal: "I ... found my father and mother and all my friends ... in good health." He described the lands of the area and declared that the country "is superior to any country I ever saw in the U.S ... and in a few years will be the garden spot of the United States." He took some pleasure in adding: "Perfect friendship and contentedness prevail all over this land." He moved his family—as did the Boudinots and the Waties—further into the heart of the Cherokee territory, leaving the border area to the Ridge.

XXVII

A COLONEL OF THE ARMY OF THE UNITED STATES CALLED the Cherokee people into a meeting to speak on the necessity of their obedience to the treaty of removal. But they stood unmoved unless it was by anger at his words. Rain fell heavily upon them as they heard words which offended them, words which struck at their motives in wanting to stay on their native lands. The Colonel did not handle the subject of their Chief with care, either. The resistance of the majority of the Cherokee people who were still abiding in their land was considerably stiffened by the Colonel's remarks.

John hoped at least to gain them more time, perhaps even stall the removal until the rising feelings against it in white America could result in some action. He did as his people asked and made yet another trip to Washington, taking with him a memorial signed by over fifteen thousand Cherokees objecting to the New Echota Treaty and their removal under it because the treaty was made by the "minority." John, deliberately trying for a delay, asked his friends in Congress to submit a new treaty to the Cherokee wherein some of the Indians' lands could be set apart for them, making the removal unnecessary.

John was certain that the proposal was receiving consideration in the Senate and that President Van Buren, who had refused to see him, was now becoming interested in such a proposal.

The proposal had no chance, however. President Van Buren heard reports from the nation that individual Cherokees were apparently settling down on their new lands to stay, planting crops, ignoring all the efforts of the federal agents, and he reacted as sternly as Jackson might have done. The President gave Major General Winfield Scott specific orders to get the Cherokees out of their native lands by the date set by the treaty. Scott was placed in command over seven thousand federal and state troops and told to get the job done.

On the twenty-seventh day of March, 1838, John was handed an official document from C. A. Harris, Commissioner of Indian Affairs, United States of America:

> Yesterday the Senate had under consideration the Memorial of the Ross delegation, which by a decision of the majority (36–10) was promptly laid upon the table, every member of the Committee on Indian Affairs, except one, voting in the affirmative. These proceedings leave no room for doubt that the legislative branch of the government concurs with the executive and will sanction him in the purpose to carry the Treaty into full effect. You will perceive the importance of giving general circulation of these proceedings in forcible language, the unavoidable conclusion that a ready and cheerful acquiescence on their part can alone save them from serious calamities.

Although all hope of resistance to the removal was gone, John and Shanawan Calvin lingered in Washington. John, centering his attention now on the welfare of his people as emigrants, determined to hold a conference with General Scott. He also spent many necessary hours with members of the United States Senate in an effort to expedite sorely needed annuity payments overdue on prior treaties with his nation.

General Scott, an enormous man whose relaxed manner belied his dedication to the military, was not eager to have a visit from the Chief of the Cherokee Nation. "I have no time to pacify him," he complained to the President. "He'll just have to get in line with the others and march."

The meeting between the Chief and the General took place in an office at the War Department. It was a small room, furnished only with three chairs and a desk, looking as though it had been unlocked that same day for the purpose of the meeting.

The General stood until the Chief was seated opposite him. "Chief Ross," he said, "it may be that this meeting serves no purpose at all except to acquaint us with each other. You must understand that I go to your Nation with my orders clear in my mind, and in writing. I shall follow them to the letter."

John nodded. "I understand. Now if you will allow me the same regard and concern for my position as Chief of my Nation. I too function, in effect, on written orders, and they are also clear in my mind. I intend to fulfill my obligations to my people at all times. That is why I am here."

The General slumped a bit in his chair. "All right, sir. What's on your mind?"

"Today—two things, in particular. I'll get to them now and hope that you'll grant me further conferences as the emigration proceeds." He got a nod of agreement from the General and went on: "There are approximately two hundred old and infirm people in my Nation, my parents among them, who cannot endure the rigors of a march west. I ask that these aged be allowed to stay in their cabins on the little land that they need and that they be treated as citizens of the community."

General Scott frowned. "I'll have to take that up with my superiors."

"What are your own feelings about it?"

The General shook his head. "I am the military commander of the removal, under orders of the War Department. I have no personal feelings in this matter." But his eyes said that he did and that he would recommend that the old people be permitted to stay, if they wanted. "What's the other problem today?"

"I ask for the release of all Cherokees now held in the prisons of Georgia. They are wrongly held. They ought to be allowed to move west with us."

"That, too, will be decided by my superiors. However, I'll submit the request. Is there anything else?"

A faint smile passed over John's face. "There's a great deal more, General Scott. But suppose we see how we do with these suggestions first? I'm sure you're burdened enough for the start, but I warn you, I'll be calling upon you whenever I feel the needs and welfare of my people demand your attention. My duty is to them."

They stood and shook hands over the desk. The General said: "I begin to understand the way your people feel about you, sir. You certainly have their loyalty."

"I have the loyalty of the majority of them, General." His eyes clouded. "I could not hold them all, and so now we are emigrants."

"The new land to which you go will bring you all together, sir. You are not a lost Nation."

John's gaze was steady: "It is that hope which keeps me alive, General."

Returning to the Nation ahead of General Scott's arrival, John and Shanawan were shocked anew. The villages were emptied of the people. Everywhere cabins stood deserted, often with windows opened, doors banging in the winds. Untended livestock roamed at will and dogs and cats searched hopelessly for families they would never see again.

The troops were doing their job, rounding up Cherokee and placing them in the stockades to await the day of exodus. There was no mercy shown anyone. Families were taken from their homes and yards, their farms and businesses, with no warning or chance to even finish their meals or dress as they might find most suitable. The armed militia came and took them, sometimes beating those who objected or resisted, shoving them along the roads to the pens, bayonets at their backs.

John and Shanawan parted at Red Clay, each riding to his home as swiftly as possible.

The Ross cabin was deserted, but the doors and windows were closed and the furnishings and personal belongings were intact. John mounted his horse and raced toward Ross's Landing, where a stockade had lately risen.

The confinement of the past few weeks was already taking its toll among the people who were so accustomed to freedom in their daily lives. The rough-hewed prison camp was crowded with the sick. The diet on which they were subsisting was largely corn, and the children and old people could not even chew it for it was hard and dry and resisted cooking.

John, identifying himself to the guards as the Chief of the people, was finally allowed to enter the stockade in search of his family. There was a threat that once in he would not be able to get out, but his cold wrath and his reference to his position as well as his acquaintanceship with General Scott put the guards at a disadvantage.

Inside, he scanned the familiar faces of the men and women and children, some sitting cross-legged on the ground, others standing, some lying stretched out under blankets. He spotted old Going Snake standing motionless staring at the prison walls, encased in a dust-covered blanket.

"My brother," John touched his shoulder, afraid to startle him from his reverie.

Going Snake put a bony hand on John's shoulder. "Ah, my son!"

"Have you seen my family?"

"They are here." The old man grunted. "I have lived too many years. I have no wish to see more."

"This will end soon. Let not your heart grieve."

Going Snake said: "It grieves for you. You, who have been betrayed. Yet still you love us."

John gave his shoulder a final pat and pushed through the groups, looking for his family, offering a word of kindness, a touch, as he went through the stockade.

Jane, grown to beautiful young womanhood, saw him, noticing the way people were following him, touching him, reaching for him in their need. She had been kneeling over her mother, brushing her long hair, their blankets spread on the flooring in a corner of the pen. She stood up, the brush in her hands, and called: "Father!"

He hurried over, seized her hands briefly, then went to his knees himself to lean over Quatie. She tried to sit up and smile, and failed at both. He lifted her frail body in his arms and told her: "We're going home." She clung to him, saying not a word, as he moved through the stockade, carrying her easily, his face set in a new expression. He did not have to tell Jane to follow.

She snatched the blankets from the ground and followed her parents. At the gate, he told the guard: "I am taking my family home to our cabin at Red Clay. I'll be back for my sons within the hour. If General Scott seeks me, he will find me there."

The guard pointed a rifle at them and whined: "I ain't heard about no Chief. My orders is to keep all Cherokee here. No one's to git out. I say that means you, too." He looked at John's red hair, observed his blue eyes. "You Cherokee?"

"If you fire that gun, you'll soon know. Now let me pass."

The guard, aware that the Cherokee people were edging toward the redheaded man, gave in reluctantly: "Awright. Go on. But you stay close to Red Clay. I'll make a report on you. Likely General Scott will be after you."

Back in the cabin, he laid Quatie on their bed, Jane helping to make her comfortable. She had lost considerable weight and her eyes seemed to have developed a staring quality which seemed to border on derangement. "I'm sorry," he told her. "I've let you come to such harm. Quatie, there's nothing left but my love for you."

Feeling better, back in her little home, she sat up amid the pillows at her back and managed a smile. "All we had in the beginning was our love. It's all I need."

"We have to move west," he told her.

"I know," she said. She surprised him with her calmness and the clarity of her mind: "It's all right, John. You've suffered treachery which you couldn't fight. The removal must be accepted. I've made up my mind to that." She smiled again. "I'm certain you'll find you have not lost the Nation. It will bloom again in the West for you just as my roses will for me." She leaned against him, sighing, "You'll have to help me with them. Could you get some of them from our home so I can plant them anew in the west? You see John, where they bloom, our love will, too. And our Nation."

He held her tightly. "The boys and I will get your roses."

XXVIII

GENERAL WINFIELD SCOTT CALLED UPON ALL THE
Cherokees who still were at large, evading the roundup and the
stockades, to cooperate with the Army and the treaty and surrender themselves to custody. At the Calhoun Agency on the tenth
day of May, 1838, under blue skies, he addressed them:

"Cherokees! The President of the United States has sent me
with a powerful army to cause you, in obedience to the Treaty
of 1835, to join that part of your people who are already established in prosperity, on the other side of the Mississippi. . . . Do
not, I invite you, even wait for the close approach of the troops,
but make such preparations for emigration as you can, and hasten
to this place, to Ross's Landing, or to Gunter's Landing, where
you will be received in kindness by officers selected for that
purpose. You will find food for all, and clothing for the destitute,
at either of those places, and thence at your ease, and in comfort,
be transported to your new homes according to the terms of the
treaty."

A week later, having been confronted with rumors and reports
of the behavior of the troops toward the Indians, General Scott
issued a stern communiqué to the combined military of the state
and federal governments:

"The Cherokees, by the advances they have made in Christianity and civilization, are by far the most interesting tribe of
Indians in the territorial limits of the United States. Of the fifteen thousand of those people who are to be removed . . . , it is
understood that about four-fifths are opposed, or have become
averse to distant emigration; and the troops will probably be
obliged to cover the whole country they inhabit, in order to make
prisoners and to march or transport prisoners, by families, either
to this place, to Ross's Landing or Gunter's Landing, where they
are to be delivered over to the Superintendent of Cherokee Emigration.

"Considering the number and temper of the mass to be

removed, it will readily occur that simple indiscretions, acts of harshness and cruelty, on the part of the troops, may lead in the end to a general war, and carnage, a result, in the case of these particular Indians, utterly abhorrent to the generous sympathies of the whole American people. Every possible kindness must, therefore, be shown by the troops, and if, in the ranks, a despicable individual should be found, capable of inflicting a wanton injury or insult on any Cherokee man, woman, or child, it is hereby made the special duty of the nearest good officer or man instantly to interpose, and to seize and consign the guilty wretch to the severest penalty of the laws."

Taking the last of the prisoners' arms, the General promised that the weapons would be returned when they had crossed the Mississippi. He carried forth the exodus plans with efficiency and with as much good will as he could legally offer. He set up special units of care for the aged, who were to go along after all. Special care was also provided for the ill and the insane, for infants and expectant mothers. The prisoners to be freed by Georgia would be placed under the authority of the Army until reaching the West, when they would be handed to whatever Cherokee law existed at the point of destination.

More than once his orders to the troops were viciously violated. The human roundup was taking place largely in remote areas where people had fled to hide; they were already disarmed and at the mercy of their conquerors. Some of the troopers held the frontier belief that the only good Indian was a dead Indian and behaved accordingly. Some were not blind to the beauties of the Cherokee women, and kidnappings and rapings were common. The troops robbed and burned homes still occupied by the Indians and dragged the resisting people bodily to the stockades.

Terrible stories swept the Nation. Two young men and two young women were taken prisoners. Camped at night with their captors, the girls were set upon and dragged into the bushes by the white men. One of the girls had a knife and she killed the two attackers. The young Cherokee men took the blame for the murders and were forced to dig their own graves.

The exodus of the Cherokees loyal to Ross began in March when John Drew led a contingent west, voluntarily before the May deadline. The Cherokees boarded two-decker keelboats, 20 feet wide and 130 feet long. Accompanied by a large steamboat, the two crafts sailed westward on the Tennessee, Ohio, Mississippi, and Arkansas rivers.

On the eleventh day of June, the deadline set by the treaty for voluntary travel west, the military forcibly placed a group of emigrants aboard other boats at Ross's Landing. The Indians, grieving aloud about leaving "the graves of our fathers," were unruly and defiant. A count of their number was required for the record, but as fast as they were brought aboard, they jumped ship and had to be captured again. At last, though, the guns and superior numbers of white men prevailed and they were kept aboard the boats and set afloat, their wailing and forlorn chants drifting to land.

The next group traveled by wagon, boat, and foot to Waterloo, where they were taken aboard government boats and moved on west.

In the midst of the removal efforts, a summer drought hit the Nation. The Indians appealed to the military for a delay in the exodus. Many were ailing from their long confinement and the dry, hot weather was causing new illnesses. The Army complied, postponing the move west until the first of September.

The misery of the people was such that it could only find help in prayer. A small church was hastily constructed at Camp Butler where Baptist ministers were allowed to tend to the needs of the prisoners. Baptisms were allowed. Guards marched the Cherokees from the stockades to the river where the ministers officiated. Among the religious leaders were the Reverends Stephen Foreman and Bushyhead, around whom the people flocked to speak their prayers.

John, appalled by the incident of the June 11 debacle on the river, made a visit to General Scott at Ross's Landing where the military officer was headquartered in a converted feed store. The General, fighting flies and mosquitoes, sat at an improvised desk—an old three-legged table supported by heavy bags of corn.

"General Scott, this exodus is going to end in a shambles unless we get in a little leadership. You can't do it simply because the people won't have it."

"Chief Ross, what are you suggesting?"

"I'm requesting. Place me in command of my people. Let us work out our own schedule of removal."

"Your own schedule?" the General frowned.

"Oh, we'll keep to the one you set. I mean, let us organize. The people will follow my orders. I'll get them moving. I promise it."

The General scratched, his gaze sleepily on John. "I think you're right. Go ahead and organize. Consult with me as you plan, of course, and if I don't see the sense of it, that will end it. But you may have the answer, you just may."

With exact figures of costs in mind, John was soon visiting again with the General. John told him: "I've divided our thirteen thousand people into units of one thousand each. Now, based on that, here's the cost for each division—"

The General protested that the figures were too high. The government had set the cost of daily rations at sixteen cents per person, and the lists of what the rations would be were also set. John had exceeded the sixteen cents and added items to the lists. "How do you explain it?" General Scott asked.

"I've added sugar, coffee, and soap to the government's lists. We'll expect all these things in our daily rations and consider them reasonable."

"Reasonable?"

"Did I say 'reasonable'? I ought to have said 'indispensable.' "

The General smiled. "Yes, I think that's better. All right, the items will stand."

He wrote his superiors that he had approved the Ross figures, and in doing so he gained disapproval in Washington.

John called a meeting of the Cherokee Council at the stockade at Aquohee on the first day of August, 1838, to tell of his appointment as the Superintendent of Removal and Subsistence. He was given power by the Council to draw upon Cherokee funds as necessary for the expenses of the people during the exodus.

There was no joy in the news at the Hermitage. Andrew Jackson was furious that John had replaced a white man, Nathaniel Smith, who had been acting as Superintendent. The Attorney General of the United States received a letter from the former President, written in a high temper on the twenty-third day of August:

> The contract with Ross must be arrested, or you may rely upon it, the expense and other evils will shake the popularity of the Administration to its center. What madness and folly to have anything to do with Ross when the agent was proceeding well with

the removal on the principles of economy that would have saved at least 100 per cent from what the contract with Ross will cost. . . .

I have only time to add as the mail waits that the contract with Ross must be arrested, and General Smith left to superintend the removal. The time and circumstances under which General Scott made this contract show that he was no economist, or is, sub rosa, in league with Clay and Co. to bring disgrace on the Administration. . . .

P. S. I am so feeble that I can scarcely wield my pen, but my friendship dictates it and the subject excites me. Why is it that the scamp Ross is not banished from the notice of the Administration?

John set up his own organization to settle the business of the Nation's people. He worked with the group in registering the claims of every Cherokee against the Union. The people had been stripped of their belongings, from elegant homes to musical instruments, and John aimed to put in claims for everything for everyone. Included were pleas for payments for buildings, houses, mills, furniture, tools, spinning wheels, and almost anything that was useful and left behind on order of the government. Livestock was a heavy item, inasmuch as pets as well as field animals were included.

The major share of his attention during August went to the actual organization of the wagon train. He hired physicians for each of the thirteen detachments of a thousand people, as well as supply contractors, wagonmasters, and artisans. Withal, John was keeping to the schedule of departure on the first of September. But when it came, the Army delayed the departure due to the continuing drought.

John had to draw upon extra funds for more food, medical, and clothing supplies, all of which would be needed in excess of the amount counted upon had the train left on schedule. The government met its obligation in the first payment to the Cherokees for removal. A messenger rode into camp all the way from Philadelphia with the sum of half a million dollars from the Bank of the United States.

The official Nation of the Cherokee received John's careful consideration. He directed the preparation of all official documents for carting west. He and members of the Council signed a declaration of perpetuity of the Cherokee government, thus taking the first step in its transfer in total to the West:

> Whereas, the title of the Cherokee people to their lands is the most ancient, pure, and absolute known to man, its date is beyond the reach of human record: its validity confirmed and illustrated by possession and enjoyment antecedent to all pretense of claims by any other portion of the human race, . . .
>
> And whereas the natural, political, and moral relations existing among the citizens of the Cherokee Nation toward each other and toward the body politic cannot in reason and justice be dissolved by the expulsion of the nation from its own territory by the power of the United States Government,
>
> Resolved therefore by the National Committee and Council of the Cherokee Nation, in General Council assembled, that the inherent sovereignty of the Cherokee Nation, together with the Constitution, laws, and usages of the same, are, and by the authority aforesaid, hereby declared to be in full force . . . and shall continue so to be in perpetuity subject to such modifications as the general welfare may render expedient.

John took his three oldest sons into his confidence. He aimed to get as many rose cuttings from the plantation as he could manage for Quatie. He sent the boys on a mission to request the cuttings of the new owner, explaining how much they meant to their mother. The owner turned them away, threatening to set bloodhounds upon them if they did not hurry off the place.

John took the problem to General Scott: "I've seen my wife deprived of almost everything," he said, "but I'm bound and determined to get those roses for her. Can you help me, or will I have to work secretly and against the law?"

The General went to the plantation himself and held a conference with the owner. The man resisted the idea, but when the General hinted that an investigation of the man's rumored connivance with a discredited lottery agent might raise questions of his right to the Ross plantation, the man cooperated. The roses were prepared for Quatie. She received them with tears of joy.

Daniel and Mollie Ross, neither very well, now in their seventies, wanted to travel with John and his family, but John feared they would not survive the long trek.

"You'll go to Philadelphia for a time," he told them firmly. "Everything's arranged. There's a comfortable house waiting for you. If we can build a proper new home in the West, we'll send for you."

"Oh, John—" his mother began to plead.

"Now, Mollie!" Daniel put an arm around her. "We'd best do as John says."

She took her son's hand. "John, you promise? In time, you'll let us come to you?"

"In time, Mother, we'll be together," he faltered a little, knowing that only in another life would they be together again.

Daniel said: "You've always made us proud of you, son." He shook his head. "But I don't understand Andrew."

John was afraid of the emotion the farewell was building in him. "Everything will be all right, Father. You'll hear from me soon."

XXIX

THE FIRST DAY OF OCTOBER, 1838, DAWNED MISTILY UPON the long line of wagons, people, and livestock awaiting the signal to begin moving westward from Rattlesnake Springs, Tennessee. Two armies were gathered there: thirteen thousand Cherokees and the nearly six thousand members of the United States Army under command of General Winfield Scott. Over six hundred wagons of the emigrants, their five thousand horses, and numerous oxen stood ready and under guard of bayonets. The Army was keeping a sharp lookout. Some Cherokees had already successfully escaped the exodus, fleeing into the wilderness they knew so well. As the hour for departure came, the sun broke through the cloudy atmosphere and the day turned bright, although heavy clouds began clustering far off over the old familiar hills.

The move was held for a prayer which John led, standing amid his people, his head bowed, his voice raised in supplication for God's blessings upon the people in their hour of need.

A bugle called the wagons to order. As its sound died away, wagonmasters shouted, "Move on!" and drivers snapped whips and pulled reins. The wagons were filled mostly with children, sick persons, old folks, and expectant mothers. Numerous emigrants began the journey on foot. Others were astride their own horses, riding beside their family wagons.

They did not move forward silently. Infants were crying and sobbing, and the aged wailed for death, mingling their cries with the moanings of the sick and injured whose bodies felt every jolt of the wagons over the ground.

Quatie sat on a blanket on the wagon seat beside John, her head covered with a wool scarf. She turned a sad profile away from her husband's view, but he had seen the tears. He took a hand from the reins and put it over hers where she had them clasped tightly together in her lap.

A woman in a wagon a few spaces behind the Ross family, screamed: "I die! I die!"

"Who is she?"

Quatie could not look at him. "Sally Parr. All her people except her grandson are buried here. She wants to die and stay with them."

John pressed her hands. "I know."

Unexpected bitter winter weather descended on the trail. The Cherokees, covered by insufficient canvass and blankets, began to suffer greatly. Deaths came almost hourly, especially among the old and infants.

John sent his brother Lewis and another man on an emergency trip to St. Louis to get more supplies and warm clothing, including shoes for the children who had worn out the pairs they had started with weeks earlier.

But the shortage of blankets was serious. It became a battle to keep the children warm during the cold night. They huddled them together in the bottoms of the wagons, heaping as many blankets as they had for them upon their small bodies, but many of the children caught cold which often developed into pneumonia. Many were buried by the trail each dawn.

The whole train was spread over vast areas, some contingents traveling faster than others. There was illness and death in each unit. Some of the people had taken to government-offered boats, but ice often blocked the water, forcing them to transfer back to wagons on the trail.

At Paducah, Kentucky, Quatie's illness became acute. She had lost more weight and she had become very silent. She could no longer rise from her bunk bed and she lay still except when uncontrollable shivers shook her. John, desperate, decided to make arrangements to have her transferred to a government boat and get her to St. Louis for medical help. Wrapping her in his own blanket, he carried her aboard the boat, his sons and Jane beside him.

"You'll be fine," he told her, settling her on a bunk in a small cabin.

"Where are we, John?"

"On a government boat. We'll get to St. Louis soon. Just don't worry." He leaned over and kissed her forehead and was shocked at its heat.

A sleet storm and high winds drove the boat ashore. It was necessary to leave the craft and take Quatie back to a wagon. John and his group made camp atop a bluff overlooking the Arkansas River at Little Rock. Other contingents joined them at the camp, looking for a place to camp out the storm. A little boy, ill of pneumonia and delirious, was brought to their wagon and laid near Quatie.

Quatie spoke, startingly. "Who is he?" She tried to rise on an elbow to get a look at the child.

"Quatie!" John's heart took a leap at the sound of her voice after so long a silence. He came to kneel beside her. "You're feeling better?"

She was looking at the child. "Isn't that Bryce? Little Bryce Calvin?"

"Yes," he said, pulling her into his arms, cradling her against the news he had to give her. "Shanawan and Lydia are dead of pneumonia. Bryce has it, too."

"Shanawan?" She could not believe her strong young cousin was gone. "And Lydia?" She was shocked. "Why, John. What's to become of Bryce?"

"I don't know. As far I can learn, he has no relatives anywhere but us."

"Then," she said quietly, "he is ours." She looked at the boy again. "He will live. And he's ours."

"Are you sure, Quatie?"

"I'm sure. He'll be a son to you," she nodded, closing her eyes, her voice drifting.

John laid her back under the covers and went in search of Jane, who would take her turn at nursing Quatie.

When he was gone, Quatie sat up, pulled the blankets from herself and went to the boy. She took a long time but managed to wrap the child in her own covers and then sat on the wagon floor, holding him. "You must live," she told the unconscious child. "I can't. I must leave. I want you to be a good son to John Ross. Take care of him as he grows old. His own sons are already grown, really, and will soon leave him. I want you to stay close to him. Bryce Calvin, you're very blessed. John Ross already loves you." She closed her eyes, rocking the child, keeping him warm. The icy shivers which struck at her back caused her no concern.

Jane found her unconscious, the blanket-wrapped child sleeping in her arms. Pneumonia was closing her lungs.

John sat on the bunk in the wagon, holding her, motionless. More than once a dread alarm raced from his heart. But each time he saw that she still breathed and, seeing it, took false hope that she would live. She moved a trifle, sinking deeper into his embrace. A shudder seized her.

"Quatie?"

He sat, holding her limp body in his arms.

Jane came and stood beside him. His sons crowded into the wagon, one by one, silently.

At dawn, General Winfield Scott ordered a grave dug for Quatie Ross. An hour later he stood beside the Chief in the icy wind on the bluff at Little Rock, to hear a brief service offered for the Chief's wife. Many friends were there to mourn. Going Snake, suffering from a cold, bowed his head in silent prayer, oblivious of the threatening weather.

John asked to be left alone for a time, and his family and friends went quietly away.

General Scott, looking back at him from a distance, thought for a moment of Andrew Jackson. The General's beloved wife,

Rachel, had been laid to rest in the rose garden of the Hermitage and the General was able to visit her grave whenever he wanted.

The lonely Cherokee Chief stood, head bowed over the grave on the isolated bluff, the fierce wind blowing his hair, and had his last moments with his wife.

XXX

THE DREARY SIX-MONTH TRAIL OF TEARS AND DEATH CAME to an end on a bright, sunny April day. At last the Ross wagons crossed over the Arkansas border into the new land of Indian territory. General Scott and his troops withdrew as escorts, encamping at Fort Smith for a short term. The government of the United States would be represented in the territory by Montfort Stokes, its Indian agent, and General Matthew Arbuckle, a soldier of long service on the frontier.

They took the old Military Road into the territory, riding directly from Fort Smith to Tahlequah, where most of the Treaty Party members had settled. John, riding a horse at the head of the wagon train, was impressed with the land. The beautiful Elbon Valley through which they were passing was snuggled between gentle hills and watered by five rivers—the Canadian, Arkansas, Verdigris, Grand, and Illinois—and numerous creeks and ponds. The trees and bushes and grasses were brilliant in spring color.

As they neared Tahlequah, a buck and doe ran across the road and disappeared into the brush, tails flicking, feet lightly crushing the undergrowth of the riverbank.

Jim and Silas Ross rode back from a scouting run to report that the settlement of Tahlequah lay just ahead. John passed the signal down the line of wagons to halt. "Ask the folks to leave their wagons and come forward."

Though their ranks were thinned, nearly one thousand came to kneel with their Chief in a prayer of thanks that God had brought them to the end of their journey.

"We are home," John told them. When the few contingents following his train arrived within a few days, the mass exodus would be completed.

At the prayer stop, John removed the saddle from his horse and placed it in a wagon. He mounted the horse, placing three-year-old Bryce in front of himself and the little boy rode in quiet-voiced but bright-eyed excitement into Tahlequah with the Chief of the Cherokee.

Tahlequah was not yet a town, but its log-constructed buildings were increasing in number. The Old Settlers, having come on their own initiative to the territory some years before, had accepted the newcomers of the Treaty Party with goodwill. The Ridge and Watie faction were fascinated by the simple, near-primitive life enjoyed by the old-timers. With no strict system of government, they imposed little in the way of law and order.

Stand sent word to the Ridge at his home at Honey Creek that John Ross had arrived. The Ridge, receiving the message, accepted it as a warning of possible personal danger. "The Blood Law will have its day now," the old man said.

The residents turned out to see the Ross wagons trundle in from the Military Road and pull to a halt in a grove of trees behind Stand Watie's supply store. The people were curious, but made no move toward the Ross wagons, leaving the approach to Stand who came out of his log-built business house and went to the grove, his stride almost a swagger.

John, holding Bryce with one hand and the reins of his horse with the other, took in the scene with a quick glance. There would be no warm welcome here. He knew that their last uneasy meeting in the hotel in Washington was fresh in Stand's mind, too. Yet, this was a new time and a new beginning. The past must be forgotten.

Stand came forward and patted John's horse. "I hope all is well with you."

John shook his head. "Death has ridden with us, every step of the way. Quatie—" He could not continue.

"Not Quatie?"

John nodded. He changed the subject. "Sequoyah advised me to bring my family to a site at Park Hill, near his own home, I believe. Can you direct me?"

"I'll take you there, John," Stand offered. "But first, come into the store. I've got coffee hot on the stove. The boy might like a little bread and milk."

"All right, thanks. We'll take the time." He looked at the wagons. The people were going about their own camping efforts, and some of the Treaty Party individuals were following Stand's lead and were mixing with the immigrants. Jane was with Silas and George, adjusting ropes on the wagon, talking to a few of the residents. "Will the wagons be allowed to stay in the grove for a time?" John asked.

Stand smiled. "Certainly, as long as it takes for the folks to locate home sites and put up their cabins. Life is easy here, John. No heavy laws. Everyone's free to do as he wants."

Stand led John and Bryce into his store. It seemed as though half the population had gathered around the barrels of food and at the counter. John's appearance stilled the chatter. The people gave way to him as he followed Stand to a small, separate room at the back of the place.

At a small table in the room which Stand used as an office, John helped Bryce with the bread and jam that Stand placed in front of him. Stand poured a mug of sweet milk and two cups of black coffee.

"You've chosen the right place to settle if you go to Park Hill," Stand began. "It's about five miles south of here. A wooded, hilly section, bordering on a healthy stream. Lots of land good for planting, properly cleared. You'd find nothing better in Georgia."

"It's beautiful," John admitted. "But it needs taming."

"This is great country. But it may never be tamed."

"Civilized people always tame a land, Stand. The first requirement is a governing body."

Stand took a deep breath. "We've got a governing body. The Old Settlers had it when we got here and we've added a few simple laws to it. A few innovations, such as a unit of lighthorsemen who ride the land, seeing to law and order. We've got all the government anyone wants or needs."

John's gaze held Stand's. "Government? What kind?"

"Well, suitable to the land—the vast area. The nation is divided into three districts and there is a chief for each district and under him, courts, councils, elected officials. The Council meets every six months at the capital city, Tahlonteskee."

"And law? Is there a written constitution?"

"Oh, we've got law. Even got a jailhouse. People behave or they go to jail. They aren't much concerned with the old things of the old Nation. Here, they're free. They'd rather hold a dance or a horse race than an election. The young have had a look at the exciting life the Comanches are leading on the plains, and they like what they see of it. They aren't interested in government and rules."

"Where have our young men met the Comanches?" John asked.

"On the Brazos at the Texas border. They ride there to trade with each other—gunpowder and arms from our youth for the wild horses the Comanches bring in from their plains. It's a new, relaxed life here, something like the old days when we were boys."

"You're right about that," John shook his head. "Riding into Tahlequah is like riding into the past. Well, we'll just have to take a hand, Stand, and get this nation organized. We'll call a meeting of the Council as soon as possible." He got up and helped Bryce to his feet.

"You haven't heard a word I've said, have you?" Stand said huskily.

"I heard, and I'm impressed. As Chief, it's time I moved to bring law and order to our Nation."

"As Chief! You aren't Chief of the Cherokee West. The old government has been declared null and void, and you know it. You're a latecomer here, John, and no more."

"I *am* Chief of the Cherokee West. Our national government merely stands adjourned *sine die*. I'll call a convention at the earliest possible moment." John carried Bryce to the door. "I believe I can find my way to Park Hill, Stand."

"Yes, I'm sure you can," Stand agreed. He made no move to go with him.

John took his wagons and horses south to the Military Road cutoff to Park Hill. Greeted by Sequoyah at his cabin home, John selected the site where he would construct his new home: a section of land dominated by a hillock and blessed with rich soil and groves of trees, bordering on a tributary of the Illinois River. He would place his home atop the hill to give it a view of the stream and woods, but until the home was built, he and his family would live in a cabin near Sequoyah's.

In the next few months, even the matter of government had to be secondary to the needs of individuals in Elbon Valley as many hands cleared land, felled trees, cut logs, hauled lumber, made bricks, built homes, laid crops, and moved livestock behind fenced areas.

But the emigrants depended upon federal government provisions until they were able to bring in their own crops. John, inspecting the goods which were deposited at Stand's store for distribution, found the meats and the flour unfit for consumption. He showed the bad food to Stand: "The flour is crawling with weevils. The meat is rotten. I won't accept this. It's unclean and unhealthy."

"I doubt that anything can be done about it," Stand told him.

John notified Montfort Stokes and General Matthew Arbuckle that he was rejecting the goods. He would use the remainder of his Cherokee government allotment to purchase supplies from an independent source.

The government agents accepted his complaint and made haste to reimburse him for the money he had spent. New supplies arrived, including ploughs and furniture. The grateful people praised John anew for his quick work in obtaining decent supplies, but the Treaty Party members were wary of him. Chief or not, he was obviously still the leader of the majority of the people.

A meeting was held at the Honey Creek home of the Ridge, who was host to Elias Boudinot, John Ridge, Stand Watie, Andrew Ross, and others. Stand, pacing the comfortable sitting room of the farm home, warned the men: "We've got to take action right away. Ross actually believes he is Chief of this nation. He intends to call a meeting to organize the old government."

The Ridge held up his thin hand to stop the disconnected discussion. "There's only one way to handle this man Ross and his people."

"How?" Elias inquired.

"Beat Ross to a convention call. Gather our three chiefs and our councilmen and invite Ross and his people. The convention will welcome them to this land and acquaint them with the elected officials of the people."

The grin on Stand's face was the first that had been there since he had heard John term himself Chief of the Cherokee West.

XXXI

ON THE TENTH DAY OF JUNE, HUNDREDS LEFT THEIR daily chores to go to the convention site at Takattokah. The weather was clear and cool and many citizens stood wrapped in their blankets. There was a restrained friendliness in the atmosphere, but the western faction made no particular effort to mingle with John's followers.

The western chiefs, John Rogers, John Looney, and John Brown, welcomed the newcomers, speaking of the good life and peaceful conditions in the territory. Chief Rogers offered the rostrum to John, suggesting he might like to respond to the welcoming words of the westerners.

John looked out over the gathering. People were jammed in the area surrounding the open-air council hall. He saw Stand and the Ridges watching him. Elias was pushing his way through the crowds to join the little group, his gaze directed anxiously to the rostrum. Certain that he would be deprived of another opportunity to speak at the convention, John made his remarks right to the point. "On the thirty-first of July and the first of August, 1838, the Cherokee Nation adjourned its Council and National Committee *sine die*. On those days, your elected officials through proper procedure, resolved that our national government, sentiments, rights, and interests, would be immediately reinstituted here upon a reunion of our people. This is the hour."

The intense hush over the crowds told that the words of the Chief were stunning some, pleasing many.

"As Chief, I make a suggestion. Our national government exists because it has been perpetuated by action of the majority. Yet we cannot overlook or disregard the system created here by the minority of our people. And there no doubt are things in the unwritten government they have been enforcing that we might well consider keeping. For this purpose, I suggest a committee be formed to effect a new code of laws for our western land. This committee could bring us a merger of our interests and create an even stronger government than that we have enjoyed in the old land. Let's work together to this end."

The reaction was immediate. Ross's people swarmed toward him, eager to speak to him. The Ridges, together with Stand, Elias, and Andrew Ross, broke away and followed the three western chiefs to another section of the camp ground, near the river.

"We will have no more to do with John Ross," said the Ridge. "He is to have no voice in this land. I see blood over this."

"Ross will not have the rostrum again," Chief Rogers assured the Ridge. "We'll hold our own meeting. He shall not enter it."

When it became apparent that the Treaty Party was proceeding with a convention session without him, at the opposite end of the grounds, John's people were fired with resentment. "Let's move in on them," someone shouted.

John held his arms up for silence. "I ask you to remain calm. Let me go to them." He strode to the campfire where the Treaty Party people were gathered. "Is this convention in adjournment?" he asked.

Chief Rogers, standing beside the Ridge, made the reply. "No. But you have spoken all that will be heard from you. You are advised we have just passed a resolution which declares that you and your people, having accepted our invitation to this convention, have already merged with our government. We are now a united people and all will live under the system of government now operating here. You and your people will be expected to live among us under our laws."

The words of Chief Rogers spread fast among the Ross people. The young men, Alan Ross among them, mounted their horses and sped away to a cabin to hold a meeting of their own. They talked about the Blood Law, the rule of death for treason. But they needed to know more about it, and so rode to consult with Going Snake.

The old man answered their questions to their satisfaction. Nothing had changed the law held among the Cherokee. "Three men are selected as executioner," said Going Snake. "They must be of the same clan as the condemned. The Blood Law is justice."

The young men met again at the cabin. Alan, though present at the meeting, declined to participate further in deference to his father. "He wouldn't want the Blood Law invoked. I won't go against him."

He reached home as the sun shot a streak of red over the horizon. He hurried to his room, his pledge of silence weighing heavily in his father's house.

John Ridge awoke. It was not yet dawn although a streak of light edged the earth. He lay quietly beside his sleeping wife, his half-awake mind wondering what had awakened him. His thoughts went to the family. Susan had told him at dinner that Becky Boudinot was not doing too well and that Alexander was a very worried young husband. The expectant grandparents, Elias and Harriet, were much concerned, not only for Becky but for her expected baby.

The bedroom door opened. He turned a startled face to it, thinking one of his children was there.

There were three shadowy figures in the doorway. Before he could even shout, they were at the bed, pulling back the covers, yanking him to his feet. He struggled. Susan screamed. The intruders said not a word but forcibly dragged him from the bedroom, in a half-sitting position, out of the house and into the yard.

Susan and the children came running from the house, the chill of the morning penetrating their night clothing. She beat at the men, trying to reach her husband, but she was shoved aside.

The first deep knife cut on John Ridge's neck brought a well of blood. He slumped to the ground. They leaned over him, slashing down at him, again and again. As they ran for their horses, they looked back to see the hysterical mother drop to her knees over the dead body. Susan's piercing scream rose above the terrified sobs of the children.

The sun was high in the sky, the hour nearly ten o'clock, as the Ridge, accompanied by a young black slave, was riding his favorite steed homeward. The long, dusty trail passed under a high, jutting cliff that extended directly over the road.

Three shots rang out. The Ridge's hands jerked free of the reins. He toppled from the horse, dead.

Using his heels as a spur, the black boy jolted his horse into a run, wheeling it away from the cliff, turning wide to return the way he had come. Not looking back, he headed for Tahlelquah, away from the three men he had glimpsed atop the cliff.

At about the same hour the Ridge died, Elias Boudinot opened the door of his home to three men who greeted him in half-apologetic urgency. "We've been told you'll help us," said one of them, "We've got bad sickness in our families and can't get hold of any medicine. We're told you can get a supply for us from Doctor Worcester at Park Hill. We're askin' you to go with us. The Doc likely won't do it unless you say so."

Knowing of the scarcity of supplies in general, Elias believed them. He would go with them and see what he could do.

At the turn in the road which would take them to Doctor Worcester's home, they seized Elias and dragged him from his saddle. He struggled but one of them held his arms behind his back. He closed his eyes. A tomahawk descended toward his skull. Their knives were not needed. Elias Boudinot was dead.

The Ridge's slave rode straight to Tahlequah and Stand Watie's store. Stand, talking to a customer at the flour barrels, turned in amazement to see the sweating, frightened boy.

"Mister Watie! They killed him dead. They did, that's a fact. The Ridge mister, he's dead, sir. He is."

Stand knew what it meant: the Blood Law! He thought: Elias! They'll be after him, too!

He rode to the home of his brother and found him stretched out in death on a couch in the sitting room, his frightened, crying family gathered together. He took Harriet's hands. They've murdered the Ridge, too! "I'll see John Ross dead for it. I'll kill him, so help me God."

"No, Stand. We don't know who did this. Three strangers came for Elias, asking for his help. I don't remember what they looked like. I'm not sure I could ever recognize them, if I were to see them. John Ross didn't do this. Oh, God, help us!"

"Ross sent them. He's invoked the Blood Law." Stand went to the door.

"Where are you going?"

"To find some men who will ride with me. I'm going to kill John Ross."

Harriet sent for one of the young slaves and scrawled a hasty note which she put into his hands with instructions to deliver it to none but John Ross.

John was at his home, hosting a committee meeting to deal with the records and muster rolls of the exodus. The War Department had requested a final report from the Chief and the accounts included his own demands for belated payments for his lands in Georgia and Tennessee. Hundreds of others were mak-

ing their claims through the committee, and the work was painstaking. When Jane called him to the door, he took the note from the messenger in person.

"It's from Harriet," he exclaimed to Jane. "Elias and the Ridges have been murdered! She warns me to leave. Stand has sworn to kill me." He looked at Jane in disbelief. "He thinks I had them assassinated!"

Jane was unnerved. "Where can you go?"

"I'm not going anywhere, Jane."

"Father, you've got to leave. You'll be killed!"

"Jane, I'm innocent."

"They'll kill all of us—"

"No, they won't." He shook her by the shoulders to stop her rising terror. "General Arbuckle will keep order. Stand's sense will return. You see that Bryce stays in the house, and stay in yourself. Round up the boys. I'll need one of them to ride to Fort Gibson with a message to the General."

John, alone at his writing table, stared down at Harriet's note. He could not deny that his followers had obviously invoked the Blood Law against the trio of leaders of the Treaty Party. All the years of organizing a civilized government had been wiped out. Thanks to the New Echota Treaty and the resultant division of the Cherokee people, the Nation was back to the ancient law of personal revenge.

John was certain he would never know the identity of the assassins. Yet they had committed murder, and if a constitutional government was to be established in the Nation, such crimes must be brought to justice. He would have to assist in the search for them.

Suddenly he recalled that just as the convention broke up, he had seen Alan riding away in the company of other young men. All of them had looked very angry. He opened the door and shouted in a manner he never used, loudly and sharply: "Alan!"

Alan's eyes were so much like Quatie's that at times John felt an ache in his heart. John handed him Harriet's note to read. "I'm sorry for her," he said.

"Do you know who committed these executions?"

"Yes, sir."

"Will you tell me what you know?"

"No, sir."

"Did you take part in the killings?"

"No, sir."

"Why didn't you warn me?"

"Father, it was none of my business. The tribal law allowed the executions. I couldn't have stopped them."

"How could you let those men die without warning them, or going to General Arbuckle?"

Alan's expression was inscrutable. "They were traitors. They betrayed the Nation. They were enemies, especially your enemies. If I'd warned anyone, I'd have rightfully been killed, too. I had no choice." He hesitated, then added slowly: "Sir, if I had betrayed the men who did it, I'd have signed a death warrant for you, too."

"So after all our struggles toward civilization, the young men meet secretly and take up the primitive law of personal revenge."

"Justice, sir. They took up justice."

"You call it justice? Justice planned at clandestine meetings, carried out by night riders, bands of unidentifiable men?"

"Sir, it had to be done. You don't understand."

"I can't change it. But now I'm in a position of defending myself against accusations of murder. I'm going to send a note to General Arbuckle at Fort Gibson. Can I trust you to get it to him at once?"

Alan bit his lip, hurt shadowing his eyes. "You know you can trust me to deliver it, Father."

He stood quietly beside the table as John wrote a message to the General. "Will you ride as fast as possible? This thing is going to be out of hand unless we get some control into the situation."

Alan was at the door when John called to him. "I understand one thing. That you've been faced with a terrible choice. To follow your own conscience or to respect your father's. I'm grateful, and proud, that you chose to put my position ahead of your own."

Alan gave him a salute of the hand and left.

After delivering the note to General Arbuckle at Fort Gibson, Alan rode swiftly to the remote cabin where he found a gathering of the young men who had effected the assassinations. "Stand Watie has threatened to kill my father," he told them. "General Arbuckle has just received a note from my father asking for protection and that peace be kept in the Nation. I saw some of Watie's men at the fort and I don't think we can trust my father's safety to the Army."

Sounding the Cherokee chortle of battle, the group saddled and rode with Alan. Along the road, and sweeping through Tahlequah, where they left word of Watie's threat against the Chief, they were joined by others, including Alan's brothers.

The posse rode quietly when it reached the lands of John Ross at Park Hill. The group moved up to the house and spread out, completely encircling the home, keeping open eyes for any sign of other riders.

As Stand gathered his armed force at his home, he received a warning from Tahlequah that Ross's faction was alerted and the Ross house ringed with an armed patrol. He was also advised that his name was on the list of traitors and that his assassination had been ordered, too. Taking the warning to heart, Stand and his men rode to Fort Gibson.

"I'm mighty glad to see you here, Stand," General Arbuckle said, escorting him into the office.

"General," said Stand, "I'm here for protection against John Ross. I'm told my name is on the blood list. He's got an army around him. Tahlequah is under arms, too."

The General's eyes glinted. "I know. And I've just had a note from him swearing he is innocent of the assassinations. I've sent a reply off to him, asking him to come here tomorrow for interrogation. The three chiefs of this territory will be here tomorrow and we can deal with John Ross together."

Stand sat back. "Then it is all right if I stay here tonight?"

"I wouldn't have it any other way. You're in protective custody, sir."

John did not like General Arbuckle's invitation to come to the fort for questioning about the murders of the Treaty Party trio. If he were to go, chances were he would be held as a prisoner.

He looked out of the window of his room. Everywhere he looked, there were armed men, his sons among them, distributing ammunition, checking out weapons, directing guards to posts of duty. Quatie would have been proud that they were standing ready to defend him, that the people were ready to raise guns in his defense. Yet he was not proud of the armed division of his Nation. He who wanted only peace for his people was bringing them to the verge of civil war.

Jim came to his room. "Stand Watie and his men have taken refuge at Fort Gibson."

"Then the men can disband and go home," he commented gratefully.

"Not yet, Father. They're going to keep watch out there for a few days yet."

General Arbuckle fumed at John's word of rejection of the invitation to Fort Gibson. "This man Ross is a tyrant. He's got a mighty highhanded way of behaving for a man suspected of murder." He picked up a desk pen. "Well, I'll just insist upon his visit here. I'll send him another note."

Stand, who had spent the early morning hours in conversation with the General, shook his head. "He won't come here. If you want to see him, you'll have to go to him. I've never known John Ross to change his mind about anything."

The old officer rode into the Ross yard with a company of ten men, flags flying, and refused all hospitable offers of welcome. He stood in the front room, his hands locked behind his back, and his gaze fixed on John. "Sir," he began, "there's no need to drag this inquiry out. Just give me a few answers and I'll be on my way."

"What do you want to know?"

"First, the obvious one: Did you murder the Ridge? Or John Ridge? Or Elias Boudinot?"

John's face paled with anger. "Am I accused of their murders?"

"Some say it." The General was not apologetic. "Do you deny murdering those men? For the record, sir."

"I deny murdering them."

"Did you order the assassinations?"

"I did not."

The General peered at him. "Can you name the assassins?"

"No, I cannot."

"Let me rephrase that. Do you know the identities of the murderers?"

"I've told you. I can't name them."

The General watched for any change in John's expression, "Do you believe in the legality and justice of the Cherokee Blood Law?"

"The record proves I believe in constitutional government. No, I don't believe in the legality or justice of the Cherokee Blood Law."

The General's eyes sparked. "You're a very brilliant man, Mr. Ross. I see that. Clever, educated, personable. And, in my opin-

ion, sir, guilty as hell in these murders!" He turned on his heel and left the room.

At the fort, he told Stand: "I'm convinced John Ross is implicated, but I don't expect to prove it. Well, we'll keep trying for evidence. I'll keep on questioning people. If I can get anything on him, I'll have him arrested at once."

Stand shook his head: "You won't get anything. The Ross people will protect him at all costs. He'll never lose their loyalty. At least the immediate threat is over. He won't make any move against me now. I'll be on my way, General, with thanks for your help."

XXXII

WHILE THE DRAGOONS OF GENERAL ARBUCKLE RODE THE territory seeking information, John and his people went ahead with plans to unite the nation under a constitutional government. Sequoyah and Doctor Worcester aided John in calling a convention to which members of the Treaty Party were also invited.

Responding to Sequoyah's appeal to meet and to settle things "amicably" was Chief John Looney, who rode to the convention on the twelfth of July at Illinois Camp Ground. Breaking with Chiefs Brown and Rogers over the acceptance of the invitation, he came to stay with the Ross forces. On the twenty-second of July, the two other western chiefs met at Tahlonteskee in a convention with the members of the Treaty Party. The Ross faction was not invited to attend.

Stand had just finished speaking when John appeared at their council, riding alone. His hand went to his gun, but when he saw that John carried no weapon, he dropped his hand and waited.

John went to the rostrum amid an ominous murmur of lowered voices. He told Stand: "I'm here to speak to this convention. I've got information of great importance affecting this gathering."

There was an instant outbreak of "No! No!" from the assembled convention.

Stand held his arms high: "Quiet! John Ross does not speak here."

John faced them, ignoring Stand. "I speak briefly. The majority of the people, on the twelfth of July, adopted in convention an Act of Union which makes one body politic for us all under the title of the Cherokee Nation—"

Rising from spectator benches, Ellis, Tom, and Bean Starr and the Bell brothers interrupted John, coming forward with guns in hand. No one made any move to stop them as they surrounded John. Bean's gun was close to John's ribs as he said: "We're escortin' you out."

John looked to Stand, who only stared impassively and stood aside as the men forced John down from the rostrum with guns at his back.

He strode ahead of them to his horse at the hitching post. Mounted, he told them: "There will be a convention of the Cherokee people on the sixth of October at Tahlequah. An election will be held for the office of Principal Chief. Tell your friends." He spurred his horse away.

The men went back to their benches and with the others voted to bar from the land any white man showing friendliness toward John Ross. They also resolved to enlarge the unit of lighthorsemen. Then, mindful of the election planned by John, they voted to hold their own convention in October to elect new chiefs.

The elections held by the two factions separated the nation even more. The majority voted for the reelection of John as Principal Chief of the Cherokee Nation West. He took the oath of office anew, receiving the instructions of the Council to proceed to Washington in behalf of the nation's unfinished business with the Union. At the convention, the people also passed a resolution which came from their own ranks: All signers of the New Echota Treaty were required to appear before the Constitutional Council to answer for their treachery. If they did not so appear, they would be banished from the land as outlaws.

Going Snake took John's hand at the conclusion of the convention. "Your people burden you. They send you now to Washington to write a new treaty. They want a million dollars in annuities, long owed them, brought back to them. They ask you to explain the assassinations to the satisfaction of the federal officers. If you can effect even one of these things, you will return in triumph."

Before he went east, John saw three of his children married at festive ceremonies. First, Jim was married to Sarah Mannion; then Jane wed a long-standing friend of her father's, Return Jonathan Meigs, who owned the flourishing general store at Park Hill; and Alan, after a whirlwind courtship, took Jennie Fields as his bride.

Jim took his bride to a farm a few miles north of Tahlequah. The log building was not new, but it was cozy and it was theirs. "I'll build you a proper frame house in time," he promised, "one with the bedrooms upstairs." Sarah cuddled in his arms, perfectly content with what they had.

Alan took his bride to a farm also, and friends raced them to the place where the wedding supper would be served, followed by dancing and singing.

Jane and Return were planning to build a home near the river, not far from John's lands where Rose Cottage would rise. They would supervise John's home while he was in the east. Since John was to take Silas along on the trip, Jane would only have George and Bryce to concern herself over. "Don't worry about us," she told John. "It's going to be a happy time for us."

"Are you certain? You may want to spend time watching your own home go up."

"Oh, I'll run down there all the time." She hugged her Father. "You just put your mind at ease. We'll manage."

The members of the delegation were delayed in leaving. General Arbuckle, pressing the investigation, made no attempt to keep John in the territory, but he detained the delegates for further questioning. His dragoons brought the delegates to the fort, where Joseph Lynch, Elijah Hicks, Edward Gunter, Archibald Campbell, and Looney Price denied any knowledge of the assassinations.

As John, accompanied by Silas, left for Washington, the Treaty Party convened. John Rogers was elected first chief, with John Smith as second and Dutch third. The new officers also appointed a delegation to Washington with instructions to visit President Van Buren and gain the Treaty Party official recognition as the legal government. Stand was appointed head of the delegation.

John and Silas were fascinated by the train on which they rode into Washington. The long, boxlike car of the train was heated by a sheet-iron stove. The warmth was welcome at first, but within half an hour they were suffering from the excessive heat blasting from it.

"Open the window, Silas," John suggested.

His son struggled with the wide glass in vain.

"It won't go," he said.

John stood up and they tried together. The other passengers smiled.

Silas shook his head. "It's hopeless."

Fumes from the anthracite coal which fueled the steam engine drifted into the car, adding to the staleness of the air. Their eyes burned from it and their heads ached and their clothing was dusted with grey residue.

But the speed of the train was worth the discomforts. The countryside passed swiftly by, but the train slowed to a crawl whenever it approached water. The rails were laid low over the rivers, perched perilously above the water on wood piles, giving the passengers the dizzying experience of looking straight down into water.

When dark came, the train pulled to a stop on the tracks and everyone debarked to walk to the nearest private home used by the railroad as a station. The houses usually offered little in the way of comfortable rest or good food. All the passengers dined at one immense table in the dining room, and service was mostly by passing dishes from one hand to another. Afterward, men and women separated into their own quarters.

John prepared for bed in a room he and Silas shared with four bearded strangers. A public towel hung by a basin filled with water already well used. "Don't touch that towel," he warned Silas. "It's foul. As a matter of fact, don't wash at all. Anything you've already got on your hands is better than that."

They traveled on the next day, wiser about private station houses, but feeling unfed and unrested and in need of a bath. Before the end of the day, the tracks came to an abrupt end. The journey would continue with a half-day's ride in a stagecoach to the point where another train would be waiting.

John enjoyed the ride along a country road, pulled by four horses. "This is more like it," he told Silas. "At least we know what to expect." Silas grunted in agreement as the coach hit a dip in the road.

Arriving in Washington, they hired a carriage. The city streets were in a state of upheaval due to a civic-sponsored digging for wells and the installation of cisterns and pumps in Washington homes. Great mountains of bricks were stacked everywhere for use in pipe building.

En route to the Globe Hotel, where they would take rooms for their long stay, they passed the National Theater, which had opened five years earlier. The coming appearance of the noted Irish actor, Tyrone Power, was blazoned on the advertising sheets posted at the front of the building.

They had not been in the city twenty-four hours when John realized that his prestige and that of his people was still low in Washington. Requesting a meeting with President Van Buren, he was refused. It was clear that the President, formerly Jackson's Secretary of State and Vice-President, was holding loyal to Jackson's policies.

John went to the War Department and asked for a meeting with Secretary of War, Joel Poinsett. The Secretary would not see him. John insisted upon being allowed to speak to an officer of the federal government about relations with the Cherokee Nation. He was kept waiting several hours in the office of Secretary Poinsett.

Finally he was ushered into the Secretary's office. No chair was offered him and no hand in greeting. He stood, hat in hand, in front of the Secretary's desk.

"I've decided it's necessary to speak to you," the Secretary told him bluntly. "It's best that you understand your position in the eyes of this administration."

John nodded: "I'll appreciate honesty."

"To that end, I'll read you part of a letter which the President has received from General Matthew Arbuckle at Fort Gibson." He cleared his throat and proceeded in precise tones, reading from the letter: " 'If Ross had not been prepared to start to Washington on business of much interest as it was understood, to the late emigrants, I would have caused him to be arrested and placed in confinement until the government was known.' "

"That's a shocking—"

"Never mind!" The Secretary held up a hand to silence him.

"There's more, to the effect that the only legally elected principal chief of the Cherokee Nation West is John Rogers. He heads the only legal government of the Cherokee people. You, sir, are in effect, an imposter and I cannot deal with you—"

"You actually believe—"

"Oh, we're aware of the division of opinion in your land. We know some consider you to be Chief. We've had a dispatch from Montfort Stokes in your behalf. He speaks of you in high terms and urges your recognition as Chief. He has vowed you're not involved in the terrible political assassinations which have taken place in the Nation. He believes you incapable of such crimes. But then, Governor Stokes is suspended as our agent to the Cherokee people."

"Suspended? For being my friend?"

"Suspended for being a biased agent. For championing a man who has no legal claim upon the Cherokee Nation. Governor Stokes has contributed to the unsettled conditions in the territory by upholding the violent attitude of your self-elected group. The passage of a resolution at your July meeting now sets up a hanging committee against all signers of the New Echota Treaty."

"The Treaty of New Echota—"

"—is a treaty ratified by the United States and representatives of the Cherokee Nation. You, sir, have overstepped your authority in allowing a resolution in your Nation which declares its signers subject to judgment and punishment by your Council. Good day, Mr. Ross."

"You leave me no recourse but to take my appeal to the Congress," John told him quietly.

He obtained an appointment with Representative John Bell, a member of the Indian Affairs Committee. After an hour of discussion, the Congressman agreed he would delve into the Cherokee situation and submit to Congress a report on his findings along with his recommendations. His confession that his sympathies had always been with the Ross faction gave John new hope. Bell's report could result in federal recognition of John's government and bring belated payment of the annuities.

Stand Watie arrived in Washington in the company of John Bell and William Rogers; and they too took rooms at the Globe Hotel. Before making their visit to the White House, they spent several days purchasing new clothing.

Stand's square figure was set off with pearl gray trousers and stockings. He chose a scarlet vest and gray frock coat trimmed in the scarlet tone, a long-furred beaver hat, and natural kid gloves. The others chose similar outfits in greens and browns.

Stand shopped, too, for the newborn daughter of Alexander Boudinot, one of his brother's sons. Alexander's wife had died when her child was born and Alexander, already stricken by the murder of his father and the Ridges, was staying with the Watie family at Tahlequah. Stand had loved the diminutive Copper, his new grandniece, on sight.

"If you'll let us," he had told Alexander, "Sarah and I will raise this child as our own. She's special, coming along a week after I've lost my brother. She's my grandchild, as well as his. Do you mind?"

Alexander was only too grateful.

Stand bought Copper luxurious items of clothing and furnishings, telling the shopkeeper: "She's the most beautiful infant I've ever seen. I want the world for her."

The Watie Delegation was received hospitably at the White House. Its plea for recognition as a delegation of the only legal government of the Cherokee Nation was taken under advisement by the President. It would take some weeks of consultation before a decision could be handed them.

Waiting was easier for Silas than for the others because he soon found himself included in many social functions through John's Congressional friends. There were few evenings when he was not engaged. Silas was bedazzled by the beauty of the glamourous young women then sporting a new fad which reminded him of his people's colorful celebration headdresses. The young women wore chains around their heads which looped onto the forehead, the loop set with precious jewels.

John, returning to his room at the Globe in the late afternoon of January 15, 1840, was encouraged by an event of the day, and found Silas dressing for a dinner party: "Governor Stokes is still battling for us. He sent a report to Congress today that our people have held a meeting at Tahlequah aimed to help us here. They have voted to rescind the resolution requiring signers of the New Echota Treaty to register with the Council. The President can't hang his case against us on it now."

A few weeks later John received word that the Secretary of War desired to see him.

Offered a seat in the Secretary's office, he tried to read the

Secretary's expression. It was a look of triumph. John braced for the words he knew were coming.

"Mr. Ross," the Secretary spoke crisply, tapping some papers on his desk with his long fingers, "this is a copy of a resolution issued by a council meeting held at Fort Gibson a few weeks ago. You'll be given a copy. It proclaims the Cherokee citizens as a sovereign and independent people. . . . The elected chief is John Rogers. It specifically states that 'John Ross and his partisans' are not to participate in the new government except through consent or by conquest. The Council expressly stated that the new government will never yield to John Ross."

John protested: "This is a personal attack by an illegal—"

"Let me finish! The Council refers to your meetings as acts of usurpation. It vows your government will never be recognized. Their claim is based upon the fact that they have merged with the old governing body of the Cherokee West. The Treaty Party and the Old Settlers' party have united into the new government."

"The Treaty Party is in violation of our constitutional government," John said quietly.

"They pledge to uphold and defend their government." The Secretary leaned on the desk, pronouncing his next words very slowly. "The government of the United States recognizes the government of the Cherokee Nation as set forth in this document on my desk."

John was on his feet. "I do not. And Congress is yet to say so." He went to the door without offering a hand to the Secretary.

The majority report of the Indian Affairs Committee of the House of Representatives was ready for public release. Representative Bell invited John to his office to give him a first look at it. "We've made a careful study of records of the United States and the Cherokee government relations over the past twenty years." He circled his desk, too nervous to keep his seat. "John, we've come up against a mighty problem. On examining all the records of the relationship, we've found such a general indictment of the policies of the incumbent President, and his predecessors, and the War Department that the main body of the House of Representatives refuses to let us file our report! It's downright uncomplimentary to the President's reputation. Yet every word of it is the truth."

John leaned forward in his chair. "What good is it, if it can't be used?"

Representative Bell got to his feet, poured two glasses of brandy, and offered one to John. "John, a toast!"

John, puzzled, held up the glass.

"To the freedom of the American press!"

"You mean the report will be published?"

"It will appear in tomorrow's edition of the *Intelligencer*, and no doubt throughout the country." The Congressman's smile was broad.

"What's in the report?"

Representative Bell clucked his tongue. "The eventual defeat of Martin Van Buren. More exactly, President Van Buren and the War Department are accused of an unjustifiable interference in Cherokee matters, causing a state of unrest, dissension, and anarchy within the Nation. You want to hear the exact words?"

"Every one of them."

"Well, in reference to the President, we have reported that 'interference by the Executive in the affairs of the Cherokee Indians by prescribing any particular form of government or interdicting any system of laws already adopted by the majority, is unconstitutional. If persisted in, it will probably lead to disorder and war.' "

"It's recognition!" John exclaimed.

"Wait, John. There's more. The Little Magician," he said, using the public's nickname for the President, "is personally held to account. We've brought attention to the fact that he is withholding the near–million dollars which was due your people upon your arrival in the new land. He is withholding it until you agree to accept the government of the Treaty Party and the Old Settlers as the only legal one!"

John was so awed that he could not find a thing to say.

The Congressman was enjoying himself. "And just to be certain, John, that we've nailed his hide to the barn door, we've noted that his allies are certain members of the Treaty Party, a few of the Old Settlers, and General Arbuckle. The conclusion of our report states that we are 'reluctantly compelled to believe, that upon no better or higher suggestions than the hope of operating upon the necessities and avarice of the Indians has the Executive of the United States been influenced in withholding the large sums of money long since due by treaty.' "

Happily stunned, John left the Congressman's office a bit later with the report in hand, his hopes soaring despite Bell's warning that even with the report in circulation, it might take the government a long time to act upon it and grant him recognition.

President Van Buren, raging at the publicity given the report, and chagrined at the shock that the American people felt upon reading the facts, took action to consolidate his policies in the Indian Nation. He refused to see John and gave disciplinary powers in the Cherokee Nation to General Arbuckle. He kept Montfort Stokes under suspension, but he had to proceed with caution because it was election year and his opponent was the military hero William Henry Harrison. President Van Buren had other matters than the Cherokee Nation on his mind as he prepared his reelection campaign. John, seeing that the issue would need more time, returned to the Nation with Silas and John Howard Payne. The famed author began a new series of articles about the Cherokee Nation.

When John presided over the first meeting of the Council at Tahlequah, John Payne was there to report it, telling the world of the deep affection the majority of the Cherokees had for their newly elected Chief.

Martin Van Buren was defeated by William Henry Harrison. At his Inaugural, the new President of the United States caught a cold and three weeks later, on the fourth day of April, 1841, President Harrison succumbed to complications. Before that day was over, the new Vice-President, John Tyler, was sworn into the office of President. A lifetime opponent of Andrew Jackson's policies, the new President brought a new age to Washington.

John's congressional friends advised him to return with a delegation to see President Tyler, and John lost no time in following the advice. Once again he left his home affairs in Jane's good hands.

In Washington, he immediately submitted to the President's office a proposal for a replacement of the New Echota Treaty. He left the proposal for the President's study without seeing the Chief Executive at all. Stand came to Washington, too, at the head of another delegation requesting official recognition and the perpetuation of the New Echota Treaty.

President Tyler read the report of the House Indian Affairs Committee which had been issued during Van Buren's administration and consulted with numerous experts and with the record. The day came when he opened the door of his office to John and his delegation of four. The President's blue eyes were kind and his voice pleasantly pitched, and he was a good host, seeing that the Cherokees were comfortably settled around his desk before he began to talk.

The President stood before them almost like a preacher at a Sunday morning prayer meeting, his hands clasped in front of him, his expression benign. "Gentlemen, I want you to know that as far as I have any power or influence, there shall be not only justice done you and your people, but a liberal and generous policy shall be adopted toward them. The ratification of a new treaty we mutually contemplate will give full indemnity to the Cherokee Nation for all wrongs it has suffered. We will establish upon a permanent basis political relations between our Nations. A new sun will dawn upon you."

Once again John and his delegates returned to the Nation without recognition and without the monies due them, but John believed that justice was to come and that, in the meantime, he ought to give his time and attention to the development of Tahlequah and his own plantation home. He made frequent trips to Boston and Philadelphia, entering into trade agreements for his own cotton products and for the Cherokee's produce and commodities, including cotton, cattle, fruits, and vegetables. The people were already trading on a regular basis with the ports of New Orleans and St. Louis, the products shipped by steamers and some along the Texas road by overland wagons.

In Philadelphia he entered into an association with James Stapler, a Quaker merchant, who was fascinated by the operations of the Cherokee people. "Thou hast a whole new market to offer the world, Chief Ross. I don't mind saying, I'm pleased at the opportunity to be a part of it."

"It may be slow, at first," John warned. "We've still got a long way to go until we can consider our lands flourishing."

"I'll wait. In the meantime, go thou ahead and draw on our new account for whatever is needed to bring thy nation to a fruitful position. We'll get our money back many times."

John went to New Orleans to purchase slaves. He took Bryce along with him, wanting the boy to see a thriving city. John's first piece of business was the hiring of an overseer experienced in slavery, Hank Dall, a physically powerful man who stood nearly six-and-a-half feet tall, wore a heavy black beard but was totally bald, and who had an ability to listen.

John instructed him: "Select the best field and house hands you can find in New Orleans. Keep in mind that as Chief, my home is open to my people and I want it to be well managed. My cotton fields will go far toward the support of the plantation, so I must have expert workers."

The new overseer bought three young blacks to be headmen. They were allowed a little power in their work, standing as driver-guards over the other hands. They were equipped with whips and were instructed to deliver a dozen blows upon the backs of any lazy or rebellious workers. If further discipline was needed, they were ordered to refer the problem to the overseer. The headmen also held keys to all the work buildings on the plantation. It was their special duty to dole out the daily food rations to each slave family, as well as to distribute winter and summer clothing.

Dall had purchased families, his long experience proving that the unbroken family unit not only provided both house and field hands but made far superior workers to those who grieved for relatives sold "down the river." Hank was also careful to check into their abilities. He brought experienced bricklayers, carpenters, mechanics, and blacksmiths to Rose Cottage, as well as field-hands and house servants.

The quarters which awaited them at just-completed Rose Cottage were the most comfortable they had ever seen. By the rise of the sun the morning after their arrival, he had them working in the fields and in the house.

Rose Cottage, set upon its little hill, its wide verandas and its pillars encircling the two-storied frame house, was dominant over the other buildings on the land. The slave quarters were virtually a small town spread beneath the mansion.

The blacksmith and cooper shops had been completed first of all because their services were constantly needed by the work crew constructing the other buildings. The cook shop was a large building with four huge chimneys. The slaves' meals were prepared there three times a day and distributed to them outside. They could eat at the cook shop or take their food to their own individual cabins, as they preferred, though most ate the food prepared for them.

The infirmary was equipped with medical supplies and emergency beds. Doctor Spencer Mattern, recently arrived from New Orleans, would stay in his own rooms available at the infirmary.

John, lying in bed at Rose Cottage for the first time, was restless. He lay on his back and stared at the dark ceiling. Quatie! What had it been like, having her? He frowned into the night. What had her softness been like? The scent of her, had he forgotten? He tossed the blankets and sheet aside and swung his naked legs over the side of the bed to sit upright in the dark.

The windows faced the east so that he could see the rise of each morning's sun, but now he gazed blankly into the night. A loneliness such as he had never known, except at the new grave of Quatie, swept into his heart. He got up, dressed, and strode out into the night, walking rapidly toward the stream below his lands. He recognized his cause of restlessness, his inability to sleep, for what it was. He looked toward the lights of the slaves' quarters. There were long-limbed, full-breasted dusky young women there, legally his. All he had to do was send for one of them. But he could take no woman without love.

He looked up at the sky again and saw that the stars had moved their positions, sliding into dawn. He walked home slowly, glancing at the Morning Star which was beginning to fade.

XXXIII

IN THE LATE SUMMER AND EARLY FALL OF 1844, JOHN MADE a visit to Washington and checked in at the Globe Hotel. He went the rounds of the offices of his congressional friends to bring himself up-to-date on progress in relations between his Nation and the Union.

Democrat James Polk and Whig Henry Clay were campaigning for the White House. Old Andrew Jackson had urged the nomination of Polk, who had served as Speaker of the House during his second term in office. To make certain that the Democrats nominated his choice, the former President called many of them to the Hermitage, where he impressed them as a host and as a political sage. But John feared the election of James Polk would mean another long delay in justice for the Cherokee Nation.

"Don't despair if he is elected," Henry Clay told him. "Just remember, the Congress has always been within a vote or two of giving you complete support. No matter who is President, the day will come when Congress sees justice done you."

During John's stay in Washington, he was invited to attend a colorful event held in the Supreme Court chamber. Along with many government officials and their guests, he was witness to a demonstration by Samuel Finley Breese Morse, inventor of the magnetic telegraph. The awed audience was absolutely silent as the instrument under Morse's fingers transmitted to Philadelphia the message: "What hath God wrought?"

That amazing event was followed by an invitation from Senator Clay to visit the newly completed National Observatory, set upon a hill between the White House and the Potomac River. John, with others, stood absorbed, gazing toward the sparkling heavens through a revolving dome.

A week later, in James Stapler's Philadelphia office, John arose from his chair at the unexpected entrance of a young woman.

She was very young, exquisitely beautiful with large, velvet-brown eyes. Her face was delicate, but her full lips were curved in a smile. Her dark brown hair was smooth under a ruffled bonnet of dark green and white, which matched her dress. She carried a Bible.

"Father," she said to Stapler, "forgive me for interrupting, but thou hast forgot thy Bible for thy prayer meeting. I know thou hast it marked for reading this evening and thou wouldst want it."

James Stapler led his daughter across the room. "Chief Ross, my daughter, Mary." The father looked at the daughter, smiling. "Mary, this is John Ross, Chief of the Cherokee Nation. We're associated in the cotton business."

John took her tiny hand in its lacy glove and bowed. James Stapler, confounded by their mutual silence, rushed into the verbal void: "Thank thee, Mary, for bringing me the Book."

Mary seemed not to hear her father. She asked John: "Thou art Cherokee?"

John's voice was a trifle shaky: "I am."

She smiled. "Thou art a strange-looking Indian."

"Mary!" her father was shocked. He turned to John: "The younger generation has no respect at all for its elders. Still, at eighteen years of age, my daughter ought to possess it."

Staggered that Mary Stapler was only eighteen, John quickly reckoned the differences in their ages and was horrified to realize that he was thirty-six years older than she. He could not collect his thoughts. He knew only that he had to get away from her presence and never see her again. "Mr. Stapler," he said, "if you don't mind, I'd like to continue our conversation at another time." He dragged his gaze away from the girl, adding a fabricated excuse: "I've forgotten an appointment at my hotel."

Mr. Stapler nodded, a little puzzled. "Certainly, Chief Ross. Any time."

The two men shook hands. John gave Mary a bow and moved to the door.

"Chief Ross!" she called.

He turned to face her, a silent pleading in his eyes. "Miss Stapler?"

"Chief Ross, I need an escort to a charity ball Friday evening. It's a very worthy cause. Wouldst thou do me the honor?"

"Mary Stapler!" her outraged father interceded.

Mary's smile fled and she looked almost frightened. "I'm sorry. Perhaps thou art married and wouldst like to escort thy wife?"

John was very solemn. "Miss Stapler, I'm a widower." He added, almost truculently: "I'm fifty-four years old. I've four sons and a daughter, all older than you."

She was smiling again. "Widower Ross, will thou be my escort? Thou hast not said."

John's grin was like a boy's, and he gave her a bow. "Miss Stapler, it would be a very great honor."

During the next few weeks John became the only escort of Mary Bryan Stapler, and when he was due to return to the Nation, he was arguing with himself to no avail. Age, race, reason—nothing mattered. He did not want to go home without her.

He hired a carriage and invited her for a drive around the city. It was a hot August night. Dark clouds had begun to move in over the city at sunset, and there was the grateful scent of a rain in the offing. When it was dark and the night hid his face a little from her gaze, he pulled the carriage to the side of a road. "Mary, I've got to go home next week."

"Father told me thy plans," she confessed her knowledge. A flash of lightning illuminated them and they saw each other clearly. She put out her hands to him. "I want to go with thee, John."

He held her off when she would have come into his arms. "No!"

Rebuffed, she held her silence for a moment. Then she lifted his hands, placing each palm against her cheeks. "Dost thou feel the warmth of me?"

"Mary—"

"My face is hot from a blush thou canst feel but cannot see. It is the only concession I make to maidenly decorum." Thunder rocked the carriage. "John Ross, I love thee."

"No, you can't! I'm too old for you! I'm Cherokee! There's no way—"

"There's a way, John," she told him, giving herself into his arms.

A little later, quietly conversing, John spoke of Rose Cottage mentioning that the slaves' quarters at Rose Cottage were the finest west of the Mississippi.

Her shock had been visible. "Slaves! Oh, John! Thou dost not own people!"

"Why, of course I've got slaves on my plantation. I assumed you knew that."

She shook her head. "No. Loving thee, I never assumed thou wouldst hold people in slavery." She was on the verge of tears.

Alarmed, he took her hands. "Does it make a difference in how you feel about me, Mary?"

She was very pale. "I'm not certain," she shook her head unhappily. "I'm disappointed, I know. Slaves! That thou shouldst enslave anyone!"

"Perhaps you want to think about our marriage anew."

"If thou canst give me a little time? I'm so sorry, John, but I must be by myself and think about it."

He thought he might never see her again, and at one point, he seriously considered leaving Philadelphia without any further talk. He was causing her trouble, the last thing on earth he wanted to do, but to leave without a word would only hurt her more.

Finally she sent him a note inviting him to see her at her father's home. A servant opened the front door of the three-storied brick home and led him to the library. For a few minutes he paced the floor, glancing at the bookshelves.

The door opened and Mary was there.

She smiled, but her eyes were moist. "I love thee. If thou still lovest me, take me home with thee."

"But—the slaves?"

"The slaves are on thy conscience, John, not mine. And the more I've thought of that, the more I've realized that I have but to leave the matter there. You, see, I know thee better than thou knowest thyself. It will be all right, in the end."

"I'm not certain I know what you're saying, except that you love me," John said. "That's all I want to know."

John was able to reach numerous relatives in the east who responded joyfully to his wedding invitation. But his happiest moment came when his parents, despite their advancing age and illnesses, accepted his invitation to attend.

On the second of September, 1844, the day of their marriage, John was plagued with the doubts he had known since the beginning. Ought he let Mary accept the life he had to offer her? She had already been shunned by some of her former friends for her intention of marrying an Indian. He knew they were whispering and joking about the differences in the ages of the bride and groom, and that many of her friends considered him an aging aborigine whose lustful desires were directed at an innocent white girl.

Mr. Stapler had objected only mildly: "The difference in your ages is tremendous. It could eventually ruin a marriage between ye."

John had asked him: "You say nothing about the fact that I am Cherokee. I would think your opposition to the marriage would be on a racial basis."

James Stapler gave him a steady look. "As a Quaker, I see only the divine light in all men. That light shines in thee, as it does in Mary, as it does in me. I trust my daughter to that light." He added, a hand on John's shoulder, "If I did not recognize God's divine light in thee, I would be a sinner."

At the ceremony, Mary was attended by her sister and brother. When she made her vows before their families and guests, he wanted to drop to his knees in thanks to God for such a gift as her love.

The bold wiles Mary had displayed from the moment of their meeting vanished when they were first alone in their hotel room. She sat fully clothed on the big bed, a tight little smile on her face, as John began to undress.

"Mary? Is anything wrong?"

"No," she replied hesitantly. She got up and went to her luggage, set on a marble-topped table at the foot of the bed, opened a bag and began searching through it. Naked, he went to her side.

Mary turned to him, her hand brushing his skin. Startled, she turned back to the luggage, her words flustered: "My nightgown. It's here—I can't find it—it's very pretty, you know—"

"I'm sure it is, Mary. But you won't need it."

Her shyness gave way to his caresses and his erotic whisperings. She gave him all that she had promised him from the very first look. When he slept, it was in her relaxed embrace.

Their marriage was a topic of interest to eastern and southern society. The sense of scandal which accompanied the news that an Indian Chief of fifty-four years had married an eighteen-year-old white Philadelphia heiress was reflected even in the story carried by *The New York Times*, which described the wedding with a tone of derision:

> John Ross, the celebrated Cherokee Chief, was married in the President's Parlor of the Hartwell's Washington House, Philadelphia, last night to Miss Mary Bryan Stapler. He is about 55 and she is only 18 years of age; she is a very beautiful girl and highly accomplished. Her father is a highly respected merchant.
>
> She was given away by her brother and attended by her sister and a niece of John Ross as bridesmaids.
>
> After the ceremony a family party of 20 of the Ross's (all half-breed Indians) sat down to a most sumptuous banquet.
>
> Ross is considered to be worth half a million dollars. He proposes to sojourn with his beautiful bride at the Washington House for a short time; after which he goes straight to his wild home in the South Western prairies.

The trip west was made partly by train, largely by river steamboat, with stagecoaches used to make connections between the two steam-propelled modes of transportation. Mary's sense of the delicate and private suffered considerably, but her pronounced interest in the people they met helped her adjust to the rigors of the travel.

Sharing a room with other women at night in strange houses or stations was the worst of it. Longing to be behind a locked door with her husband, she was thrust into the midst of women who seemed to be from another world.

At a private house in Louisiana, she stood in a line outdoors to await her turn at the water bowl. The morning air was a welcome relief from the stuffiness of the room in which she had been confined all night. Sleep had been practically impossible.

The owner of the house, a gray-haired woman dressed in calico, approached her. "This be your first trip west, honey?"

Mary nodded. "Yes, it is."

"You look a mite peaked," the old woman said, shifting her glance to a plug of tobacco she held in her wrinkled hand. She lifted her skirt to pull a stick from her garter. Giving Mary a snaggletoothed smile, she plunged the little stick into the plug of tobacco and offered it to Mary. "Here, child, this will put the roses in yer cheek."

Mary backed away from the offering. "No, thank thee."

"Don't chew, eh? Well, I ain't one to offer no snuff box. That powdery stuff's bad fer ye. A good chaw is better, I says."

Mary smiled. "I thank thee, ma'am, but I don't use tobacco at all."

The old woman nodded and spat. "Just makin' me civilities, lady."

Mary was glad to leave the trains and station stops behind and to sail aboard a well-equipped steamboat where they had their own cabin and their privacy.

John, still disturbed by the stir their marriage had made, was becoming uneasy about the reception Mary might receive in Tahlequah, about the attitude his sons and Jane might take toward his bride, younger than all of them. Mary noted his increasing silence.

"Thou art troubled. I think I know why, John. Thou art not certain thy family will be happy to meet me."

He took her into his arms. "They'll be surprised."

"I'll love all of them because they are a part of thee."

They came to Fort Gibson's docking in the twilight hours of an early fall evening. Soldiers from the fort and a dozen civilians were there to bring the steamboat into its harbor of natural rock.

General Arbuckle, called from his dinner by an aide, came hurrying from the fort to greet John as he guided Mary off the steamer. The General showed his surprise and bowed to the couple, his shrewd eyes on the beautiful young bride.

John's pride was obvious. "General Arbuckle, may I present you to my wife?"

The General took Mary's hand. "An honor, Mrs. Ross," he murmured.

"It's a pleasure to meet thee, General." Mary looked up at the fort on the crest of the hill beyond. "John has told me Fort Gibson is a welcome sight in this land, and so it is."

John asked: "Is there a carriage available to us, General, or shall I send for one?"

General Arbuckle put aside any thought that he might have a discussion with John regarding the continuing problems of the Nation. "Certainly we've got a rig." He turned to Mary: "We'll get you home speedily, Mrs. Ross."

The carriage sped away from the fort, leaving behind the General and a group of young soldiers who, not without envy, remarked laconically among themselves upon the beauty of the bride and the age of the groom. A sergeant took the privates to task: "What the hell—he's got to be performin' as good as he looks, or she wouldn't look so damned in love."

"Half-breeds brag they got ways with wimmen. This one sure has—enough money to buy any white girl."

An aroused young private licked his lips. "Whatever it took, he's got her to crawl into his bed. That's more than we got, boy!"

Crossing a bridge over the stream running the lower lands of Park Hill, the carriage headed up a slope and rounded a shrub-covered curve in the road. Ahead, standing grandly on its hill above the newly harvested fields, was Rose Cottage. The house was agleam with lights both upstairs and down. Unseen smoke drifted from the chimneys, scenting the crisp air.

Mary leaned forward on the seat of the carriage. "How beautiful!"

"I told you about Quatie's roses. Well, I've had them planted along the drive. I'm hoping they will bloom next spring."

She squeezed his hand. "They will," she said. "For her, they will. Thou failed to describe Rose Cottage in adequate terms, John!"

He smiled at her. "Well, how could I do better than *The New York Times*, Mary? This is your wild home."

A servant assisted them from the carriage, bowing to them. Mary realized this man was John's slave; and a shiver went over her. John told the servant to bring in the luggage stowed at the back of the rig and in the morning to send a wagon to Fort Gibson for the rest of their baggage.

John led Mary to the spacious dining room lit by a glittering chandlier. The long table was beautifully set with silver, lace cloth, and flowers from the fall garden.

His family turned to him. Alan and Jennie, Jim and Sarah, Silas, George and Bryce, Jane and Return stared at him, surprised. There he stood, hand in hand with a young and gorgeous woman, a stranger.

Jane was the first on her feet, but she stood stunned, unable to speak. Mary smiled at them. "I'm Mary, thy father's wife. I'm so happy to be home with ye."

Jane came around the table to approach the couple. Her solemn face was radiant with a smile. She went to Mary and hugged her, her words almost sung: "Oh, Mary! Mary! How glad we are to have you!"

One by one, the Ross children came forward to be clasped in the arms of their new mother. Eight-year-old Bryce hung shyly in the background until John fetched him forward. "This is our youngest, Mary. This is Bryce Calvin."

Mary's hand touched the boy's dark hair. She said: "Bryce Calvin, thy father loves thee very much. I love thee, just as he does. Wilt thou give me a kiss?"

"Well, mostly I don't kiss."

She smiled, and bent over him, offering him her cheek. He responded, giving her a light touch of his lips. She said: "Thank thee, Bryce. That was a lovely welcome home."

His children accepted his new marriage with such enthusiasm that it was obvious they had been hoping he would find a woman to share his life.

As Jane had said, "I've prayed there would be someone like you for Father, and here you are!"

Discussing the marriage with Alan, John said: "I wasn't certain how you all would take it. Especially because of the vast separation in our ages. And because she's white."

Alan grinned. "Oh, we were surprised, all right. But Mary is just right for you, Father." He winked. "I suppose you'll be raising a whole new family before long."

"Nothing could make me happier."

Alan laughed. "Or keep you younger!"

"It looks to me like nothing is going to keep me from becoming a grandfather. Jennie's blooming, isn't she?"

Alan beamed. "You noticed? She thought you did. Well, it's true. The Ross family is expanding, come late spring. Not just through us, either. Jim and Sarah think they're well on the way, too."

John was vastly pleased. "Maybe God will bless Mary and me in the next few years."

XXXIV

BUT THE GOOD LIFE ON THE PLANTATION WAS NOT matched in the welfare of the Nation. The legacy of the three assassinated national leaders continued in terrible spasmodic episodes of personal revenge and counterrevenge. The Nation's reputation suffered as word of thirty-three new murders swept the vast Indian territory. The tribes of the Creek, Seminole, Choctaw, and Chickasaw looked askance at the violence in the Cherokee Nation.

Chief Opothle Yohola of the Creeks, long an admirer and friend of John, sent him word suggesting that action be taken against civilian disorder at Tahlequah before it spread to other areas of the territory.

John sent a report of the situation to Yohola, detailing his effort to gain recognition as Chief of the constitutional government of the Cherokees. As it was now, he headed a divided people subject to the military discipline of General Arbuckle at Fort Gibson.

On the eighth of June, 1845, Andrew Jackson expired at the Hermitage. But his policies lived on in the White House. The following April, President Polk responded to an appeal of a committee of the Treaty party, led by Stand Watie, and asked Congress to divide the Cherokee Nation West into two separate political areas. The division would create a Cherokee government for each section, abolishing the Nation as it now stood.

John hurried to Washington, leaving Mary, who was expecting her first child, at home. In the capital city he immediately went into consultation sessions with his congressional supporters on a plan to defeat the presidential proposal.

In May 1846, a month after John's proposal was submitted to Congress, President Polk answered the argument the American nation was having with the Mexican government over land claims with a request for a declaration of war from the Congress. The Mexican Army had fired upon American troops en route to California on presidential order, under General Zachary Taylor. The President claimed the American troops were on American soil, contrary to the claim of the Mexicans.

Henry Clay told John that the President might be too concerned now with the Mexican War to give much time to pressing the division of the Cherokee Nation. "But I swear, Henry, if I have to stand and fight him, I will do it. I aim to preserve, protect, and defend my government, as I have taken an oath to do before my people and God." He shook his head. "I'll never accept the division of the Cherokee Nation. The United States Congress will not accept it, either."

Senator Clay was right. The legislation was defeated, the Congress upholding Chief Ross's militant opposition of the idea of division. Stand Watie and his delegation went home in bitter defeat.

President Polk was not through, however. As Jackson might have done, he created a commission with authority to investigate the Cherokee national situation and sent west a three-man board in the persons of Colonel Rogers Jones, Adjutant General of the United States Army; Lieutenant Colonel R. B. Mason of the United States Dragoons; and Governor Pierce M. Butler, who was appointed to the position formerly held by Governor Montfort Stokes.

George Lowrey, John's Acting Chief in his absence, placed himself and the office of Chief at the service of the military board. They met at Fort Gibson and at Rose Cottage where Mary, upon Lowrey's request, opened the Nation's files to the men. Lowrey had a letter from John advising and guiding him through the talks with the American officers.

There was swift action on the matter, and on the sixth day of August, 1846, John, totally triumphant, took a major role in a ceremonial signing of a new treaty between his Nation and the Union. The Treaty of New Echota was declared null and void. The struggle was over.

To honor his position as recognized Chief of the Cherokee West, John went to the White House ceremony in white buckskin and a feathered bonnet of scarlet and white—the colors of success and peace united. Tiny bells of silver were intertwined in the fringes of his outfit.

President Polk, raised in Tennessee by Scotch-Irish parents, bore a physical likeness to John. Dressed for the treaty occasion in a new frock coat and white silk shirt with a broad cravat of black silk, he was dignified and respectful toward his guests. Stand was conservatively clothed in a dark broadcloth suit, but his expression was unhappy and his face a deeper hue than usual.

The new treaty gave the Cherokees all that John had long fought to obtain. The new treaty would also give his people their long due monies. Their independence as a nation was established. A military agreement of mutual interest and responsibility now existed between the Indian Nation and the Union.

President Polk remarked that the treaty would begin a new era of progress for the Indian Nation and guarantee a brotherhood between the white and red nations. "My congratulations, Chief Ross. Your constancy toward the principle of peace and unity has never faltered and brings your people now to a new beginning."

Clasping the President's forearm in the Cherokee form of friend touching friend, John added a pledge: "The Cherokee Nation will honor the treaty signed today for as long as stars shine down upon our mutual lands. This is my word."

When it was Stand's turn to take the President's hand, he did not smile. "The Treaty is very fine for John Ross and his people. It is very bad for the Treaty Party. Yet we accept it that there may be peace among us."

"The Treaty requires immediate payments to the heirs of the Ridges and Mr. Boudinot," President Polk reminded him: "In this we have tried to show our concern for all the Cherokee people."

"It is appreciated, Mr. President."

The President looked from Stand to John. "Would you shake hands with Chief Ross, Mr. Watie?"

Stand stepped back from the President. It seemed that he was not going to answer. Then, flicking a barbed glance at John, he shook his head. "I am defeated in politics this day. Yet my heart and my will stand aloof from John Ross, and I oppose him now, as always. No, Mr. President. The new treaty does not require that I take the hand of John Ross. I will not."

John said: "So be it." From this moment, he could no longer deceive himself: he and Stand Watie were to be eternal foes.

John became eager to get home and the trip had never seemed so long. As he neared Rose Cottage, he felt the weight of the world on him, a new responsibility. There was so much to be done.

Within two weeks after his arrival home, Mary gave birth to their son, dark-haired, blue-eyed, fair-skinned John. Named for his father at Mary's insistence, the baby was adored from the beginning.

Ten-year-old Bryce, looking down at the infant asleep in its cradle beside Mary's bed, commented: "When he's big enough, I'll teach him many things."

Mary smiled, "What dost thou want to teach him, Bryce?"

"That he is Cherokee."

Mary repeated the remark to John, who was touched. "Bryce is afraid the baby is going to be spoiled. He told me he thinks John is treated as though he were a girl child."

"So he is, for a time. But when he's ready, I'll send him out to hunt with Bryce."

Mary and John had both believed their second child would be another boy, but within sixteen months, they were delighted by the birth of Annie Bryan. Annie was a tiny baby, her health of some concern during her first few months of life, but by the time she took her first steps she was in robust health.

The Treaty of 1846 brought a peace to the Cherokee Nation.

Tahlequah, incorporated the same year John brought Mary home as a bride, was booming as the capital city. Word of the modern town reached the other nations in the territory where civilization was not so spectacularly evident. Chief Opothle Yohola traveled to Tahlequah at John's invitation to see all that was being accomplished there.

Riding through the streets with John in the fancy black victoria John had recently imported from Philadelphia, the blanketed, aging Chief of the Creeks was astounded at the sight of Tahlequah. The Negro driver turned back the top of the victoria so they could have a better view of the sights as they rode.

John and the Council had guided the rising of the downtown section. Stores and business houses were built around the public square. Prominent among the buildings were those of the *Cherokee Advocate*, the weekly newspaper; the jail; the Supreme Court; the Temperance Hall; and the Masonic Temple. A brick building housed offices of two dentists, a doctor, and several lawyers.

One of the showplaces on the public square was the National Hotel, a two-storied edifice designed and constructed by a Mormon who, passing through Tahlequah on his way to California, stayed long enough to give the town its grandest building. Within days of its opening the National and its dining rooms offered meals on a par with those of any hotel in St. Louis.

The people of Tahlequah were colorfully dressed, most of them mingling between white and Indian fashions. One bronze-skinned fellow, his dark hair parted in the center and braided, tipped his tall silk hat to the Chiefs as they rode past. The women wore calico dresses, their full skirts swinging as they walked along. There were a few turbaned heads, but many wore buckskins and headbands with a decorative feather or jewel.

"You see," John smiled, "one thing we agree upon in our dress here in Tahlequah is color."

"I see that your people are just like the whites. The Creeks have no sense this way."

They drove to the sites of men's and women's seminaries which were being constructed near Park Hill. The buildings were designed much like southern mansions in style, featuring great pillars and chimneys. Their cost was great, but little considered against the effect they would have upon the youth.

As evening neared, John took his guest to the National Hotel

for dinner. The old man enjoyed every bite of a steak dinner, taking his time. It was late when at last he sat back and said: "Enough."

John wanted him to stay another day, but the Chief shook his head. "No. I go home. I have seen enough. Now I must light my pipe at home and sit and think about what I have seen."

In 1851, another girl was born to Mary and named for her. There was another wedding, George marrying Nancy Ottolifter. At the same time, Silas was engaged to marry Nannie Stiff. There were new grandchildren, nieces, and nephews. Lewis's daughter wed George Murrell, who gave her Hunter's Home, an exquisite mansion that gained a reputation as one of the finest in all America.

But in spite of everything, a crisis was building at Rose Cottage. John, sensitive to Mary's every mood, became increasingly aware that she found it impossible to live with slavery. One day she was tending the roses in the driveway when the sound reached her ears of a whip on a bared back, followed by the cry of the victim. Mary had run to the house and locked herself in her bedroom. Later, she told him: "If I hadn't fled to the bedroom, I'd have tried to take the whip from the headman's hand. I know what that would have done to thy authority, so I ran and hid."

The day little Mary was a year old, Hank Dall came to the door and requested an interview with Mary. Puzzled, since John handled all matters pertaining to Hank's work, she had him brought to the library.

He came to the door carrying a very-dark-skinned little slave, a girl who wore a clean cotton dress but no shoes. She was sucking on her thumb and had been crying, her large eyes still tear-filled.

"Is something wrong?" Mary asked.

Hank grinned. "Ma'am, this is Tobia. She's a gift for little Miss Mary." He half-apologized, "Well, just a pet now, mind you, but later on, a valuable servant for her. She can raise her just as she likes." He added: "She's a year older than Miss Mary."

Mary's voice shook. "A pet! A gift! For my daughter! This infant—" She reached for the child. "Give her to me." There was such anger in Mary that her hands were shaking. Hank put the baby into her arms, backing away. "Whose child is she?"

"She's out of Tinya, by Parry."

"Thou means that Tinya and Parry are her parents?"

"Yes, Ma'am."

"Thou mayst go, Hank."

Holding the child, Mary went to John's office, next to the library, and knocked on the door.

"Who is it?"

"Thy wife," she told him through gritted teeth.

She swept past him and stood in the large room, dwarfed by the size of it and the heavy furniture. John closed the door, not certain whether she was going to faint or pick up some object and hurl it at him. "Hank Dall has just brought this baby to me as a birthday present for Mary. Dost thou hear me, John Ross? This innocent child—a pet, he called her."

"It's a gesture well meant, Mary. In the South, most women of slave-owning husbands have small slaves as pets. They keep them in their bedrooms and consider them their toys. By the time they're five years old, they send them back to their own quarters. It's just a custom."

"A custom! There is a more ancient custom, Mister Ross, that I honor. It is the custom of mother love and humanity. This child is going back to her mother's arms. As for me, I am going to have to leave this place, John! I can't endure it any longer, the cruelty and the hopelessness of thy slavery."

She ran past him, eluding his reach, hurried out of the house and across the wide lawns, carrying Tobia, who was beginning to cry. John ran after her, heedless of all the dark faces who turned to look at them.

She went to the cabin area of the slaves' quarters. She did not have to search for Tinya. The young black woman, surrounded by a half-dozen other slaves, was kneeling in front of her cabin, Parry leaning over her imploringly as one of the headmen advanced on them, a whip ready in his hand.

Mary took the child to the weeping woman. "Tinya, here is thy little baby. Don't grieve, she is not to be taken from thee."

The black girl was on her feet. "Oh, Tobia!" She took the baby in her arms and sobbed.

"Take thy baby into thy home. She needs thy love and attention."

John finally reached her. "Mary, come. We've got to talk."

For the first time she pulled away from his touch. She looked at the headman who stood by, his gaze leveled angrily at Parry.

"Wilt thou give orders that Tinya and her family are not to be touched by the headman?"

John nodded at the headman: "Get back to the fields. You're not to lay a hand on Tinya, Parry, or their child. Do you understand?"

The big black man backed off. "Yes, sir."

John said to the baby's parents: "You two, do as Mrs. Ross asks. Take the child into your cabin and close the door. The day is yours. Tobia will not be taken from you."

Mary walked ahead of John all the way back to the house, her back stiff. She headed toward the staircase, but he took her by the hand. Back in his office, he spoke very quietly: "Mary, I can't bear to see you so unhappy. All I want is your love and respect, and if I don't have it, nothing else matters."

Her eyes were full of pain. "Oh, John! Thou knowest I love thee and respect thee. But lately, I've come to see this slavery as a flaw in thy character that terrifies me. John, how canst thou, who lovest freedom for thyself and thy people, enslave others?"

"Mary, I've seen how you feel in the past few months. It's making you pale and quiet. Now, God forbid, it threatens to take your love from me!" He led her gently to his desk, opened a drawer, and pulled out a bound stack of papers. "Look at the papers, Mary. There is how I feel about slavery."

She read the paper on top, and her face lighted. Quickly she leafed through them, reading a bit on each page. She lifted a face of joy to him, "These are emancipation papers for thy blacks! Every one of them!"

"Yes, Mary, I'm giving them their freedom." He smiled, as she came into his arms. "Thou hast made a Quaker of me in my heart."

"No, thou hast seen the holy light in each of them, as thou seest it in me and in thy family."

In the next days John consulted with Mary, Hank Dall, and the headmen, evolving a liberation plan at Rose Cottage. The freedom was officially granted on a bright Sunday morning at a gathering on the lawn in front of the house. The Ross family and Hank Dall stood on the front veranda, facing the blacks below on the grass.

John stood at a table on which lay the documents of liberation. Mary sat in a chair beside the table, holding her youngest daughter. Jim, Alan, Silas, and George stood at the veranda railing, their wives and children seated on the grass to the left of the steps, apart from the blacks. Bryce perched on the railing.

John spoke to the slaves, "My family and I are giving you freedom." He touched a stack of the papers. "There is a liberation document here for each of you. Your names appear on the papers and I have signed mine, declaring you are free. In a few minutes, I want you to come forward and get your papers. Mr. Dall will help us."

The blacks, kneeling on the grass, linked their arms and began a chant which sounded like a moaning, and they started a rocking motion.

"We are not sending any of you away if you don't want to go." He told them of the plan of paid work for them, if they wanted it, adding he hoped most of them would decide to stay. "For those of you who stay and learn a trade with which you can earn a living away from Rose Cottage, we'll have a money bonus. If any of you ever need help, come home to Rose Cottage. We will be ready to lend you a hand. If there are some of you who want to farm, we'll show you how and help you build it."

Hank came forward and told the blacks: "The fields at Rose Cottage still need good hands to work them. The Chief's home still requires service. You're needed here and we hope you'll stay."

John then introduced Mary, saying: "Mrs. Ross has a word to say to you." The blacks quieted and got to their feet, facing her, smiling.

"We just want ye to know that whether ye go or stay, we ask God's blessing upon ye." She looked over their faces. "Would one of ye come forward and offer a prayer for all of us at Rose Cottage?"

A bald young man, his sweating head shining, came slowly up the steps, to stand beside the Rosses. His prayer was brief: "Lord, you been good to us. Help us to be free folks." He lifted his head, raised his arms, spreading his fingers heavenward, and fervently shouted: "Jesus! Jesus! Jesus!" He went down to his knees, covering his face with his big hands while the blacks on the lawn chanted, "Praise the Lord!" over and over.

Mary turned to John, tears on her face. He put an arm around her. They watched together as the freed people swung from their religious chants to singing and dancing.

Their emotional celebration kept on for hours. At their quar-

ters they prepared and enjoyed a special meal. The sun was sinking when they finally came back to the veranda to receive their papers one by one.

That night, John admitted: "I've been liberated, too. Mary, it's a great feeling to be free of slavery." He kissed her mouth and murmured against it: "Thanks, for freeing me."

"Forgive me for not knowing that thou wouldst free them. I ought to have known."

"How could you?"

She shivered a little, and moved closer against him. "I'm so proud of thee, my darling." She stroked his shoulder. "But I'm not free."

"What do you mean?" he asked huskily against her throat.

"I am thy slave," she whispered.

XXXV

IN THE FOLLOWING DAYS, JOHN AND MARY WERE GRATIFIED to learn that almost all the former slaves had chosen to stay at Rose Cottage. A number left to establish their own small farms, with the financial and moral support of the Rosses.

That fall Bryce was sent east to school, and for the next six years he excelled in schools in Philadelphia and Virginia. But he longed for the territory and was brought home during any prolonged vacation. During those days at home he was a constant companion to John, riding with him wherever he went. John Junior, a studious boy more white than Indian, was often invited along, but he was still very young and obviously more interested in books than in the trail.

The sight of John and Bryce riding the Nation became a familiar one. They needed no other company for days on end and they could pass long hours without even having to speak to each other.

It was always John's longing for Mary which turned them back to Rose Cottage.

In 1857, the federal government made a surprising move and removed all of its military command, vacating Fort Gibson entirely and turning it into the hands of the Cherokee.

At first Fort Gibson had been a frontier post with only a few men assigned to it for one purpose: protection against the wild Indians for white hunters. It was rugged duty and the Army took to sending its young career officers there on their first active assignments following graduation at West Point, to toughen their hides. Jefferson Davis had come there directly from the Point and gone on to fame as a military leader with his Mississippi Rifles.

In its last years of activity, Fort Gibson had developed into a real community as officers and men fanned outward to establish homes, which in turn brought stores and schools. Many Americans took Cherokee wives and half-blood children home with them. The homes they left behind were soon filled with Cherokee citizens, and the fort became a community center.

"There were times when I would have been glad to see the military go," John told Mary. "But now, with something like revolution approaching in the states, I'm not certain the Union ought to have abandoned the fort."

In the spring of 1859, Bryce graduated from the University of Virginia and returned to the Nation to discuss his future plans with John. He wanted to serve the Indian Nation through the federal government, selecting the War Department as a place where he could seek employment as scout and interpreter. "I feel I can do a great deal for our people by working from inside the federal apparatus."

John, seeing the sense of it, nevertheless argued that the Nation needed him too.

"In time, I will come home," Bryce replied. "First let me get the background I want."

In July John and Bryce had an experience which was to affect the younger man for life. Canoeing down the Illinois River late one afternoon, they beached their craft and carried some of their gear ashore to make camp for the night. Looking for a clearing in the heavy underbrush, they found an adequate tree-locked area halfway between the river and a dirt road they had often ridden which angled off to Tahlequah, about five miles away. They built a campfire and were cooking dinner when footsteps told them someone was approaching.

A voice called: "Brother, we come in peace! We'd like to share your campfire for—" the words stopped. Stand Watie stood in the ring of firelight, followed by a young woman in a white doeskin jacket and trousers. Her long black hair fell unhampered to her shoulders and her golden-skinned beauty suggested that she was a full-blood Cherokee.

Stand, totally surprised at the identity of the campers, said to the girl, "Go!" and gave her a shove toward the underbrush. Saying no more, he turned and followed her.

Abruptly, they heard a scream come from the unseen girl in the brush, and Stand's shout: "Copper!"

John and Bryce dropped the utensils and rushed to them, oblivious of the thorny underbrush. Stand had the girl in his arms and was heading back toward the fire. "She's been snakebit!" He put her down beside the fire, tore her moccasin from her foot and sliced the doeskin legging covering her left leg.

The snake bite, near the inside of her knee, was like two small pin punctures; blood was rising in them as the edges turned white. She tried to sit up but fell back, sick with shock.

Stand looked up at John. "I'll have to slash it!"

A shot sounded in the underbrush. John put a hand on Stand's, holding back the knife. "Wait! She would bleed too much from the knife, it's too close to a vein. There's a better way."

"What other way? There's no time to lose."

Bryce came to the fire, carrying the carcass of a rattlesnake, its head shot off. The writhing body stretched over three feet. Bryce tossed it onto the ground, took Stand's knife, and, ignoring its revolting gyrations, butchered the reptile.

Kneeling beside the girl, Bryce turned her over onto her stomach and taking a large section of the snake meat, he pressed the wet mass against the wound, holding it firmly.

John and Stand exchanged glances. Bryce was calmly applying an ancient tribal cure for rattlesnake bites. They stood silently over him as he waited until he was certain the poison had been drawn out of the wound, into the snake's remains.

Copper stirred. She peered up at Bryce and said: "I want to sit up." He and Stand helped her.

"In spite of the old tales, " John said, "I never was positive that this method was a remedy. It seems to be, in this case."

Stand was appalled. "You weren't sure? And you let him do it?"

"So did you, Stand, so did you. We both know your knife would have caused her death as surely as the snakebite. Bryce took the chance he had to take, and you owe him thanks."

"I knew it would work." Bryce said: "No thanks are necessary." He wiped off the knife and returned it to Stand.

Copper looked at Bryce. "Thank you."

"You'll be all right," he told her.

"You saved her life," Stand said. "I'm grateful. Now we go. Our canoe is not far."

"She ought to rest," John protested. "And it's too dark on the river."

Stand carried her past them, headed for the brush. "The moonlight will guide us. It is not far to Tahlequah. We do not stay in the camp of our enemy."

John put out a hand to Bryce, who would have answered Stand. "Let them go. It is as he says."

Stand took Copper away into the night.

"To lose a friend to death is always sad," John told Bryce; "yet I think it can't compare to the bitterness of losing one to enmity. Stand and I will never be friends again. It is painful to me to admit that we are enemies and will remain so."

Bryce, picking up one of the utensils, went to the fire. "She's very beautiful."

John had seen the way the two young people had looked at each other. "Forget her, Bryce. For a Ross to become interested in a Watie or a Boudinot would be courting trouble."

Bryce said no more, busying himself with the cooking of their dinner over the embers. But the following day, Bryce saddled his horse and rode the trail to the campsite beside the river, hoping Copper had returned there, too.

Copper was there, standing quietly beside her horse, waiting. She let him lead her by the hand to a fallen log where they sat close together. "I'm leaving for Washington next week to work for the War Department," he said. "I'll be gone until the Christmas holiday."

"You have to go?"

"Yes. In a year's time, I'll be transferred here as an agent. Until then, I must be in Washington."

She dug a moccasined toe into the leaves. "I will be lonely."

He turned her face to his. "You promise me you will be lonely? We're pledged, one to the other? They'll take you away from me, if they can."

"I know," she said, "My uncle told me he would rather see me dead than betrothed to any of the Rosses."

"He knows about us?"

She smiled. "He said he is not blind, that one look at us told him of a warmth between us."

"We'll have to meet here secretly, until I can plan our lives. Do you mind?"

Mary and John accompanied Bryce east to Washington, where he reported to the War Department and was immediately assigned to work.

John was astounded at the change in the capital. There were so many new buildings that he found it difficult to locate the old landmarks. The new Capitol building did not yet have its dome, and enormous marble blocks, with which it was to be constructed, stood waiting on the grounds to be lifted into place. The Library of Congress had been rebuilt from the fire of 1851 which had leveled its main building. The city was lighted by new gas lamps, and Mary prevailed upon John to walk with her along the avenue at twilight to see the lamplighter turn the gas flames up. The city was developing a sewer system, too, although the lines were not yet extensive enough to service the entire area.

They glimpsed President James Buchanan in his open carriage, returning from a visit to the Soldier's Home on the edge of the city where he spent some of the summer.

The long stay in Washington, which included attendance at plays at Grover's and Ford's theaters, was marred by an event which scandalized the country. Philip Barton Key, son of Francis Scott Key, was publicly murdered in Lafayette Square by Congressman Daniel Sickles. The younger Key had been the secret lover of the Congressman's wife. Having discovered his wife's adultery, the enraged Sickles went in search of the man and killed him on sight.

The trial resulted in the acquital of Congressman Sickles. The verdict's popularity was evidenced by the heavy applause from the audience in the courtroom.

Returning from Philadelphia, where Mary enjoyed a brief reunion with her relatives, John and she were made acutely aware of the political and emotional turmoil seizing the American people. Hurrying home, John knew that the rising crisis would be reflected among the Cherokee people.

XXXVI

BY THE EARLY WINTER OF 1861 THE AMERICAN STATES WERE divided, and armed men stood in a rebellion against the Union. As John had believed, the conflict moved into Indian territory, as people took personal stands for or against the Union's cause.

John, to demonstrate that the Cherokee Nation was bound by treaty and intent to the United States, erected a flagpole on the front lawns of Rose Cottage and personally raised the Stars and Stripes to the top.

Stand rode to the mansion accompanied by fifty young men, every one an expert rifleman and rider.

Each wore a decorative gold pin, a star encircled in gold, the symbol of the prosouthern Knights of the Golden Circle. They rode to the towering flagpole, forming a circle around it. Their voices lifted in the Rebel yell, bringing workers from the fields and servants from the house.

Stand broke his horse from the moving circle and rode to John and Mary. "We ask you to remove that flag. There has been no vote by the people that this nation is allied to the Union."

John's hands were clenched at his sides but he kept his temper. "This Nation is allied to the Union through treaty. The flag stays."

Stand pulled on the reins of his horse, kicked his belly with the heel of his moccasined foot, and raced away, waving his men after him. They sped away from Rose Cottage, traveling out to the Military Road toward Tahlequah.

Mary took John's arm. "I thought he was going to fight thee!"

"Stand *is* fighting me. He came here just to be certain I meant the raising of the flag as an official act in support of the Union. When he had his answer, he took off. The Cherokee Nation is divided again. I pray to God I can keep it from disaster."

The wind blew hard against them as they walked back to the house. Mary's concern was aroused. She asked: "Dost thou think Stand will sign a treaty without authorization or approval as he did before?"

"I don't know about that," John frowned, leading her by the hand, "but I'm certain he'll make contact with the Confederacy. He may already have done so. At least, he'll insist upon a vote of the people for or against the Union Treaty."

"John, dost thou believe the Confederacy is strong enough to move against the Union forces in the Southwest?"

"Yes, and they may seize the forts before President Lincoln can move to stop it. The southern troops are closer to them than reinforcements from the Union. It's very bad, Mary."

"Then, the territory is in extreme danger? And thou, John? How canst thou hold the Nation to the Union, against such odds?"

He shook his head. "I'm going to do it, Mary, because I must. But how?"

XXXVII

IN WASHINGTON, PRESIDENT LINCOLN SAT AT HIS DESK AND interrogated three government officials—Simon Cameron, Secretary of War; William Dole, the Commissioner of Indian Affairs; and Senator Jim Lane of Kansas—regarding the civil and military situation in the Indian territory. The President was a bit vexed by the lack of information he was receiving in response to his questions, and he was coming as close to sarcasm in his remarks as he had ever done.

His long-fingered hands pressed down firmly on a copy of *The New York Times* which lay on his desk. "Gentlemen, the *Times* is very inquisitive about our relations with the Indian Nations. And so am I.

"Now, your reports tell me that the Indian country south of Kansas is in the possession of insurgents from Texas and Arkansas. You say that the few loyal agents we have—those who volunteered to replace the agents who have joined the Rebels—have not been able to reach their posts! You say there is no communication now with the Indian territory or any of the governments within that territory, that we actually don't know what is happening there. Is that the sum of what I've just heard from you?"

Secretary Cameron moved uneasily in his chair: "It's about all we can give you now, Mister President. It's possible that the entire Indian territory, behind the blanket of silence, has gone to the Confederate flag."

President Lincoln shook his head. "No, I'm certain that's not so."

The Secretary asked stiffly: "Sir?"

"My study of the Indians assures me of one thing: If John Ross, Chief of the Cherokees, is alive, he will hold his Nation and the territory to our flag. I am certain he will honor our treaty. He will never desert it."

Commissioner Dole was excited: "John Ross! Mister President, his adopted son, Bryce Calvin, is one of our interpreters and scouts. He's given us his resignation just this day, said he was going home. I'm sorry, Mister President," the Secretary was abashed, "I failed to realize his importance in this crisis."

"Mister Secretary, you have time to make amends," the President told him. "Kindly send for the young man at once."

The Secretary arose and left the room.

The Chief Executive arose and went to look at a wall map which had been tacked near his desk for the meeting. Hands locked behind his back, he peered at it over the rims of his glasses.

The noise of a long column of soldiers straggling down from the river, along Pennsylvania Avenue, dragging guns on wheels behind them, was heard as clearly as though they tramped through the office. The curtains lifted gently on the warm wind.

Jim Lane, the enormous man from Kansas, shifted in the chair. He had come to the meeting with his own purpose in mind and was only tolerating the President's concern with the Indian territory. Lane had already petitioned the administration to enlist

Indians as fighters against the South. He argued vainly that the Confederacy was openly recruiting warriors and predicted that within weeks the Indians would be riding with the Confederate Army.

His gaze on the President, Senator Lane took advantage of the wait to speak persuasively again on the subject of Indian recruitment.

"Mister President, if you were to recruit Indians, you'd only be repeating history. Washington, Madison, Jackson all used Indian warriors at one time or another for the defense of this Nation. The type of Indian who killed your grandfather, Mister President, now exists only on the far western plains, and I'm not speaking of his kind when I urge you to employ Indians as soldiers for the Union."

The President turned a mildly amused face to the Senator. "Jim, sometimes I'm convinced you feel I've never left Kentucky. Believe me, I am not questioning the civilized status of most of them. The only question before this meeting, Senator, is what is happening to our forts in the Southwest and what is going on in the Indian territory? You, unfortunately, cannot tell me."

The Senator persisted in his stubbornness: "Why not let the red men fight for the Union, as white and black men are doing?"

There was a sharpness in President Lincoln's voice. "Jim, no! In the first place, we don't know for a fact that the insurrectionists are recruiting Indians." He went to the desk and looked down at the copy of the *Times*. "It says here only that a portion of Indians have been organized as a military force, attached to the army of the insurgents. But I have no official information confirming this story in the press. Do you, Jim?"

"It has to be official?"

"It's got to be more than an unverified newspaper report. I'm not running our Army on press stories but rather on official reports of my officers and agents. I want either a military report or an agent's. Right now, I have neither."

The Senator commented: "And if you did have such a report, would you recruit Indians?"

"I'd have to consult with my officers. I personally would rather leave it alone. I know what Indian warfare can become."

Commissioner Dole was about to speak when a knock came on the door and with the President's invitation Bryce entered the office.

The tall, dark-haired, dark-eyed young Cherokee was introduced to the President by Commissioner Dole. Lincoln, arising from the desk, drew Bryce toward the map on the wall, saying: "Mr. Calvin, take a look at this—"

He spread his hand on the map. "Here is the Southwest, including the Indian territory. As you know, we have forts throughout the area."

Bryce nodded: "Yes, sir."

The President folded his long arms across his chest and gave Bryce a worried look. "Well, Mister Calvin, as President of the United States, I have no information at this moment as to any military movements occuring in that entire vast land. All I know is that the insurrectionists have seized Santa Fe. I am forced to conclude, due to the silence, that all of our forts in the Southwest are inoperative, either through capture or desertion. I have not one word of what is occuring in Indian territory. Rumors are drifting to my desk that the Indian Nations may have signed military pacts with the Confederacy. What do you know about it?"

"Very little, sir."

"Do you have any knowledge of what is happening in the Cherokee Nation, or in the others in the territory?"

"Not recent knowledge, sir. It's been several months since I've had a message from my father. I'm concerned about it and I'm going home. You see, sir, the last word I had, my father told me that our Nation is divided again. Stand Watie, as leader of the Old Treaty Party, is dealing with the Rebels."

"Mister Calvin, I'd like to send you to the Cherokee Nation as my special agent. Your assignment is to bring me Chief Ross. I need to confer with him as soon as possible. It is imperative that I do so. Will you accept the mission?"

Bryce responded without hesitation. "Yes, sir!"

Commissioner Dole spoke: "Mister President, no one else has been able to reach his post in the territory. It's a very dangerous assignment. And perhaps to no avail. Chief Ross may be allied with the insurrectionists."

Bryce looked at the Commissioner and his bronze face went darker hued. "Sir, John Ross has never reneged on his word of honor no matter what the provocation. He will not be the one to dishonor the treaty between his Nation and yours."

President Lincoln smiled and took Bryce's hand: "I'm not giv-

ing you an easy task, my boy. But since there is no communication existing between Washington and the territory, it is the only way in which we can get our necessary facts. Take care and come back as quickly as possible with Chief Ross." The President looked at Commissioner Dole and Senator Lane. "When he returns with the Chief, we'll meet again. Bill," he said to Dole: "see to it that Mister Calvin has whatever he may need in the way of supplies and papers. Get him the fastest horse you have. He'll make better time riding that way than waiting on public transportation which is about as poor as communication now."

Bryce followed Commissioner Dole out of the office. Jim Lane, getting to his feet, said: "Now that's the kind of Indian I've been talking about, Mister President."

"If I could have an army of young men like him, I'd recruit every Indian today," President Lincoln conceded. "We'll see what he does."

XXXVIII

RIDING IN FROM ARKANSAS ALONG THE MILITARY ROAD, Bryce took a cutoff road to get a look at Fort Gibson before traveling on to Tahlequah. He wanted to be able to tell the President the condition of the place as he saw it.

The high, wooded palisades of the fort revealed its location, about 150 yards from the Grand River in the midst of tangled brush. The fort was silent, although the community beyond and around it was apparently lively enough. Bryce, pacing his horse to a slow walk, removed his shirt and stowed it under a saddle strap. The sun on this hot day of July 21, 1861, was made bearable by a breeze crossing the wide water of the three rivers of the Nation which flowed nearby. There had been a rain the night before and Bryce enjoyed the air on his skin. Huge clouds were

forming in a darkening pattern against the vivid blue sky, and
shadows moved over the land.

Pulling his horse to a halt, he looked at the Army post. Even
though he knew it had been deserted, the sight of it now hit him
hard in the pit of the stomach. The fort, which ought to be
bristling with Union activity, was lifeless. The garrisons were
empty, the soldiers vanished, the guns spiked, the flags furled,
the bugles stilled. The Stars and Stripes did not fly from the
ramparts.

Down the Texas Road lay the Creek Nation. At North Fork
Town there would be men who were plotting against the Union
and against John Ross, and there would be men who would be
ready to fight for both. Division, the plague of the Nations,
would be in evidence in the Creek Nation, too.

The Chickasaw Nation, situated on the Blue and Clear Boggy
rivers, would be split, too, with the Rebels eyeing their chances
there.

Down on the Red River, the Choctaw Nation would be bitterly
divided over the coming American civil war. The Seminoles,
living in the heart of the territory, would be likewise divided.
In each of the Nations, Bryce thought, men were waiting to see
what course John Ross would pursue, and, seeing, would follow
him.

Now Fort Gibson was in the path of the ambitious Confederacy and President Davis would be among the first to want it in
his ever-growing string of military bases. The Rebels would be
riding into it as fast as they could make a pact with the Nation.
Stand Watie would see that the fort was placed at their command.

Bryce urged his horse on, leaving the silent fort behind. As he
came into the public square, he found to his astonishment that
there were many people about, with an air of near-holiday excitement. Though it was normally a school day, a number of children
crowded the streets along with adults. The people jamming Mus-
kogee Street, the main thoroughfare of Tahlequah, were in mixed
moods.

Then Bryce spotted the gray-uniformed and armed men in
front of the log-structured Council building across the street
from the National Hotel. One of the young southern soldiers
stood at the door of the building, holding a Confederate flag. The
other troopers were at ease, watching the people.

Obviously the Rebels had come to town to talk to the Cherokee officials, who must be meeting with them as the Rebels stood on semiguard duty outside. What was John Ross doing?

Leaving his horse tied to a hitching post, Bryce pushed his way through the crowds beginning to swarm around the Council hall. He returned the greetings of many acquaintances as he passed through the mob, but he did not stop to talk.

It was a feisty-tempered crowd with a loud, argumentative shouting. A fist fight began in Bryce's path and he had to duck to avoid a blow meant for another man.

Entering the Council building without a challenge, he went past the offices of the councilmen, including the chiefs', and into the enormous meeting hall. The benches were filled with citizens and an overflow of spectators lined the walls.

John, seated on a bench at a long table on the platform, was engaged in a discussion with a bearded man on his left. Next to the other man was Stand. The meeting had not started and members of the Council were still coming to take their places at the table. John glanced to the door, saw Bryce, and excusing himself from his conversation meet Bryce halfway up the aisle.

"You don't know how I've hoped you'd come home, Bryce! I need you here."

Bryce told him: "I came as soon as I realized your messages weren't getting through the lines."

John took him into his office and closed the door. "There's trouble here. Stand has brought Albert Pike, the Commissioner of Indian Affairs of the Confederacy, here to discuss a military alliance with the Rebels. I've been stalling them, but today I've got to meet the issue. I've sent a courier to President Lincoln asking him to send troops here to protect us against any invasion by the Confederacy. I sent a message to you, along with the one to the President." He stopped, his face stricken: "You didn't get it? The President doesn't have my message?"

Bryce shook his head. "No. There's been no word from any part of the territory or the Southwest for some weeks. Father, your courier was either captured or he defected."

"But that means there won't be any federal troops here!"

"Can you stall this issue out there today?"

John shook his head. "I don't know. I've got to reconsider everything—"

"President Lincoln has requested that you come to Washington as fast as you can get there. He wants me to escort you at once. He says he must confer with you."

John's expression changed from one of desperation to renewed hope and determination. "Well, then, Bryce, We'll go to Washington!"

"Father, I don't have to say that the Washington trip is to be kept secret?"

John smiled, "Hardly, Bryce, hardly!"

They took their places on the bench and Bryce greeted Albert Pike, who sat to the left of the Chief. He was a disheveled-looking individual, with long hair and unkempt beard, baggy clothing and shaggy brows, but there was a warmth in his manner that affected even Bryce. Bryce also gave his nods to the councilmen, but Stand gave him no chance, turning his head away as he would have spoken to him.

John remembered Albert Pike. The man was known to every tribe and highly regarded by all of them. The southerner was well-educated, fearless, and honorable, a philosopher and poet whose words and frontier deeds had a tremendous appeal to all Indians, particularly to the young. His word was reliable—and that was everything to men who had often been the victims of lies. He walked freely among all red men. His association with the Confederacy gave its cause an advantage among the Indian tribes.

When John directed his own attention to the paperwork in front of him, Bryce looked at the audience, searching. He saw the Rosses gathered on a bench a few rows to the left of the platform. Mary's smile for him was a glad one. He exchanged a wave with the Ross men.

Then he saw Copper seated with Stand's family: Sarah and daughters, Minnehaha and Jacqueline; and the sons, Watica and Saladin. Neither Bryce or Copper showed a smile or a nod of the head as they looked at each other. What was the need? Seeing each other was sufficient for the moment.

Bryce dragged his gaze from her, giving his attention to the meeting which was to begin.

He glanced at the Chief and was impressed with his calm look of dignity. There were signs of the years on John Ross now, but they gave him an even more impressive appearance. His extra weight added to the breadth of his shoulders and matured his entire body effectively. The red hair, gone silver, contrasted with the dark brows, and his aristocratic facial lines were heightened with the touch of time.

The Chief arose to address the Council; the audience quieted.

John placed his hands on a cashbox on the table and spoke coldly.

"The Confederate States of America have sent an emissary, Albert Pike, to petition the Cherokee Nation for a military alliance. Before we go further, it is my duty to remind everyone that our Nation is now bound by treaty to the United States of America." He looked down at the box under his hands and then at the audience. "This box contains one hundred thousand dollars in gold. It's proposed as a gift to our Nation by the Confederacy: a most generous and unacceptable gift."

The vocal reaction was a wild humming in the hall. Stand conferred quickly with Pike.

John continued: "In answer to it, the Confederate government will hear officially of our existing treaty with the federal Union. Further, I have to report to Commissioner Pike that a week ago our Council voted a position of neutrality in the division of the United States, a position which we aim to hold. Therefore, this money gift must be returned to Commissioner Pike."

Commissioner Pike stood up to speak by leave of the Chief, who sat down beside Bryce. Pike was relaxed, and he stood with one hand in the pocket of his trousers. "The Chief of the Cherokee has rejected the Confederate offer without advising you of all the facts. There is more—the Confederate States want a close relationship with the Cherokee people. To prove it, Chief Ross is personally offered a commission as a full general in the Confederate Army with command of his own troops."

A smile played around Pike's mouth as he darted a look at John. When he could be heard again, he lifted his head cockily. "The Confederacy wants to honor the Cherokee people by inviting them, under the treaty suggested, to send their own elected representatives to sit with the Confederate Congress. Have you had such an offer from the Union? No, and you won't!"

Cheers swept his words away. Men were on their feet, pounding each other on the back. The young men standing at the walls gave a wild Rebel yell.

John arose and banged the gavel, demanding silence. It took a few minutes to regain order. It seemed that a demonstration might empty the hall. But the gavel prevailed and quiet came.

John asked the Commissioner: "Your government would have us exchange our peace for its war? You would have us raise an army for you?"

"Under the treaty which would place Cherokee warriors in the field beside their Confederate brothers, we would help you raise your troops and arm them. All we ask is to welcome the Cherokee Nation as an ally."

Amid the new burst of cheers, John pushed the money box a little toward the Commissioner. "The Cherokee Nation is a republic. As Chief, I cannot either accept or reject these things. They must be properly submitted for consideration to our legislative bodies and to our people. We are not an uncivilized tribe which can be bought—or sold—with beads or any other prize."

It was obvious that John had maneuvered the meeting into a stall. The Commissioner recognized the tactic but there was no way he could challenge it without causing open enmity. John Ross had bested him and he would have to retreat for the time being.

Looming large, Pike took the box back, shoving it to a position in front of him on the table. He shook his head and apologized. "I'm sorry, Chief Ross. I've handled this badly, I'm afraid, in my eagerness to claim the friendship of your people." He grinned at the audience. "I've tried to speed the pace of government, I suppose, and that hasn't worked yet."

The audience laughed with him and a few cheers went up. He turned to John again. "A proper formal document will be prepared for presentation to the noble Cherokee Council and people. You are right, of course, to insist upon it, Chief Ross."

He sat down amid applause. Stand Watie was rising to his feet to be recognized. John reluctantly gave him the forum.

Stand's once-black hair was now gray. His white cotton shirt was open at the throat and tucked into black broadcloth trousers belted with a wide leather girdle, clasped at the left side with a silver buckle. He wore boots with silver spurs, and a gun holster with a silver-decorated Colt hung from the belt.

"Brothers!" the voice came strong and steady. "It's not easy to speak here but the issue must be met.

"Since the early days of the removal west, our people have been divided. John Ross has never brought us together. You hear him now—he follows the same old course, stubborn as ever. John Ross is an illusionist! He prattles about neutrality in a land torn by passions. He seeks peace in the midst of war."

The sound of distant thunder was easily heard in the silence which had fallen on the hall. Lightning flashed across the valley.

Stand moved closer to the people and lowered the pitch of his voice, shaking a finger at them. "What you don't know is that the neutrality he mouths to us today—the peace he longs to hoard—is a curtain of deceit. He plans secretly for war!"

John was on his feet. "Now, wait a minute—"

Stand waved a hand at him angrily: "No! I'll have my say." He turned back to the aroused audience. "Chief Ross has appealed privately to the President of the United States for troops. He has requested that Union troops be ordered here at once." He whirled on John: "Can you deny it?"

John was appalled. Bryce had been right when he suggested the courier had defected. It was the only way Stand could have come by the information. John spoke to the audience: "Mister Watie, in revealing state business which has apparently come into his hands in an unlawful way, has not given you all the facts. Yes, I have asked the President of the United States to send troops here to protect this territory and this Nation against any attempt by the Confederacy to seize our lands and our government. I have done this under the requirements of our current treaty with the Union. I would have been delinquent in my duties to my people if I had failed to ask for troops to protect them against aggression."

Stand was furious. "Protection! The Union troops would imprison us, as they did once before."

John said: "It was the southern states who demanded our removal from our native lands. It was Mister Watie and his followers who signed the false treaty with President Jackson which resulted in our exodus. The same southern states now court us."

"The exodus was on order of the federal government," Stand protested. "We dealt with it when you would not. Then, and now, you were concerned only with that hopeless, worthless dream of yours—statehood in the white man's Union! You would keep us tied forever to that Union, as a slave to a master." Stand faced the people, raising his arms high, and shouted: "Let John Ross follow his elusive dream. As for me—and those who will join me—there is the Confederacy!"

Many of the young men were on their feet, cheering. John came from the table to the front of the platform and stood, waiting. Stand gave his young followers a sign to be seated and most of them complied.

Their Chief told them: "When the Cherokee Nation becomes a state in the federal Union; when there is a star in the American flag which represents our land, we will at last be a truly free, independent, and united people, equal to all the world. To be a part of the American Union would be to see all our sacrifices vindicated. When we become a state in the great Union, there can be no more trails of tears for us. Yes, I follow that dream. Still, that is not the issue here today. Now we are concerned only with the action we must take in regard to the war between the American states. As your Chief, I am pledged to honor the treaty we now hold with the Union."

He bowed his head to the people and went back to the table.

Stand left the platform and moved down the aisle, and most of the young men left the benches and gathered around him. With roars of approval, they lifted him to their shoulders and carried him out to the rainsoaked street where they were quickly encircled by grinning young Rebels in uniform. The break had come. The Cherokee Nation was divided.

The storm was lifting, the sky showing blue through the clouds, and the sun shone suddenly down upon Stand Watie and his celebrating followers.

John formally adjourned the meeting. The already depleted audience filed out of the hall almost before the gavel banged for the last time.

Albert Pike stood with John and Bryce at the table. "Watie and his men will be welcomed by the Confederacy," Pike said. "Yet I know they come to us now without the approval of their Chief. I can only hope that you will change your views. I'm going west now to arrange alliances with other tribes, but I'll be back here within six weeks. I hope you'll be ready then to sign the treaty with the Confederacy."

John was polite. "You're always welcome in Tahlequah, Commissioner. But don't come back expecting me to sign that treaty."

Albert Pike gave him a bow. "I will at least hope for it, sir. I'd rather have the Chief of the Cherokee as my ally than any other man I can name."

XXXIX

THEIR CAMP HAD BEEN DAMP FROM THE AFTERNOON RAIN but in their brief hour there they hardly noticed it. They had hardly spoken. She had been there waiting for him. "I thought you'd never get here!"

He frowned. "I don't like having you come here alone. We're not going to meet this way any more. When I return, I'm going to see your uncle and let him know how it is with us."

"Oh, Bryce! It's no use. You saw it today, even if you hadn't known before. If Uncle Stand ever found me with you—"

He stroked her hair. "No one can take you from me, Copper. I promise. No one."

She moved in his arms, looking up at him. "Bryce? You said something about returning? You aren't going away again, are you?"

"For about a month, Copper."

"But why?"

"I can't tell you," he hurried his words. "I don''t want to go. You will just have to trust me, and I ask you to say nothing to anyone about me. All right?"

"It's got something to do with your father and Uncle Stand and the treaty, doesn't it?"

"Please, Copper? No questions?"

"But a month is such a long time," she protested. "Do you want me?"

He took a deep breath and his hands dropped from her. "Of course."

Once more she gave him a direct look. "Then, why don't you take me?"

His words were hoarse. "Don't! Don't ever ask me that again. Don't you know how much I want to have you. How close I've come to taking you in the last weeks? Oh, Copper! We just have to wait, that's all."

She backed away from him, her fingers wiping tears away.

"For what? For my Uncle Stand and your father to become friends? Oh, Bryce, they'll never let us have each other. Don't you know that?"

"We'll find a way," he vowed.

They had parted near the church at Park Hill with his promise that he would see her as soon as he returned to Tahlequah. He would settle things then. She waved to him and sped her horse toward her uncle's home. Now, as he rode the drive to Rose Cottage, there was no sound except the clip-clop of the horse's hooves on the road and the call of nesting birds.

Rose Cottage was straight ahead, its lighted windows sending shafts of golden light out toward him. The cabins of the freed people glowed with lanterns and candles, and overhead the starry sky showed no signs of the afternoon storm.

Smoke from the cooking fires in the valley drifted to him. Taking the curve of the driveway which brought him to the front door of Rose Cottage, Bryce was enveloped in the tantalizing aroma of roasting beef from the big kitchen in the rear of the house. He knew at once that Mary had ordered his favorite meal prepared to celebrate his homecoming.

She was at the open door, dressed in a pink cotton gown, a band of tiny pink roses fitted to her smooth coiffure. "Bryce! Welcome home, son!" she greeted him with a kiss and a hug, drawing him into the reception room.

The dinner was excellent, but John would not linger over it this evening. He asked Mary to serve their coffee in his office.

The room had always been one of their favored places. It was here they had read books together; here John had first instructed Bryce in gunnery and the fine points of hunting. They had often sat before the enormous fireplace to clean their guns and to check on the working mechanisms of the weapons. It was in this room that they held their private talks. A green-globed lamp stood on the dark wooden desk, illuminating the huge wall map of the Indian territory and the adjacent southwestern territory of the United States. John went to the map and studied it a moment. "It's not a bright picture for us, is it?"

"It amounts to a hundred circling enemy camps," Bryce conceded.

"I'm wondering if we ought to travel by way of Missouri? Arkansas is probably well patrolled by the Rebels now." He shook his head sadly. "Too bad they joined the Confederacy. You know that only one man held out against the vote for it in May?"

"I heard." Bryce got up to study the map closely. "I think you're right about going east through Missouri. I had a few close pursuits on my way through Arkansas. They're mighty touchy just now at the sight of a stranger."

John nodded; "Yet Missouri is a regular battlefield right now. I've heard the roads are jammed with refugees fleeing from both the Rebel and federal armies. The people are caught in between."

"General Fremont is bringing order out of the chaos, though. He's running the war there by his own rules and he's tough," Bryce remarked.

"We're really set down in the midst of Confederate land," John pointed out. "Texas, Arkansas—members of the Confederacy. Missouri—divided. The Territory of New Mexico—falling to the Confederacy. To the west of us, the Seminole, Choctaw, Chickasaw—all threatening to form an alliance with the Rebels. Pike may return with their treaties in hand." He looked at the lines marking the borders of the Creek Nation. "Commissioner Pike will have some success there, to start. The McIntosh brothers are not friendly to me or to the Union and I suppose they'll be eager to join the Rebels."

"I know," Bryce agreed. "Chief Opothle Yohola is facing dissension. They say he's too old to rule. They'll have no patience with him if he insists on staying with the Union."

They planned to leave the Nation secretly and ride their horses to St. Louis. Their absence would be explained as a camping trip into the wilderness, their usual custom every summer. If anyone thought otherwise, there would be little proof, and they would return within a month, before Commissioner Pike came back to Tahlequah.

At midnight, John turned down the lamp. "If Mister Lincoln will see the necessity for federal troops here, we'll have a proper greeting for Commissioner Pike."

"He's got something in mind, Father, or he wouldn't have asked to see you."

Turning in to bed, Bryce thought that he should have told him about Copper. He went to sleep knowing that he would have to face the problem first by discussing it with John. When he returned from Washington, he would go see Stand Watie.

XL

AS JOHN AND BRYCE BEGAN THEIR JOURNEY NORTHWARD TO the Missouri border, Commissioner Albert Pike moved west accompanied by Confederate troopers. Pike rode into the wilds where other white men were killed on sight, with an escort of mounted Texas Riflemen under the bright banner of the Confederacy. He rode with wagons loaded with gifts and arms for the Indians he would visit. He had conferences with portions of the civilized tribes, making pacts with the Chickasaw, Choctaw, and Seminole. The McIntosh brothers, in the Creek Nation, promised him the eventual overthrow of their old Union-loyal Chief and agreed to provide troops for the Confederacy.

The Commissioner rode on to the uncivilized tribes where he held powwows on the plains. He rode to Jesse Chisholm's settlement on the rim of the far west. Chisholm, a white man, was a friend of the Comanches. Pike greeted him with gifts and an impressive array of documents to prove that he had military pacts with a faction in every tribe but the Cherokee—and that one was pending there. He needed Chisholm's help to bring the wild tribes to the cause of the Confederacy.

Jesse Chisholm, chewing a wad of tobacco, spat a stream of it past Pike, and said: "I can arrange what you want. If my Indians can help lick the Union, let 'em." His eyes narrowed on Pike: "It'll take some talkin' on my part and lot of giftin' on yours."

"No more than I expected. I'm prepared. Are you?"

The trader gave him an exaggerated bow: "At your service, Commissioner. Make use of my post all you want." He waved an arm at the log buildings of the Chisholm Trading Post.

"All right. I'll take whatever your shelves hold that you can spare. We'll see that your friends are well supplied with whatever they want: food, drink, clothing." He glanced at his own wagons. "I've got the weapons."

Jesse Chisholm spread the word of the visiting white man named Pike who had gifts to offer and weapons to trade. The

Comanche appeared at the post, coming in from their villages of hide-covered wickiups, their bodies painted, their nearly hairless heads decorated with feathers.

When Pike and Chisholm came forth from the main cabin of the post to greet them, the Indians circled them astride their ponies. Jesse Chisholm waited. The ponies were bridled to a stop and the Comanches were absolutely quiet, keeping their circle, holding the two white men in their silent ring.

Jesse turned slowly around so that he spoke to all of them in turn: "My friend, Albert Pike, a white man from the land beyond yours, is in need of warriors. He will give you many things for warriors to ride at his word in a time he says. He has words to speak."

The Comanche kept their silence, but their gaze shifted from the white men to the supply wagons packed at the door of the post.

"The white men of my land are at war with each other," Albert Pike began. "My people are united in a great Confederacy. We fight the Union. We need warriors. For men who will ride to battle with us, we have many gifts—"

The Comanches came to life. As though they had rehearsed their action, they raised their beaded and bell-decorated arms and shouted in unison: "Gifts!" They began to ride again in the circle movement, faster and faster.

"Give them the gifts," Jesse Chisholm advised quickly. "There'll be no more talk today."

Reluctantly, Pike agreed. With the help of Chisholm's hired hands, food and clothing and some paste jewelry were distributed to the Indians.

A lean-bodied young warrior with eyes as cold as a rattler's rode his pony close to the Commissioner. He pointed a long-fingered hand at the wagon which held the guns and ammunition: "We take!"

Pike gave him a look to match his, frigid and calculating. "No you don't take now. When I have warriors, you take. The guns and ammunition stay. You come back some time soon with gift of warriors. Then you take."

The young Comanche thought about it. Kicking his pony with his bare heels, he turned and gave a call to the others, a signal they understood. With the gifts seized, they sped away from the post and disappeared.

Pike despaired of ever seeing them again, but Jesse Chisholm assured him: "They'll be back. Right now they're celebrating. They'll have a wild night of dancing and singing. The drums of war will beat and their blood will grow hot. They will ride back and deal with you. You'll have your warriors."

They came to the post the next afternoon. Under the beat of the drums, the fever of promised war was upon the young braves. The whoops announcing their coming sent shivers along Pike's spine. He watched with Jesse Chisholm as the Indians circled the post, running their ponies at a breakneck speed, giving a terrifying show of their enthusiasm.

The Comanches agreed to raise a battalion of warriors for service with the Confederate Army, and the bareskinned allies left the post with a wagonload of guns and ammunition. Chisholm turned shrewd eyes upon the southerner: "I've heard tell there's plans for a real Indian uprising, something like never has been seen. They say every tribe from Minnesota to Texas will take part in it and they'll swarm on the border states, killing everything that's white and moves, all along the way."

Commissioner Pike pulled a pipe from his shirt pocket. "Is that so?" He gave Chisholm a sideways glance. "A thing like that could discourage the border states right quick. That would be some scalping party, all right." He shoved his pipe into his mouth, unlighted. "Let's hope it's not so."

It was impossible for him to go any farther west and also keep to his schedule for the return to Tahlequah. He sent couriers to the Osage, Apache, Cheyenne, and the Arapaho, and his call to join the war against the hated white Union met with spectacular success. The Confederate cause swept the tribes like a raging fever. All of them promised warriors.

In a tent pitched on the plains of the New Mexico Territory, Pike wrote a letter to John Ross, noting the success he was experiencing among the wild tribes. He carefully pointed out that the Cherokee Nation was the only tribe not yet offering troops to the Confederacy, and he directed the Chief's attention to the ring of Rebels around the Nation.

"Both Kansas and Missouri are a shambles from dissension and battles with outlaws riding behind both Armies to complete the destruction. Surely you don't look to them for assistance. General Fremont in Missouri is beset with trouble, and Missouri may yet be won by the Confederacy. To maintain neutrality in such a position as you find your Nation would be impossible.

"Upon my return to Tahlequah within the month, I expect you and I will be able to settle the matter of a military treaty between our governments in an amicable and satisfactory manner."

He sent the sealed message by courier to Rose Cottage.

XLI

THE ROLLING HILLS, VALLEYS, AND RIVERBEDS OF SOUTHERN Missouri provided scenes of beauty and horror to John and Bryce as they rode upstate. The farther north they moved, the more pronounced became the pitiful evidences of war and death. The roads were filled with weary refugees, families whose farm homes or small towns had been under fire of the opposing military forces, or burned to the ground by looters.

Many of the refugees had fled northward toward St. Louis to get away from the vicious outlaws who committed robbery, rape, and murder on a wholesale scale. St. Louis was their only hope of security, for there General Fremont held the city with a ring of guns and barricades and there his word was law. There was food there, too, and the hungry, scared, diseased people, to reach the sanctuary, went north by foot, horse, or wagon. Many were dying along the way.

On a warm, sunny day John and Bryce reached Springfield, Missouri, on the summit of the Ozarks. They had come in the hope that there would be some kind of food supply, but there was nothing. Both the Union and Confederate armies had swept through the town in the recent weeks, and the stores stood empty, the homes vandalized. Refugees stood in the streets of the town.

They camped outside the town that night near the skeleton of a burned farmhouse. John hardly spoke at all as they prepared a meal of hardtack and coffee from their meager supplies. Bryce unrolled his blanket, and asked, "Do you feel all right?"

John kicked some dirt onto the fire, so that its light would not attract visitors. "I'm all right, Bryce," he said quietly. "It's just that seeing all these refugees—these helpless people—reminds me of the exodus. The people we lost—"

"A night's sleep will help, Father."

John said nothing, but he thought: It never has.

At dawn they saddled and rode to the main road linking the towns of Missouri. Their progress was slowed by the numbers of footsore and hungry who held to the road as they would to life itself.

They suffered from many of the same things which plagued the armies: lack of food, contaminated drinking water, chiggers, bedbugs, wood ticks, mosquitoes, and flies. The sun blazing down on the long road to St. Louis felled men, women, and children. Families walked with their hands linked together so that the small children and the older people would keep each other awake and moving.

Blistered feet were common and dreaded because dangerous infections spread fast, crippling the victims. Those who had the luxury of both smeared the inside of their shoes with soap.

There were wagons, carriages, and farm rigs of all sorts on the road, but the oxen were soon slaughtered for food and many hungry refugees cast resentful eyes toward those who insisted upon keeping their horses alive and moving.

The sight of the small children, stumbling along amid their elders, homeless and hungry, affected John and Bryce the most. They stayed with the plodders for a time to let some of the children ride their horses. Others they carried in their arms and the little exhausted ones slept. They gave the babies the last of their good drinking water. Word came down the line that there was a stream several miles ahead, and the people hurried their pace.

All along the line of march one word was heard above all others: Fremont! General John Charles Fremont, commander of the Army of the West, would chase the Rebels from Missouri. He would give the refugees housing and food and welcome them to St. Louis.

John, in conversation with a bearded father, each of them

carrying a sleeping child in his arms, asked why General Fremont was held in such high regard. "Rumor has it that he's looked upon as a troublemaker and that President Lincoln is threatening to remove him from command."

"To hell with Fremont's enemies," the Missourian said. "He aims to make Missouri safe for Missourians. He's chased half the Rebs out already and he's after the other half." He squinted at John: "He's got a feeling for the folks and they have a feeling for him. Ain't no politician can hold a candle to him. Why, man, it's a fact that he's run the Secesh people right out of their mansions in St. Louis and give the folks whose homes been burned, like ours, the right to live in them places for a time. That's why we're all walkin' to him on bleedin' feet, we know he'll help us. We got a real man in Fremont, yessir!"

General Fremont was sending the Union's administration into concerned conferences. He had issued a proclamation freeing the slaves of all Confederates in Missouri. He drew the Union lines in Missouri as extending from Leavenworth, by way of Jefferson City, Rolla, and Ironton, to Cape Giraddeau on the Mississippi. In those lines, any civilian found north of them with arms on his persons would be tried by court-martial and, if found guilty, shot.

The freeing of the slaves gave President Lincoln a serious problem. General Fremont had defied the presidential order to the military that the rights of all American citizens to their life and property were not to be abridged. The political consequences of Fremont's proclamation were embarrassing to the President, who had not yet even decided whether the slaves should be freed.

There was talk in the Union that Lincoln would do well to follow Fremont's example. And many people now believed that Fremont, who had been the first Republican candidate for the presidency, ought to be in the White House instead of Lincoln.

When they could not reach him directly, Fremont's enemies turned their fire on him through his loyal followers. They verbally attacked Captain Lewis Merrill, of the 2nd Dragoons, who had formed a regiment of light cavalry at Benton Barracks to serve as Fremont's bodyguard. The General's wife gave the regiment the official name of "Merrill's Horse." The sharpshooters, excellent in riding and swordsmanship, were a crack unit operating out of St. Louis, sending the guerrillas and the "Secesh" into hiding, gaining an envious reputation, never once acting on the defensive. Their love of battle and of their General caused his political enemies to charge that they were the nucleus of a personal army which might turn at any time against the Union itself.

St. Louis was in a state of blockade, roads into the city closed to anyone who did not have a proper military or personal pass. Gunworks were dug in ugly circles around the city and Union guards walked the areas with orders to shoot any person who tried to bypass the barricade.

"St. Louis will not permit the entry of a Trojan Horse," the Commander was quoted as saying in defense of the blockade. He allowed refugees to enter only after they had been screened by his soldiers. The process was tedious, but handled as fast as possible.

The breastworks around the city also served as a defense measure. The city was ringed with mounds of mud and mortar where guns were held ready for any use. Pickets seen and unseen guarded the city and the beloved General day and night. It was impossible to keep all southerners out, since many were longtime citizens of the city. But Fremont knew most of their identities, and if they were not imprisoned they were watched. There were many arrests and the jails were filled with southern sympathizers.

At one of the gates of the roadblocks, John and Bryce came face to face with an efficient, freckle-faced guard who took his duty seriously. All around them at the gate, hundreds of others in miserable camps waited their turn for admission to the city.

The guard shook his head sadly. Everywhere the exhausted and hungry young were whining and crying, fighting with each other, exasperating their burdened parents. Now, so close to relief, the sick and tired fought each other to be the first in line for entry into St. Louis.

Bryce gained the gate for himself and John simply by using the method everyone else was using: pushing. He shouldered aside strong men, ignoring stronger language, to get to the gate with John right behind him.

Bryce told the guard: "Chief John Ross of the Cherokee Nation requests an interview with General Fremont. The General will understand the urgency of such a meeting."

The guard looked at the dark-haired Cherokee and the gray-haired Chief. "You got papers?"

Bryce brought out a leather case and found the document signed by President Lincoln proclaiming him his special Indian agent. The guard read it, handed it back. "Yes, sir," he said, "that sure says who you are. Now how do I know your friend here is John Ross, the Chief?"

Bryce looked him in the eye. "Because I say so."

The guard grinned. "I believe you, sir. All right, you two. I'll sign passes you may be needing in the city. Pass."

General Fremont's headquarters were rented from Colonel I. B. Brant, a noted citizen. Fremont's twenty-eight-member personal staff was established in Brant's former mansion on Choteau Avenue in an elegant neighborhood. The upper floor of the house was given to the General's personal use as office space. The lower floors were occupied by his staff, and the basement was stocked not with the fine wines and foods of Brant's day, but with guns and ammunition.

Numerous critics claimed the staff of the General was living in luxury, but actually the mansion had been stripped to a military bareness, and the routine in the offices was as strict as that at Jefferson Barracks, where Union troops were bivouacked and trained. The Brant mansion drew endless numbers of citizens to the door with a variety of personal petitions for the General. Finally it had become necessary for him to take a stand and let the word go out: "Fremont is a General—not a Mayor," ending many unnecessary demands upon his time.

The General had just concluded a meeting with some of his men when John and Bryce took the steps to his suite. Captain Lewis Merrill, a large man with a friendly personality, turned for a last word to Fremont, who stood in the doorway of his office. "It's as good as done, sir," Captain Lewis assured him.

General Fremont was advised by a guard that Chief Ross and his son were next to see him. He extended his hand in welcome: "I ought not be surprised about anything any more, but I am, to see you here, sir. I understand the Rebels are taking over the territory."

John gave a quick briefing on the situation, explaining without detail that they were on their way to Washington. "Frankly, I'm hoping that you may be able to alleviate some of our troubles. If you could send some troops to Tahlequah from St. Louis, providing the President approves, it would save us a longer wait for help which would otherwise have to come from further east."

The General gave a whistle. "Damn, if only I could! My friend, I'm scratching to keep my men armed, and I'm only a hop, skip, and jump ahead of my critics in Washington who want my neck in a noose. I'm given next to nothing to fight this war. Do you know, if I had not purchased five thousand stands of rifles when I was in France at the outbreak of the war and had them shipped here, there wouldn't have been a Union gun available and St. Louis would have fallen? Sir, the guns you see are my personal belongings!"

John and Bryce exchanged glances. "All along the road from Springfield to St. Louis," John said, "we heard the people speak of you in near-reverent terms. We begin to understand." He stood up. "General Fremont, we've imposed upon you. Our thanks for your time and hospitality but it's obvious we'd only add to your burden."

The General shook the Chief's hand. "Good luck to you, sir." He gave him a wink of an eye. "If you can manage to slip in a good word for us in Washington, it will probably be the only one the President hears."

"We'll do it," John replied.

Bryce gave the General his hand. "Sir, when I was young and you were exploring the far west, I wanted to follow you." He grinned, shaking his head: "I used to pretend I was the Pathfinder!"

"I wish you could have been there. You know, the skies and the waters of the New Mexico Territory are incredibly blue. And the air so clear! More than once, I've followed mirages." He smiled, giving Bryce's arm a friendly slap. "I don't suppose those mirages would have fooled a Cherokee! Well, it's a dramatic land out there, dramatic!"

Parting from the General, they settled for a hotel in the heart of the downtown section. Their room was on the third floor, overlooking a busy avenue. They had dinner in the hotel's dining room and were amazed by the choice of foods and by the atmosphere of luxury. The perfume of well-dressed women lingered on the air. The men, most of them in uniform, indulged in good cigars or well-filled pipes. Many couples were planning an evening at the theaters. It was difficult to believe that within a few miles there were people near starvation bedding down on the ground for the night.

Stretched out on their bed after bathing, they tried to sleep, but the noise of the traffic moving through the city streets and the heat and high humidity kept them awake.

Suddenly there was the sound of drums and horses' hooves on the brick pavement. John and Bryce came to the window to look. Down the street past the hotel, by the light of flaming torches, came a brass band, and behind it, resplendent in dress uniforms of blue trimmed in red and gold, came three companies of Fremont's Guard, astride their handsome mounts. Each man, a battle veteran was armed with two Colt revolvers, a rifle, and a sharp-edged saber, and rode proudly, carrying a torch in his left hand. Their voices were raised in one patriotic song after another, awakening the city.

Even Rebel sympathizers were joining the throngs now on the streets. Young women ran after them, shrieking their delight and admiration. No one worried about the fact that normally a nice girl was not seen on the street after dark. Never had there been such a parade in St. Louis.

John and Bryce dressed and went down to the street to join the crowds, following the torchlights to the Brant Mansion.

Word circulated: Washington had hinted, through the War Department, that the special bodyguard was to be disbanded. The parade was the answer of Fremont's men.

General Fremont stood in the doorway of the house, his wife beside him, totally surprised at the appearance of his troopers. On the front lawn, the men, still astride their horses, faced their commander and raised their sabers aloft in a salute, the fine steel of the weapons catching the light of the torches in brilliant reflection.

The Captain of the Guard dismounted, reached up to his saddle to grasp a sword which had been carefully attached there, and strode to the General, who stood quietly on the steps of the mansion. The Captain shifted the sword to his left hand in order to salute General Fremont.

The General returned the salute, a look of puzzlement in his eyes. Mrs. Fremont smiled but she was obviously as surprised as her husband.

"General Fremont," said the Captain, "I have the honor to present you a token of the esteem of the men of your command. Sir, this sword is yours." He handed the General the sword, hilt first.

General Fremont ran his hands over the scabbard, noting every detail. The scabbard was pure silver and it held a bust of himself, sculptured in gold, bordered with sparkling diamonds. A setting of blue enamel above the bust bore the initials J.C.F., each letter formed by diamonds.

The General unsheathed the sword, holding it up to the torchlight, and he saw the engraving on the blade: "To the Pathfinder, by the Men of the West." He looked at the men and choked out: "Thank you!" He tried to say more but he could not speak. Sheathing the sword, he stood before them, not hiding his tears.

The soldiers gave him another salute before turning their mounts out of the yard and down the street. The drums beat their march but there was no other music now. The General and his wife, Jessie, stood on the steps and watched them go. He was still speechless.

Jessie put a hand on his arm. "No one can ever take their devotion from you."

He spoke through hoarseness: "Jessie, no man deserves such devotion." He looked at the sword, and she saw anguish in his eyes. "This glorious gift—it cost them a fortune! And if our enemies in Washington prevail, they'll be mustered out of service, the regiment disbanded, without pay. They may go hungry for a time, in order to have given me this sword."

"They have fed their souls, my dear."

XLII

THE CONSTANT FLOW OF CONVEYANCES OF ALL KINDS GAVE Washington a murmur "like distant thunder," John told Bryce. The city was noisy and sprawling, its streets busy with wartime traffic. Farm wagons, painted carriages, mammoth stagecoaches, covered wagons, army rigs—everything on wheels rolled over the streets in a perpetual parade.

They spent an hour walking the streets. The Potomac glistened like a silver-crested arm around the city. Standing on the steps of the Capitol, they could see the White House gleaming behind the trees. Overhead, scaffolding still topped the building where the new dome would soon be completed.

John Hay, confidential secretary to Abraham Lincoln, met them at the bottom of the stairway leading to the rooms of the President. If the secretary was surprised at the sight of them, he managed to hide it. Still, he could not hide his interest.

John wore his tribal chieftain's outfit of white buckskin and his magnificent feathered headgear. He carried an heirloom cane which had belonged to his father: a shining black stick with a silver head, not unlike the silver-headed canes President Lincoln was to send to all the Indian governments as tokens of recognition.

To match with John's choice of tribal vestment, Bryce wore a Cherokee hunting shirt with fringes cut across the wide shoulder line and down the length of the sleeves and the matching buckskin trousers.

John's only hesitation in wearing his outfit was that it might draw unwanted attention to his presence in Washington. However, as soon as he saw the jammed condition of the city, he told Bryce: "No one is going to notice us. I go as Chief to the President and I choose to wear the clothing of my people as they would expect me to do."

The President of the United States left his desk to meet them midway across the room. His hand was strong-boned and warm, and the dark shadows under his light gray eyes told that this man of the outdoors missed the sun and air. "I've hoped for this meeting," President Lincoln said.

John gripped the President's hand: "Sir, so have I."

The President, indicating chairs for them, giving Bryce a quick handshake, turned to his secretary. "Would you send for Secretary Cameron and Commissioner Dole?"

John briefed the President on the military situation in the territory. "The South is forcing a military treaty upon my government," he concluded, "and unless I am sent troops by the federal government, I will be powerless."

Secretary Cameron and Commissioner Dole arrived and took their seats. Following a hasty briefing by the President, the Secretary asked, "Will the Cherokee Nation leave its neutral position and fight for the Union?"

"Simon, that's the reverse of the question," the President said. "I believe Chief Ross wants to know if the Union will fight for the Cherokee Nation."

John was worried by the Secretary's sullen silence. "Why don't I outline our exact trouble spots on the map, Mister President?" he quickly put in.

With pins the President handed him from a desk box, the Chief worked at the map, explaining as he operated. His nation's predicament, subject to Confederate seizure either through immediate military action or by enforced treaty, brought a new look of concern to the Secretary's face.

The President asked the Secretary: "What are the chances of sending our troops to Tahlequah for its defense, as our treaty demands?"

"Not a chance, Mister President! You know, sir, we can't spare a company, let alone whole regiments. The Missouri situation is already taking more men than we can afford to lend the western command. There's no place from which we can currently withdraw troops."

"We're going to do something, Simon. We've got to keep the Indian territory safe for us."

The Secretary shook his head. "As Commander in Chief, will you order troops away from active battlefields to an area merely threatened?"

Not bothering to reply to the last question of Secretary Cameron, the President shifted his attention to Commissioner Dole. "Bill, a few months back, weren't you visited by several members of the Creek Nation?"

"Yes, sir," the Commissioner nodded. "They came to say the Creek Nation is loyal. They wanted us to know that their Chief will not sign a treaty with the Confederacy. They were worried because their Nation is split and a powerful faction in it is working for a treaty with the Rebels."

Lincoln pursued the subject: "The Creeks carried the word of their Chief to you in which he praised John Ross as the greatest strength and hope of the Union in the Indian territory?"

The Commissioner nodded. "Chief Opothle Yohola is very weak and old and he cannot do much to help. He has sent this message: 'Look to Chief John Ross of the Cherokee, above all others, for loyalty and cooperation against the Rebels!'"

Keeping his steady gaze on the Chief, President Lincoln asked

the Commissioner, "Did he say how Chief Ross can be a source of strength to us since he is not in a position to fight the insurrectionists?"

"The Creek Chief suggested Chief Ross could carry on a secret war within the ranks of the insurrectionists just as he has conducted a passive resistance to their treaty proposal."

John was appalled. "It's true that I've stalled the proposed treaty. But to fight an underground war!" He looked at the President. "How can I wage a war of any kind? I have not arms or a united people."

"Underground warfare *is* war without arms or a united people," the President replied.

It was as though John were arguing against his own thoughts: "To fight a war of subterfuge against the Rebels, what would I have to do? Sign the treaty of military alliance with them. Then, from within their ranks, destroy their battle plans, one way or another. I'd have to deceive them. I'd have to give my brother, my enemy, my hand in friendship and then defeat him by turning a gun on him." He turned a stricken look upon the others. "I don't see how I can do it!"

"I won't ask you to do that which you cannot," the President said. "Yet, if there is any way you can give me time, I can give you a special Union column within six months to defeat the Confederates in the territory. But I need the time. Can you gain it for me, Chief Ross?"

John, receiving a nod he looked for from Bryce, took the President's hand: "We'll do it, Mister President, though at this moment I'm sure I don't know quite how."

"I'm grateful beyond words, my friend."

The meeting ended on that note, but John and Bryce were back the next day to detail the plans. It was determined that communications would be handled in Missouri and Kansas by federal military officers and in Washington through Senator Jim Lane's office; the officers of the special Union column would be appointed by the President from his regiments; the troopers would be recruited by John from the Five Civilized Tribes in the territory; the United States would train and outfit the column at a secluded site in the foothills of southern Missouri. In the late spring of 1862, the column would proceed to the territory in pursuit of Confederates, and John Ross and his family would be placed under "arrest" and escorted to Washington. The arrest would be a protective custody only, with John and his family returned to the Nation at the end of hostilities between the states. The status of the Cherokee government and its Chief were not to be changed.

When the conference was over, Lincoln clasped the hands of both John and Bryce at the door of the office. "Before you leave, can you give me a translation of Tahlequah? I've often wondered, lately, what it means in Cherokee."

John smiled: "It's not easy to translate, sir. It means, 'Two will do.' Our people pride themselves on the idea that it takes only two Cherokee to master any problem. Two alone surveyed our new capital site. The name evolved—Tahlequah."

The President was pleased. "Is that so? Well, as far as I'm concerned, it's well named. Two will do—in this crisis: John Ross and Bryce Calvin."

"There will be some bad days ahead," John said. "I want you then to remember my hand in yours as now it is, and this pledge I give you: The cause of the Union shall prevail in the Indian territory."

XLIII

NEWLY COMMISSIONED AS AN OFFICER IN THE CONFEDERATE army, Captain Albert Pike, looking more enormous and disreputable than ever, came to Rose Cottage with treaties to spread before Chief Ross.

As his troopers stood outside, Captain Pike conferred with the Chief of the Cherokee informing him of his new military rank in the Rebel army. John installed his visitor in a leather-covered chair beside the fireplace filled with green pine boughs. Over the fireplace hung the guns and bows collected by John and his sons through the years. Bryce was there at John's invitation, but as the interview progressed he kept his opinions to himself.

The Captain peered at his host with sun-reddened, dust-irritated eyes and bit off the end of the cigar John had given him. "I've got some interesting trophies to show you, Chief Ross," he tapped the portfolio on his knees. "When you look at 'em, keep in mind that the Union is disintegrating fast. There won't be any, soon enough. Nope. Your best chance is with the Confederacy." Pike untied the leather thongs binding the portfolio and lifted out some papers.

After a few minutes of study, John asked: "These represent only factions in each tribe, don't they?"

Captain Pike blew a heavy cloud of cigar smoke into the air. "They're signed," he retorted. "Are you ready to accept our treaty? I've got to have an answer." He added, almost apologetically: "Time is valuable."

Time was the only weapon. It was impossible to stall the negotiation of the treaty any longer, but he could delay the necessary national vote on it and the consequent ceremonies. He would drag every hour he could out of the situation.

"I'll call a special session of our Council to consider your proposed alliance," John told Captain Pike. "If the Council recommends it, the issue will be taken to our citizens for their vote. The vote of war or peace is always in the hands of the people themselves."

"I know," Pike conceded, "but I want to know what you are going to recommend."

"Captain, I've made up my mind. The Cherokee Nation must join its brothers of the South. I'll recommend that the people vote for the military alliance with the Confederacy. And I'll ask authority from them to raise troops to be attached to the southern army to serve under my personal command."

"Welcome to our tribe, sir," said Captain Pike, extending a hand to him.

Within minutes, Captain Pike rode away from Rose Cottage and headed for Texas to report to General Ben McCulloch, whom the Confederacy had appointed in supreme command of its troops in the Indian territory. McCulloch, already well known and much admired for his work with the Texas Rangers, was to cooperate with Captain Pike in his special mission among the

Indians in behalf of treaties. Both were under the immediate orders of Commissioner David L. Hubbard of the Confederate Indian Bureau.

Watching the Rebel troops ride away, led by the Stars and Bars whipping out on the wind, John observed to Bryce: "A man could die from inner rage and helplessness in this kind of war."

Bryce gave him a wide grin: "If you think you're feeling defeated, how do you think the Captain is going to feel the day he realizes he's been outfought by the Chief of the Cherokee?"

"Well, if we're going to speed that day, we'd better begin by calling the Council to meeting within the week. That will delay it as long as I dare."

In that week, emotions were to run high at Rose Cottage. Jim came to see his father in privacy and strode the room nervously. "Nothing's really wrong, Father. I'm going to St. Louis to join the Union Army. I'm leaving today, and I've come to say good-bye. I hope it won't cause you any trouble—that I'm joining the Yankees?"

"You must know how proud I am of you, Jim."

The young man frowned. "I know." He lowered the pitch of his voice. "Mary has told me a little of your crisis. Father, if you need me here—"

"No, you do what your heart tells you to do. My position here is unsettled, but it's something that only time will solve." He had a plea in his eyes: "Jim, no matter what you may hear as time goes on about my activities in this war, will you trust me? I'm not free to say more, son. But I have to know that you are with me, no matter what happens."

"Father, I was born trusting you, and that's the way it's always going to be."

"We'd better get Mary in here—"

Jim shook his head: "We've said good-bye, Father. I told her about this yesterday, before you got home. It would be difficult for us to say it again. You know how women are, sir."

After a request that John keep a watch over Sarah and the children, and a quick embrace, Jim hurriedly left.

Bryce came to the office within an hour of Jim's departure. John was going over the official papers for the call of the convention. Bryce put it bluntly: "Sir, I aim to marry Copper Boudinot. We've been meeting whenever possible at the river campsite but I'm not going to be secretive about this any longer. I'm riding

over this morning to tell Mister Watie about us. I wanted you to know."

John got to his feet. "It just can't be, Bryce. You know there's no way for a marriage between you. Stand would take drastic steps to prevent it."

"Are you going to, sir?"

John shook his head. "What can I say? You know as well as I do that we've got all the trouble with Stand Watie and the Confederates that we can handle. If Stand's hatred of all Rosses is stirred just now—well, I leave it to you, Bryce."

"The only trouble he could stir would come to me, sir, and I'm determined to tell him the truth."

Sarah Watie was a gentle woman, her dark eyes soft with compassion. She was wholly surprised to see Bryce Calvin on her doorstep.

"Mrs. Watie, I'd like to see your husband. It's a personal matter, ma'am."

There was no need for her to call Stand to the reception room. He was there, dressed for riding in white shirt, black trousers, and boots. He put a firm hand on his wife's round arm. "Sarah, leave us alone." The woman left them, glancing back with worried eyes.

"Is there a room where we could talk, Mr. Watie?"

"Say what you've got to say and get out."

Bryce stood unflinching. "All right. I'm going to marry Copper Boudinot."

Stand took a deep breath and shouted: "Sarah!"

She hurried back. "Yes, Stand?"

"Fetch Copper."

"Mister Watie, I've said what I came to say—"

Bryce got no further. Copper was in the room. Stand took a tight grip on her arm.

"Copper, this Ross claims he's going to marry you. I want to know where he got such an idea." Stand shook her a little. "Have you been seeing him?"

"We've been meeting at the campsite on the river," Bryce interrupted. "We've had to, since you've refused to let us see each other openly. But I'm not going to ask Copper to do that any more. We're going to be married, regardless of our families."

Stand's heated fury was turning to an icy truculence. "You, a Ross! You've dared compromise a Boudinot!" He thrust Copper

aside toward the white-faced Sarah, and moved menacingly on Bryce. "I'd rather you had murdered her, as your father did my brother, than make love to her!"

Bryce took the blow on his raised forearm, and shoved Stand backward. Before Stand could regain his balance, Bryce backed to the door and was gone.

Copper turned in Sarah's arms, crying now: "We haven't done what Uncle Stand thinks. Bryce hasn't touched me!"

Stand came to her and slapped her face. "You, a Boudinot! Giving yourself to a Ross! Letting him take you—"

She stood very straight, the mark of his slap on her cheek. "I wanted him to take me. I asked him to! He told me we have to wait. But if I can get to him, I won't let him wait any longer!"

Sarah's cheeks were pink in shock. "Oh, Copper!"

"You're never to see him again," Stand told her. "There's only one thing to do to set things right, and I'm going to see it done. Lock her in her room for now."

Copper, alarmed, stopped her efforts to get away from Sarah. "What are you going to do?"

"The Rosses have put dishonor on the Boudinot name for the last time. And, as John Ross used the Blood Law against my brother and the Ridges, so will I see it work against them. I'll see Bryce Calvin dead for what he's done to you!"

He left the house, and Copper's shrieks did not deter him.

XLIV

IT WAS A MEETING OF THE CHEROKEE COUNCIL AND NATIONAL Committee which John had never expected to call.

It was a warm day in August but John was wearing his ceremonial buckskins and feathered bonnet. He stood at the rostrum as Chief of the Cherokee.

The rays of the sun slanted through the blinds of the window to point at him like quivering fingers, fine dust swirling in the shafts of light. The hall was hushed as he began his address.

Briefly he reviewed the points of the proposed military alliance, drawing attention to their merits. "I recommend the people of the Nation vote favorably for the treaty," he concluded. "It is generous." Most of the legislators, knowing of the serious crisis which faced their nation, were not surprised at the recommendation their Chief made to them. A few who had stood with him in a position of neutrality looked upon him in disillusionment as they heard his plea for a Confederate military alliance. They would follow him anywhere and did so now, but with heavy hearts. They had expected Chief Ross to put up a fight, even if a hopeless one.

A councilman stood. "What about our treaty with the Union. Why do you turn from it?"

John showed only the slightest hesitation. "The United States has failed to honor the treaty. I have appealed in vain for troops with which to maintain our Nation in a desirable state of neutrality. Since we cannot remain neutral, we must choose sides. It seems that our destiny is now involved with the Confederacy."

After some further consideration, a vote was taken. The legislators agreed that the proposed military alliance with the Confederacy be submitted at a general convention of the people for approval or disapproval. A date two weeks ahead was selected for the people's meeting to be located at the public campgrounds on the Illinois River, a mile from town.

When the hall was emptied of all but himself and Bryce, John banged the gavel down hard on the table. "Damnation!"

Bryce gave him a grin. "Would that be a word from your Scottish background?"

"Bryce, I don't know that I can go through with this." A wild hope sprang into his eyes. "Maybe we could fight them, instead, from the hills: a hit-and-run war."

Bryce's eyes clouded. "I may have to take Copper to the hills and fight from there to hold her."

"I'm sorry, son. I don't see how you can do anything but forget her. There's too much against you."

"Even you, sir?"

"For now, even me. We've got to work with Stand and I fear

your involvement with Copper, if continued, could end in disaster for us. I don't want anything to imperil our course of action, you understand?"

Bryce gave him a steady look. "Yes, sir."

Four thousand members of the Cherokee Nation answered the call to the late August convention at Tahlequah. They gathered beside the river in a holiday mood. The contagious fever of war swept through the Nation, arousing the young and the old alike. On the grassy slopes of the valley along the edge of the river rose an immense tent city, spreading in all directions.

Stand Watie's mounted Knights, their new status of volunteers to the Confederate Army merely awaiting the confirming treaty, rode with the 4th Texas Calvary under General McCulloch, the Confederate outfit to which they would soon be officially attached. Some of them already wore the gray uniforms of the Confederacy, having made their private purchases from the Rebels.

The citizens were awed by the splendid appearance of the Cherokee riders, and the young warriors gave them a show, racing through the streets and over the hills, emitting the chilling Cherokee battlecry and the weird ascending notes of the Rebel yell.

At noon the crowds gathered at the public square where had been erected a rostrum and a half-dozen benches for the speakers and the government officials. There were also benches situated in the square for women and children. With all traffic detoured to side streets, the place had the look of a park.

Copper came out of the National Hotel alone, where she had lunched with her family. She saw Bryce near the rostrum. Across the distance, they looked at each other. He made no move to go to her. She turned her profile to him. Stand came out of the hotel, escorting Sarah. He was in the uniform of a Confederate, lacking insignia, although rumor had it that he was to be commissioned as a General as soon as the treaty was in effect. Minnehaha, holding the hand of her little sister Jackie, came behind her parents. Stand took Copper's arm and the family group approached the rostrum.

The convention was in order. John met the strange and difficult moment with dignity, speaking of the Nation's political and military crisis. He recommended they vote for the Confederate treaty and made a formal request that they empower him to raise troops to serve under his personal command.

The Cherokee people, standing to be counted, lifted their hands high in vote. The Confederate treaty was accepted.

Captain Pike, taking John's hand as they stood before the citizens, shouted: "Now we are one!"

Stand Watie was immediately commissioned Brigadier General by personal order of Jefferson Davis, President of the Confederacy. The treaty was ready for the formal ceremonies which would see its signing.

One of John's increasing worries was the worsening situation facing the old Chief of the Creek. The Confederates had not been able to bring him to a treaty, yet Chief Opothle Yohola had no way to fight the threat of open rebellion in his land. The Confederate cause in the Creek nation was in the hands of the McIntosh brothers, Daniel and Chilly. Separated in age by twenty years, the brothers were nevertheless devoted to each other. The younger, Daniel, was a Baptist minister who had broken with the old Chief over his insistence upon his people clinging to the old tribal life.

Chief Yohola, however, had an unshakable faith in the treaty existing between his Nation and the Union. He had given his word on it, and he would not swerve from it. He was not at all coerced by the sight of the McIntosh brothers in new gray uniforms or by the strange flag they carried.

Nor was he moved by the threats upon his life. "I am an old man who has fought more than one battle. If I must fight again, there will be a way. I will not abdicate, as my enemies ask. The young men will have to defeat me, if they would have me leave my position as Chief of the Creek. I do not faint before them."

John asked Bryce to ride to the Creek Chief with a plan which John believed was now the only way the old man and his loyal supporters could survive in a territory fast being overrun by armed Confederates. "He may not want to listen to my words," John said, "because he will believe that I've deserted the Union. You tell him the truth. Then plead with him to do as I suggest. Tell him there is no other way than what I say to save his people, and that if he follows my plan he will serve the Union. He will prove he is my friend now, as always."

Preparing to leave for the Creek Nation, Bryce stayed long enough to consult with John and Alan on the recruitment of

Cherokee warriors for the Union column. Alan, Silas, and George were advised of the predicament in which John was entrapped and pledged themselves to silence. They assisted in the recruitment.

John brought forty-year-old John Drew, a full-blood Cherokee, long a friend and long in favor of the Union, into the secret war. Behind the locked office door at Rose Cottage, he asked: "Will you accept a dual responsibility, which carries a deadly risk, for the cause of the Union?"

Drew said simply: "If it comes through you, Chief Ross, you know I will."

"What we have to do," explained the Chief, "is recruit loyal men for two separate duties. First, we need men to ride with us and the 4th Texas Cavalry. They must be men whose loyalty to the Union and to me is unquestioned."

John Ross detailed the plan which had evolved from his meeting with President Lincoln. "Do you think we can do it, John?"

"There's only one weakness in the whole plan, to my mind."

"Name it," John urged.

"You, sir—that is, your reputation. I can hardly believe that Stand Watie, and many of the others, will believe that you have actually turned against your treaty with the Union. You've never been swerved from your word or principles before, and if I were Watie or Pike, I'd doubt that you have been now." He grinned. "I suspected you were working in your own way for the Union, before I came here to hear it's so."

"I suppose we can't expect to carry on with the subterfuge too long, but if we can destroy their efforts for a time, it may be long enough. We'll have to try."

A trio of men was dispatched secretly to the foothills of Missouri to locate a site for the training of the Union Column.

Recruitment of men for service with the Confederate regiments began in Tahlequah. Hundreds of young men flocked to the town, anxious to follow their Chief in whatever cause he was involved. It was no problem filling the ranks of the Texas troops and the regiments which would ride with him.

Recruiting men secretly for the Union column took a little more detailed work with tedious interrogation, but there was no real difficulty. The young men chosen for the column were enthused and ready to ride.

While John and Colonel Drew worked on recruiting and arming the men, Stand Watie, his troops already well trained, turned his attention to Bryce and Copper.

Early one afternoon the dining room of the National Hotel was closed to the public for a few hours. There were sixteen men in attendance, including Brigadier-General Stand Watie, who sat at a small table with his wife and grandniece. A large dinner table served as the conference hub, and the man with the gavel was Richard Barber, a newly appointed officer in General Watie's regiment. The fate of Bryce Calvin now hinged on the testimony of Copper Boudinot.

She walked slowly to the witness chair set beside the table, her face very pale. Her plain blue dress and bonnet added no years to her youthfulness. She sat down, keeping her gaze resentfully on her uncle.

The chairman wasted no time with formalities. "Miss Boudinot, you've heard the charges here against Bryce Calvin?"

She looked at him and said not a thing.

He glanced at her uncle, then banged the gavel again. "Miss Boudinot, please answer."

She lifted her chin. "I've heard the charges."

"And what do you say? Do you offer a defense for Bryce Calvin?"

"None of you have a right to question me. But I'm proud to testify: I love Bryce Calvin."

The chairman banged the gavel noisily. The committee members gave up their husky whisperings and looked to the chair again. "Tell the court the truth, Miss Boudinot. Did Bryce Calvin meet you in secret in an isolated place on numerous occasions?"

Sarah stood: "Leave her be! She's only a young girl—"

Stand reached up and pulled her down to her chair.

Chairman Barber tried again. "Miss Boudinot, answer the question. Did Bryce Calvin lure you to meetings alone with him in the wilderness?"

Pink mounted her cheeks and her eyes flashed, but she did not speak.

A middle-aged man nudged another in the ribs. "I wouldn't mind crawling through the underbush after that, either."

His huskily built companion smiled, his gaze traveling over Copper. "It might even be worth the punishment."

Chairman Barber banged the gavel. "You're excused," he told Copper. "We'll take our vote on the basis of what we know."

The chairman waited until Copper had passed through the aisles toward the door. Stand arose to intercept her and brought her back to the table. Copper sat down and let her aunt hold her hand, but she turned her face away from her uncle.

Barber again spoke: "The question to be decided is: Did Bryce Calvin, a son of Chief John Ross, commit the seduction of Copper Boudinot, bringing dishonor upon her name, when he lured her on numerous occasions to an isolated area where they were alone? The testimony has included the admission to General Watie by Bryce Calvin that he has met the girl secretly and often. Is Bryce Calvin guilty or innocent of the charge? You will make your decision in the knowledge that a vote of guilty carries the punishment of death under the Blood Law."

The vote of guilty was counted as unanimous. The two middle-aged men who had studied Copper with roving eyes were appointed executioners.

Copper, without a glance at any of the men, walked out of the room, head held high, her aunt hurrying along behind her. On arrival home she retreated to her bedroom while her aunt went to the kitchen to prepare tea for her, her own nerves in need of soothing, too. It took Copper only a little time to change into riding clothes, leave the house undetected by her aunt, corral her horse, saddle it, and ride toward Rose Cottage.

She spotted Mary working on her knees among her favorite flowers. She knew Chief Ross's wife only casually, but because of Bryce she felt she knew her well. She pulled her horse to a stop in the drive near the flowerbed where Mary gazed up at her in surprise.

"Mrs. Ross! Is Bryce here?"

"Why, no, Copper! He isn't. I'm not certain when he'll return. What's wrong?"

Copper dismounted and felt a sudden faintness, and was grateful for Mary's steadying hands on her. "There's been a committee meeting—"

The pain in her eyes melted into tears and she broke down sobbing.

In the front parlor of the mansion, the whole story came out to Mary in Copper's halting words, alternating between embarrassment, anger, and pride.

Mary was moved. "Thou wast subjected to such a public meeting of men on such an intimate subject—"

Copper explained nervously: "I didn't care about myself. Uncle Stand believes in the old ways of the tribe, you know. Mrs. Ross, he really loves me very much, as I do him. He actually believes he's protecting me from a family enemy." She steadied her gaze on Mary. "The hate my uncle holds for Chief Ross transcends everything else in his life, even his loves."

Mary's hands were trembling. "Yes, I see. Then, in invoking the Blood Law against Bryce, he'll be striking at John Ross. He'll avenge the murder of his brother, as he sees it."

Copper arose: "I'd better get home, Mrs. Ross. I certainly don't want Uncle Stand to start a search for me."

Mary rose. "He won't hurt thee?"

"Oh, no! My uncle won't touch me. He may make it difficult for me to get away again." She frowned. "Mrs. Ross? Will Bryce be protected?"

"Thou hast done all that is necessary, Copper. Bryce will be all right, but he is going to be worried about thee, though. He'll want to come to thee—"

"No! Tell him I ask him to stay away. For now. Please?"

Mary nodded. "Yes, thou art right. For now."

Copper gave Mary a quick kiss on the cheek and left.

XLV

IT WAS ONLY WHEN THE COOLER TEMPERS AND MINDS OF Mary and John prevailed in the matter that Bryce agreed to stay away from the Watie home for the time being.

The thought of Copper's ordeal at the public meeting disturbed him deeply. His hands gripped the reins tightly, thinking of the things she had faced: the staring men, the accusations, the questions. All those men looking at her, thinking the worst of her! But there was a mission to be accomplished for the sake of the Creek people, and Copper's plea to him to stay away gave him thought: It was going to take time to claim her.

He was not unaware of his own peril. Somewhere in the land were two men looking for him with instructions to kill him. He rode with guns and a knife; his eyes and ears open.

The night was dark around him when he bedded down on the first stop of his lone trek. He camped in the protection of a small gulley where the mud slopes of the nature-made trench acted as windbreaks. He made no campfire, eating food from a knapsack prepared at Rose Cottage.

He was closing his eyes when his ear, cradled on his arm close to the ground, picked up the sound of approaching horses. Instantly he was awake, on his feet. Hastily he gathered his equipment and saddled his horse.

Guessing the intruders to be at a distance from which they could not yet see him, he pulled buffalo grass from the ground and collected some of the dry wood which littered the area. He quickly built a sizable fire and lit it. While the flames raced skyward, he shaped his buffaloskin blanket beside the fire so that it resembled a man's body in sleep.

He put his ear to the ground again and determined that the riders were moving more slowly, coming in cautiously toward the fire. They would not ride into the camp until the flames died down and their intended victim was supposedly asleep beside the embers.

It was a ruse, a temporary escape only. They would come after him again, more determined than ever. But when they came again it would be on his terms and in the light of day. He rode swiftly away.

By noon the next day he knew they were closing in on him again. A yellow cloud of dust rising on the horizon behind him announced their impending visit.

He liked the time and the place. The area was flat for miles around. He slowed his horse. He turned in the saddle now and then to look back. Their figures in the distance were getting larger.

He brought his horse to a halt and dismounted to stretch and to check his weapons. Taking his knife from the scabbard at his belt, he looked at its cutting edge and was satisfied. He sheathed

it, drew it forth, sheathed it again, drew it, making certain his fingers knew their business. He gave his gun the same exercise. He was ready.

The killers were much closer now, riding hard. He swung into the saddle and set his horse off at an easy run, deliberately allowing the pursuers to gain on him.

Believing their quarry was within their grasp, the riders spurred their horses to a racing stride over the hot, dry land. They were soon close enough to fire at him.

Bryce bent low in the saddle, loosening the reins, letting his horse take it easy, as bullets whined around him. When they were almost at his heels, Bryce jerked the reins of his own mount and pulled the animal around abruptly.

The sudden braking of Bryce's horse caught the gunmen by surprise, ruining the aim of their gunfire. The two men could not check the speed of their horses and, helpless to stop them, they rushed past Bryce.

As they sped by, Bryce drew his gun.

The killers made wide turns to come riding back to face him. The first rider to wheel his horse around rode straight at Bryce. For a second they faced each other at close range, almost knee to knee. The bearded man had his gun aimed at Bryce's heart.

Bryce fired and a bullet struck the volunteer assassin in the chest. He pitched forward in the saddle and fell heavily to the ground, dead.

Bryce turned his horse in a semicircle to dodge the erratic firing of the other frantic rider. Now with his Green River knife in hand, he charged his adversary. Spurring his horse to a run, he tossed the weapon at the gunman. The knife hit the man in the heart, and he died trying to reach for it, toppling from his horse.

Bryce buried his attackers in the only way he could, wrapping them in their blankets. He took the saddles from their horses and turned the animals loose on the open range.

Chief Opothle Yohola waited for him in the tent pitched in a hunting camp some five miles from the Chief's frame house. The old man was glad to see Bryce, and his wrinkled face held a smile. He wore buckskins, and though the day was warm he had a blanket tossed over his shoulders. His headgear was a caplike covering sporting a dozen peacock feathers. Long gold earrings hung from his pierced ears. His hair, long and white, reached to his shoulders and he looked ancient although his eyes were ageless. Despite his age, he had been hunting, and his bows and arrows were stacked nearby.

After he had seen that his visitor had a meal, the Chief lighted a pipe and offered Bryce a draw on it. Bryce was able to smoke it without revealing his complete distaste.

When they had sat in silence for a time, alone with the pipe, the Chief signified he was ready to talk. "Speak," he invited.

They conferred for several hours. The old Chief of the Creek explained the critical situation in which he was plunged:

"The McIntosh brothers threaten to kill every Creek who will not declare loyalty to the Confederacy. They promise death to me, their Chief, for opposing them. They say I am old and new ways must take my place. They warn me they will let blood flow everywhere in this, my Nation."

"Will you do as the Chief of the Cherokee advises? Take your loyal people north to Kansas until hostilities are ended in the States and Territory?"

The old man rocked a little, pondering the question. "I would die before I would surrender to the McIntosh brothers and the white Rebels. To take my people north—this would be a removal, as before. Many would die on the way. The weather turns cold soon. Yet such a flight would confound my enemy." He turned a quizzical look upon Bryce. "The Confederates would not let us go if they could prevent it. This would draw their troops from other areas, would it not?"

"Chief Ross asks me to say to you that the flight north would be full of terrible risks. Yes, it would be a military action, in effect, and the enemy would be after you. You'd take them from other potential battles, yes."

The dark eyes were lively. "That is very good. In this way, I shall fight them." He put a hand on Bryce's knee. "You tell Chief Ross that the Creek Chief fights beside him in this silent war."

In further talk, they contrived a letter, to be delivered to Albert Pike, meant to camouflage the true intent and actions of the Creek Chief and his people. Admitting to Pike that "a large segment of the Creek Nation is loyal to the United States" and that he, their Chief, stood with them and would "so stand forever," he added that he was much too old and ill to take any action against the Confederates, and that he was too ill to travel.

When John welcomed Bryce home again and heard about the

Creek Chief's agreement to take his people north, he was overcome with feeling for the old man.

The Creek Chief's situation was no worse than what John
himself faced, and yet the tragedy of it seemed worse. For a man
to see his life's work destroyed, his government overthrown, his
friends become his enemies was a supreme cruelty—but at the
age of Chief Opothle Yohola, nearing ninety!

John turned his back on Bryce to stare with unseeing eyes at
the wall map. It was likely the valiant old Creek, uprooted once
more, would never see his home again.

XLVI

THE FIRST WEEK OF OCTOBER 1861 SAW THE FORMAL
alliance ceremonies between the Cherokee Nation and the
Confederacy. It was a week of holiday festivities with a school
recess declared so the children could enjoy the excitement.

The weather cooperated with the mood of the people and the
valley was turned scarlet and gold by frosty nights which became
warm sunny days. There was a fragrance of burning maplewood
from the fireplaces of Tahlequah. Fleecy clouds cast moving
shadows over the land, and the brisk winds had just a hint of the
cool weather which was coming.

The ceremony was held at Rose Cottage, the place the people
considered not only the home of their Chief but their national
house. The speaker's stand, raised beside the towering flagpole
on the front lawns, was decorated with bunting. The flag of the
United States still flew from atop the pole, but this occasion
would see it lowered. Benches had been placed on the grass for
the use of those who wanted them, but almost everyone sat on
the ground, gazing up at the speaker's platform.

They came to their Chief's home in varied dress, from tribal outfits trimmed with feathers and beads to fancy suits and dresses. Almost without exception, the men wore their hair long and many of them braided it, twining ribbons, feathers, or beads in it.

Stand Watie was handsome in the dress uniform of his rank of Brigadier General. Commanding his regiment of Mounted Rifles, he rode his horse up the driveway of Rose Cottage with all the pomp of a military hero. His well-trained men paced him, preening before an appreciative citizenry.

Colonel Drew's regiment joined with Watie's in forming lines around the platform. A rivalry had already developed between the regiments, but Colonel Drew had cautioned his men to act with reserve at the ceremonies.

Bryce looked for Copper but she was not seated with the Watie family. His disappointment was nothing compared to Stand's surprise at seeing him seated on the stand beside John.

As Stand took a seat in the front row of the speaker's benches, Albert Pike was introduced by a Council member. The Confederate spoke well, telling the people of the bright future they were moving toward in the company of the Confederacy. He welcomed them as allies. "Now, too, your own nation is no longer divided. Only weeks ago, you were two factions, best symbolized by those of you who called yourselves Knights of the Golden Circle, and wore pins to prove it. Your opposition simply called themselves 'the Pins,' wearing plain pins as emblems of their loyalty to the old treaty with the Union." He grinned, waving his arms. "Now you are all Confederates and brothers once again!"

When he finished speaking, John arose. He kept his remarks brief, referring only in a formal manner to the treaty itself. But at the conclusion of his address, he reminded them: "Union is strength. Dissension is weakness, misery, and ruin! In time of war, fight together! As brothers live! As brothers die!"

An officer came forward to John at the front of the platform. He carried a folded Confederate flag, presenting it with a bow to the Chief of the Cherokee Nation.

John took it, his face solemn, and turned to Colonel Drew to lay it carefully on his upturned hands.

Colonel Drew bore the flag down the stairs of the platform to the base of the flagpole, where he was met by a sergeant of Watie's regiment. The enlisted man, saluting the officer, took the flag and stood by with it as another soldier began to lower the Stars and Stripes.

The Chief stood at attention on the platform, Bryce behind him, as the Union's flag came slowly down the pole. John felt drained of life as Old Glory was taken from its pole lines and passed from hand to hand of the Rebels.

The sergeant stepped forward and attached the Confederate flag to the ropes. As he pulled, the Stars and Bars began to climb the pole, snapping out on the breeze prettily. The soldiers and the citizens shouted and called out, the Rebel yell ripping through all the noise. Drums sounded, a bugle blew, and men saluted as women smiled or cried.

A sudden commotion in a part of the crowd near the platform caught everyone's attention. Some of Watie's troopers had snatched the fallen Union flag and they were motioning the crowds back. They tossed the flag on the ground and set it afire.

John turned away from the sight. Bryce shared the pain and the resentment. Neither said a thing, but anyone closely observing their eyes would have known they were suppressing an inner rage.

Within a few weeks, John and Bryce were summoned by courier to a meeting with Senator Jim Lane and the officers assigned to duty with the Union column. Their courier-guide led them to an old abandoned farmhouse on the outskirts of Neosho, Missouri, in the Ozark foothills, close to the Cherokee border. They passed the campsite of the proposed column a short distance back in the hills from the farm. It was a snug spot, called Fox Hills, not easily accessible, perfect for its private purpose.

A wet snow, driven by a rising wind, fell on the hills. The roof of the aging farmhouse was sagging from its years and the added load of snow fast piling on it.

Colonels James Blunt and William Weer awaited them, along with the Senator. Blunt was to be in general command of the special project, with Weer in specific command of the column itself. Each had a few members of their own staffs with him.

Senator Lane, whose tenacious abilities had gained him a reputation as a troubleshooter, had suggested the assignments of Blunt and Weer to the President. He believed in them as much as he did in their mission.

Colonel Blunt, Napoleonic in physical attributes and tough as saddle leather, had a mind which the Senator said "has the edge of a Bowie knife." His dark-eyed face was dramatized with a drooping black moustache and a small goatee. Heavy-chinned, with a protruding underlip, he normally presented an unsmiling expression. He was an acknowledged military strategist and was eager to get to work on the assignment at hand. His orders from President Lincoln were to "restore the federal authority among the Five Tribes" of the Indian territory. Blunt was in that deserted Missouri farmhouse to take the first steps ordered by his Commander in Chief.

Weer was a man of contradictory character. He, like Blunt, was as flinty as Missouri hardtack, but he hid the fact under a relaxed veneer, giving the erroneous impression that he was lazy and maybe mentally slow. There was a rumor that he drank more than enough. He seemed to be in no hurry to accomplish anything.

Colonel Weer would command the Indian column which would be expected to carry out Blunt's strategy to recapture the territory. Weer's particular task would be the seizure of Tahlequah, a separate but vital operation under the presidential order to restore the territory to federal authority

John and Bryce were welcomed into the house as the bleak winter day surrendered to the freezing night. An orderly lighted the candles and placed new logs on the fire, brightening the room.

In the front parlor, the officers and the Cherokees got down to business. Colonel Weer took his jacket off and rolled it into a pillow, stretching himself on the floor in front of the hot fireplace.

John was at ease in the depths of a chair fashioned from barrels by the departed owner of the farm.

Surprisingly, to John, Colonel Weer was opening the conference. "We're planning to assign approximately fifteen hundred white men to the column. Will there be a matching number of red men?"

"Yes. We're recruiting enough men to form a regiment from each tribe."

Weer sat up, drawing his long legs up to rest his forearms on them. "You seem sure."

"I am. We're recruiting well at Tahlequah. They're anxious to get here. Most are awaiting orders as they go about their normal lives. Many have joined Colonel Drew's outfit and will transfer quietly when the time comes. Drew's men are directly under my supervision, so we have no problem."

Blunt thrust his booted feet toward the fireplace. "You don't doubt their loyalty?"

John shook his head. "No," he bragged, "I'm going to send you the best fighters in the world—Cherokee warriors with a secret cause."

"We'll match them," Blunt assured him. "Are you satisfied with the location of the camp?"

"It's adequate. Secluded, water source, plenty of open space, yet well into the hills."

Weer asked: "How long to finish recruitment?"

"Maybe another month. Working secretly delays us some. We'll be ready when the camp is equipped and open for operation."

They conferred on through the night. Senator Lane had the least to say. He listened because he would have a report to hand the President. They retired late and were up at dawn. The cold, blue sky was clear and the sun shone with a scintillating brilliance on the ice-glazed countryside.

They met again over breakfast and reviewed their assignments, making certain that each man knew his own task. They set plans to meet again at the camp by the end of January and went their separate ways. Colonels Blunt and Weer would ride back to St. Louis to work on the immediate problems of equipping and staffing the camp where the training of the recruits would begin within a month.

XLVII

THE CRISIS WAS UPON THE CREEK NATION. THE REBELS WERE moving through the land, and the McIntosh brothers raised the Confederate flag over the area and proclaimed that Chief Optohle Yohola and his followers would be liquidated.

Having buried his personal treasures and the ones of his Nation, slaughtered his cattle and emptied his home of his personal effects, the old Chief mounted his horse and rode at the head of a long line of wagons, riders, and pedestrians, all refugees of war.

The Chief led his people into the wilderness, moving north. The pace was slow. He was much burdened with the old, the sick, the very young. His greatest strength were the slaves of many of the families. The blacks could have stayed behind, but their loyalty was with the people plodding northward.

The Creek people knew they faced the terrors of cold weather and lack of food and fires. Disease might strike. If the enemy pursued, many would die. But on the frozen trail north they followed the vein of liberty and life.

The Chief sped a message to John at Tahlequah, telling him the flight to Kansas had begun. If the Confederates followed him, he promised to fight. "I will do whatever I must to get my people safely to the fort in Kansas. I promise I will deal in war if the Rebels pursue us. We are weak and we are not well armed, but there will be a way to fight, we must."

The pale sun of the mid-December day thawed the frozen mud of the trail. The Creeks, stumbling ahead, left their footprints and wagon-wheel imprints behind. Many wagons were hopelessly mired and a few overturned in the rough path. The people were plagued by frostbitten feet and hands, and many children and old folk were suffering from colds and coughs.

The miserable trek was not long under way when a report of it reached the McIntosh brothers. They spread the word and joined the white-haired Colonel Douglas Cooper and the 4th Texas Cavalry for an immediate pursuit.

Fourteen hundred troopers, Indian and white, left Fort Gibson with Cooper to find and destroy the fleeing Creeks. The bright red banner with its blue bars and white stars was a flash of warmth against the sad gray winter sky.

Cooper's troops were followed closely by the Creeks riding under command of Daniel McIntosh. His long hair, blowing free in the wind, was iced more than once as sleet began to beat down and the temperature dropped. His warriors rode with their faces set grimly, but high excitement and hate for their old Chief gave them a kind of warmth in the bitter cold. Opothle Yohola, who had taken a stand with the detested white Union, had run away.

Old and useless, no longer a leader of men, he deserved to die.

The Seminole troops came riding behind the Creek, under the authority of Major John Jumper and Chilly McIntosh.

The pursuit went on relentlessly for four days and nights. The Confederates found evidences of the Creeks' camps in cold ashes and frozen wagon marks in the trail. At the end of the fourth day of pursuit, Cooper's advance guard signaled that he had the Creeks in view. The Creeks were encamped across a stream at a place known as Round Mounds, their campfires twinkling among the trees. On the opposite shore, from the vantage point of high ground, the Confederates stayed in their saddles and gazed silently down on the Creek camp.

The Creeks were apparently preparing their evening meal. No guards stood to be seen anywhere.

Daniel McIntosh moved quietly to the side of Colonel Cooper. "The scouts report they have guns. But they don't appear to be expecting an immediate attack."

"We'll move in before we're discovered," the Colonel said. "Their only protection is that afforded by the trees and the cane-brakes. It's not enough."

Large flakes of snow were pelting down as the troops crept forward to the river. The crunch of iced grass made an alarming sound as they crawled downslope on the flats of their stomachs to the water.

Colonel Cooper was in their midst. He gave the order to charge, spurring his own mount.

The flares of the ignited gunpowder lit the riverbank like lightning. The bullets were nowhere near the target, slicing into the banks.

Cooper's "hold fire" order was heard all down the line. He listened, waited, looked, his arm upraised at the river's edge, his horse restless under him.

A few lights in the enemy camp had gone out. There was a babble of voices ashore among the Creeks. No answering shots came. Darkness went deeper as the last fires were smothered.

Chilly and Daniel rode to Cooper's side. "Go on!" Daniel urged. "Don't give them time to rally!"

The Colonel, standing in his stirrups, shouted: "Forward!" He swung his arm to signal the move.

The troops responded and men and horses plunged into the icy water which all but paralyzed their bodies.

Now, from shore, from the camp of the Creeks, came the sound of rifle fire. In the stream, Confederates were toppling from their saddles, victims of the surprise defensive fire. The refugees were aiming with deadly accuracy, making every bullet count, knowing the Rebels were too numb with cold, too surprised to react well.

The McIntosh brothers made it back to the other shore and rode up a slope to safety.

Colonel Cooper was in a daze. He turned his horse back, and when a young Texan trooper was thrown from his saddle into the river, his head bleeding, the Colonel leaned down from his saddle, hoisted the man up, and rode back to land with him. He laid the man down on the ground and wiped his own wet forehead. Although uninjured himself, Cooper was covered with blood. The young soldier died on the ground, and the Colonel walked away dizzily. A few minutes later, he would look at the blood on his uniform and wonder where it had come from. He had no recollection of having brought the youth to shore.

The sound of a bugle calling retreat shivered through the night as men staggered from the numbing, death-choked river.

Through the long, cold night the Confederates tended their wounded and collected their dead. Colonel Cooper stood beside the river, a blanket tossed over his shoulders, and stared across the dark waters. The Creeks had relighted their campfires.

Daniel McIntosh came quietly to watch with him. "They won't be able to hide behind the trees at dawn."

"They expect us now," said the Colonel, eyeing the moving figures around the campfires across the stream.

"We'll repay them in the morning," Daniel promised.

Colonel Cooper sat down on the ground and watched. Sleep was impossible. There was nothing to do but wait for the light of day.

As soon as there was a scarlet line of light edging the gray clouds, the Colonel ordered another attack upon the Creeks. The Texas 4th, somewhat depleted in its ranks, crossed the river, guns blazing.

They rode unchallenged. Not a sound came from the Creeks. The Rebels rushed the grounds, expecting a hand-to-hand battle. The camp was all but empty. Chief Opothle Yohola and his people had escaped during the night.

"What kind of scouts do we have?" Colonel Cooper demanded

to know of the McIntoshes. "I had a report the Creeks were here. I saw them! They paced this camp all night long."

Daniel was stunned. He had a black man by the collar, dragging him forward to the Colonel: "This man belongs to the old Chief. He'll tell you what happened."

"They gone," the slave said, a pride in his eyes which he did not try to hide.

"How?" the Colonel demanded. "How did they do it? I saw men walk the camp all night long."

The Negro grinned. "You want I should show you?"

"Yes!" the Colonel exhaled.

The slave went to a horse standing near. Taking the bridle in hand, and flashing his wide grin at the Confederate officer, he walked the horse back and forth in front of a fire. "The Chief said, walk the horse all night. The enemy will be fooled. The horse will look like many men, walking. The Chief is wise."

"You are a prisoner," the Colonel told the black man.

"I don't mind. The old Chief, he rides free."

The snow during the night had turned to rain and it erased all traces of the Creeks. Finding them again would entail long hours of travel. The men were in no condition to pick up an immediate pursuit. Further, General Hunter was reported traveling toward the direction of the territory from Missouri. Rumor or not, the Colonel needed time to reorganize his troops and his plan of pursuit. He did all that he could, sending a squad in pursuit of the Creeks just to keep contact with them until he was ready to attack, and returned to Fort Gibson.

Not many days later his pursuit squad returned, too. The Creeks had taken to the wilderness, and they could not be found.

The Colonel called the McIntosh brothers to his office in the fort. "When we go after the Creeks this time, I want John Ross and John Drew with me. Go to Tahlequah and bring them here."

John was inwardly exultant at the news the McIntoshes brought him at Rose Cottage. But when Daniel told him Colonel Cooper needed his troops to "reinforce him for the pursuit and capture of the Creeks," John was hesitant.

"What about Watie? Where are his troops?"

"He's been scouting near the Missouri border. He's been called back."

Having assured the McIntoshes that he and Colonel Drew would respond with troops, John watched the men depart.

"We've got to find a way to help Yohola," he told Bryce. "This time he's going to be confronted with a superior force."

He amazed the troops when he appeared not in the uniform of the Confederacy, or even in his tribal outfit, but in Scottish kilts, tunic, and tam-o'-shanter, the colorful plaids of the Ross clan, giving him the look of a Scottish war chief.

The regimental band included bagpipers who enlivened the short march to Fort Gibson with the exciting piping of martial music. The throb of it filled a need in John's heart.

The weathered old tower of Fort Gibson loomed ahead, and the gates of the fifteen-foot stockade opened wide to Ross and his troops. The Stars and Bars flew over the place which had once been the military cradle of many Americans who were now enemies. The 4th Texas Cavalry was temporarily housed there.

Colonel Cooper told John he had lost all contact with the Creeks. "Do you have any idea which route he might take to reach Missouri or Kansas?"

John shook his head. "None."

A lone Cherokee scout, loyal to the Confederacy, sat his horse high on a bluff which jutted over the Verdigris River, to the west of the camp where Cooper had attacked the Creeks. Clem Rogers looked down, solemnly studying the surrounding area where stood cabins of an isolated Creek village. The place was called Big Bend, obviously named for the wide bend of the river which wound past the village. Below him, stringing out for some distance along the river road, were halted the battered wagons of Chief Opothle Yohola, headed north now in escape from the Confederates. The wagons were being swarmed over by Creeks welcoming their old Chief and his people. The refugees had found a temporary haven where they could care for the sick and the dying.

Clem Rogers lifted the reins and rode straight for Fort Gibson. His word to the Colonel would bring warriors to Big Bend and the deaths of the Confederates at Round Mounds would be avenged.

Colonel Cooper hastily conferred with his fellow officers and mapped a pincer-type maneuver against the Creeks. The regiments would separate on the trail before reaching Big Bend. The McIntosh brothers would lead the veteran Indian fighters and Colonel Drew's regiment, accompanied by Chief Ross, up the

Arkansas River toward the bend. Colonel Cooper would take the white soldiers up the Verdigris River and a semicircling movement would be effected.

The day after Christmas brought subzero weather, with heavy clouds lowering over the hills, spitting a wet snow which sifted into the clothing of the troopers.

Once again, water separated the enemies. The McIntoshes rode the lines swiftly, inspecting, issuing preliminary orders. They rode into the heavy thickets of the riverbanks at the bend. Troopers were strung along the shores of the Arkansas and Verdigris; at their confluence stood a high bluff of land jutting over the waters.

John and Bryce sat astride their horses, looking across the waters to the tree-protected campsite of the Creeks.

Sitting on his horse, dressed now in his white buckskins and scarlet-feathered warbonnet, John was an impressive figure. His face was painted with red and white stripes. He held a rifle in his hands, resting on the saddlebow. The large white horse he sat on was also streaked with vermillion paint, like gashes of blood, and red bits of wool were interwoven in the braided tail of the animal.

"Now is the time," John told Bryce. "I'll wait here. Come back when they have the message."

"Yes, sir!" Bryce replied and rode his horse carefully, moving downslope toward the river.

John was sitting quietly, observing the Creek camp below for any signs of activity, when Chilly McIntosh came up the slope to see him. He viewed the Chief with a grudging admiration.

Chilly looked down at the campsite, too, and remarked: "Looks like we've got him trapped all right. He can't escape this time." When the Chief made no reply, Chilly asked insolently: "Are your troops ready?"

The Chief did not turn his head. "Colonel Drew is in command. Ask him."

Chilly swallowed the rebuff and rode back down the bluff to the river, checking the fact that Drew's men were hidden in the canebrake along the river, guns in hand.

The general advance was ordered quietly, and troopers begn to move. Their hands tended to freeze to the barrels of the guns, but gloves were useless because they were too clumsy for triggering weapons. Drew's troops, having approached the river on their bellies, as ordered, held their positions now in the thickets, a new order having come from their Chief.

Bryce moved silently among them, and they passed the word from man to man in hushed tones. The heavy sky pressed down upon them. There was only the sound of their whisperings upon the wind until the startling sound of a child's cry came from the Creek camp.

"I hope to God the old Creek Chief has the children out of range of our guns," Colonel Cooper said to Chilly. He raised his arm in a signal to charge.

Out of the underbrush came the Texans, braving the cold water, firing as they moved forward, their first bullets flying harmlessly into the mudbanks below the camp.

Downriver, Daniel McIntosh responded to the order to move and slid down the muddy banks to join the Cherokee troopers of Colonel Drew. Daniel held his rifle high over his head as he hit the water. Heading toward midstream, he turned to look back. There was not a single Indian Confederate to be seen. Not a man of them had emerged from the canebrakes.

Daniel stood in the cold water, his head twisting from shore to shore, stunned. He waved frantically to them to come forward, to join the attack, but there was no answer. Appalled, he shouted hoarsely to them. There was no response.

On the opposite shore, Colonel Cooper and Chilly looked back to the river, searching for sight of the supporting troops. Cooper went back across the river, slipping several times, soaking himself thoroughly. The frigid water numbed his legs, but he was too furious to care.

From upriver came the sounds of loud gunfire, mixed with screams. The odor of gunpowder drifting downstream added to his nausea at the realization that the Cherokees and Creeks serving with Colonel Drew, and under the command of John Ross, were not going to fight.

Shaking from head to foot, he waded to shore and made his way up the bluff where he knew Chief Ross was sitting astride his horse in a strange silence. He was there still, the rifle unused. He looked down at the approaching officer with calmness.

Seeing him, Colonel Cooper shivered anew. Gone was the white John Ross who had advanced to battle in splendid spirits, seemingly eager to fight the enemy. Here, beyond the reach of any white man, was a silent-tongued Indian Chief with eyes too deep to read, face too set to understand. This was not the John Ross he knew. This was Cooweescoowee, the "Great White Swan," a man apart. Cooweescoowee, the Indians called him, the word's descriptive meaning so accurate: a large white bird of uncommon occurrence! This was much more than a man he confronted: this was a symbol, and he could not cope with it.

The Indian did not even notice his presence. Still, resentment burned through the Colonel. "Where is Colonel Drew?" he asked coldly.

"I do not know."

Purple veins bulged in the Colonel's neck. "You know! There's been a mass desertion. Not one of your men has responded to the attack call. They are nowhere to be seen."

Bryce came riding up the slope to the side of the Chief, his horse and his clothing water-soaked and mud-splashed.

Colonel Cooper looked past him to the Chief. "Sir, without my full complement of troops the outcome of this engagement stands in doubt. I'll need a detailed report on the desertion of your troops to hand to my commanding officer, General McCulloch."

"Tell him what has occurred," the Chief told Bryce.

Bryce patted the neck of his wet horse, calming him. "Sir, the Cherokee troops under the command of Colonel Drew will not fight. They have heard the voice of the Great Spirit warning them not to join the battle. They will hear no other voice now. Sir, you know that Indians hear the Great Spirit as much with their hearts as with their ears. Now they are deaf to mere mortal orders."

"They *have* deserted!" the Colonel said. He looked from Bryce to the Chief, hopelessly. He said no more but turned his horse and rode down the slopes without even looking back.

John and Bryce stayed on the bluff, knowing they had done all they could for Yohola. Now they had to endure an agony of waiting.

After taking the south bank of the river, the Confederates pushed ahead. They made the Creeks fall back from the river area, forcing them into the doubtful shelter of bare trees.

The Rebels were determined to capture them or kill them and they went about the work well. They pursued them into their hiding places and either shot them on sight or forced them to surrender, man after man. The routing of the Creeks became a full-scale retreat in the black night.

Colonel Cooper stood in the center of the captured camp, with wounded and dead around him. There were huddling groups of frightened and sick women and children, staring at him, pitifully uncertain of their fate. "Get me a count fast of the living," he ordered a soldier. "Post sentries over them and keep an eye on the wounded men. I don't want anyone escaping."

A young lieutenant saluted him: "Sir, Chief Yohola and most of his people have escaped."

"Then we'll pursue—"

"Sir?" the boyish-faced officer was almost apologetic.

"Yes, Lieutenant?"

"The Creeks have disappeared. Sir, there's no trace of them." He looked into the dark beyond. "We'd need daylight, sir, to find them."

Standing in the scarred camp amid the suffering people who were his captives, the Texan weighed his course. Should he continue the pursuit of the Creek Chief or should he stand and take care of the sick and wounded, the desperate and the dead? Could he risk another battle now? The failure of the Cherokee troops to support him had cost him the total victory he had counted upon. Did he dare ride into the wilderness with his weakened outfit?

Cooper was interrupted by the arrival of Stand Watie and his troops. Coming in from the Missouri borderline, General Watie had intercepted some of the escaping Creeks. He took none alive. Leaving bodies on the path behind, he had ridden swiftly to give Colonel Cooper the support he suspected he needed.

Splashing across the Verdigris, their voices raised in the spine-chilling war cry of the Cherokee, Watie's men raced into the embattled camp. In spite of their Confederate uniforms, the warriors wore warpaint.

Watie reined his horse beside the Colonel, calling out: "Colonel, where is the old Chief?" His dark eyes searched the bloody camp.

The Colonel put a hand on the bridle of Watie's horse to steady the excited animal. "He's escaped."

"Then I go to bring him back!"

The Colonel halted him. "Wait! We're in trouble. The Cherokee troops of Ross and Drew have deserted. They never fired a shot."

General Watie's words were more hissed than spoken. "We

have much to settle with John Ross! But now I go after Chief
Yohola." He stood in the stirrups, saluting Cooper and waving
his men forward, hurrying on.

Colonel Cooper watched them disappear in the dark. Did the
Confederacy have much to settle with Chief Ross? Was the Cherokee Chief responsible for the failure of his men to fight? If so,
then the Colonel was faced with a problem which would reach
into the halls of the Confederate Congress and require the personal attention of President Davis. A conspiracy between John
Ross and the Union, if such existed, could wreck the Confederacy's plans in the Southwest.

He looked up to the bluff across the river. There were some
kind of lights burning there now. The Chief was still there.

He went back across the river and pushed his way through the
frozen canestalks to climb the bluff to the camp of the Chief of
the Cherokee. The Chief was seated on the ground, Bryce Calvin
beside him, a dozen other troopers with them. A circle of a dozen
rifles were plunged into the cold ground by means of attached
bayonets, and on the butt of each rifle a candle had been set and
lighted, giving light and a hint of warmth to the encircled men.

The Chief looked up to the Colonel with no surprise. However, he gave a wave of his hand to the young troopers, and they
got up, leaving the circle of rifles to vanish in the dark. "Come,
join us," he said to the Colonel.

Slowly, wearily, aware of every tired muscle and bone in his
body, the Colonel edged through the rifles and took a half-kneel-
ing position in front of the Chief and Bryce. "I want the truth.
What happened today?"

Chief Ross did not hesitate: "You have heard the truth, my
friend. The Great Spirit spoke to my warriors. It told them they
must not kill. They were warned not to harm their red brothers."

Colonel Cooper licked his lips and tasted dry mud. "You seriously offer this as an excuse for the cowardly desertion of your
men? Come, now, Chief Ross! You're a Christian! You don't
believe in such things as voices giving military orders, or coun-
termanding them, do you?"

"Yes, I am a Christian, as I am Cherokee. Because I am, I
believe that a man can be spoken to by the Great Spirit. God does
speak to the hearts of men. It happened here today. The men
obeyed," he repeated solemnly. "They could not kill."

Colonel Cooper was appalled. "Do you realize what you're

saying? You're telling me that I can't rely on my Indian troops!
If it happened today, it can happen tomorrow! If this is so, there
can never be a Confederate victory in the territory."

"My warriors will not fail again. The next time, I can persuade
them to fight even their brothers."

"*Persuade* them to fight!" The Colonel was aghast. "Chief Ross,
there's a treaty between our nations which declares your men
will fight upon order. You signed it. You agreed to give us your
Cherokee warriors."

"The treaty has been honored. You were given my warriors."

"But they wouldn't fight! There are men who will term the
desertion today deliberate and willful treason. Some will say you
planned it."

The Chief looked at the Colonel and his blue eyes were like
a winter pond. "And you, Colonel? What will you say?"

The Colonel was not really certain. "I will say they are wrong.
There are men who have much to learn yet about their red-
skinned brothers. The white commanders must learn what is in
the heart and mind of his red warriors."

"Colonel," the Chief spoke the title quietly, bowing his head
to the man.

"In order to avoid a repetition of this day, I'll use the Drew
warriors only in battles against white men. They will not be
required to fire upon their red brothers."

When the shrewd Colonel was gone, John's young warriors
returned to the circle and sat with him through the long night.
"A major battle was won here this day and not a shot was fired,"
John told them. "An underground war is surely justice without
trumpets. We have sown the seed of doubt, and it will flourish."

General Stand Watie picked up the trail of Chief Yohola and
his people and made vicious attacks upon them as they kept
moving north, killing them without mercy when he came upon
them.

The Creeks fought valiantly and, for civilians, with a brilliant
touch of the military. Men, armed and determined, kept dropping away from the wagon train with its old people, women, and
children. They rode back to meet Watie's men on the trail, letting
the wagons move ahead while they played a deadly game of delay,
sniping at Watie's troopers from trees. The Rebels had to account
for every foot of the trail they took, and if many Creeks died, so
did numerous Confederates.

It was not the policy of General Stand Watie to take prisoners. Death was dealt by his troopers when they cornered a Creek. He was determined to kill Chief Yohola, enraged that the old man had thus far outwitted, outmaneuvered, and outdistanced all the Confederate troops which had come after him. If he were to reach Kansas alive, the Confederate cause in the territory would suffer a real blow. So General Watie rode hard, pressing on after the Creeks. Word drifted throughout the territory about his bloody, relentless pursuit.

But the bleeding wagon train kept on moving north. Their suffering was terrible. They no longer had any supplies, their cattle long lost. The horses were weakening, many falling dead from starvation, and there was no time to butcher them with General Watie pushing closer. The weather stayed below freezing. There was no time to linger over campfires. Food was so scarce that some of the hungry children were found eating droppings from the horses. Walking, stumbling along on feet wrapped in rags, they went on.

Finally the ailing and aged Chief led his people across the border to Leroy, Kansas, where doctors and friendly hands awaited them at the fort. Behind on the trail lay the grisly testimony to all that the Creeks had suffered. Seven hundred Creeks were dead at the hands of Watie's troops.

One doctor, treating the near-frozen victims of the miserable trek, spoke in awe of their flight through the wilderness. "The old man did not head an exodus—he wrought a miracle."

The word of the majority of the Creeks' safe arrival in Kansas spread throughout the territory. The young men who were riding to Fox Hills to quietly volunteer for duty with the Union column heard.

As they took their training, Yohola! was their battle cry.

XLVIII

THE FLOW OF SUPPLIES FROM ARKANSAS TO THE Confederates in the territory was in jeopardy. Wagons used the main road that skirted along the Arkansas-Missouri-Cherokee borders, winding around the range of hills through that area called Pea Ridge, where Union guns overlooked the road, and the Confederates' wagons were finding it impossible to get past. Unless the Union could be ousted from its position atop Pea Ridge, the Confederates were going to face a crisis in the acquisition of provisions.

The Yankees on the Ridge were headquartered in a building which had served for many years as a tavern. Its commanding view and highly defensible location made it an excellent fort. Marching orders from Colonel Cooper were not long in coming to the Ross and Drew outfits. There was to be a combined attack upon Pea Ridge.

The Colonel consulted with John at Rose Cottage. "This mission must not fail. We need the road below the ridge not only for supply wagons but we can use it as an attack route into Missouri. And since the Yankees on the ridge are white, I don't believe your warriors can desert on the grounds that they will not fire upon their red brothers. I expect them to rally to the attack orders."

When he was gone, John called Bryce to his office and handed him a written message. "Ride to Fox Hills. Give this message into the hands of Colonel Blunt, and do whatever he orders."

When a messenger rode up to the front door of Rose Cottage just a few minutes later, John thought that Bryce had returned, but in a moment he recognized the courier as a member of Drew's force. He gave the Chief a salute. "Sir, Colonel Drew requests you read this with his heartfelt sympathies."

John took the little piece of paper, knowing what was written there. "Thank you, sergeant." And he went into the house, to his office.

He did not hear the courier leave the driveway. He did not hear Mary enter the room and close the door behind.

"John?"

He got up, the message crumpling in his hand. "It's Jim."

"Oh, John! No!"

"I've seen death so often. I've faced it myself—thought of it, many times. But—Jim!" He shook his head, remembering Quatie and Jim, together.

"It happened in battle?"

"Yes," he put the crushed note in her hands.

"I'll have to go to Sarah right away. I can spare you that."

He kissed her forehead. "She'll need you."

Riding to join Colonel Drew and his troops in Tahlequah, John hardly remembered the trip into town. All his memories of Jim brought only a deeper pain. The firstborn son! How proud he and Quatie had been at his birth! Wasn't it only yesterday? Jim, gone!

While the Confederate troops were organizing their march to Pea Ridge, Bryce was conferring with the Union officers at Fox Hills. In response to Chief Ross's message, Bryce and twenty-four Creek and Cherokee volunteers of the Union column were ordered to Pea Ridge. Bryce was given special orders which he communicated to the warriors. They rode fast to the Union stronghold and had reported for their special duty by the time the Confederate troops under General McCulloch, Albert Pike, Stand Watie, John Ross, and Colonel Drew arrived at the base of the Ridge.

Colonel Cooper rode to John's side, "Your troops look good, sir. I hope they'll perform with valor."

John gave him a frown. "Pea Ridge stands within the borders of the State of Arkansas. Our treaty promised that the Cherokee warriors would not be required to serve outside their own national lines."

"My God, Ross!" the Colonel exploded. "You aren't going to take your troops out on a technicality?"

"I ought to," John retorted. "Some of them aren't happy about this duty, but I expect no trouble. If there should be some erratic behavior, however, look to your own source, Colonel."

The Colonel jammed his hat on his head and rode off briskly to inspect the lines—troopers of the 1st Regiment Cherokee Mounted Rifles of Colonel John Drew, the 2nd Regiment Cherokee Mounted Rifles of Colonel Stand Watie, the Choctaw and Chickasaw Mounted Rifles under Colonel Daniel McIntosh. Albert Pike rode over to meet Colonel Cooper, and at the foot of the ridge they completed their plan of attack.

A bugle sounded in the Indian ranks in the heavy underbrush—the call to attack.

In the hushed moment which followed the fading of the bugle call there came the weird sound of the Cherokee chortle drifting down from the fort, loud and clear.

At the top of the Ridge were positioned Cherokee soldiers in blue Union uniforms, calling down to their Cherokee, Creek, Choctaw, Chickasaw, and Seminole brothers. Red man called to red man.

The answering chortle came from the Confederate lines, chilling the bones of the white troopers who moved past the Indians to start their advance on the Ridge.

The Indian warriors made no move to follow their white comrades. Not one lifted a gun. Instead, Indians in blue uniforms kept calling to Indians in gray uniforms, shouting through the distance in their native tongue. There was no barrier, no war between them.

Colonel Cooper was back at the side of John. "Why aren't your troops advancing as ordered? Now what's happening?"

Chief Ross was having some difficulty in keeping his horse quiet. "Do you understand Cherokee?"

"Hell, no!"

"Too bad, Colonel. The Confederate and Union Indians have just declared peace between themselves. They will not fight each other."

"They've got to fight! We can't take the Ridge without all our guns."

John shook his head. "They won't go against each other. But you'd better keep your eye on Pike's Indians. They've armed themselves with bows, arrows, and tomahawks. I think they've got their own war in mind."

"You mean half the Indians won't fight, and the other half is planning a scalping raid?"

Chief Ross shrugged his shoulders.

The Colonel pulled rein, riding toward General Watie, whose troops were advancing bravely upon the Ridge, eager for the battle.

The seige raged for three long days, but the outnumbered Confederates could not overcome the loss of their Cherokee troops. General McCulloch was killed. Individual Indians reverted to Indian warfare, terrorizing the whites on both sides, descending with awful screeches upon their victims, murdering, scalping, and running. At the end of the third day it was over.

A Confederate trumpeter sounded the retreat which always lingers to haunt the ears of fighting men. The Rebels pulled away from Pea Ridge, leaving the superior guns of the Yankees behind.

Stand Watie and Albert Pike, seated in a room of the National Hotel in Tahlequah with Douglas Cooper, heard the Colonel express their own views: "John Ross cost us Pea Ridge. He is operating against us at all times. He is guilty of treason against the Confederacy."

"What can we do about him?" Pike asked.

"Try him," Stand said. "Hang him for treason. His son Bryce was at Pea Ridge with the Yankees. I had word on that which I trust."

The Colonel held up a hand of caution. "We can't take the law into our own hands. This is a matter for the Confederate officials in Richmond. Perhaps even the President—"

Albert Pike nodded. "You're right. I'll go to Richmond right away. We'll see what kind of action we can take. Meanwhile, keep Ross out of our plans."

XLIX

THE DAY JOHN AND BRYCE WERE TO DEPART TO JOIN THE Union expedition force at Fox Hills, John gave some last hours to the problems Mary faced at home. She had to pack all the necessary official papers and personal belongings and decide which would be transferred to their temporary Washington residence and which could be left at Rose Cottage to await their return at the war's end.

When John came back from Fox Hills, it would be ostensibly as a prisoner of war and actually as the legal Chief of the Cherokee in protective custody for the duration of hostilities. Mary had to arrange for their comfort in faraway Washington and still see that Rose Cottage was maintained efficiently in their prolonged absence. Hank was to be in charge of their plantation, directly responsible to three Ross sons who would be staying in the Nation, as well as to Jane, whose home stood so close to the mansion.

Bryce, knowing only that his duty required that he go to Washington and his feelings for Copper urged that he stay in the Nation, saddled and rode upriver alone.

He saw the bright yellow of her cotton shirt through the screen of shrubbery at the old campsite. Dismounting, he pushed through the brush to break into the clearing.

They moved to each other, embracing. There were no words, just repeated kisses, a few tears. At last he told her, "Copper, there isn't much time. There are things we've got to discuss."

"Oh, Bryce, I know! I prayed you'd come here today. Bryce, my uncle and Captain Pike actually believe you and Chief Ross are traitors to the Confederacy! Captain Pike has gone to Richmond to report you both. My uncle has said you'll both be shot!"

"You're certain he's gone to Richmond?"

She stepped back from him, her eyes wide in fear. "They're right about you! You and Chief Ross *are* working for the Union!"

"Copper, please—"

She pushed at his hands, retreating to her horse. Grabbing the reins, she mounted the big animal.

"Copper, give me a chance—"

"No!" A sob carried her words from her throat: "It's no use. You're a Ross and I'm a Boudinot, no matter what else happens. Nothing will ever change that!" And she spurred the horse away from him, forcing him to step back, crashing the mount through the underbrush.

L

JOHN AND BRYCE JOINED IN THE LAST FEW WEEKS OF THE training of the troopers at Fox Hills, demonstrating on the open range their own skills with the Sharp rifle, the Green River knife, the bow and arrow. They showed the men how to combine the use of the weapons with riding. They taught them how to tumble from their horses without injury and how to swing into the saddle from a running or downed position.

With the field training went military lessons in the theory of teamwork; the necessity of sometimes dropping a prepared plan and initiating a new one, even in the midst of battle.

The troopers learned to act together as one man under simulated battle conditions. They swam the river, climbed trees, marched over hills, rode prairie lands, charging each other with sabers and gunning each other in mock battles. They could let an arrow fly straight to its mark, as deadly as a bullet.

Now, having learned all the lessons of war which could be taught in the hills, they were eager to ride to free their Nation of the Confederate rule. Especially, they wanted to avenge the Creeks and prove their loyalty to their Chief against Watie's forces.

The first week in July 1862 the outfit was joined by a tall and angular man, the Reverend Evan Jones. He came in from St. Louis, easing himself slowly from the saddle to extend friendly hands to John and Bryce. Troopers stood by, gaping at the strange man who had just arrived all dressed up in Sunday meeting clothes: long black frock coat, tall silk hat, white gloves, silk tie—all befitting a church service more than a military camp.

In John's tent the Reverend handed a saddlebag to John. "Chief Ross, President Lincoln requests that I deliver this to you. He said this: 'Tell him I give it to him with my grateful thanks.' "

John opened the bag and brought forth a carefully folded American flag.

That day also brought the exciting news that General Stand

Watie and his troops were encamped on an independent raid expedition of their own scarcely twenty miles away, apparently hovering near the Missouri border in a plan to attack a wagon train bearing supplies for Union troops operating in Arkansas. The news served better than a rousing marching band to inspire the troopers. General Watie was in the direct line of their march.

The Union expedition moved out of its camp at dawn on a clear July day. Four thousand men, regiments of white men and Indians, rode together on the mission to Tahlequah.

The Indians wore blue uniforms, which had not been designed for their lean bodies, and the fit was generally bad. Under the military caps of the Union, their black hair hung in braids highly decorated with feathers and cornhusks. Their faces were streaked with crimson paint. In his youth, John remembered ironically, he had identified the color blue with tragedy and defeat.

As the column picked up its marching rhythm and crept south along the bottomlands of the valley, they lifted their voices in the breathless, fluctuating chant of tribal battle hymns.

To the south of the column, a Confederate scout rode to General Watie's camp pitched near the same river. The scout flung himself from the sweating horse before it came to a halt and saluted the General. "Sir! A Union column is headed this way. Fifteen miles distant, to the north, sir."

General Watie was cool but puzzled. "I don't see how that's possible. We're aware of the location of every Yankee outfit from Tahlequah to St. Louis. Are you certain of the identity?"

"Yes, sir!"

"The number of men?"

"Approximately four thousand," he shook his head, "I'd guess, sir."

"Come with me, sergeant, and give me the details." The flap of the General's tent was dropped behind them, shutting out the curious faces of the troopers who were gathering outside.

Hearing that Cherokee and Creek troops were riding with the Yankees, and that Chief John Ross and Bryce Calvin were accompanying the expedition, the General was stunned. He had been right, then. John Ross and Bryce Calvin were serving the enemy! So the war had become one between them, after all.

The General saw things clearly—outnumbered, he could not surprise them. He must retreat now, not running from a battle but, rather, choosing the time and the place.

The Confederates pulled out, riding all through the night in a racing drive to Tahlequah. The General put considerable space between his force and the Union column.

Due to excellent scouting, however, the Union column never lost contact with the fleeing Confederates. The Yankees did not expect to overtake the Rebels until they reached Tahlequah.

"I believe General Watie will send the main body of his troops on toward Texas," John advised Colonel Weer. "He'll want to pick up reinforcements. But he'll keep a force behind in Tahlequah to do what he can to delay your troops from taking the whole Nation."

General Watie, having indeed cut out a regiment of his troops from the whole force and sending the majority on southward, had a further plan in mind. It had to be done expertly and in short time. He rode with his remaining troopers to his home, entered, and called: "Sarah!"

She came from the kitchen, drying her hands on a blue apron tied to her waist, surprised to see him.

"I don't have much time, Sarah, but I want you to know what's happening. I may have to go on to Texas for a time. Sarah, John Ross and Bryce Calvin are riding toward Tahlequah with a Union column. They'll reach town soon."

"A Union column!" She was appalled. "You mean they've been captured?"

"Hardly! It's as I said. They're agents for the Union—have been all along."

Copper came into the room to stand behind her aunt. She listened to her uncle with her fingertips pressed to her lips.

"I'm going to pay the Chief for his loyalty. Before I head for Texas, I'm going to burn Rose Cottage to the ground."

"You wouldn't do such a barbaric thing!" Copper exclaimed.

"Barbaric!" He took hold of her, shaking her. "It was John Ross who had my brother murdered! Yes, I'm going to burn Rose Cottage, and if I can, I'll kill Ross and Calvin! Now, you get to your room and stay there."

Stand, persuaded by his wife to eat a quick meal at the kitchen table, did not see his niece slip past the door. Sarah did, but she busied herself with serving her husband at the table, keeping her silence.

The citizens of Tahlequah gathered in the streets, at their doors and windows, to see the arrival of the Union troops. These

were the people who had never understood their Chief's acceptance of the Confederate treaty. As in the old days, they looked
for the arrival of their beloved Chief with eager eyes and glad
hearts.

Copper banged on the front door at Rose Cottage. Her fast ride
up the drive had attracted the attention of the black people in
the fields and many faces were turned toward her.

The door was opened by a black servant. Copper swept past
the woman, calling for Mary, and met her hurrying down the
stairs.

"The Chief and Bryce are riding toward Tahlequah from the
north with a Union column. My uncle is coming to burn this
place. He says he will kill them both!"

Mary reacted fast. "Help me, Copper. There's a bell outside
the kitchen door; go pull the rope on it. It will bring the help
we need to get our personal things out of the house. There are
things upstairs—and everything in John's office. Go right
through the dining room and out the kitchen."

As Copper ran to toll the bell, Mary raced upstairs, calling to
the servant who still stood at the front door: "Warn everyone in
the house to get out. Miss Mary and Annie are in their rooms,
I'll get them!" Young John was away in an eastern school, for
which she was grateful at the moment.

There was barely time to carry out the personal papers of Chief
Ross when General Watie and his troops cut across the lawns,
the summer roses trampled under the hooves of the horses. Some
of the troopers, acting on prior orders, raced to the servants and
service buildings, where they rushed the people, herding them
into the corrals at gunpoint.

General Watie, with a dozen men holding blazing torches, rode
to the front door. Mary and Copper stood with the other members of the household in the driveway.

"Uncle Stand! Please! Don't!" Copper cried out.

Watie was totally surprised to see Copper there, but he said
nothing.

Although Mary's face was very white and in her eyes there was
a pleading for compassion, she uttered not one word to General
Watie. She would not beg.

Stand moved his arm in a wide circle and, standing in his
stirrups, tossed a flaming stick into the front window of Rose
Cottage. Giving the Rebel yell, the other men, one by one, rode

past the windows of the Ross home and flung their torches through the glass. Clouds of black smoke burst from the shattered windows. Rose Cottage was burning and the flames were spreading from the first floor, up the stairs, and on to the roof.

Coming in on Military Road, north of Park Hill, Bryce was the first to spot the high-climbing smoke. He pulled his horse beside John's and pointed off to the left.

John, riding some distance ahead of the troops, took one look and knew what it was: "Rose Cottage! Stand must be there." He spurred his horse and took off, Bryce racing beside him.

General Watie and his men were ready to leave when up from Military Road came John and Bryce, their horses at a full gallop.

The General wheeled his horse around to shout at Copper. "Get on your horse! Ride!" He reached for the reins of her horse, took them in hand, waiting for her to mount.

Copper saw Bryce racing toward them, but she obeyed her uncle. As soon as she was in the saddle, Stand led the animal along behind his, not trusting her to hold the reins. The General and his troops raced across the lawns, cutting off into a ploughed field toward Military Road.

Bryce raced after them. John headed alone for the burning mansion and his family.

Drawing up beside Copper's horse, still being led by General Watie, Bryce leaned out of his saddle, grabbed Copper around the waist, and lifted her from her horse, holding her firmly to his side as he made a circle back toward the flaming house.

General Watie rose in his saddle, reached for his sidearm, and aimed. Copper was clinging to Bryce, her arms tight around his neck, her cheek against his. The General did not fire his gun. He let go of Copper's horse and spurred his own ahead; his men encircled him protectively as they sped away from the Ross plantation.

Bryce lowered Copper from the saddle, dismounted, and joined her at the family group. Mary held out her arms to Copper, drawing her into the family circle.

John, holding Mary, their crying daughters pressing against them, stared numbly at the destruction of his home. The flames soon died, the ruins smoking, sending forth a suffocating air.

Colonel Weer cantered his horse up from the fields. He left the saddle, and led his horse toward the Rosses. "The pursuit and capture of General Watie is going to become a career." He looked at the blackened, smouldering timbers of the fire-collapsed house. "Watie's fierceness will never allow him to be captured. He'll be the last to surrender."

John nodded agreement, "He's a strong man, as a friend or enemy."

Colonel Weer put a compassionate hand on John's shoulder. "You know you're my prisoner, sir?"

"I know."

"There's not much point in lingering here, is there, Chief Ross? Perhaps we might as well get organized and send you people on your way to Washington."

John glanced at the flagpole. "Colonel, before we leave, I'd like to raise the flag the President sent me. And before we leave Tahlequah, I'd like an hour with my sons and my overseer."

"Certainly, we'll see that you have the time you need to confer."

John and Bryce worked together to haul down the Confederate flag and attach the Stars and Stripes to the ropes, and Old Glory slowly climbed the pole to the top and unfolded on the wind.

"I'm hopeful President Lincoln will want a new star added at the end of hostilities," John told them. "A star to represent the entire Indian territory as a state."

Colonel Weer mused aloud: "A state of red people. Okla Homa—red man, right?"

"Right. Choctaw words," John agreed. He turned his attention to Mary. There was not a tear in her eyes as she turned her gaze from her demolished home. He wiped some soot from her forehead. "Why don't you cry?"

"Because I still have thee," she replied.

Elsie
Oct. 9, 1983

EPILOGUE

"No danger appalled him. He never faltered in supporting what he believed to be right, but clung to it with a steadiness of purpose which alone could have sprung from the clearest convictions of rectitude. He never sacrificed the interests of his Nation to expediency. He never lost sight of the welfare of the people. For them he labored daily for a long life, and upon them he bestowed his last expressed thoughts. A friend of law, he obeyed it; a friend of education, he faithfully encouraged schools throughout the country, and spent liberally his means in conferring it upon others. Given to hospitality, none ever hungered around his door. A professor of the Christian religion, he practiced its precepts. His works are inseparable from the history of the Cherokee people for nearly half a century, while his example in the daily walks of life will linger in the future and whisper words of hope, temperance, and charity in the years of posterity."

The Cherokee People
1866